The GIRL *and the* STARS

MARK LAWRENCE

The First Book of the Ice

HARPER
Voyager

Harper*Voyager*
An imprint of HarperCollins*Publishers* Ltd
1 London Bridge Street
London SE1 9GF

www.harpercollins.co.uk

HarperCollins*Publishers*
1st Floor, Watermarque Building, Ringsend Road
Dublin 4, Ireland

First published by HarperCollins*Publishers* 2020

This paperback edition 2021
8

A catalogue record for this book is available from the British Library

ISBN: 978-0-00-828479-4

Typeset in Sabon LT Std by Palimpsest Book Production Limited,
Falkirk, Stirlingshire

Printed and bound in the UK using 100%
Renewable Electricity at CPI Group (UK) Ltd

MIX
Paper from
responsible sources
FSC™ C007454

To the succession of English teachers who kept this scientist from forgetting that there was more to learn at school

PROLOGUE

Many babies have killed, but it is very rare that the victim is not their mother.

When the father handed his infant to the priestess to speak its fortune the child stopped screaming and in its place *she* began to howl, filling the silence left behind.

Omens are difficult and open to interpretation but if the oracle that touches your newborn dies moments later, frothing at the mouth, it is hard even with a mother's love to think it a good sign.

In such cases a second opinion is often sought.

On the diamond ice out past the northern ridges is an empty place where the wind laments and no one listens. Alone in all those miles is a cave where a witch lives. Or rather where she exists, for little about her might be called living. Agatta waits, nothing more. With the blood frozen in her veins she waits, moving only to crack the ice that forms around her and to let it fall.

The father and the mother came wrapped in sealskins and the furs of hoola, so bulky that they might be great bears

1

roaming from the south. They set the salt price before the witch, and then the baby, swaddled in skins.

'Go.' Agatta creaked when she moved. She sniffed the air, and scowled, her face cracking. 'The present.' She looked down at the baby through frozen eyes. 'This smells like the present to me. Such a thin slice between what was and what will be, and yet always so much going on in it . . .'

The witch waited for the parents to retreat from view. She watched the silent baby, aware of its pinkness. Her hand, in contrast, was the white of early frostbite.

'What have we here? A little drop of warmth in a cold world.' Agatta reached for the child, stretching her senses into the future and the past as she did, seeking out the roots leading to the seed and following the shoot across the years, branching into possible tomorrows.

'Let me see . . .' Icy hand touched warm skin.

Instantly there was fire. A fierce bright fire consuming frozen flesh.

The parents returned, cautious, summoned less by the single piercing scream than by the silence that followed. They entered the cave, blinking at the gloom and wrinkling their noses against the stink of burned meat.

Agatta stood where they had left her, one hand pointing at their infant, the other behind her back, still smouldering.

'Take your child and go.' Her voice creaked like the pressure ridges where the ice flows.

'A-and the oracle?' The father stuttered the words out, wanting to run but having come too far to leave without answer.

'Greatness,' Agatta said. 'Greatness and torment.' A pause. 'And fire.'

CHAPTER 1

In the ice, east of the Black Rock, there is a hole into which broken children are thrown. Yaz had always known about the hole. Her people called it the Pit of the Missing and she had carried the knowledge of it with her like a midnight eye watching from the back of her mind. It seemed her entire life had been spent circling that pit in the ice and that now it was drawing her in as she had always known it would.

'Hey!' Zeen pointed. 'The mountain!'

Yaz squinted in the direction her younger brother indicated. On the horizon, barely visible, a black spot, stark against all the white. A month had passed since the landscape had offered anything but white and now that she saw the dark peak she couldn't understand how it had taken Zeen's eyes to find it for her.

'I know why it's black,' Zeen said.

Everyone knew but Yaz let him tell her; at twelve he thought himself a man, but he still boasted like a child.

'It's black because the rocks are hot and the ice melts.'

Zeen lowered his hand. It seemed strange to see his fingers. In the north where the Ictha normally roamed the whole clan went so heaped in hide and skins that they barely looked human. Even in their tents they wore mittens any time fine tasks were not required. It was easy to forget that people even had fingers. But here, as far south as her people ever travelled, the Ictha could almost walk bare-chested.

'Well remembered.' Yaz would miss her little brother when they threw her into the pit. He was bright and fierce and her parents' joy.

'You've spotted it then?' Quell came alongside them. He had no sled to drag and could move up and down the line checking on the thirty families. He nodded towards the Black Rock. 'I remember how big it is, but still, it always surprises me when we get close.'

Yaz forced a smile. She would miss Quell too, even though at seventeen he boasted nearly as much as Zeen.

'*Always?*' she asked. Quell had been to the gathering twice. Once more than her.

'Always.' Quell nodded, almost concealing his grin. He held her gaze for a moment with pale eyes then moved on up the column. He passed Yaz's parents and uncle, who between them pulled the boat-sled, pausing to swap a comment with her father. One day soon he would have to ask her parents for permission to share Yaz's tent. Or so he thought. Yaz worried what Quell might do when the regulator picked her out. She hoped he would prove himself grown enough to embrace this fate and not shame the Ictha before the southern tribes.

'Tell me about the testing,' Zeen said.

Yaz sighed and leaned into the sled traces. She had of course told Zeen everything a hundred times over but she had been the same herself before her first visit to the hole.

'You'll be fine.' Zeen's worries were nothing, it was just the mind turning on itself when there wasn't anything to do but pull a load mile upon mile, day upon day. The journey had proved difficult, the ice rucking up before them in pressure ridges as if seeking to impede their progress. For the last week the pace had been gruelling as the clan-mother sought to make up lost time. Still, they would arrive a day before the ceremony. 'Don't worry about it, Zeen.'

On Yaz's first trip south she had been sure the regulator would sniff out her wrongness. Somehow she had passed inspection. But that had been four years ago, and what had been starting to break within her back then was now fully broken. 'You'll be fine.'

'But what if I'm not?' The sight of the Black Rock seemed to have opened the gates to her brother's fear.

'The southern tribes are not like the Ictha, Zeen. They have many that are born wrong. We have to be pure. Weakness was bred out of us long ago,' she lied. 'When you walk the polar ice you are either pure or dead.'

'Strangers!' Quell came hurrying back down the column, excited. 'We're getting close!'

Yaz looked to where her parents had turned their heads. Faint in the distance a grey line could be seen, another clan trekking in from the east. And between the two columns, a single sled closing on the Ictha at remarkable speed.

Zeen stopped to stare in amazement. 'How can—'

'Dogs,' Yaz said. 'You'll get to see your first dogs!' Even now, as the distance narrowed, the hounds pulling the sled resolved into dots in a line before it. Soon she could make them out against the snow: heavy beasts, silver-white fur bulking them up still further, their breath steaming before them. In the far north the cold would kill them, but south of the Keller Ridges all the tribes used dogs. The Ictha said that a true man pulls his own sled. The southerners laughed at that and called it something that only a man with no

5

dogs would say. Even so, everyone gave the Ictha respect. Anyone who has known cold understands that only a different breed can dare the polar ice.

'Get along!' Behind them the Jex twins shouted. Zeen started forward again just in time to avoid having them drag their boat-sled over him. Yaz kept level with her brother, watching the strangers approach.

Within a few minutes the whole column came to a halt while at the front Mother Mazai greeted the men dismounting their sled. Yaz could smell the dogs on the wind, a musky scent. Their yapping rang in ears unfamiliar with anything but the voices of men, of the ice, and of the wind. The sound had a strangeness to it and a beauty, and she found herself wanting to go closer, wanting to meet with one of these alien creatures, bound just like her to a sled by strips of hide.

'They're so different!' Zeen struggled out of his harness and broke from the line to get a better view. He meant the people not the dogs.

'I know.' It had been the first thing to strike Yaz at her previous gathering. It wasn't so much the difference of the southern tribes from the Ictha, it was that even among themselves they were varied, some with the copper skin of an Ictha, some redder, so dark as to almost defy colour, and some much paler, almost pink. Their hair varied too, from Ictha black to shades of brown. Even their eyes were not all the white on white that Yaz saw at almost every turn but a bewildering range. Many had eyes almost as dark as the mountain behind them where the rock won clear of the ice. 'Don't stare!'

Zeen waved her off and edged up the column for a closer look. She understood his fascination. Mazai said that where there are many tasks, many kinds of tools are needed. The

Ictha, she said, had a single task. To endure. To survive. And to survive a polar night required a singular strength, one recipe. The clan-mother spoke of metals and of how one might be mixed with others to gain particular qualities. There was, she said, a single alloy fit for the purpose of the north, and that was why all who dwelt there held so much in common.

Yaz edged out to join her brother, ignoring her mother's hiss. Soon they would cast her down the Pit of the Missing into a darkness from which there was no return. She might as well see as much of what the world had to offer as she could before they took it away from her.

'That one's the leader.' Zeen pointed to a man who stood taller than any Ictha and thin, too thin for the north. In places strands of grey shot through the blackness of his hair.

In the months-long polar night the breath you exhaled through your muffler formed two types of frost, the normal southern one, and a finer ice that would smoke away into nothingness within the tent's warmth. The Ictha called it the dry ice for it never melted, only smoked away. In places, in the depth of the long night, dry ice would drift above the water ice and, when the sun's red eye returned, a great cold fog would rise in clouds miles high. The storyteller had it that dry ice formed when part of the air itself froze.

Yaz knew that if the thin grey-haired southerner were to draw breath on a polar night the cold would sear his lungs and he would die.

'Back in line, you two.' Quell came up behind them, the gentleness of his voice taking the sting from the reprimand. He steered Zeen back into place with a hand on his shoulder. Yaz wished that Quell would lay his hand upon her shoulder as well. The sight of naked fingers still amazed her. If she were going to die then she should experience a man's touch too.

She had thought many times about pitching her own tent and inviting Quell in. Of course she had. Too many times and for too long. But in the end two things had always stopped her: sometimes one, sometimes the other, sometimes both. Firstly something in her rebelled at the idea that fear should force her hand before she was properly ready. It was not the Ictha way. And secondly there was the pain that Quell would feel when they took her from him. It would not be fair to use him like that.

Three things. Something else had held her back too. And might have been enough on its own even without the other two. A rebellion against a choice that seemed already to have been decided for her.

But Quell and Yaz had walked the ice together since the days when they could first stand on their two feet, and many of her dreams were filled with thoughts of the bold lines of his face, the strength of his hands, and the mix of kindness and bravery with which he tackled the world. She did not want to leave him. When the regulator cast her down her heart would at last be broken like the rest of her, though at least the pain would not continue long, and in death she would join the spirits of the wind.

Yaz returned to the line and watched Quell go forward. Like Zeen he wanted to listen to the southerners. She found a smile on her lips. The regulator might declare a man grown, but they were still just taller boys.

Perhaps she should have set her tent for him. But in any case she was still counted a child and properly they could not be bound until she had endured the regulator for a second time. Almost every broken child was culled from their clan at their first gathering, but even though it was as rare as melting, sometimes it took a second, and no child was truly counted as grown until their second gathering. So in many ways Quell had been a true member of the clan since he was thirteen whereas Yaz, at sixteen, was still seen as a child and would be until tomorrow when the regulator turned his pale eyes her way.

Her mother offered Yaz a knowing smile then looked away as the wind picked up, laden with stinging ice crystals. There had been sadness in that smile too.

Yaz looked down at her hands. Fear prickled across her. It seemed cruel that just one sleepless night away the hole waited for her, an open mouth that would devour all the days she had thought she owned. A future taken. No tent of her own, no boat to set upon the Great Sea, no lover taken to the furs. Maybe there would have been children. At least now Yaz would not have to harden her heart and watch while they in turn stood beneath the regulator's gaze.

The clan-mother said it wasn't cruelty. All the tribes knew that a child born broken would die on the ice. Their bodies lacked what was needed to survive. As they grew, the weakness in them would grow too. Some needed too much food to keep warm and would starve. Some would lose their resilience to the wind's bite and the cold would eat at them, taking first the tips of fingers, nibbling at the nose and ears, later taking the toes. Flesh would turn white, then black, then fall away. In time the fingers and face would be eaten, dying then rotting. It was an ugly death, and painful. But the worst was that the weakness in that adult would pass into their children, and their children's children, and the clan itself would rot and die.

There was a wisdom to The Pit. A harsh wisdom, but wisdom even so. The burden that Yaz had carried with her out of the north, which had hung from her shoulders each and every mile, was the same weight that set sorrow along the edges of all her mother's smiles. Years had not blunted the sharpness of Azad's death. Yaz should be leaving her parents with two sons to support them, but when the dagger-fish broke the waters her strength had not been sufficient to hold her youngest brother, and in what now seemed one long moment of horror he had gone, leaving her alone in the boat. If the regulator had seen at the first gathering that she was broken, Azad would have known his eighth year, and would have had many more to come.

A muttering ran down the column, one passing the news to the next, with a rumble of discontent echoing in its wake.

'What? What is it?'

Yaz's father ignored Zeen and told her instead, while the Jex twins leaned in to hear, 'The Quinx clan-father says our count is out. The ceremony is today.'

'Why aren't *they* there then?' Yaz's hands began to tremble, a sweat prickling her skin despite the freezing wind. In the months of polar night it was difficult to keep track of days, but she had never heard of the count being out. 'Was their count out too?'

'A hoola attacked their column. They had to observe the rites for the dead. They're force marching to get to the ceremony in time.'

The Jexes were already passing the news back. As the sun began to set, the regulator would commence his inspection. He would be finished by full dark. If they missed it Yaz would have four more years, albeit forced to remain as a child. From where she stood four years looked like a lifetime. 'What will we do?'

'We'll march too,' her father said.

'But . . . it's twenty miles or more, and it's nearly noon.'

'The Quinx are going.' Her father turned away.

'The Quinx have dog-sleds to carry the young and rest the grown!' Yaz protested.

'And we,' her father said, 'are the Ictha.'

The endurance of the Ictha was a thing of legend among the tribes. The Ictha husbanded their strength. Nothing could be wasted on the polar ice. Not if you wished to survive. But when called upon to do so they could run all day. Yaz began to flag after the second hour. Quell ran beside her as she started to labour, his brow creased with a pain that had nothing to do with effort. He was trying to shield her from notice, she knew that. Somehow hoping that he could drag her along by sheer power of will. Behind her the Jex twins' relentless strides devoured the distance. Quell could try to hide her weakness. Others could turn a blind eye, perhaps not even admitting it to themselves. But the regulator would see. There was no hiding from him.

The Ictha could not let the Quinx open too large a lead even if they did have dogs. Old rivalries ran too deep for that. The Quinx didn't even recognize Ictha gods but held their own, some of them twisted versions of the true gods, others entirely foreign. It was a duty of the regulator and his kin in the travelling priesthood to settle disputes and keep the peace. They witnessed oaths, blessed unions, and ensured the purity of all bloodlines. The priests knew all the names of every god, both true and false, and even had a god of their own, a hidden one whose name was secret. The clan elders told stories in which priests of old had channelled the power of their Hidden God to devastating effect, blasting the flesh from the bones of oath-breakers.

Yaz dug deep. Whatever recipe made the Ictha so suited to their environment had gone astray in her. She lacked what the others had. The cold reached her before it reached her friends. Her strength failed against tasks that others of her age could master. She had begun to notice it about a year before her first gathering. Around the same time that she found the river.

There are, impossibly, rivers that run beneath the ice. Yaz's father said they were the veins of the Gods in the Sea and that enchantment made them flow. Yaz had seen, though, that if you press on ice with enough force it will start to melt where you press hardest. In any case, Yaz's river was not one of those that run beneath the ice and are seen only where they sometimes jet forth into the Hot Sea of the north or the three lesser seas of the south. Hers was a river seen only in her mind. A river that somehow ran beneath all things, and through them. When she was ten Yaz had started to glimpse it in her dreams. Slowly she had learned to see past the world even when it filled her waking eyes. And everywhere she looked the river ran, flowing at strange angles to what was real.

Now, as she ran, her heart hammering at her breastbone for release, her lungs full of exhaustion's sharp edges, she saw the river again. And she touched it. In her mind's eye her fingers brushed the surface of that bright water and in an instant its terrifying power flooded through her hand. The river sucked at her, reluctant to let her go, but she pulled free before she burst. Heat and energy filled her, flowing up her arm and into her body. This was how she lived. Touching the forbidden magics of the first tribe to beach on Abeth, driving away the cold and the hunger and the weariness. It wouldn't last and she would not be able to find the river again for days, but for now she felt as if she could run forever with a boat-sled on each shoulder, or dance naked in the polar night.

'I'm fine.' She made a smile for Quell and picked up the pace, hardly noticing now that she was even running.

'I know you are.' Relief washed over Quell's face and he fell back to check the line.

Yaz fixed her gaze on the sled before her, making sure not to run too fast. She kept her bare hands in fists, knowing that the tips of her fingers would still be glowing with the power now pulsing through her veins.

Around the gullet that the tribes name the Pit of the Missing the ice is rucked up in concentric circles of ridges like the waves left when a leaping whale has returned to the ocean. Yaz always thought of the ridges as curtains, positioned to hide something shameful.

The ice around the outer slopes was littered with the sleds of many clans. Dogs waited in groups, tethered to metal stakes, and here and there a warrior stood guard.

'Don't stare.' Yaz's father cuffed his son without anger and pointed the way.

The Ictha would drag their smaller sleds up among the ridges. Yaz's people had few possessions and the loss of any of them was often fatal, so even though theft was a great rarity among the tribes, the Ictha always kept what little they had close to them.

'Quell will have pretty words for you at the gathering tonight.' Yaz's mother stood beside her. They were of a height now. It felt strange to stand eye to eye. 'He's a good boy, but be sure he speaks to your father first.'

Yaz's cheeks burned, though a moment later sadness washed away any embarrassment. She almost broke then, almost sought the warmth and safety of her mother's arms and cried out to be saved. But her mother had already turned to go, and there was no saving to be had. The world had no place for weakness.

* * *

More than half of the sun's huge red eye had sunk behind the horizon by the time Yaz started to climb. The energies that had sustained her for hours began to fade, leaving her to labour up the slopes. Suddenly each breath burned in her throat, sweat froze on her skin, every muscle ached, but she endured, and all around her the clan kept pace. Behind her she could hear Zeen struggling too. Unencumbered the boy was the fastest of any of them, his hands were just as swift, falling to any task with blurring speed. Harnessed to a load, however, his stamina was less than the others of his age.

By the time they reached the top of the first ridge Yaz was helping to pull her brother's sled as well as her own. By the third ridge she was pulling both almost by herself. She worried that her strength would fail and she would arrive at the testing having to be carried by her father. The fact that she lacked the full hardiness of her people was the first sign of being broken. The next common sign was that a child would grow too quickly and eat too much. Perhaps these ones were destined to become giants but giants had no place on the ice. Others lived too fast for the ice; they moved more swiftly than anyone should be able to, but they aged quickly too, and grew hungry quickly, and however fast a person is the cold cannot be outrun. Rarer still, they said, were the ones that developed strange talents. Yaz had never seen such a witch-child but whatever magics they had at their disposal were no match for the night freeze, and be they witch, quickling, or giant they paid a price, losing their ability to endure the white teeth of the wind. Yaz wasn't particularly tall for her age, neither was she unnaturally swift, but her Ictha endurance had been eroding for years. The river gave her ways to hide these failings. They wouldn't fool the regulator though. Clan-mother Mazai said that the regulator could see through lies, she said he could even see through skin and flesh to the very bones of a person, and that all weakness was laid bare before him.

The Ictha left their sleds at the base of the final ridge and Rezack, who was strong and keen-eyed, remained to watch over them. Yaz descended into the crater around the hole, exhaustion trembling in her legs. She and Zeen were towards the rear of the column now. Quell had fallen back to watch over them, his brow furrowed with concern, but this was not the time to be seen helping. That would do nothing for Yaz's chances with the regulator.

The tribes had shaped the crater to their purposes, cutting a series of tiers into the ice. The space encircled by the ridges was maybe four hundred yards across and more than two thousand people crowded the level ground, an unimaginable number to Yaz who had spent almost every day of her life with the same one hundred souls.

At the last moment before they reached the crowd below, Quell pulled Yaz to the side, standing precariously on the slanting ice while others passed nearby with the practiced indifference of people with few chances for privacy.

'Yaz . . .' A nervous excitement, most un-Quell-like, haunted Quell's face. He released her hand, struggling to make his mouth speak.

'Afterwards.' She placed a hand against his chest. 'Ask me when it's done.'

'I love you.' He bit down as the words escaped him. His eyes searched hers, lips pressed tight against further emotion.

And there it was, out in the open, delicate hope trembling in a cruel wind.

Quell was good, kind, brave, handsome. Her friend. All an Ictha girl could dream of. Yaz thought that maybe the first sign that she was broken wasn't the weakness but that she had always wanted more. She had seen the life that her mother lived, the same lived by her mother's mother in turn and on and on back along the path of years. She had seen that this life of trekking the ice between closing sea and opening sea was all that the world had to offer. In all the vastness of the ice, with small variations, this was life. And yet some broken thing inside her cried out for more. Though she stamped upon that reckless, selfish, whining voice, pushed it down, shut it out, its whispers still reached her.

I love you.

She didn't deserve such love. She didn't deserve it for many reasons, not least that the broken thing within her called it burden rather than blessing.

I love you. Quell watched her, hungry for an answer, and behind her the last of the Ictha shuffled past.

The Ictha knew themselves each as part of the body, and they knew that the body must be kept alive, not its parts. Sacrifice and duty. Play your part in the survival engine. As long as the flame is kept alight, as long as the boats remain unholed, as long as the Ictha endure, then the needs and pain and dreams of any one piece of that body are of no concern.

'I . . .' Yaz knew that if she somehow walked away from the pit this time then she was more than lucky to have Quell waiting for her; she would be more than lucky to resume her trek along the life that had always stretched before her across the ice.

Her heart hurt, she wanted to vanish, for the wind to carry her away. She did want Quell, but also . . . she wanted more, a different world, a different life.

'I . . . Ask me at the gathering. Ask me when this is done.' She took her hand from his chest, still worried for the heart beneath it.

She turned and followed the others, hating herself for the

look in Quell's eyes, hating the broken voice that gave her no peace, that left her dissatisfied with the good things, the voice that told her she might look the same but that she was different.

Quell followed at her heels and Yaz walked on, unseeing, understanding a new truth on her last day: Abeth's ice might stretch for untold miles, but there was, in all that emptiness, no room for an individual.

The ceremony was already in progress as Yaz caught up with her brother. On the lowest tier, with only the dark maw of the hole below them, the children of seven clans belonging to three tribes queued in a great circle. Every few moments the line shuffled forward as each boy or girl presented themselves to the regulator in turn.

The old priest stood cloaked in an inky black hide that belonged to nothing that Yaz had ever seen hauled from the sea. Hoola claws reached across his shoulders and fanned out across his chest, threaded on a cord around his neck. His head was bare and bald, marked like his hands with a confusion of burn scars, symbols perhaps but complex and overlapping.

The Ictha said that Regulator Kazik had overseen the gathering for generations. While the other priests came and went with time's tide, growing old, retiring to the Black Rock, Kazik it was said remained immune to the years. A constant, like the wind.

Today he was the regulator, merciless in judgement. Tomorrow he would be Priest Kazik and he would bless marriages, and laugh, and mix with the clans, and become drunk on ferment with the rest of the grown.

Yaz and Zeen joined the rear of the queue with a score of other Ictha children. One more came up behind, delayed by his mother's arms. At the front, around a third of the crater's circumference from them, another child escaped the regulator's scrutiny. She scrambled away to join her parents watching from some higher tier.

Yaz shuffled forward with the line. The climb still burned in her legs and her chest felt sore from panting.

'That was tough!' Zeen smiled up at her. 'But we made it.' He stood close to the edge where the ice sloped sharply away towards the hole.

'Ssshhh.' Yaz shook her head. It was best to avoid any thoughts of weakness. They said the regulator could read a child's mind just by staring into their eyes.

'Has anyone been thrown in?' That was Jaysin behind them, just nine, as young as any Ictha were tested. The younger children remained at the north camp with the old mothers. 'Has anyone gone down yet?'

'How would we know, stupid?' Zeen rolled his eyes. 'We just got here too.' He moved behind Yaz to stand with Jaysin.

Yaz glanced at the hole and shuddered. Even here in the south the ice lay miles deep. She wondered how far she would fall before she hit something.

'Are they down there?' Zeen kept glancing at the pit. The closer they got to the regulator the further Zeen positioned himself from the edge. 'Are the Missing watching us from down there?'

'No.' Yaz shook her head. Most likely all the pit held was a sad pile of frozen corpses, the broken children properly broken at last and removed from the bloodline. Some of the southern tribes spoke of the Ancestor's Tree and of pruning it, but Yaz didn't know what a tree was and her father, who had spoken to southerners at gatherings across the years, had never met any who had seen such a thing.

'But they call it the Pit of the Missing,' Zeen said.

'It's the children who are thrown down there who are missing.' Little Jaysin spoke up again from behind Yaz. It seemed fear had made the boy brave. He rarely had the courage to speak outside his own tent.

'It's a different sort of . . . Oh, never mind.' Yaz would let someone else explain it to him after she'd gone. Instead she looked up at the sky, pale and clear above her, laced with strips of very high cloud, their edges tinged with the blood of the setting sun. The Missing had lived on Abeth an age before the tribes of man beached their ships upon its shores, but they were all long gone by the time men navigated the black seas between the stars and came to this world. Many southerners treated them as if they were gods, though the Ictha knew that the only gods were those in the sea and those in the sky, with the ice to keep them from warring upon each other.

'I'd rather just be left out of the tent,' Zeen said. 'If I was broken I'd rather just be left out.'

Yaz shrugged. A quick death beat a slow death, and at least this way you gave honour to your tribe. Also there was the issue of metal. Clan-Mother Mazai said that the priesthood was the only source of metal in a thousand miles, and not just pieces of it as might sometimes be traded between the tribes, but worked metal, fashioned to meet demand, be it knife or chain. The ceremony honoured the god of the Black Rock and that in turn earned the clan favour with the regulator. Dying here would help the clan.

A sudden cry jerked Yaz from her thoughts. The regulator was standing alone, the wind tugging at the tattered strips of his cloak. There was no sign of the child that had failed his inspection, just the faint and diminishing echoes of their screaming that still escaped the hole. A stillness pervaded the watching crowd, and they had already been still.

With a bored gesture the regulator beckoned the next in line.

'I'm scared.' Zeen's hand found hers. He had been scared all along of course, but this was the first time he'd spoken the words.

The world turns whether we will it or not and everything, longed for or feared, comes to us in time. The queue leading to the regulator advanced slowly but it didn't stop, and at last Yaz's world narrowed to the point towards which it had spiralled for so long.

'Yaz of the tribe Ictha and the clan Ictha,' the regulator said. He never needed to be told name, clan, or tribe. The other tribes had several clans, but in the north they shrank to the same thing.

'Yes,' she said. To deny your own name was to cut a small piece from your soul, Mother Mazai said.

The regulator leaned in towards her. He had the familiar white-pale eyes of her own clan and seemed unconcerned by what the southerners called cold. The burns across his face, head, and hands looked as if he had been branded with some kind of writing, but with lines of symbols at differing angles and sizes, overwriting each other into confusion. He bent closer, showing his teeth in something that was not a smile.

'Yaz of the Ictha.' He took hold of her hand with hard, pinching fingers.

His scent was unfamiliar, sour and as different from the Ictha as the dogs had been. He was old, stringy, gaunt-faced, and looked displeased with the world in general.

The regulator had not touched Yaz on her first visit. Now he seemed unwilling to release her. The tattered strips of his cloak blew about them both and for a moment Yaz considered what would happen if she grabbed them when the time came that he threw her down. The image of his surprise at being hauled in with her struck through Yaz's fear and she struggled to suppress the burst of hysterical laughter that was pushing to escape her.

'You've seen it, haven't you, girl?' He looked up from his inspection of her hand and met her eyes.

'N . . . No.' Yaz shook her head.

'You should have asked "what?". All the ice tribes are terrible at lying but the Ictha are the worst.' The regulator ran his tongue over the yellowing stumps of teeth worn down by years. Without warning he jerked Yaz's hand to his face and began to sniff at her fingertips. She tried to pull away, disgusted, then realized that if he were to release her as she tugged she would fall back with only the slick gullet of the pit to receive her.

'Seen what?' she asked, too late to be convincing.

'The path that runs through all things.' He let her go with a last sniff. 'The line that joins and divides. Seen it and . . .' His gaze fell to the hand she now clasped to her chest. 'And touched it.'

'I didn't . . .' He was right though. She didn't know how to lie.

'That makes you rare, child. Very rare.' Something ugly twisted on the regulator's thin lips: a smile. 'Too good for the pit.' He nodded to the other side of him. 'You stand over there. You'll come with me to the Black Rock.' Excitement tinged his voice. He had thrown children to their death without affording them the respect of caring. But now he cared.

So, numb and trembling, with her wrist still pale where the regulator had gripped her, Yaz moved on. She stood on the flat ice of the tier, watching without seeing while the others shuffled forward one place. She had survived. She was grown and equal to any in the clan. But still she stood here, forbidden to return to where her parents waited. To where Quell waited. Her gaze tracked back up the stepped ice, across the sea of faces, towards the heights where the Ictha families stood.

'No.' The regulator's quiet announcement drew Yaz's attention back to the line. His skinny old hand was clamped over Zeen's face, fingers spread across the boy's forehead and cheekbones. 'Not you.' And with the slightest shove he sent Zeen stumbling back. For a moment Yaz's brother stood, caught on the edge of balance, his arms pin-wheeling, and in the next he was gone, sliding down the steep slope of the gullet then pitched into the near-vertical darkness of the ice hole. He fell with a single short cry of despair.

Silence.

Yaz's face had frozen in shock, her voice gone. The thousands stood without sound. Even the wind stilled its tongue.

It should have been me. It should have been me.

Still no one spoke. And then a single high keening broke the silence. A mother's cry from somewhere far up near the crater's rim.

It should have been me.

The Ictha endure. They act only when they must. They guard their strength because the ice does not forgive failure.

It should have been me.

Yaz glanced at the blue sky, and in the next moment she threw herself after her brother.

CHAPTER 2

At first Yaz slid, then the black throat of the pit was before her and in the next moment she was falling, all the air escaping her lungs in a hopeless scream. The blind rush of dropping through empty space stole all her thoughts. Her body contracted against the inevitable impact. She grazed one wall, grazed another, continued hurtling down with the ice scraping at her all the way. She was sliding again, moving at impossible speed, every part of her clenched in terror. When she hit bottom all her bones would shatter.

The ice wall pressed on Yaz, and in doing so made her still more aware of her awful velocity. Suddenly the pressure increased, everything spun, and somewhere in the spinning she lost herself.

There are stars in every darkness. They are the mercy of the Gods in the Sky.

Yaz jerked in shock, crying out and thrashing her limbs. She was lying in water deep enough to reach her mouth. Coughing and spluttering, she tried to orient herself, slipped, and went face first into the pool. A moment later she was on all fours, choking. The water seemed to be about four inches deep and she was soaked. To be wet on the ice without a tent and dry clothes to hand was a death sentence. A hysterical laugh burst from her. She shook the water from her hair and looked for the light. There was no light, no distant circle of sky above her, just a velvet darkness filled with the constant sound of dripping.

Yaz got to her knees, trying not to slip again. She patted herself. All of her hurt a little; none of her hurt a lot. It seemed impossible that she could fall so far and break no bones.

'Hello?' She whispered it and wasn't surprised when no one answered. 'Zeen!' Loud enough to be heard over all the dripping.

Nothing.

Yaz knelt and blinked at the darkness. 'Zeen . . .'

It wasn't cold. Even wet she could feel the warmth rising around her. Enough warmth to melt this great pit and to keep it open despite the relentless flow of the ice. 'Hello?'

Darkness didn't scare her, not in and of itself. In the many months of the polar night there was never sufficient oil to light all the tents, no matter how many whales were caught and rendered while the Hot Sea remained open. She longed for a flame now though.

'Why am I not dead?'

Now that she thought about it Yaz realized that she had slid most of the way rather than dropped. Whatever heat had melted the hole it was a heat that stayed put while the ice continued its slow journey. The hole must slant.

She listened, her mind racing, pursuing erratic thoughts. She wanted Zeen. Long ago she had let their younger brother die. Her weakness had let him die. Now in the blackness a vision of Azad returned to her as he had been at four when Zeen was eight and she was twelve.

'I'm sorry.' Spoken to the empty space around her.

She wanted light. She needed to see.

Among the Ictha three elders were charged with carrying the flame. Three heavily shielded and slow-burning lamps, such that if disaster caused any one or two of them to go out the fire could still be relit. If the Ictha lost their flame it would be a journey of months to find another clan who might rekindle them. But there were no elders in the pit and nothing to burn in this wet hole even if she had fire.

Mother Mazai had a thing called glass, clear like diamond ice but refusing to melt even above a lamp flame. It had been fashioned into a disc, fat at the middle and thin at the edges. One summer she had shown Yaz that it could gather the sun's red light into one bright spot that would burn against her palm. In the far south, Mother Mazai said, the sun blazed so hot that the bright spot the glass made could light a lamp wick.

Yaz shook the memories from her head. Despite being soaked in meltwater she was still dazed. The fall had rattled her brain around in her skull.

It occurred to her that somehow the darkness was not total. A variation in the blackness hinted at shape and form, though none of it made much sense. Perhaps some fraction of the day's light filtered down through the ice . . . though it seemed hard to believe given how far she must have fallen. Even so, as she moved her hand before her face she had some sense of it passing.

'What have I done?' She moved slowly, feeling ahead. Even on all fours she felt unstable on the wet ice.

It seemed that she was in a large ice cave, its smooth floor dimpled with shallow pools. After just a few yards she found the first of several slick throats where the meltwater drained away, gurgling into unknown depths. The first was large enough to swallow a child, the second would have taken a man and his sled too. There appeared to be no walls as such, just the floor curving smoothly up until she could make no progress.

The illumination was fainter than starlight and seemed to come from all directions at once. It gave Yaz the impression that the chamber was a bubble trapped in the ice. She wondered how many times she had circled it when she shot in along the main vent. If each of the darker patches was a hole then it was amazing that she had missed them all.

'Zeen?' She shouted his name, realizing that one of the ice shafts that had failed to capture her must have swallowed him.

Yaz crawled to the nearest hole. The smooth slope made approaching dangerous, a little too far forward and she would start to slide. She fumbled at her belt for her knife. The blade was a tooth from a dagger-fish. The same kind that had dragged Azad from the boat. She could never draw it without thinking of her lost brother.

Using the knife-point to gain a little purchase Yaz moved closer to the hole, lying flat on the ice now. She listened, trying to untangle any meaning from the constant dripping and the chuckle of distant water. 'Zeen!'

It occurred to Yaz then that she would have to throw herself down another hole, and that this time she would have to choose. More than this, the quick death she had imagined, smashed against an ice floor, might now be replaced with drowning in a flooded shaft, blind and struggling to keep afloat, until exhaustion claimed her and water filled her lungs.

She didn't want to do it. Now that the moment of passion had left her she found that she lacked the courage to throw herself into one of these dark holes.

Alone and trembling in the black Pit of the Missing, Yaz began to weep for everything that she had lost, and from the fear at how her life would end.

Yaz gathered herself, time had passed, she wasn't sure how long but the cold was starting to seep into her. A true Ictha would hardly have noticed but she had begun to shiver. She considered her options. Returning to the surface was not one of them. Even if there had been a flight of stairs carved into the ice she couldn't return . . . What would the tribes think of that? They would push her back in or send her wet out into the wind to die. Yaz remembered the peculiar excitement in the regulator's eye. He might welcome her. He might even keep the tribes from harming her . . . But there were no steps, just hundreds of yards of near-vertical ice running with meltwater.

'No.' Her options were to remain in the chamber and to see whether she froze before she starved, or to continue the pursuit of her brother, a pursuit that only chance had delayed.

Yaz peered at the hole before her. It seemed that the faint glow was coming from the ice itself. Her hand made a black shape before her eyes, too dim for definition. Fear returned as she inched towards the wet, yawning mouth. She didn't want to die. It had been easy to throw herself after Zeen in the heat of the moment. In the cold of the cavern it was almost impossible to release the anchor provided by her knife and to let the drop take her.

'I can't.' But she had no choice.

Yaz ground her teeth together and pulled the point of her blade from the ice. She returned it to its sheath as she started to slide feet first towards the hole. Even certain death couldn't stop an Ictha caring for what little they owned.

A moment later she plunged once more into devouring night.

CHAPTER 3

The fall was almost all vertical this time with only glancing blows from the walls to punctuate a terrifyingly long drop. The shock of impact was so violent that Yaz knew she had hit ice and was smashed beyond recovery. A moment later though she was thrashing in deep water, seeking the surface to replace the air that had been hammered from her lungs.

Yaz broke clear with a heaving gasp, both arms still churning the water about her. She gave a cry of frustration. Her worst fear had been realized. She would drown in the dark.

Yaz had learned to swim in the Hot Sea of the north. For much of the year hot upwelling from the ocean depths kept a circle of water open, nearly ten miles across. Like the three smaller seas to the south the Great Sea teemed with whales. Fish thronged there too, but it was the whales who had to return time and again for air after their long hunting trips beneath the ice.

Being able to swim was a curse. It offered hope. Yaz would still drown, but first she would struggle and suffer. The water she now swam in was only slightly colder than the Hot Sea.

Not quite cold enough to freeze, but almost. She would be able to endure it for hours before exhaustion claimed her and the weight of her clothes dragged her under.

Yaz spluttered and reached for the wall of the shaft. If she stretched out her arms she should be able to touch both sides. Her fingers met no resistance and so she struck out in a random direction, hunting the edge. Three or four strokes brought no contact. She stopped, spluttered for breath, and shook her head to try to get the water out of her eyes. The sound of meltwater splashing down came from behind her now rather than all around.

Perversely it was lighter at this depth than it had been in the chamber far above. The walls had a faint glow to them and seemed much further away than she had thought they would be. Yaz swam towards the edge and realized that she was in another chamber rather than a shaft.

When she banged her knee on something hard Yaz gave a startled cry, missed a stroke, and began to flounder. It was then that she realized the water had grown shallow. Moments later she crawled out onto a shore of black rock, still yards shy of the glowing ice walls.

Yaz lay gasping, as much from the shock of it all as from the battering she had taken. Her body felt like a singular bruise, her ribs hurt, and she was cold. 'Zeen.' She spoke her brother's name through gritted teeth and forced herself back onto hands and knees. The ground beneath her was rock, scoured into ridges. Apart from pieces collected from the slopes of the Black Rock and shown at the gathering Yaz had never touched raw stone before, just the smooth pebbles the Ictha kept for luck and the ones that Mother Mazai wore on a sinew about her neck, polished to a high shine and shot through with lines of colour.

She crawled further from the pool, water streaming from

her parka, dripping from the black veil of her hair. Where the ice walls rose from the bedrock it was light enough for Yaz to count her fingers. They trembled with more than the chill. Her options had narrowed from a quick death crashing into ice at the bottom of a fall or a slower death drowning in a hole back to the slowest of all: starvation.

'Zeen!' She bellowed it and the loudness of her own voice made her flinch. The fall of water overrode any echoes and there was no reply. 'Zeen!'

Yaz frowned and leaned towards the ice, almost close enough for her forehead to rest against it. She squinted, trying to see where the light came from. It wasn't the red of sunlight, this was a more varied, richer illumination, carrying undertones of blues and greens. Close to the wet surface the ice was clear, further back it became misty and fractured. Buried in the body of the ice like a constellation of cold stars were motes of light, none of them seeming any larger than her smallest fingernail, most considerably smaller. The larger ones burned more brightly, though none of them by itself would illuminate much more than her palm if it sat in her hand.

The ice-locked constellations exerted a hypnotic draw. It was the smell that finally broke their spell. Yaz looked away and sniffed. *Blood.* The scent of slaughter. She stood, wincing, and scanned the chamber. The pool dominated, the excess flowing away lazily on the far side along a channel with just a few inches of clearance. The beach onto which Yaz had crawled occupied a third of the perimeter, the pool lapping up against the ice elsewhere. A pair of tunnels led away from the beach into the ice, smooth and carved by meltwater.

Yaz went to the nearest tunnel. She crossed the rock like an old woman. Not that anyone got truly old on the ice, but Yewan, her father's eldest brother, was past fifty and starting to slow. She felt like he looked, stiff, making each move with care as if avoiding hidden hurts.

The blood looked black, spattered across the glowing tunnel walls. This had been an attack, not the butchering of some animal. Yaz touched a finger to one of the larger splats.

'Fresh . . .' She stared at her fingertip, feeling a new kind of coldness deep inside her. 'Zeen.' She started forward but stopped, her foot knocking something soft aside. Yaz crouched and patted the rock. She lifted the warm object for inspection. A thumb. Smaller than her own. The flesh chewed, splinters of bone jutting from it. She dropped it with a shudder, curled her lip, and followed the tunnel.

The sound of dripping from the pool chamber faded behind her and Yaz found herself folded in an eerie silence. The rock-floored tunnel was around fifteen feet wide and ten feet tall, the ceiling fringed with icicles. The longer ones had been broken off with none reaching quite low enough for her to touch. Whatever hunted down here had to be big, but it made no sense that it could be something like a hoola or a bear: they could hardly survive on a dozen children every four years.

For hundreds of yards the tunnel ran on, barely turning from the straightness of its path. Occasionally the groaning of the ice disturbed the quiet. Yaz had heard the noise all her life, deep-throated and rising into her family tent through the sleeping skins. The ice was never still and at every moment some part of it creaked in complaint. Down here though, actually in the ice, the sounds were louder, stranger, as if a great beast were waking from its dreams.

The wet rock beneath her feet wasn't the pristine, ice-scoured rock that might be expected but slick with a thin film of grime, and though she had left the blood behind her the air held a faint but undeniable animal stink, not much different from that of the dogs she had met earlier.

Further on, the tunnel was intersected by another, then another, then a third. The first narrowed rapidly, old and squeezed by the flow of the ice, the second plunged into water lit from below by a ghostly radiance. The third was perfectly round and led upwards through the ice sheet at an angle steep enough to make for difficult progress on the slick surface. Yaz paused at the entrance, listening hard, hunting for smears of blood.

On her journey she had noticed that the tiny stars bedded in the ice ran in seams. In some places more thickly clustered and therefore brighter, fading away in others. The rising tunnel looked to grow utterly dark after just a few dozen yards.

Yaz turned from her inspection of the blackness. She stared intently along the tunnel she'd been following, sure that she'd heard a noise, something other than the grumbling ice. In the gloom ahead something moved. Then again. A shape, huge and black, lumbering towards her.

The tunnels offered nowhere to hide. She could run back to the pool or try to follow the dark side passage, all the time struggling not to slide back into the clutches of any pursuit. But neither of those would help Zeen if the beast had him, and even if she gained a lead any predator would just follow her scent.

The Ictha waste nothing, energy least of all. If there is a point to running then they will run with all their heart, but an Ictha will not run from fear. Even so, Yaz wanted to run. Instead, she drew her knife. If the beast was going to kill her it would have to do it here while she could still make a fight of it.

Fear clutched at her stomach but it was a different kind

from the hopelessness she had felt in the first chamber. The anger that had begun to rise in her at first sight of the blood now started to burn, and the warmth felt good. Yaz had never been in a fight before. Life on the ice was all the fight her people needed. But it had been the worst day of her life, and likely it would be the last, and she was prepared to learn quickly.

Yaz hadn't ever been far enough south to see one of the bears that roamed between the Shifting Seas but from the saga plays acted out by the elders she knew this must be one. Black against the glow, the thing shuffled closer, head bowed, brushing the broken stumps of icicles. The creature stood twice as wide as her and more again, huge within the shagginess of its coat. A rank odour reached ahead of it. Yaz's knife suddenly looked very small. Quell had told her that a bear's claws were longer than a man's fingers. The dagger-fish tooth wasn't more than four or five inches itself.

The beast stopped a few yards from her and raised its head. The great mane of its hair moved across what seemed now to be a mass of skins and furs sewn together in confusion to create one huge shaggy coat. The face lifted to regard her was human, the mouth red with blood. A black stain, darker than any bruise, covered one cheek. It seemed almost the shape of a hand, its fingers reaching across nose and brow in sharp contrast to the pale skin beneath. The woman roared, a great open-mouthed roar, exposing teeth that had been filed to points. She took a pace forward. Something reddish swung from the hide straps around her waist. Yaz stood transfixed, forgetting the danger. A head hung by its hair from the huge woman's belt, not a neatly severed head but one torn from the body, trailing strands of meat. And the face that swung towards her was one she knew.

The cannibal charged and Yaz, frozen with horror, was too slow to evade her. Even among the variety of the southern tribes Yaz had never seen anyone tall enough that the top of their head would come close to this giant's shoulder. She stood as wide as two men and when she brought both arms up before her in a double-handed blow it lifted Yaz off her feet and flung her back along the tunnel.

Yaz slid a fair way but before she could rise, or even haul a breath into an empty chest that felt as though every rib had shattered, the woman was on her. She reached down for Yaz with a hand that could close around her whole head.

The Ictha cannot afford to lose anything. Yaz had looped her knife thong about her wrist and the hilt lay within inches of her fingertips. As the massive hand descended for her Yaz snatched up the dagger-fish tooth and plunged it through the palm.

The woman snatched her hand back with a roar, nearly taking the knife with it. A heartbeat later a great hidebound foot came thundering down to crush Yaz's skull. The cannibal's heel slammed onto stone, pinning Yaz's hair as she rolled aside. She yanked free and drove her knife through the woman's other foot, losing her grip on it when the point struck the rock beneath. The monster roared in pain and Yaz saw her chance. She scrambled between the woman's legs and took off, running down the tunnel behind her.

CHAPTER 4

Yaz ran the way the huge woman had come, sprinting at first, then with more caution. Behind her the roaring had faded into nothing, the cannibal slowed by her injured foot.

The glow from the ice gradually lessened and the circle of Yaz's vision drew in about her, a tightening noose. Imagination began to paint her fears into the thickening gloom. She saw the head dangling from the cannibal's belt, its frozen stare horrific and familiar. Whatever taint had caused little Jaysin to be thrown into the pit would never show now. Yaz hoped it had been the fall that had taken his life rather than the creature that had been eating him.

In her escape the thong securing Yaz's knife had snapped, leaving her only weapon transfixing the woman's foot. She frowned at the murky tunnel ahead, glanced back the way she had come, then carried on, empty-handed against whatever the darkness hid.

She jogged on, careful of her footing on the grimy floor. The animal stink seemed to be increasing rather than decreasing as she opened a lead on the giant. Several times she passed other tunnels but she kept to the largest, wanting room for manoeuvre if she found herself trapped in a dead end.

The big chamber took Yaz by surprise. The tunnel didn't widen, it just opened into a much larger space without warning. Yaz had no idea that caverns so vast could exist beneath the ice. She got a sense of scale through the change in the quality of the sound and through the slight motion of the air. Also there was the marbling effect of half a dozen seams of the tiny stars that offered the walls and roof in glowing bands, too faint to illuminate the contents of the chamber but bright enough to be seen across its width.

Yaz stood, wondering, wanting to shout out Zeen's name but lacking the courage. Who knew what other terrors the darkness held?

Quite what made her turn her head Yaz couldn't say. It wasn't something she was conscious of hearing. By the time she looked back over her shoulder and focused on the great dark mass rushing at her out of the tunnel's gloom she could finally hear the rush of its footsteps. The cannibal gave a bloodcurdling roar. This time, rather than freezing Yaz to the spot, the roar galvanized her and she ran, sprinting along the edge of the cavern where the faint illumination might at least warn her of rocks large enough to trip her or to turn an ankle on.

Wounded foot or not the huge woman came after Yaz with terrifying speed, fuelled by rage and pain, devouring the yards in great strides. The monstrosity pounded ever closer, narrowing the gap between them, roaring giving over to a determined silence punctuated by laboured breaths. Soon Yaz could hear nothing but her own gasping for breath and the thunder of her heart.

The ground before her began to rise in a slope of ice-worn shingle, channelled and heaped by some ancient flow. Yaz started to scramble up. The shifting stones sucked away the last of her strength and she slowed to a crawl. Behind her the giant followed, sounding like an avalanche.

'Hey!' A voice from somewhere in the gloom. 'Hey! Up here!'

Yaz glanced around wildly but saw nothing.

'Here! Catch the line!'

Yaz swung her head and saw something dangling to her left. A rope! And high up on it a clot of darkness hung. A person! She veered towards them but in that moment the cannibal made a last desperate lunge and fastened a hand about Yaz's leg, encompassing it from the ankle almost to the knee.

For a second both of them lay there, sprawled on the slope of shifting stones, too winded to do anything but pant. Yaz only found the energy to struggle once she felt herself being hauled back towards her enemy. She rolled onto her side and looked down. Close up the giant was still more fearsome; the charnel stink of her filled Yaz's lungs. The ink-black stain across her face seemed to have moved, forming a band across her eyes now, stark against pale but grimy skin. The woman's gaping mouth began to descend towards Yaz's thigh, the points of her teeth gleaming wetly. Feeding on Yaz rather than finishing her off seemed to be the priority. Whether it was hunger or cruelty that drove the cannibal Yaz didn't know, but she clearly intended to eat her alive.

Yaz grabbed a rock and hammered it down, not on the fingers but on the nerve cluster in the wrist. Quell had shown her the trick years before. Yaz struck home with all her strength and with a wordless prayer to the Gods in the Sea. She yanked her leg free just as those jaws snapped shut inches from it, and rolled away.

The rope hung less than ten yards off, vanishing up into the gloom. The figure on it had gone. Yaz ran, knowing even as she did that she wouldn't have time to climb high enough before the giant hauled her down.

She grabbed the rope, a crude thing of twisted hide strips studded with knots, and turned to check her opponent. To Yaz's surprise the giant hadn't advanced. A much smaller figure danced around her, throwing fist-sized stones. The missiles seemed only to annoy the giant but when she lurched towards her assailant the boy just danced away. His speed and timing were breathtaking.

'Climb!' A girl's voice, high above. 'Bring the rope with you!'

Yaz reached up, taking hold just above a large knot, and began to climb. It was not something she had done before. The ice tends to be flat. But fortunately the Ictha are strong and what she lacked in technique she replaced with muscle power. A short way off the ground Yaz reached down, groaning as her bruised body complained, and grabbed a lower section of the rope to tuck into her belt. Then, bringing it with her, she continued upwards. She had to assume the boy had another means of escape. If he could run as swiftly as his dodging implied then the giant would have no chance of keeping pace.

Yaz reached the top of the rope in darkness. For some yards she had been climbing alongside an ice wall, presumably a vertical shaft in the roof of the cavern. Hands reached out to help her over the lip. More hands than she had expected. A number of strangers crowded around her, drawing her back from the hole.

'Zeen?' Yaz asked. Nobody answered, they only hustled her along, blind in the dark. Yaz frowned, then stopped moving. She braced herself against the slickness of the ice. 'How did you do all this? Make a rope? Get up here? We weren't *that* late to the gathering. You couldn't have been more than an hour ahead, maybe two.'

Suddenly there was light. All around her figures shielded their eyes, some gasping as if it had been unexpected for them too. Shadows swung as the light moved, a bright point held between two prongs at the end of an iron rod clutched in a young man's fist. Yaz squinted and could see that the source of the glare was one of the stars she had seen locked in the ice, though this was a larger one, considerably larger than her thumbnail. Despite its dazzle Yaz found herself staring at it, ignoring what its light revealed. It looked like a hole in the world, opening onto some bright place. For a moment the air seemed full of whispers just beyond hearing, the space between them strange and echo-haunted, as if a heavy stone had dropped, rippling the fabric of everything.

A cough broke the spell.

Six strangers surrounded Yaz. She spun around. Zeen was not among them. Two were younger than her, two around her own age, one a man in his twenties, carrying the light, and beside him a scar-faced woman in her thirties perhaps.

Yaz's frown deepened. What was a grown woman doing here?

'We had more than an hour's head start on you, girl,' the woman said. 'The younglings came down last gathering.'

Yaz blinked. 'Four years?' Four years in the blackness. Four years under the ice.

The woman coughed a bitter laugh. 'I've seen five drops since that old bastard gave me the shove. It's still Kazik, is it?'

Yaz nodded. Kazik had been regulator even before her grandmother's testing.

'Shame. He's lived too long.'

Yaz looked about her at the others. All of them were lean, cheeks hollow, eyes bright, all grimy, all wrapped in gut-sewn skins. The two boys of her own age held makeshift clubs, smoothed stones the size of a fist lashed with hide to the end of bones that looked suspiciously like the thighbones of a large man.

'My brother?' She held a hand to indicate his height. 'Where is he?'

The others looked down, their mouths in grim lines. Yaz grew suddenly cold, stomach knotting, a twitch coming to her cheek. The scar-faced woman shook her head. 'Hetta got him.' She pursed her lips in the direction of sympathy. 'Nearly got me once.' She indicated the parallel lines scored across her face as if torn by claws. 'Nearly got you too.'

'No.' Yaz drew a breath, understanding. 'That was Jaysin. Zeen is bigger.' As she said it the anger rose in her again. Little Jaysin, timid, eager to please, now torn apart and half eaten. 'The giant didn't have Zeen. It was Jaysin's head on her belt.'

'Gerant,' the young man with the light said.

'What?'

'Gerant, not giant. The ones that grow too big. They're gerants.' The harsh shadows made something sinister of his face.

Yaz shook her head. She didn't care about that. 'My brother?'

'He must have come down somewhere else,' the woman said. 'The shafts change between gatherings. We can't cover them all. We didn't expect anyone out here, but Hetta must have known somehow. She's cunning, that one.'

'The taint told her.'

Yaz glanced back, it was one of the younglings that had

spoken, a fair-haired boy now holding his hand to his face in mimicry of Hetta's black stain. Yaz had never seen hair so pale before, but then she had seen a dozen new things in less than an hour. She turned back to the woman. 'My brother. Zeen. He's all I care about.'

The woman nodded, biting her well-bitten lower lip. 'The other search parties might have got him.'

'Or the Tainted did,' whispered the young girl standing beside the fair boy.

The woman shrugged. 'We'll join up with the rest of the Broken and find out.' She held up a hand as Yaz started forward. 'Once we're sure the regulator has finished.'

'He has,' Yaz said. 'The Ictha were the last clan. And I was near the end.'

'Three Ictha.' The man with the light looked at the woman. 'I can't remember the last time there was even one.'

The woman shrugged again. 'Two now. Or maybe just one. We'll go find out once Petrick is back.'

'The boy who attacked the giant?' Yaz asked. 'Gerant.' She corrected herself at the young man's frown.

Back down the tunnel something rattled. 'Speak of the devil.' The woman nodded to the girl who had whispered about 'the Tainted'. 'Jerra, go let the rope down.' The girl ran off into the darkness. 'Check first!' the woman called after her. 'And don't fall down the hole.'

The woman turned back to Yaz. 'I'm Arka. That's Pome.' She motioned towards the hard-eyed young man with the star. There were other names but somehow they didn't stick. Zeen was the only name she wanted to hear.

The girl, Jerra, and the boy Petrick, who close up didn't look much older, came hurrying back, the girl clutching the rope. Yaz wondered how it had been secured. Her mind always threw in tangential questions at unhelpful moments.

'Hetta?' Arka asked. Yaz saw the cannibal's mouth descending towards her leg again, drool hanging from pointed teeth.

'Still raging.' Petrick grinned. 'I lost her in the threads. The new girl stuck her good. Hand and foot!'

Yaz frowned, her hand returning to her side where her knife should be. Even now the loss weighed on her.

'And the pools? Any more arrivals?'

Petrick shook his head. 'Think that's our lot.'

'Let's go then.' Arka led the way, Pome at her side, holding his light-stick aloft as though he were some grand official at a clan ceremony.

Yaz followed, her mind still spinning. Twenty years. That's how long Arka said she'd been down here. Twenty years. It was as far beyond Yaz's imagination as a tree. Or the thin green belt the gods were said to have put around the world's waist, a place where the oldest tales said there was as much life on the land as in the sea.

Arka took the group along a series of tunnels. Many were clearly the work of meltwater but others seemed to defy logic, rising, falling, and twisting in a way that flowing water never would, and yet smooth and round, bearing no mark of pick or chisel.

Yaz jogged in the middle of the band. The Broken they had called themselves. Her new clan, she supposed, bound together by the fact they had survived the drop and wished to keep on surviving.

The darkness gave way to a dim and diffuse illumination as the ice began to be populated once more by the tiny stars. The others seemed to take the same comfort in this that Yaz did, even though they must have seen it every day for years. Little Jerra paused to gaze into the ice and dark-haired

Petrick had to give her a tug to get her started again. 'Slowcoach.'

'Everyone's slow next to you.' The girl blinked, glanced at Yaz, and carried on.

Shortly after that, Arka sent Petrick ahead to warn of their arrival. The boy scampered off at speed and was soon lost in the gloom.

The further they went the more dirty the ice beneath their feet. Eventually they emerged into another rock-floored cavern, not so large as the one in which Yaz had escaped Hetta but still large and better lit.

The air here was warmer than in the tunnels and the soft drip of meltwater filled any brief silence. A crowd of maybe four dozen of the Broken stood in an arc around the entrance, lean, grimy, their clothes cloaks of woven hair over old hides and crude patchworks of small skins. Here and there points of light winked among their number, tiny ice stars sewn onto clothing or dangling from an ear.

More than half of those gathered were huge. Not as big as Hetta maybe, but larger than anyone Yaz had ever seen before. More gerants, given time to grow. For a moment she wondered what they found to eat, and what had originally worn the skins they dressed in.

Between the Broken's reception party and Yaz a group of four new arrivals huddled together, wet, shivering, some clutching injured limbs or sporting angry red marks that would be black bruises soon enough. Zeen was not among them.

Yaz turned back towards the tunnel, meaning to leave. 'Let me pass.' She advanced on the boys blocking the passage.

A hand clamped on her shoulder. 'You can't go!' Arka tried to pull her around. 'You have no idea where you are or what's out there.'

'Zeen's out there.' Yaz jerked free of Arka's grip.

Pome, the young man with the light-stick, slipped between her and the exit. He stood nearly a head taller than her, brown hair scraped back. His mouth held a brittle smile that put her in mind of the hook-eels that play dead right up until the moment they're hauled into a boat then unsheathe a hundred claws and start to thrash. 'Tarko is going to speak to all the wets. After that he will decide what to do about your brother.'

Arka moved to stand beside Pome. 'I don't know if Zeen can be got back, but I do know you can't do it by yourself.' She set her hand to Yaz's breastbone as she tried to advance. 'I remember the Ictha being famed for making the best of bad situations . . . like everything north of the Three Seas.' She allowed herself a smile. 'So let's see some of that alleged common sense.'

Yaz ground her teeth but the sting of the rebuke managed to reach through both her anger and her resolve. She had let her clan down in a dozen ways since the sun rose. Every act she had taken unwrote the Ictha code. She bowed her head. Her recklessness and sacrifice had been as foolish as she had always been taught they were. She would do it right this time. Wait, plan, gather resources, and strike only when reason dictated. The Ictha way. Slowly she turned back and went to stand with the others who had fallen today.

Yaz joined the new arrivals. The gerants she passed to reach them made her feel as though she were a child again despite it being the day she was given her adulthood. She went to stand at the back of the group. The girl just ahead of her turned to see, teeth chattering. She looked to be just a little older than Zeen, of slight build with long brown hair and curious brown eyes. It was the different eyes that would take the longest to get used to.

'S-So you're the special one.' The girl's voice shook with cold. Yaz hardly noticed her own damp clothing. The cavern was warmer than her mother's tent in winter. 'T-The one they're excited about.'

Yaz frowned. 'Me?'

'T-The boy said he saved you from a hetta. I don't know what that is but he made it sound bad.'

'It was pretty bad.' An image of Jaysin's dangling head flashed across Yaz's vision again. She hadn't considered why they would risk themselves to help her. They hadn't helped little Jaysin. She shook the thought away. 'Why would they care about me? I'm not special—' She bit the word off. They were all special down here, she guessed. Just not in a good way. Broken. Unfit for the ice. 'Why? I'm not worth saving.'

'You don't see it?' The girl hugged herself, hands to her shoulders. 'I guess maybe you wouldn't . . . I saw it as soon as you came in.'

'Saw what?'

'The stars,' the girl said. 'They burn brighter when you're near.'

CHAPTER 5

'You stand before us still wet from the drop. Your tribe and your clan have thrown you aside and not one of them raised their voice to save you. They called you flawed, wrong, unworthy, and you were cast into darkness to die.' The man who addressed them was neither tall nor old. Yaz had thought one of the gerants would lead, for who could stand against them? Or failing that, the eldest would hold sway with the wisdom of years. But the man who paced back and forth before the crowd seemed unremarkable save for the darkness of his skin which gleamed blacker than the rock itself, something Yaz had never seen even among the many tribes of the gathering. Even his head gleamed, lacking any hair. 'We are your family now and we have all fallen here. We are the unwanted, the things of such little use that they are thrown away. We are what is beyond repair. We are the Broken.'

'The Broken!' The name rang in dozens of mouths.

'I am Tarko. I command here by the will of the Broken. You have questions. We have answers. You are wet, and the cold will kill you long before you starve. We have heat and food. You were given no choice at the mouth of the pit. I give you a choice. A hard choice.' He shrugged and pressed his lips together in apology. 'A hard choice, but still a choice. You may join us or . . .' He raised a hand towards the tunnel they had entered by. 'Or make your own way.'

Tarko watched them, the handful of shivering southerners, and Yaz. She glared back at him, boiling with her fury at . . . everything . . . and as angry at having nothing and no one to blame as she was at the rest of it. A short silence reigned. Yaz felt the pressure of many eyes upon her, and still Tarko held his arm towards the dark tunnel.

'No?' His arm fell. 'Then welcome, brothers and sisters.' Tarko turned his gaze on the rest of Yaz's new tribe. 'Five . . . it is not what we hoped for. A single drop-leader will be sufficient—'

Pome stepped forward, raising his light-stick. 'I was first to be selected! Arka and—'

'Arka will be drop-leader for this group.' Tarko singled out the woman who had brought Yaz in.

'This is nonsense.' Pome wasn't done. A gerant moved to stand at his shoulder, glowering at Tarko, one eye filled with malice, the other milky white. This one looked as if he could crush ice in his fist, the muscles of his arm mounding beneath his furs. 'We should have taken the centre pool back. We can't survive on . . .' He gave Yaz and the others a withering look. '. . . five.'

'The Tainted are too many—'

'And how many of us will there be in ten years if we only gain only five each gathering?'

Tarko sighed. 'More than if we fight the Tainted for the centre pool each time.' He looked away. 'Drop-Leader Arka, dry these wets off and let's see if they were worth the price we paid.'

* * *

'Come on, I know where it's warm.' Arka strode past them and the children hurried after her. Yaz paused, gazing back at the dark entrance that had been the other choice Tarko offered. She watched the Broken, crowding around their leader and around Pome who had spoken against him, most of them trying to make themselves heard. Some were angry, some stern, but most just looked worried. It seemed that the ripples spreading from the arrival of Yaz and the others had not stopped at the edges of the pools into which they had fallen.

'You, Ictha girl!' Arka called from the rear of the cavern. 'Come on!'

Yaz frowned then hurried after the group.

She caught up with the last of them. The girl glanced back and offered a nervous grin. 'I'm M-M-M-aya.' She stuttered the name past her shivering. Maya, who had said that thing about the stars shining brighter. Beyond the girl a boy more than a head taller than Yaz and broad with it, owning a man's size but a child's face, then another also tall but slender.

The cavern narrowed, then widened, then spread to join a maze of other wide, low-roofed caverns. It appeared that the warmth, which eventually found its way out through the Pit of the Missing, created an air gap above the bedrock of between one and five yards, leaving an ice sky above them supported here and there by still-frozen areas. Seams of the dust-like stars mottled the glacial ice above them providing a faint illumination, brighter here, darker there, and in some places a larger star, like the one Pome carried in his stick, seemed to have been deliberately sunk into a wall to provide better light.

Yaz swung her head from side to side, trying to take it all in, trying and failing to keep her bearings in case she should need to leave in a hurry. The glowing bands overhead kept distracting her, fascinating her eye and putting her in mind of the shimmering veils of light that haunt the polar night. The Ictha called those dragons' tails, though it seemed each tribe had its own story to tell about them.

'Down here.' Arka led the way into a ravine in the bedrock. Rough steps had been carved into the stone and the sound of rushing water rose from far below.

Yaz brought up the rear, stepping cautiously, unused to having rock beneath her feet. Somehow it felt more treacherous than ice. Pinpricks of light broke the darkness ahead of them. Yaz shivered, not so much from the dampness of her clothes but from the thought that this was her life now. Rock and wet ice. She tried to imagine how anyone could live down here not just for days and weeks but for decades, without the ocean to supply hides and fur, sinew and oil, food and fuel . . . all the materials a people needed to construct their lives.

'This is the hothouse.' Arka's voice drew Yaz from her thoughts and from focusing on her feet as she negotiated the last of the steps. The woman stood before a structure made from neither rock nor ice nor bone nor hide. Yaz had never seen anything like it. She found herself gawping and took comfort that at least the others seemed similarly amazed.

'What is it?' Yaz was the first to find her words.

'The hothouse,' Arka said. 'Follow me.' And she ducked inside through what seemed to be a tent flap but didn't look like one.

'It's a door,' said an older girl, suddenly scornful now that she realized she knew something the rest did not. She went in after Arka. One by one the others followed.

Yaz came last, running her fingers over the walls and 'door'. They were flat like stretched hide though much thicker, vertical like the cliffs of the Hot Sea, hard like rock, smooth like bone. The whole structure sat upon a ledge with the ravine carrying on down to unknown depths, and backed against a rock wall. The small girl, Maya, went through ahead of her and Yaz followed.

'Gods below!' The blast of heat that met her was like nothing Yaz had ever experienced. As if every oil lamp the Ictha owned were lit and placed side by side in the same tent. She joined the others, noticing that unlike the rest of them the thinner of the two boys wasn't wet or shivering. He had a narrow face, high cheekbones and, beneath a shock of black hair, dark eyes with a haunted look to them.

'You come wet into the world and the next time you get wet will be your last.' Arka's tribe clearly shared some of the Ictha's sayings. 'That's how it is up there where we came from. Down here things are different.' She stepped aside and they saw behind her the rocky cave that the small building fronted. The space was both large and crowded, and it was lit by the light of stars set in what looked to be bowls of glass, a thing only Mother Mazai owned, and then just a small disc of it. For a moment, her vision still blurred by the heat, Yaz thought it was people crowding the space beyond, but she soon saw that only the skins they wore hung there, on lines strung from the ceiling, dozens of sets.

'We dry our clothes here. Hang yours on the wire.' Arka pointed to a line strung across the width of the cave. She walked into the centre, pushing aside sets of hanging skins as she went and setting them swinging. The shadows swung too and for a moment it looked again as if they were people, the Ictha perhaps, dancing for the sun at the end of the long night. Arka clapped her hands. 'Hurry!'

She turned her back on them, bending to retrieve something from the floor. When she turned to face them again she seemed surprised that none of them had moved. In a silence broken only by the chattering of teeth she lifted the object she'd retrieved. A clan's wealth in iron, a squat, heavy cylinder of the stuff, thick-walled and gripped by two bone handles. Deeply etched symbols covered the outside. Yaz knew that the priesthood had a writing that they used to put words on hides. That had always fascinated her. The idea that words, such fleeting things, gone almost as they left your lips, could be trapped and lie there bound in black lines inked into permanence such that they could outlive the one who gave them life. But these symbols were something else again. Like the ice stars they seemed both more real and more distant than the world around them. Complex as the many-legged spider-fish that crawl beneath the sea ice, each was different from its neighbour and yet the same. Each tangled her eye, trying to draw her through . . . to somewhere.

'If you don't warm up soon you may well never warm up.' Arka frowned at them. 'What? It's a pot. You've seen a pot before, surely?'

Yaz hadn't.

Arka set the iron tube on the floor and using a long metal rod she took one of the glass bowls from its niche in the wall, putting it on the floor. With a small scoop at the end of the rod she removed the star from the bowl and dropped it into the iron pot. Immediately the symbols carved into the metal began to glow. The heat radiating from them made Yaz's face burn. It was as if she held her hand just an inch from a lamp flame. 'Hang those clothes up! Now!' Arka barked the order like a woman used to being obeyed. 'You stay there, Thurin.' She raised a hand to the black-haired boy as he moved forward with the others.

Yaz stayed with Thurin, though she backed away from the heat. Even Arka seemed surprised by its fierceness, raising an arm to shield her face. 'I must have used too large a stone

. . . ah . . . there, it's easing off.' She relaxed, then lifted her voice to address them all, falling into her role as their teacher. 'The sigils set into the iron convert the energy the stone gives off into heat.'

'I call them stars,' Yaz said. She tried to look anywhere but at the naked flesh being exposed. The Ictha generally only took something off in order to replace it with something warmer. They would shed layers in their tents but never retain fewer than three. Only in the Hot Sea would they strip, and there the mists shrouded everything, hiding one end of a small boat from the other. The drying, when the Hot Sea closed, was a time of great hardship and more died in that handful of days than in the rest of the year together. 'Stars. Not stones . . .' She faltered under Arka's hard stare.

'Some do call them that. Heart-stones, core-stones, ice stars, it's all the same. Strip.'

Yaz hesitated. With the exception of Thurin the others had moved among the hanging skins, seeking privacy.

'Why isn't *he* wet?' She pointed an accusing finger at Thurin, who frowned, almost in pain.

'Because he didn't drop today. He's here for . . . other reasons.' Arka folded her arms and looked Yaz up then down. 'Do the Ictha have something under their hides that the rest of us don't?'

Yaz scowled. If she protested further they would all be watching her as Arka wrestled her out of her wet skins. With a snarl Yaz walked into the area where the clothing already strung up offered the most shelter. She stripped off her outer skins, wrestling with tight knots. Her innermost layer was sewn on, requiring a knife to remove and a needle to replace. She would not need it down here out of the wind. The wind was the true killer. It amazed her not to hear it. Its absence was a silence battering at her ears. Once when Yaz was little the wind had stopped. Not dropped or weakened, but stopped. It was a thing that even the grey among them had never seen. The elders thought that it might be the end of the world. Some wept. Some tore at their hair. And then the wind blew again and it was as if that moment of stillness had never been.

Yaz shed her sodden outer hides. Her best sealskins were still stored on her sled. The Ictha would make good use of them. She peered back at Arka around a hanging coat. 'I need a knife.' She said the words through gritted teeth.

'Hey! We're not that dangerous!' A girl's voice from among the drying clothes, Maya perhaps.

'I am!' A boy. Laughter followed that one.

'She thinks we can't resist her without her furs.' Another girl.

More laughter. A slightly hysterical edge to it. Yaz reminded herself that they were children and she an adult. And that the pit had taken them all from their lives. If they didn't laugh they would cry. She shook her head, trying to press a smile from her lips. It *was* funny, she guessed, to find herself next to naked in the Pit of the Missing and to still be sweating.

'That's all I can get off without a knife.' Yaz walked back out wearing only the black mole-fish skins that her mother had sewn her into at the onset of the long night. 'At least they got a good wash today.' More laughter.

Arka sighed and shook her head. 'Ictha!'

Yaz moved closer to the burning heat of the pot until the skins began to steam. The mole-fish hides had been softened with nagga venom, giving them a velvety feel, but they resisted water and wouldn't stay wet for long. Yaz stretched. She had never felt so warm and lacked any inclination to ever step away. Then, remembering herself, and feeling the black-haired boy, Thurin, trying not to look at her, she hunched again, to present as small a target as she could for others' stares.

Arka called to the three now naked among the hanging skins. 'There are capes at the back, to wear when you've hung your clothes to dry. Then come out here and join us.'

Maya and Yaz sat with the iron pot between them, the huge boy and a black-haired girl completed the circle, the heat making their faces glow. Arka and Thurin sat further back, knees drawn up before them. The boy, Kao, had shrugged his cape from his shoulders and gathered it around his waist. His arms were so thick with muscle that it had to fight for space along his bones, heaping itself up. He watched them all with disdain from blue eyes that sheltered beneath a yellow fringe.

'The old man made a mistake.' Kao's voice rumbled deeper than Yaz's father's. 'I don't belong down here. I'm as strong as any man in the Golin clan. Stronger than most. I'm not some broken thing. I don't belong here with you . . .'

'Us what?' The dark girl was called Quina. Her face reminded Yaz of a hawk, eyes like black stones.

'Rejects.' Kao spat the word. 'There's nothing wrong with me. I'm going to climb out and throw that scrawny priest down his own hole then—'

'If you can climb out of the pit it shows that Kazik was right about you,' Arka said. 'If you can't then maybe he was wrong, but nobody will ever know. It's the perfect system.' She raised a hand to forestall Kao's hot reply. 'But I would enjoy watching you do it.'

'Me too.' Yaz hadn't intended to speak but the words left her mouth. She dropped her gaze as the others glanced her way. In the heat of the moment she had forgotten that not only was she bare-handed before strangers but she was showing more of her skin than an Ictha sees on their wedding night.

'In any event,' Arka said. 'We are all here, rightly or wrongly, and there is no returning to the surface. My task is to educate you in the ways of the Broken so that you can become useful and earn your keep. Our lives are . . . hard. You will have noticed that fewer of us grow old than even the Ictha.'

Yaz bowed her head as the others looked her way again. She hadn't spotted even a single greyhead among the Broken. At perhaps thirty Arka looked as old as any of those Yaz had seen.

'There should be more of us,' Quina said. 'I saw a dozen pushed and there were many still behind me.'

'Did the hetta eat them all?' Maya asked, round-eyed. Yaz guessed her to be the youngest of them, around thirteen. Quina might be fifteen. Kao her own age or a year younger. Despite the size of him his was a boy's face.

'Where did you hear about Hetta?' Arka frowned at Maya and glanced towards Yaz.

'The boy said it.' Maya looked nervous. Yaz suddenly wondered why the girl was the youngest of them. Most got the push at their first gathering. There should be plenty of smaller ones. 'Petrick. He said a hetta got someone . . .'

'Hetta is one of the Tainted. A wild one even for them. A rogue. She hunts alone,' Arka said, and beside her Thurin, dry and fully clothed, shivered despite the heat. 'And to understand the Tainted you have to understand that the stories told to scare little children are true. The black ice is real.'

Kao snorted with laughter, Maya paled, Yaz quietly made the sign invoking the protection of both the Gods in the Sky and the Gods in the Sea. Quina, however, just nodded.

'The Ictha have never seen such a thing,' Yaz said.

'Nor have the Golin.' Kao leaned into the heat. 'Because there is no such thing.'

'My people have seen it in the south. Far to the south. A grey scar in the ice, black at its heart.' Quina narrowed her eyes at Kao, daring him to dispute her.

'It is rare for black ice to reach the surface. But down here it exists.' Arka turned towards Thurin as if checking on him. His gaze had fallen to his hands and he made a slow study of his fingers, a twitch in his cheek giving the lie to this show of disinterest.

'They say if you walk on the black ice it fills you with terrors,' Quina said.

'And if a man touches it' – Maya's voice trembled – 'it can make him murder his children.'

'The Tainted are people who have touched the black ice?' Yaz asked, and once more she saw Jaysin's head dangling by the hair from Hetta's belt.

'Worse.' Arka looked grim. 'They swim in the pools that form where it melts.'

Maya gasped. Yaz, an adult grown, allowed herself no expression of horror but drew her knees up under her chin, feeling even now the touch of Hetta's vast hand as it had closed around her lower leg and begun to pull her towards those teeth.

Thurin had grown still and very pale. And he was pale enough to start with. 'It takes more than a touch of the black ice to taint most people. There are spirits in the ice, looking for a way inside you, looking for cracks. Anger will let them in, cruelty, greed, any weakness, even fear will invite them in eventually.' He stood and turned to leave.

'Thurin. Sit.' Arka motioned for him to return.

'And the Tainted do worse than swim in the black pools.' Thurin had his back to the others now. 'They drink from them.' And he walked away, with Arka's demands that he stay ringing in his wake.

'What's up with him?' Kao snorted.

Arka made no reply and they joined her in silence, soaking up the heat until at last a distant clanging reached the cave. Arka cocked her head to listen then relaxed. 'It's the signal for night. We keep our own cycle down here. I'll take you to the settlement. You can collect your clothes here tomorrow.'

'What about Zeen?' Yaz was no longer sure why she had thrown herself down the pit. In the moment she did it it had seemed that it was for her brother, though quite how it might have helped she couldn't have said. But now, against all odds, she really did have a chance to help him and she was damned if she would just shut up about it and go to sleep.

'The Tainted have him,' Arka said.

Even though she had guessed the answer a cold fist still clenched around Yaz's heart. 'Then I need to find him before they eat him.'

'They won't eat him.' Arka shook her head. 'They are vile but none are quite as crazed as Hetta. They'll taint him along with the rest of those they caught from today's drop.' Arka stood to go. 'You don't have to worry about finding your brother, Yaz. You have to worry about him finding you.'

Yaz got hurriedly to her feet and caught Arka's shoulder. 'There must be a way to save him.'

The woman turned, the scars on her face very white against heat-reddened skin. 'Oh, there's a way. It's just very hard, is all. It's a lot easier to taint someone than to untaint them. I've been here twenty years and only seen it work once.'

'Then I need to meet that person,' Yaz said. 'The one who was saved.'

Arka pulled free and started towards the door. 'You already have,' she said. 'He's called Thurin.'

CHAPTER 6

Arka led them from the ravine back into the ice caverns. Their footsteps echoed through the endless twilight, each breath steaming up before them. To her amazement Yaz saw that what she had first thought to be fallen lumps of ice scattering the floor of these long halls were in fact something very different. Roundish objects, in shades from white through grey and brown, lay here and there, varying in size from an eyeball to a head, all of them smooth-skinned, some beaded with water drops.

'What are they?' she asked as they drew closer to a place where scores of them clustered.

'Are they dangerous?' asked Maya, moving closer to Yaz.

'Rocks,' Kao declared.

Quina reserved her judgement.

'Fungi. They grow where the stones . . . the stars . . . give enough warmth.' Arka bent to pick up a small one from the shadow of a larger one. It made a faint tearing sound as if it were attached to the rock.

'It's an animal?' Yaz wondered why it didn't run away.

'A plant. You can eat them.' Arka took a bite from it and winced. 'These sort taste better cooked.'

'Plant?' Maya asked. Yaz thanked her silently, not wanting to always be the one showing her ignorance.

'Plants . . .' Arka waved her hands at the things helplessly. 'They don't move and they don't bleed but they live . . .'

'Like a tree,' Quina said quietly, rolling something small between her fingers.

Arka frowned. 'I don't know about those. But Eular says plants grow anywhere that there is warmth and water and light. He says everything living depends on them for food.'

'I bloody don't,' Kao growled. 'I eat meat like everyone else.'

'Yes, but the fish you take from the sea eat plants or eat other fish that eat plants and—'

'There are plants in the sea now?' Yaz asked.

'Yes and—'

'But there's no light under the sea,' Quina said.

'Well . . .' Arka grew flustered. 'There must be . . . Eular knows these things. Ask him!' She thrust the rest of the fungus ball into Quina's hand and strode away. 'Come on!' As she walked she offered more advice on the mysterious world of plants. 'The brown ones aren't bad raw. Brown ones with reddish spots will have you vomiting blood for a week. Purple ones will kill you. We weed out the bad ones from the groves but out in the more distant caves you'll find them, sometimes mixed in with the good ones.'

The settlement sat in an enormous cavern whose entire roof glowed faintly with innumerable stars. Instead of tents, angled to resist the wind, the Broken lived within strange, blocky dwellings fashioned from a variety of materials each more foreign than the next. Glass was the only building material Yaz recognized, gleaming in ill-advised openings in walls. Many of the walls were made from what might be rock but of a lighter colour than that underfoot. The rock had been shaped into blocks much like those the Eskin clan made from snow to construct shelters.

'Do we have to sleep in one of these?' Maya's voice echoed Yaz's own mistrust of those hard flat roofs and sharp angles.

'Is there nothing you're not afraid of, girl?' Kao snorted. 'No wonder Clan Axit wanted to drop you down the pit!'

Maya put her head down and said nothing. Clan Axit were the largest of all the clans and many said they all thought themselves kings of the ice. Although life in the wastes left no room for war the Axit had a reputation for fierceness. Blood and more blood had been spilled in the long ago and some said they trained in secret for a war still to come. Yaz gave Kao a hard look until he coloured and turned away.

Yaz couldn't tell how large the settlement was, only that it seemed to cover a bigger area than the Ictha used when pitching their tents. Perhaps there were more of the Broken than she had first thought. Or maybe there had been more of them in the past.

As they drew closer to the buildings Yaz sniffed at the familiar smell of humanity, stronger here than in camp where the wind scoured the ice between the tents. She saw figures moving in the gloom, making their way along the clear pathways between the various structures. Closer still and she heard the drip, drip, drip of water on rooftops. Every surface close to horizontal glimmered with a light so subtle that the eye almost missed it, stardust falling with the meltwater.

Arka directed them to a low building, one of the first they reached. 'You'll all be sleeping in this barracks tonight. And

I will be in that hut over there.' She pointed to a smaller structure whose door faced the barracks door. 'To keep an eye on you.'

Arka followed them into the barracks. Unlike some of the other buildings this one had none of those glass-covered openings, a fact for which Yaz was grateful. A single small star-stone hung from the roof support in a wire cage, providing a weak light. A dozen bedrolls had been laid out on pallets of the same stuff the walls were made of. The rolls themselves were patchworks of worn skins, sewn and resewn to the point that Yaz wondered if she would wake to find hers in a hundred pieces. She didn't recognize the fur, not hoola or harp whale.

Maya yawned and Yaz found herself suddenly exhausted. She had no idea how long had passed in the first ice chamber she'd dropped into. Would the gathering far above be in full swing or breaking up as the sun rose? For a moment the weight of all that ice seemed to crush her. She bore it though, along with the weight of sorrow for her mother and her father and Quell and maybe for some of the others she would never see again. Would they be grieving amid the celebrations, even though they were not supposed to? The music and the ferment were meant to help in the forgetting but she hoped they would each at least shed one tear for the girl they had lost.

'You stay here until I come for you.' Arka opened the door, pointing. 'That hut way over there by the entrance to that side chamber. That's where you go in the night. Nothing freezes down here so we don't take care of our business near where we sleep. And nothing is wasted. What we have no use for helps grow the plants we eat.'

'The fungi eats dung?' Kao pushed up the blond mop of his hair in disgust. 'And you eat the fungi?'

Arka shrugged. 'You will too if you don't want to starve. It's the circle of life. The dead go into the pits too. It's how life is. Eular says that on the ice that circle is broken because Abeth is dying. What you take from the sea does not return. But down here the cycle still turns life into death and death into life, and will do so as long as the stars shine.' With that she left them. Yaz sat, watching Arka walk away and wondering who this Eular was who seemed to know everything.

'Well, I'm not eating that . . . muck.' Kao slammed the door behind Arka.

A low chuckle brought their attention to the gloom at the far end of the barracks where what had seemed to be a heap of bedding now raised its head.

'So this is where you ran off to.' Kao snorted at Thurin and shook his head. On the ice nobody stormed off in a temper. The wind would cool you down quicker than you liked, and if your anger took you out of view then you might never find your way back.

Thurin shrugged. 'I have things to prove before they let me back.'

'Back?' Quina went to take a sleeping place not far from Thurin's.

Thurin said nothing, only lay down and turned away. Maya went to take a place near the door.

'Not that one,' Kao said, looming over her.

Maya moved to another, and Kao scowled at her retreat. Yaz watched, wondering that someone so large would feel the need to push a small girl around. Kao could have made an issue of Thurin laughing at him, if he wanted a fight, but there was something haunting that one's eyes that might give a mad dog pause.

Taking a pallet a good distance from Kao's Yaz settled herself down. 'I'm going to find my brother and rescue him from the Tainted.' She said it with more confidence than she felt and looked through the gloom at the shapeless heap that was Thurin.

'If you see him you should run,' the heap replied.

'Arka told me that the rest are not as bad as Hetta,' Yaz said. 'They don't eat people.'

'Let them catch you and you'll wish they had eaten you.' A long silence. 'Theus is worse than Hetta. Much worse.'

It was as if Thurin were daring her to ask. She held her tongue. She wasn't sure if it was pride that kept her lips sealed. Or maybe it was just knowing that since she *had* to go after Zeen it was better she didn't hear anything which might make it harder to leave.

Thurin told her anyway. 'Theus has a plan. He leads them. All of them. Even Hetta is scared of Theus. He's looking for something in the black ice. Been looking for it a long time. A very long time.'

'Who is he? What tribe? How old is he?' The man had taken her brother. Yaz found herself needing to know, however bad it might be.

Thurin didn't speak for a while and the barracks seemed to hold its breath, as if the others were listening too and feared to betray themselves.

'Theus is as old as the body he wears. When I first saw him he was wearing Gossix, a boy I used to know.'

'Wearing?' Yaz shuddered. She could only think of a flayed skin, just as the Ictha wore the skin of mole-fish, the hides of tuark, and seal furs traded from the Triple Seas far to the south. 'None of the tribes would—'

'Theus is not of the tribes.' Thurin's voice fell to a whisper, haunted with memory. 'He comes from the ice itself.' He seemed about to say more but the door burst open and light flooded in, chasing shadows to the corners.

'On your feet, drop-group!' Pome stood, revealed in the light of his own star.

He watched, hard-faced, as they stood, Thurin last of all, favouring him with a dark look.

'Inspection time.' Pome strode in between them. 'Let's see what sorry excuses we've been given this time.'

Maya shrank away from the star as Pome waved it past her on the end of its iron rod. Pome swung back to Kao by the doorway. 'Big fellow, eh? Golin?'

Kao nodded.

'I should have been leader of this drop-group,' Pome said. 'But Tarko has his politics to play. In the end though, drop-groups aren't here or there. You come sit with us sometime, down at the Green Shack, and I'll tell you how things are under the ice. The Broken are listening to me these days and they like what I'm saying. Tarko has me marked for great things.'

Kao nodded and Yaz found herself starting to nod too. She stopped. There was nothing she liked about this young man: not his attitude, the things he said, or the way his gaze slid over her, and yet somehow his words had been carrying her along with them.

'Get out, Pome.' Thurin spat. 'Take your pretty lies with you.'

Pome curled his lip in annoyance and strode towards Thurin, thrusting his star before him. 'Was that you talking, Taint? Or did you let a demon take your tongue again?'

Thurin backed from the starlight, shielding his face as if it were a fierce heat.

'See?' Pome looked back at the rest of them. 'The Tainted can't stand the stars. The light is what keeps us safe.' He glanced at Kao. 'Never go where it's dark, boy. Not down here. They'll have you in a moment.'

'Yessir.' Kao gulped and nodded.

Pome turned and jabbed his star at Thurin, who was pressed to the back wall now. The light made him gasp as if in pain, forcing him to slide into the corner on his rear.

'Stop that!' Yaz found herself moving forward. However convincing Pome's words felt, she didn't like what he was doing one bit.

'Or you'll stop me?' Pome swung round, thrusting his star at her chest.

Yaz squinted down to where the star blazed against her mole-fish skins, brighter even than before. It was just light though, no heat, no pain. The star gave off a faint sound, like the strains of a distant song, with a rapid beat beneath it. 'You should leave.'

Pome frowned and jabbed the star against her. He looked puzzled.

'Pome!' It was Arka at the doorway. 'Get out here.'

Pome's face tightened. He forced a smile over gritted teeth and left without saying anything more.

'Are you all right?' Yaz tilted her head, not sure if she should offer Thurin her hand to help him rise. Outside, Arka and Pome's raised voices diminished into the distance.

'Fine.' Thurin got to his feet, not looking at Yaz or her half-offered hand. He brushed himself down and went to his bed.

Thurin didn't speak again until they were all settling to sleep. 'People think Pome's special because he can withstand the stars, but that's not why he's dangerous. He's dangerous because his words get under your skin. Listen to him too long and you start believing what he says. And if he doesn't manage to hook you that way then watch out for the ones he does hook.'

Sleep took an age to find Yaz. Imagination chased her through her exhaustion. Strangers' eyes watched her from tainted faces, laden with malice. At last she turned her thoughts from Thurin's words only to rediscover the unsettling warmth, the dampness in the air – something she knew only from the Hot Sea – the irregular splat of meltwater drops falling upon the roof, the distant groaning of the ice always on the move. All of it conspired to keep her dreams away and instead her mind replayed the events of the pit and the screaming rush of her fall, over and over.

Yaz lay in the gloom staring at the roof above her. In her whole life this was the first time she had tried to sleep anywhere but within her family tent. She needed the constant complaint of the wind against the hides. She needed her father's growling snore building to the familiar snort then temporary silence. She needed the cold and the knowledge that Zeen and her mother pressed her, hide-wrapped, to either side. Yaz thought of her mother then and a tear ran from the corner of her eye. What must it be like in the tent now with just the two of them in all that space? Father, grim-faced, hands in fists upon his lap, knuckles white. Mother, proud, her face carved by the endless wind, iron in her long dark hair, eyes as pale as the wastes. Four years ago she had two sons and a daughter. Now they were gone. Would her pride still carry her over the ruin of her family? A second tear rolled after the first.

Finally Yaz dozed, woken periodically by a gnawing hunger, not helped by regular gurgles from Kao's stomach. Hunger reminded her that however suicidal her mind might have been in throwing her down the Pit of the Missing, her body intended to live and was demanding that she look after its needs or things would go hard on her.

When a dark shape crept past her Yaz imagined that whoever it was was heading for the distant hut Arka had pointed out. But the figure, too slim to be Kao and too tall for Maya, left the door ajar and turned the wrong way. Curious, Yaz slipped from her covers and moved to follow.

She saw now as she left the barracks that it could only be Thurin ahead of her. On the ice he wouldn't last long, too thin to resist the wind's assault. Yaz herself lacked the full solidity of the Ictha but Thurin looked as though he might be blown away before the wind froze him.

The gritty rock felt curious underfoot, sticking to her damp feet. To leave a shelter without boots and liners was to lose toes to the frost, but here a lifetime's learning could be undone in one drop. Yaz stumbled as she followed Thurin away from the settlement, stubbing her big toe on a fold in the rock. She cursed as quietly as she could, hobbling along a good thirty yards behind her quarry.

Thurin crossed the length of the cavern, jumping two small streams, and came to an archway that led to some new chamber, darker than the one they occupied. Near the entrance a single light burned, a star-stone larger than any of those Yaz had yet seen, bedded in the ice at a level she might reach if she were to stand on Thurin's shoulders and stretch.

Thurin came to a halt near the arch. 'You're not doing a very good job of spying on me, you know.' He didn't turn towards her.

Yaz froze and said nothing.

'Stealth isn't really a skill you need on the ice. I'm told the wind hides every other noise and that there's nothing to hunt.'

Still Yaz remained motionless, the air trapped in her lungs.

'You should have told me that you weren't trying to be quiet.' Thurin at last turned to face Yaz and she released her breath. 'But I have heard that the Ictha can't lie.' He cocked his head. 'Is that true?'

'Yes,' Yaz lied, and they both smiled.

'You can't sleep. Most can't on the first night. Maybe the others are just faking it. The big lad, Wayo?'

'Kao.'

'Kao, then. He can't really snore like that? I'm sure it must be some kind of a joke . . .'

Yaz found herself chuckling and made herself stop, suddenly stern. 'What are you doing out here?'

'Answering questions.'

Yaz didn't smile this time. 'I have more. I want to know—'

'Aren't you cold?' Thurin asked.

'I—' Yaz looked down, mortified at the reminder she had nothing on but the mole-fish skins she'd been sewn into. She should have stolen Kao's cape but it was so warm she hadn't noticed her state of undress. Now beneath the brightness of the nearby star she felt next to naked. 'No!' She had hoped the word would come out defiantly but it ended up as more of a squeak. 'Too hot if anything.' Not a lie. Under Thurin's amused gaze every inch of exposed skin felt as if it were burning.

'It's a breath away from freezing.' Thurin shook his head. 'The stories about the Ictha appear to be true. Are you all as strong as bears too?'

'I don't know. I've never seen a bear, let alone wrestled one.'

Thurin smiled, though there was a sadness in it, the same sorrow that had been haunting him when they first met and ran beneath his laughter. He turned back towards the ice again.

'I have more questions.' Yaz moved closer.

'I didn't come here to answer your questions,' he said.

'But you said—'

'I have questions of my own.' He crossed to where the rock held a puddle and crouched before it.

Yaz bit back on her impatience and went to stand behind him. Shouting at Thurin was unlikely to get her the answers she needed. Though she was prepared to knock his head against the rock as a last resort if that was what it took. 'Well?'

Thurin reached out to the water, putting his hand into it, flat against the rock at the bottom, long fingers splayed.

'Ah . . .' Something twisted inside Yaz, a curious sensation, as if she were a pool into which a ball of ice had fallen, sending out ripples. Only she was the ice and the ripples as well as being the pool.

Thurin let out a small gasp, pain perhaps, and raised his hand. Somehow the water rose with his hand, a slowly undulating glove, inches thick on every side, beautiful where the light came through to project moving lines of light and shadow across Yaz's stomach and thighs.

'You're a witch-child!'

Thurin laughed and the water fell away in sparkling drops. 'I'm not a child. And it's an old blood that runs through us. Older than the Ictha or any other tribe. Marjal blood.'

'Us?' Yaz wasn't sure she wanted this strange young man as her kin.

'Well, you're too small for a gerant, unless you're twelve . . . and you don't look twelve.' For a moment Thurin's gaze ran the length of her.

Yaz let anger burn away any sense of shame at her state of undress. 'I've seen the long night sixteen times. None but the Ictha can endure it.'

'Ah, but that's why the regulator threw you down, is it

not?' An eyebrow arched. 'You wouldn't have lasted many more. You don't strike me as a hunska even though you have the black hair. Your eyes are too pale. Are you quick?'

'Quick enough.' Yaz thought of Zeen. Her brother made her seem slow. In the hand-slap game there was no beating him, and although his eyes weren't the night black of some southerners like Quina, they were the darkest she knew among the Ictha.

'Not gerant huge or hunska fast, and yet thrown down here with the rest of us. You're a marjal, Yaz.'

She hadn't been sure Thurin had even registered her name. It sounded strange in his mouth, the southern tribes blunted the edges of their words.

'Will I be able to do . . . that . . . then?' She nodded at the rippling puddle.

Thurin pursed his lips. 'We marjals have many tricks; the gods reach into their bag of marvels and scatter us with this gift or that, but never too many. The most common are skills to work with shadow or air. My talent is the most prized of the basic skills down here. We can influence the ice, even in its molten form.' He waved a hand at the puddle and the ripples vanished. 'I can also work with fire, that's a rarer skill than ice-work but useless. There's nothing to burn here.' He shook his head, smiling ruefully at the gods' joke. 'The rarest elemental skill is rock-work. But there's no rock on the ice and no fire beneath it.'

'How do you even know you can work flame if there's no fire down here?' Yaz asked.

Thurin smiled. 'At the forge they melt iron down. I can understand the heat, move it around. It feels the same as when I manipulate the ice. I think my flame-work might actually be stronger than my ice-work.' He shook his head again at the irony.

'Are there other magics?' Yaz asked. None of this sounded like the river that runs through all things, the source of her strangeness.

'Some. Oddities that crop up now and then. Welaz could make things float in the air. Anything. Even people. But he's dead now. Old Gella can make a wound heal faster than it should. Dekkan can find things that are lost.' He shrugged and pulled his coat around him. 'How can you not be cold?' he asked.

'Why did you come out here?' Yaz tried to turn the conversation in a new direction.

'Maybe I wanted to spy on someone.' Thurin met her eyes with a frank smile and Yaz turned away. 'Or maybe I needed to check I still had value.'

'Do the marjals lose their powers then?' Yaz asked. 'I know the Tainted had you. Is that why they let you go? Your power got weak?'

'We don't lose our skills, no. If anything they get stronger. Once ice-sworn, always ice-sworn. But I'm exhausted and underfed.' He looked down at his own thinness. 'And the Tainted don't let anyone go. Ever. Arka led a raid to get me back. A woman died. Another man lost his eye. They should have left me.' He stared out into the darkness, bleak and silent for a moment. 'Tarko wouldn't have let them risk it if I weren't valuable to the Broken.'

'But why? The trick with the water is pretty but—'

'They need me to dig through ice. I can dig faster than three gerants put together. For a tenth of the food ration.' Thurin forced a smile and patted his narrow stomach. 'I like the digging too. If I don't use my ice-work regularly then the energy builds up inside me and when I do eventually use it . . . well, it can be dramatic.'

Yaz looked around at the echoingly large space about

them. 'These caverns are huge. Why is it so important to dig new ones?'

'For these.' Thurin turned back towards the wall, thrusting his hand out. High up the ice shattered and the brilliant star fell within a cloud of glowing fragments to strike the rock beneath.

'Should you have done that?' Yaz glanced back towards the settlement, alarmed. For all that she wanted to find Zeen she knew she needed help from the Broken. Getting banished on her first night would cap off, with one stupid move, a day's journey that had started with another very stupid move.

'Relax. It's us ice-workers who put the things up there in the first place and they're always being re-sunk. All of the stars generate a very small amount of heat even without sigils around them. They sink through the ice very slowly. The tiny ones, little more than dust really, sink so slowly that the current of the ice can lift them. The big ones all end up on the bedrock given time.' He advanced on the star as he spoke until he was reduced to a silhouette with the light streaming all around him.

Thurin's steps grew slower and closer together as he approached the star, almost as though he were fighting to make progress against a great wind. Yaz could hear the strain in his voice when he spoke. 'This is the largest of the stars we use as lights. People don't like to get near them, especially the bigger ones, so we use smaller ones in town.'

'You . . . you're not worried someone will steal it?' Yaz wondered if that might be exactly what he was doing right now.

'The Tainted? No, the Taints can't abide them. Won't go near one if they have a choice.' There was real pain in Thurin's voice now, and still he had a yard to go if he were to pick the stone up.

'What are you doing?' Yaz called, squinting into the light. 'Why are you doing it?'

'Proving . . . something . . . to . . . myself.' Thurin took another step then fell back with a cry.

'Thurin!' Yaz ran to help him as he crawled away, the light flaring behind him.

'I'm all right.' Thurin pushed her hand from his arm and staggered up.

'You don't look all right.' He looked like a rag that's too worn to be used as anything but stuffing. She glanced towards the star, still blazing on the rock. 'How can you put it back if you can't even touch it?'

Thurin waved a tired hand at the star and the water rushed from the puddle to set it rolling back against the ice wall. He made a fist and twisted it. Somehow the ice drew the star half into it and began to lift it. Fascinated, Yaz edged closer while Thurin continued the slow upward flow of the ice, raising the star above her head towards its former position. Creaks, groans, and small splintering noises accompanied the star's gradual ascent, the ice protesting just as it did on a larger scale as the great sheets moved across the rock.

Glancing back Yaz could see the effort it was costing Thurin. In the twilight she could almost see the threads of magic connecting Thurin to the wall. Suddenly he faltered, the gossamer network of his magic fell apart, and with a sharp retort something high above Yaz snapped.

The star fell, hit the rock, and rolled, coming to a halt by the side of Yaz's foot. She heard Thurin cry out in shock then find his words 'Get away! Quick!'

The star blazed so bright Yaz could see nothing but its brilliance. The power and nearness of it sang in her bones, a wordless roaring, beautiful but wild enough to drown in. Despite its smallness and outpouring of light the star seemed a wider and deeper hole than that into which she had thrown herself only hours before. Unable to stop herself Yaz crouched and reached to pick the thing from the floor. The light made black lines of her finger bones and a rosy haze of the flesh around them. Her whole hand tingled, then burned, then closed around the star, so small that she could almost hide it within her grasp.

'Be still,' she told it for it seemed to her that the star was a racing heart, beating beyond its limits. And suddenly the blaze vanished, replaced by a molten reddish glow like that of the setting sun. There was a silence too. She had barely heard the star's song before, but now that it was gone the air seemed to ache for its return. Yaz looked for Thurin and saw nothing but blackness swimming with after-images.

'What have you done?' Thurin, aghast, speaking from her blindness.

'I asked it to be quiet.' Yaz blinked and was relieved to see Thurin as a dark shape moving against a less dark background.

'You shouldn't be able to do that!' He sounded scared. Amazed, but scared. 'Make it work again.'

Yaz went right up to the wall and held the star above her at arm's length, stretching. She pressed it to the ice. 'Make it go in.'

Thurin's magic fluttered around her and the ice swallowed the star as easily as if she were pressing it into fresh snow. 'It's still not working!' he hissed.

Yaz stepped back. The star's red glow gave the ice around it a bloody hue. 'Sing,' she told it. And in an instant the light returned, bright as it had ever been.

'Come on!' Thurin grabbed her shoulder, nails biting into bare skin. 'We need to go back.' He pulled her with him. 'Pray nobody saw that!'

Both of them stumbled into the settlement, exhausted. Yaz found herself unable to stop yawning and Thurin seemed barely able to stand. 'Working the ice . . . takes something out of me.' He straightened with effort.

Yaz just nodded and followed as he led off again. Her sight had yet to recover entirely and the cavern's twilight pulsed around her. Amid it all a mysterious clot of shadow moved across her vision like a person wrapped in night.

'I'm not normally so weak,' Thurin muttered. 'But when I was . . .'

'With the Tainted,' Yaz supplied.

He nodded. 'My ice-work got used, but it wasn't me using it. I was a passenger in my own body. I'm out of practice at being me . . . if that makes any sense.'

Yaz said nothing. Part of her was thinking of Zeen, demon-haunted, wandering out there somewhere in the black ice. The other part ran Thurin's words through her mind. *Out of practice at being me.* She felt adrift. She had, for her entire life, been a small but vital part in a single organism dedicated to survival against the odds. Just like every other member of the Ictha she'd carried out her duties in the certain knowledge that should she fail they would all suffer. On the edge of extinction every mistake carried a fatal edge, every waking moment had a purpose, every hour was occupied. It seemed strange that after what should have been a fall to her death she had for perhaps the first time in her life a chance to practise being her.

On the outskirts of the settlement Thurin turned and looked out across the great cavern sleeping in its own starlit twilight. A dozen openings led from it into other caverns or tunnels. 'It's pretty, but seriously though, don't wander off.'

'I might get lost?' asked Yaz, trying not to bristle at the suggestion she couldn't look after herself.

'You might get taken.' Thurin made a flat line of his mouth. 'Hetta will only eat you. Theus haunts the dark, and those they can't fill with demons . . .'

'What happens to them?'

Thurin turned away. 'Sometimes we hear them screaming, even here. It can last for days. They do it to tempt us out there.'

Yaz hung her head. The shadows and starlight seemed suddenly less beautiful and she shivered despite the warmth.

Thurin led off wearily without saying more.

They reached the barracks and almost fell through the door. Yaz found the energy to close it behind them, noticing as she did so that the door to Arka's hut stood ajar. She wondered for a moment if the woman had watched them return together. She decided that she was too tired to care, about anything, and crawled beneath her thin blanket with a sigh. She thought of this Theus, this nightmare creature waiting for them in the darkness, and was sure she would lie awake until the next day. But she was asleep before she drew her next breath.

CHAPTER 7

Hua, least of all the Gods in the Sea, made Zin, the first man, from salt water, the bones of a tuark, and the skin of a whale. While Aiiki, least of all the Gods in the Sky, made Mokka, the first woman, from ice, clouds, the whispers of four lost winds, and a colour stolen from the dragons' tails.

Zin climbed from the waves and scaled the great cliffs to find that Mokka was there on the heights before him and had already set her tent. Zin asked if he might enter for the wind was a stranger to him and cruel. Mokka knew the wind as she knew herself and let the man come within, for he would die without.

Zin brought fish from beneath the water and he ate to restore his strength. Mokka asked if she might eat for the sea was a stranger to her, showing its face but rarely. Zin knew the waters as he knew himself and let the woman eat, for she had known only hunger.

Hua and Aiiki were the least of all the gods and neither spoke nor touched, but the children of their minds came to walk all corners of the world, and their

*work was in its way as mighty as that of any in the sky
or in the sea.*

*None walk ice but for the sharing of Zin and Mokka.
None survive there alone for the wind is cruel and the
sea is a stranger. All their children are taught this lesson
in their cradle hides. To forget this is to forget ourselves.
To forget this is to go into the ice before your time.*

A clanging sound drew Yaz from the depths of her dreaming.
An alien noise. The Ictha owned little metal and what they
did own came from the priests of the Black Rock, iron pins
that could be driven into the ice where bone would prove
unequal to the task, knife-blades for those who could afford
the trade goods demanded for such things. Yaz's uncle owned
an iron knife but it had been her grandfather who purchased
it with the horn of a narwhal and a stack of bundled tuark
skins as tall as himself. Even so, Yaz had heard the sound
of metal on metal before: it clanged.

CLANG.

Yaz sat abruptly then clutched her blanket to her. On all
sides her fellow newcomers were sitting up, remembering
where they were, and realizing that they had no idea what
to do until someone arrived to tell them. Yaz drew up her
legs and hugged herself, not against the cold but against the
memories of the previous day.

The clanging stopped but Arka failed to appear.

'What was that?' Maya asked.

'It's to wake up the day shift.' Thurin yawned and stretched.
'Not that we have nights and days down here. But Tarko
likes to keep things ordered.'

'So, we're awake.' Kao hulked in front of the star-
lamp throwing everyone into shadow. 'Where do we go for
breakfast?'

The others grinned but Kao's answering scowl showed that he wasn't joking, and now that Yaz thought about it she discovered herself to be ravenous. She went to dip a hide cup into the water bucket at the end of the barracks and drank. The bucket was made of no substance she knew. The water tasted clean but everything here was strange, nothing felt right.

'Where did all the young ones go?' Quina asked suddenly.

'They fell to the Taints,' Thurin answered in a quiet voice.

'She told us that yesterday. The scar-faced woman . . . Arka.' Kao sneered, though whether at Quina's stupidity or some distaste for Arka, or both, Yaz couldn't tell.

'But why?' Quina persisted. 'Why are all of us here nearly grown and all the young ones . . . none of the older ones . . . with the Taints?'

'It's a good question.' Thurin closed off Kao's retort with a raised hand. 'It depends on how the pit is. The vents form, stretch and twist as the ice flows, and then are abandoned as the heat finds a new more direct route to the surface. There can be many ways down and sometimes who falls where just depends on how heavy they are. The shafts sort them like . . .' He wriggled his fingers as if trying to pluck a good analogy from the air.

'Fish in a sorting basket,' Maya offered.

Yaz and Quina grunted. It was well said. In a sorting basket the fisher shook their catch in the right way and the largest rose to the top, the small fry packing the tail.

The door banged open. Arka leaned in. 'Come on then, eat!' She frowned at Thurin. 'You know this stuff. Show some initiative.'

The five of them followed her out into the same gloom that had seen them to bed. Kao, Quina, and Maya clutched their capes about them, and Yaz brought her blanket. Arka cast a disapproving eye over them. 'All right, all right, you can go fetch your clothes from the drying cave. I want you back here before I get bored of waiting. Thurin, make sure they don't get lost.' She clapped her hands. 'Run!'

Thurin led off at a steady pace, weaving around the larger puddles. Quina kept easily at his shoulder, Yaz next holding to a straighter path, Kao and Maya labouring at the rear, one too heavy for speed, the other too short-legged for it.

Yaz slowed considerably when they reached the ravine. The narrow path down into it gave onto a decidedly fatal-looking drop on one side. Quina was nearly dressed by the time Yaz joined her and Thurin. The heat immediately made Yaz sweat, droplets beading the redness of her skin and making her wonder why she'd bothered drying the clothes. In the north an Ictha could not afford to sweat. Even that small amount of moisture could see them freeze entirely. Here in the heat and dampness she seemed to do little else.

'Be quick about it,' Thurin advised. 'We don't want to make Arka look bad. Pome is just itching to find fault and get himself put in charge of us. If he put half as much effort into defending us against the Tainted as he does into fighting Tarko and agitating then we'd still have them confined to the black ice.'

'He . . . he's not dangerous though?' Little Maya looked worried. She looked worried most of the time.

Thurin made a half-shrug. 'Arka thinks he is, but Tarko doesn't see it. Arka isn't convinced that everyone who's disappeared lately has been taken by the Tainted or while scavenging. But that's hard to prove. Just because some of those who vanished were standing in Pome's way doesn't mean he had a hand in it. Life down here is dangerous . . .

So don't go making enemies of Pome or anyone else. Especially Pome.' He glanced at Yaz, a warning look, as if standing up for him last night had been a foolish thing.

Yaz dressed in a hurry, haste making her clumsy, and then had to wait for Maya and Kao to finish before Thurin would lead them back.

'Why dry clothes all the way out here anyway?' she asked.

'The stone keeps the heat in better than any shelter. And we don't like to make too much heat under an ice roof. Sometimes they don't just drip. A chunk can fall. And that tends to hurt.'

Yaz winced.

Quina stood, fully dressed in her clan furs. Their clothes identified their clans both by design and composition. Nothing but men survived on the ice in the far north so the Ictha had no furs save the few they traded. They wore hides and skins. Among the Broken, though, the differences were lost amid years of repairs. The coat and leggings that wrapped Thurin's narrow musculature were a patchwork of furs and leathers in which Yaz saw no clues at all to his clan.

Quina offered her a narrow smile, quick then gone. 'More speed less haste. We'll get your brother back from the Tainted. They got Thurin back after months. So you can take the time to match your ties up.'

Yaz looked down to realize she had mismatched one side of her outer coat to the other. 'Dung on it!'

Quina's grin returned. 'Is that how they curse in the north?'

Yaz felt her cheeks colouring but she nodded. She found herself liking this narrow girl with her guarded ways and swift smiles.

'I thought the Ictha would be good at swearing, what with all those long nights to practise!' Quina went to the doorway. 'I'll teach you some better ones later.'

Maya's struggling head emerged wide-eyed from the top of her parka. 'You're going to rescue your brother?'

'Yes.' Yaz frowned. The Ictha would call it throwing good spears after bad. The Ictha couldn't afford grand gestures. Weakness had to be abandoned on the ice. Grow too old, get sick, become injured, become a burden and the harsh equations of wind and cold dictated that you be left. No one would come after her. She had committed the crime of weakness and the Pit of the Missing was her sentence, though somehow the regulator had commuted it. She set her jaw defiantly. This was a new world. New rules applied. 'Yes, I am. And soon. Coming with me?'

Maya paled at that and edged towards Thurin, waiting in the doorway. Thurin shot Yaz another glance, this one unreadable. Quina had already left the hut.

'Come on!' Thurin waved to go, even though Kao was still struggling to get his other over-boot on and lace it.

'I feel better like this.' Yaz stamped her boots, the rock no longer grating against the soles of her feet. Back in the clothes she'd been wearing when she dropped Yaz felt like an Ictha again. She looked like one too. The mix and colour of her skins declared it. She wondered how long it would take for her differences to fade into the patched oneness of the Broken. She wondered if the guilt would ever fade. If she would ever lose the feeling that it had been her fault which dragged her here. Her failure that deprived the Ictha of a pair of able hands and took her parents' first and last child from their tent.

The others started up the path at a half-run, laughing as Kao bellowed curses after them. Yaz followed, deep in her thoughts, Kao labouring behind her, still snatching at his boot. He began to catch them up in the second great chamber, puffing and blowing.

'Call that running? Arka told us to hurry!' Quina sped off, showing a remarkable turn of speed. 'Come on!'

Thurin made to chase after her but paused when he saw that Yaz had come to a halt. 'The Ictha girl needs to rest?'

'No . . .' Yaz wasn't sure what it was but it was . . . something. The river that runs through all things remained hidden from her; she had used its power on the previous day to match the endurance of her tribe and it would be some time yet before she could find it again. But even when the river lay beyond her reach there were echoes of it everywhere, lines, infinitely many and infinitely fine, running from and to every part of every thing. She only had to defocus her vision to see those threads, and sometimes, like now, they encroached without her asking. They had pulsed in the air around Regulator Kazik while he inspected her at the mouth of the pit and they vibrated now, throughout the cavern, as if they were a net across which something heavy were advancing. 'Over there.' She pointed without seeing.

'No?' Thurin spoke the word in disbelief.

'What is it?' Maya moved to stand behind Kao, who joined them, puffing, and with angry words waiting only on the breath with which to express them.

Yaz could now see two points of light in the direction she'd aimed her finger. Far across the dark cavern. Hard white light of a kind she had never seen. Not the soft red of sunlight or the warm orange of flame.

'With me!' Thurin shouted. 'Run!'

Yaz took off after Thurin, the others following, all but Quina who had gone off ahead and become lost from sight in the gloom. 'What is it?'

Thurin saved his breath for running. Yaz pounded after him, praying no unseen fold of the rock would trip her, and from behind came a growing clatter of hard feet hitting stone, a clattering and a clashing and a thrashing. Whatever the thing was it was gaining on them at a frightening rate. In seconds it would be on them, and with the cavern wall looming ahead they had nowhere to run in any case.

'In! Crawl!' Thurin reached the cavern wall at a point where the base failed to quite meet the floor, leaving a narrow gap between ice and rock. Yaz threw herself after him, cutting her hands on the grit to save tearing the knees from her leggings. Skin grows back, hides don't, was an old Ictha saying.

'Deeper!' Ahead of her Thurin was on his chest, scraping further in.

Kao and Maya launched themselves after Yaz and a heartbeat later their pursuer hit the wall with a thump that shivered through the ice. A shower of pulverized fragments fell in a white veil across the entrance to the gap.

'Quick! Get in deeper!' Thurin sounded desperate.

'I can't!' Kao's thick body was jammed two yards short of Yaz's position.

'Grab hold!' Yaz had already half turned to wedge herself deeper and now turned further to reach back for Kao's outstretched hand. Behind the boy she could see what seemed a forest of black legs through the clearing debris.

'Pull!' Kao screamed.

Yaz hauled, trying to anchor herself, but Kao proved more tightly held and instead they only succeeded in dragging *her* forward a few inches.

Behind Kao's scrabbling feet something large and black clanged against the rock and a blinding white eye filled the crevice with light.

'Try again!' Thurin shouted and above Kao a layer of ice several inches thick shattered and fell away as Thurin exercised his power.

Yaz hauled and Kao lurched forward.

Through slitted eyes Yaz could see a variety of limbs invading the gap, some sinuous like black metal tentacles, others rigid and articulated, iron arms with too many elbows and skinning knives for claws.

Kao jerked his foot back as one of the clawed arms reached for it.

Thurin shouted behind them. 'Back further! It opens up!'

In a nightmare of squeezing and pushing Yaz and Kao burrowed deeper until at last, as Thurin said, the ice roof lifted slowly, then swiftly, and they found themselves in a bubble the size of an Ictha tent, the almost-dark broken by the faintest glow from the walls.

'What in the long night is that thing?' Yaz almost had to shout to hear herself above the grinding and fracturing noises coming from the cavern wall even though it was now separated from them by ten yards of ice.

'A hunter from the city,' Thurin said. 'It shouldn't be here. They hardly ever leave the ruins.'

'But what is it?' Yaz demanded.

Thurin only shook his head. Behind him the glare from the hunter's eyes was a diffuse white glow reaching through the yards of ice.

Yaz crouched down to peer back the way they'd come. The hunter had lifted its head to get in close and was reaching for them blind. The longest of its arms raked the rock two yards shy of their chamber but could reach no further. The only light now was a deep red one, so deep it was almost black at times, radiating out from between the plates of armour covering the creature's body. Yaz couldn't make sense of the thing; it looked like a random collection of segmented pieces joined together. 'How long will it stay?'

'I don't know. It's not supposed to be here.'

'City?' Yaz looked up, suddenly realizing that Thurin had mentioned a city. 'What city?' Men had had cities before the ice swept them aside. The legends said so.

'A city of the Missing,' Thurin said. He leaned back and shook his head. 'You really don't know what goes on down here at all, do you?'

'No!' Suddenly she was angry. 'And neither did you before you were pushed down the pit, so don't play so high and mighty with us!'

'I wasn't pushed.' Thurin said it so softly she wondered if she had misheard him above the hunter's clawing. He'd thrown himself down, like her?

Kao snorted, recovering some of his composure. 'Of course you were, you lying sack of—'

'I was born here.'

CHAPTER 8

'How long do we have to stay here?' Kao had been pacing for what seemed like hours. One pace, two pace, turn. One pace, two pace, turn.

'I don't know.' Thurin had given the same reply the last several times and it didn't seem to stick.

'Try sitting,' Yaz suggested from where she sat.

Kao made no reply. He seemed more scared of the narrowness of the space confining him than of the hunter outside. And he had been pretty scared of that. Yaz didn't blame him there. No amount of muscle is going to make a difference against a creature of iron with knives for claws. But fear of enclosed spaces was not something the Ictha knew. Anyone who couldn't spend three months inside a tent would not last long among her people.

Outside, the grinding continued as it had continued the whole time.

'Will it dig its way to us?' Maya asked, eyes wide in the darkness.

Yaz would have said no, nothing could, but the sounds did seem to have grown louder, as if the beast were actually making progress. Certainly when it reached in every so often its claws seemed to scrape the rock much closer to their hiding place each time. Either it was burrowing through ice at a remarkable rate or its limbs were growing longer!

'The others will come,' Yaz said. 'Quina will have told them.'

'Unless that thing got her,' Kao said.

Yaz shook her head. 'Then Arka would have sent someone to check on us already. Arka said we should hurry.'

'They'll all know by now,' Thurin agreed. 'One way or the other.'

'So they come and find us and . . .' Yaz still marvelled that they were being attacked by a mass of iron that would outweigh all the metal owned by even the largest of clans. Her life could soon be ended by a sharp-edged heap of treasure of incalculable value. 'How do you beat these things?'

'We don't. We hide and eventually they go away.'

'And if they don't?'

'Then someone draws them off. But they always go away in the end, and if you can make it to the long slope they hardly ever follow you past the gateposts.'

'So . . . why hasn't someone drawn it off?' Maya asked. Now that they were in real trouble she sounded perfectly calm, no sign of the wide-eyed nervous girl from before.

Thurin didn't speak for a moment, and then, as if deciding on honesty, 'I guess they've tried to draw it off but it just wants us more than it wants them. Sometimes that happens. It's one of the reasons you won't see many grey hairs among the Broken.'

Kao stopped pacing. 'I've got to get out,' he muttered to himself as if it were a sudden realization. 'Got to get out.'

He fell to his hands and knees and began to crawl to the gap.

'Don't be stupid.' Thurin grabbed the boy's shoulder and tried to haul him back. He made almost no difference against Kao's strength but the boy lashed out anyway, sending Thurin flying back into the wall of the chamber.

Yaz stepped between Kao and the gap just before he could enter it. 'That thing out there will tear you apart!'

Kao showed no signs of having heard her. Somehow his fear of being trapped in such close confines had overwhelmed his fear of the hunter. He jumped to his feet with a strangled cry and reached to grab Yaz as though intending to toss her aside too. Bracing herself against the wall she caught both his wrists. The boy growled and tried to fasten his hands on her shoulders. He stood well over six feet, his arms heaped with muscle, and his strength was frightening.

'What?' Kao grunted with effort and pressed down even more forcefully.

Yaz ground her teeth, breathing heavily and held him where he was, hands just inches from closing on her. In the main chamber a great crash rang out.

'How . . . are . . . you . . . doing . . . this?' He eased the pressure, amazed.

A pained laugh rang out behind them, Thurin back on his feet, clutching his side. 'She's of the Ictha. The northmen are a different breed.'

'Listen!' Yaz let go of Kao's wrists. A second great crash sounded outside along with an unearthly howl more chilling than any the wind ever made. The light dimmed, nothing but the faint glow of the surrounding ice reaching them.

'It's not normally like this.' Thurin's voice sounded beside her, closer than she had thought he was. 'Even when hunters do leave the city they stick to the fringes. I've never heard of one this far in. We're practically at the settlement.'

Yaz shrugged, trying to offset his worry. 'This sort of thing has been pretty normal for me lately.' The hunter scared her less than Hetta had, though it looked even harder to overcome. Somehow it was Hetta's hunger that terrified her more than iron claws and spikes.

'Ha.' Thurin snorted. They faced each other, just two handwidths between them but still not close enough to make out each other's expression.

'It's stopped.' Maya crouched low and peered through the gap. 'It's gone!'

Kao bent to join the girl but Yaz turned from Thurin and shoved him back with a grunt. 'It could be a trick. We wait!'

Kao straightened but thought better of testing his strength against hers again. Yaz was glad of that. Her arms hurt. She had always been told the Ictha were stronger than the southern tribes but had thought it meant only that they could endure the cold better. However strong the Ictha might be, though, Yaz knew that a couple years more growing would see Kao able to brush her aside without effort.

'What's going on out there?' She directed the question at Maya, still on her belly looking out.

'I can only see ice. The way out's blocked. But I hear digging.'

'The monster?'

'I don't think so . . .'

The four of them waited, crouched and ready, listening to the crunch of ice, quieter and less violent than it had been before.

'Halooo?' A woman's voice from outside.

This time nobody stood in Kao's way as he threw himself at the gap and began to wriggle out beneath the ice.

The rest of them followed, Thurin bringing up the rear. Many hands reached to help them from the mass of crushed ice mounded around the base of the wall. Yaz rose to find herself surrounded by the Broken, scores of them, hulking gerants making their neighbours look like children. Arka led her from the debris as others helped Thurin out. Quina was among them and had taken charge of Maya, brushing fragments from her long brown hair. Pome was there with his star-on-a-stick, others also bearing lights, some holding smaller stars in glass bowls on the end of long poles. Their leader, Tarko, stood among them in hurried conference with a series of his people who took off running once they had their orders.

'This!' Pome stepped forward as Thurin stood dusting sparkling fragments from his skins. 'This is what comes of toying with the Taints! Theus will come for us all. His numbers are growing and we sit back and let him plan our destruction! We leave him to choose when to lead the Tainted against us.' Pome singled Thurin out, pointing in accusation. 'Instead of a war to eradicate their kind and take back the drop pools, we capture one of their number and try to cleanse him. Wasting months' worth of stones and losing a good warrior in the process.'

'That good warrior was my mother!' Thurin roared, and about him the crushed ice writhed as though some great serpent were moving just beneath its surface. 'I don't need some surface walker one drop from his fall to tell me—'

'Peace!' Tarko boomed. His voice rolled out deep as glaciers groaning. 'The Tainted did not bring a hunter to our caves. Tainted do not go to the city.'

'And hunters don't come this far into our territory!' Pome shouted to mutters of agreement from behind him. 'But still we have a hunter on our doorstep hard on the heels of

Thurin's restoration. We have challenged the order of things, against the will of many here, and now we see the price. The Tainted are lost to us and a quick death is all the mercy we can afford them.'

Tarko rubbed both hands across the back of his neck as if seeking to ease some tension. He looked tired – close to exhaustion even – but when he answered it was with a measured tone. 'And what would you have me do, Pome? Return Thurin to the Tainted? Leave him to the hunter? I thought you were eager to fight. Today we have driven off a hunter. When have the Broken known such a victory?'

This time the mutters were for Tarko and they were louder. He continued, 'I've set a watch on the long slope so we will know if a hunter comes our way again. But we've shown that here at least we have some defence against them.' He nodded to himself and looked out across his people, waving them on. 'Now, each to their task. The ice does not mine itself.'

The gathering appeared to be over. Slowly the crowd began to break up, moving off in threes and fours, some deep in their silence, others talking animatedly among themselves to the accompaniment of the drip drip drip from above and the distant groan of moving ice.

'What happened?' Thurin asked Arka, amazed. 'How did you drive off a hunter?'

'Tarko worked the ice,' Arka said.

'Tarko has marjal blood, like Thurin?' Maya asked.

'Someone's been paying attention. Tarko is the strongest ice-worker among us.' Arka gave the girl an approving look and Maya beamed up at her. 'He broke a block from the ceiling bigger than Hetta and let it drop on the hunter. That got its attention. The second one seemed to hurt it. Anyway, it retreated after that.' She pointed to the far end of the cavern where more caves opened out. 'Let's go.'

Yaz ignored the woman and kept her gaze on Thurin. His mother had died in the effort to rescue him, perhaps on the same day Yaz fell. It explained the sadness in him. And he was tainted but was rescued from that too. She needed his help if she were to rescue Zeen. Guilt rose, the old Ictha guilt that always reached up to run its claws through her whenever she thought about herself rather than others. She'd been looking at Thurin as someone who might be a friend. Or even more than that. Those were the sorts of dreams that saw you die on the ice, the sort that hurt the clan. Thurin was her means to recover Zeen. That was her focus. Nobody would know the Tainted better than someone who lived among them. 'I'm sorry about your mother.'

Thurin frowned, uncomfortable. 'Nobody lasts long down here. But I will miss her. Very much.' He paused and added, 'I'm sorry about your brother.'

There seemed nothing else to say. Sometimes all your words are the wrong shape and none of them will fit into the silence left when the conversation pauses. Yaz looked away from Thurin, her stomach a cold knot. Zeen would be poisoned and insane when she found him. She would need to do whatever had been done for Thurin. The knowledge ate at her. Each new thing she learned only bound her tighter to the Broken. She needed them, and while every instinct told her to go out now and get her brother to safety, her head told her to stay, to listen, and to learn.

'How—' But already Arka was leading the others back towards the settlement. Yaz hurried to catch up with her. 'How do you make someone who's tainted better again? And what's this city? And why can't you just bring ice down on them there too?'

'Because in the undercity the ceiling is made of stone,'

Arka said. 'And the rest will have to wait until I've eaten. Maybe the Ictha don't need food but I'm starving.'

'Food!' Kao said it as though remembering a lost love. 'Hells yes.'

Arka led them to the settlement, past the barracks and further in amid a confusion of huts and larger buildings, all different both in design and orientation. They looked almost to have been made from discarded pieces of larger, more complex objects, like the child's doll Yaz's father had fashioned for her when she was little. The thought stung her and she wondered what her parents were doing now, what Quell was doing, and how far away they were from her now, up in the freshness of the wind.

She looked around and sniffed in distaste. The settlement lacked the order of an Ictha camp, it was dirty, and it smelled . . . it smelled delicious! Yaz sniffed again. Arka had led them to one of the largest halls and as she opened the door a wave of warmth rolled out along with the most wonderful aroma. All five of the drop-group suddenly found themselves as hungry as Kao had declared himself to be. They wasted no time installing themselves around a platform that Arka named a table on objects she named chairs, designed to allow them to sit while at the same time being raised to be on a level with the table. Yaz wondered what was wrong with the floor but she made no complaint.

An older woman with dark hair that fell in a strange curling way came in hefting a huge bowl that seemed to be made of iron, blackened with fire on the outside and steaming from within, the source of the wonderful aroma. Yaz was as amazed by the woman's curls as she was by the fact that metal was so plentiful here that it could be used to make bowls to keep food in.

Arka held up her hand. 'Two things. One: don't touch the pot, it will burn you. We serve food hot here. Madeen will bring bowls. Two: this is Madeen. She cooks the meals. Never upset her or you might get something nasty in yours.'

Madeen gave the lie to these words with a motherly smile as she hefted the pot onto the table, then swung round suddenly to aim a narrow-eyed scowl at Maya who jumped and nearly fell from her chair. Laughing, Madeen went to fetch the bowls.

'Oh, and three: these are spoons.' Arka showed off a metal scoop.

The pot contained what Arka described as stew. Yaz stared at the steaming and complicated pile of . . . pieces . . . in the strange bowl before her. 'But what is it?'

'Stew. Eat it. It's good.' To prove her point Arka scooped up a lump and put it, still steaming, into her mouth.

'But . . . won't it burn me?' Yaz could feel the heat rising off the stuff.

'No.' Kao spoke the word oddly, trying to fit it around a large mouthful while rapidly sucking and blowing air into and out of his lips. 'Is good.'

Yaz, Maya, and Quina joined Thurin, Kao, and Arka and started to eat. Yaz had only ever eaten fish before, hot from the sea or cold on the journey from a closing sea to an opening one. The Ictha ate their travel rations frozen. As far as she knew all the other tribes did too.

The warmth was delicious on its own. Whether it made the slices of fungi taste so wonderful or whether they tasted that good cold Yaz couldn't say, but she knew for a fact that a burned mouth was a small price to pay. She ate with a dedication that nearly matched Kao's. She'd never tasted anything so full of flavour, so complicated, savoury with a slight saltiness to it.

Towards the bottom of the bowl, as Yaz mustered the strength of will to slow down, she discovered small chunks that seemed familiar, though far more tasty hot and soaked in the stew's dark juice. 'This is fish!'

'It is.' Arka nodded. 'You can't live on the fungi alone, not for too long. Without fish and salt you fall sick and die. Fish livers hold most of what you need to live.'

'And where do you get fish? Where do you get salt down here?'

Arka met her gaze with serious eyes. 'Where do you get iron up there?'

'I . . . The priests trade it with us.'

'And we trade it with the priests.' Arka had all their attention now, though Kao still pushed in another mouthful as he stared at her. 'Some say it's the only reason they put us down here.'

'But . . .' Yaz ran out of words.

'Broken children die if they stay on the ice. A slow, cruel death,' Quina said. 'That's what the pit is for, to keep the bloodlines pure.'

Arka shrugged. 'Maybe. Maybe not. Have any of you ever seen a gerant, hunska, or marjal child given the chance to try?'

Nobody answered.

'They throw us down here,' Yaz said slowly, 'and we search for metal from this city, and in return they give us some salt and fish? We work for the priests. Slaves in a hole?'

'Stars too,' Arka said.

'What?'

'We mine the ice for stars too, and trade them for the food we need, and sometimes skins. Though mostly we use rats for that.'

'Rats?'

'Like tiny bears . . . only different.' Arka waved the question off. 'But yes, you're right. We're slaves working for the priests of the Black Rock.' She pursed her lips. 'I'm impressed. It normally takes several days for wets to figure it out, and you've just dug most of the answer out with a spoon from a bowl of stew!'

They finished eating without further talk, each held by their own thoughts.

'Is there more?' Kao was the first to speak again.

Arka snorted. 'Gerants! Three times as strong, five times as hungry.' She shook her head. 'You got the largest bowl. There's more later. We eat when we rise and again just before we sleep.'

'How do we know when that is?' Maya asked. 'The light never changes here.'

Thurin frowned. 'You just know.'

'You'll learn to "just know".' Arka walked to the door, beckoning for them to follow. 'It can take a while, but you have the rest of your lives to learn.'

CHAPTER 9

In the story days the first of men, Zin, who climbed from the sea to Mokka's tent, rose from his sleeping hides and found himself old. He saw in his hands the lines that told a lifetime. With a sigh he set down his dagger-tooth beside the many kettan he had carved in the long night. Zin left his shelter and saw a brittle dawn in the east. The cold had bound itself tight across the ice. A knowing came then into the first of men, a shout and a whisper, carried by the cruelty of the wind, borne by the strangeness of the sea. This would be his last day. And so Zin walked into the whiteness that was the world seeking to know what had become of his many sons and daughters.

Though he had grown old Zin bore the wind and the miles upon his shoulders and in the morning of his last day he found three of the four tribes that had sprung from his seed. In the west the Axit had grown broad, their eyes dark, their hearts fierce, and they knew him not. They followed the seas and their fine nets caught small fish in great number and variety. With octar ink his Axit sons tattooed the flames of dragons' tails across their necks, licking up over their cheeks. Their threats cracked the ice. His daughters wore bones through their eyebrows and came running before their men with spears in hand.

In the east the Quinx had found a dog and it had become many, as dogs will when fed. Zin's Quinx sons were tall and wore their hair in warrior braids. His daughters there drove dog-sleds and with their teams hauled even the green whale from the sea. No memory of Zin remained in all of the Quinx. They prized stone beads from such rocks as the Gods in the Sky sometimes cast upon the ice, and because he wore none they counted Zin as lesser, despite his age and the whiteness of his beard.

Far to the south Zin's Joccan sons walked beneath strange stars in such heat that sometimes molten ice would run and flow even outside a tent and delight the children before it froze again. Joccan wives painted their eyelids black and their hair grew in many shades. The Joccan had forgotten the face of their father and replaced the stories of their mother with lies of the green world that only the gods know.

At last, growing weary, with the sun falling, Zin turned north and walked to the lands where the cold is born and where it hunts. Here the ice grew hard, the landscape fractured, the voice of the glaciers sharper, louder, more fierce. Zin's Ictha sons turned their pale eyes towards his approach and were amazed for the first of men came among them bare-chested and they knew him for their father and wept. And as the sun descended on the last day of the first man his children of the north feasted him with harp-fish and tuark and *the eggs of the great loach, and sang the oldest songs that told of his love for Mokka and the days of his youth when Zin had taught his offspring what secrets of the sea the gods had given into his care.*

And come the night the Ictha gave back to the sea that had birthed him all of Zin save that which they held in their hearts.

Yaz stood with the others outside the food hall. She found her shoulders hunched and forced them to relax. It wasn't cold. It was just the strangeness of the place, the twilight gloom, the glistening ice sky lit with its own stars, the constant dripping, and on all sides the shadow-wrapped buildings full of strange angles and built from gods knew what. Here and there the occasional star-stone hung, alive with light and whispers, drawing Yaz's eye, reminding her of the star she'd held on the previous night, burning in her hand, its song pulsing through her.

Arka coughed for attention. 'There are six main tasks we turn our hands to here. On the surface we all did everything. Here we choose a role and we stick to it. You can change, but not from one day to the next. We have . . .' She raised her hand and spread the fingers, closing the first one as she began. 'Harvesters, who seed, protect, and collect the fungi. Hunters, who catch rats for meat and skins, and blindfish from the rivers. Scavengers, who gather metal and building material from the city. Smiths, who melt down the metals and work them into new forms. Miners, who hack star-stones from the ice.' With four fingers and a thumb closed in Arka now held a raised fist. She brought it smacking down into the palm of her other hand. 'And warriors, who keep us safe from the Tainted.'

'The warriors don't have to do anything except fight?' Kao asked.

'They patrol and practise their weapon skills. Actual fighting is rare, thankfully, but still too frequent for us to replace our losses.'

'I'm going to be a warrior!' Kao nodded as if the matter were settled.

'First we do the tour,' Arka said. 'Spend some time seeing what goes on here. Sometimes the dullest-sounding tasks are more interesting than the most exciting. Harvesters always have something to do, warriors can find themselves bored, then terrified, then bored.'

'A warrior! Not grubbing around with those . . . plants,' Kao said.

'They do get to eat as many as they like . . . as long as no one sees them do it.'

Kao's truculence weakened as opposing desires waged war. Arka allowed herself a small smile then led them on. 'First we visit the foundry!'

'The foundry is the closest area to the main pit shaft that we still hold.' Arka had led them for what felt like an hour and couldn't have been anything like that. 'Can any of you guess why we keep such valuable industry out here where the Tainted contest us?'

'To show them who's boss,' Kao grunted.

'It's too difficult to move?' Maya asked.

Yaz frowned, puzzled.

'The heat,' said Quina. 'It needs to escape without drowning you or bringing the roof down.'

'Fast brain as well as fast feet,' Arka said.

At the exit to the low cavern they had been traversing

101

Arka led the drop-group past three gerants and a short dark man heading in the opposite direction. One of the gerants must have been close to nine feet in height and was built like a bear. All three of them wore metal plates linked together by iron rings, each plate no bigger than Yaz's hand so that together they formed a flexible metal skin over the warriors' chest, arms, and upper legs. Rust patterned them like frost rings on a closing sea.

The smaller man wore no armour. All four carried iron spears, not bone shafts tipped with an iron blade but iron throughout. And at their hips they bore huge knives with small arms spreading from the hilt.

'Swords,' Thurin said, seeing her surprise.

Arka led them on through a perfectly round tunnel that went up and later down, gently undulating through the ice. Broken rock had been scattered on the floor to give purchase in the steeper sections. There seemed no way to account for the conflicting gradients. Meltwater would only flow down.

Arka paused where one tunnel pierced another, listening.

'How are these tunnels made?' Yaz had seen similar ones before, shortly after crawling from her drop pool.

'Coal-worms.'

'What-worms?' Yaz knew of worms that swam beneath the ice surrounding the Hot Sea but none of them were much longer than her arm and she didn't think they burrowed.

'Coal.' Thurin waved his hands. 'Black rock, but not like the mountain. Eular says it used to be forests . . . trees . . . and you can burn it just like whale oil.'

Thurin said *whaleoil*, as if it were one word and he had little idea of what a whale or oil were. Which Yaz supposed was true. 'Good for burning but hard to light, Eular says . . .' He looked at Arka for support.

'Coal-worms eat coal. They generate heat and melt their

way through the ice. Though mostly it's the young ones who travel, looking for new deposits. The big ones only move on when they've exhausted the seams.'

'Lucky for us a big one chose to head where we're going then!' Yaz said.

Arka frowned. 'This was made by a baby. Pray you never meet a full-grown worm.'

'What were you?' Yaz kept close behind Thurin in the tunnels and asked her question quietly.

'What was I?'

'You know, hunter, harvester, warrior—'

'I was a miner. Mostly.' Thurin glanced back at her, his face curiously lit by bands of stardust in the ceiling just above them. 'Ice-workers have to be. Well, they are "encouraged". Miners produce most of the stars that we give to the priests. But the biggest stars are scavenger finds. Like the one we . . . the one that lights the settlement cavern. And those are *dangerous*.' His voice carried the warning. 'Not all the Tainted were stolen from us. Some went willingly. A star can do that to you. A big one. They break your mind up and fill you with demons.'

'What sort of demons?' little Maya asked from behind Yaz, proving to have sharper ears than expected. She was shy but curious, always watching. 'What do they look like?'

'Imagine all your hate broken away from you and given its own voice,' Thurin said. 'Living under your skin as a separate thing. Or all your greed, or lust. I've seen it happen, once. A demon made just of you. Crawling over your body like a stain. That's what it looks like, just a stain, no bigger than your hand. A taint. So be careful around the stars. Even the smaller ones. They weren't made for us. They aren't good or evil. Just dangerous. Like fire.'

* * *

103

The coal-worm's tunnel eventually descended to the bedrock again and connected with a melt chamber. The air was warmer than back at the settlement, the dripping faster, small streams wound their way across the rock, vanishing beneath the ice at the chamber walls. Yaz led them past more warriors into a cavern lit by half a dozen bright stars whose glow revealed a collection of sheds beside a lake, and above them a ceiling that funnelled up into a steep but slanting shaft vanishing into darkness.

'This is where I fell,' Quina said, her narrow face growing tight at the memory.

'Me too. But I made a bigger splash!' Kao slapped his belly and chest.

'What's that smell?' Maya sniffed. Ever since coal-worms had been mentioned she'd been jumpy. It was hard to remember that the timid child came from the Axit. If she had not been dropped she would soon have worn their bone piercings through her eyebrows and allegedly, beneath her furs, blood tattoos recording the clan's victories over past enemies. Walking close behind Maya it seemed to Yaz that something odd happened each time the girl flinched at a new sound. A subtle change, so slight it might just be imagination. The twilight seemed to flinch with her, as if just for a moment the shadows themselves drew in their breath. Maya sniffed again. 'What is it?'

Yaz inhaled slowly through her nose. The air smelled of blood and fire and harsh, alien scents with sharp angles to them. 'I don't know.'

'Metal, being melted down,' Arka said.

'Metal melts?' Yaz blinked.

'If you get it hot enough. A lot of things do. Even rock!' Arka took them towards the huts.

As they drew closer a man in a thick hide apron emerged.

The skin on his bare arms glistened with sweat and black smudges decorated bulging muscle. He grunted at Arka and took two handfuls of random metal pieces from the bin beside the hut. The mixture included toothed wheels of unblemished silvery metal, thin black wire in coils, and rusting iron rods with traces of some coating that had been stripped away.

'That's Ixen. He doesn't say much.' Arka caught the door before it closed and took them inside.

The heat hit Yaz like a blow and she staggered beneath it. The shed was a longish hall whose central feature was a large bowl of what looked like stone, supported on thick chains that ran to the ceiling. Ixen dumped his collection of metal pieces into the bowl, discarding one and adding some more iron rods from a nearby stack.

'It's like cooking,' Arka said. 'You have to get the mixture right.'

While Ixen added his finishing touches a bony woman, also in a scorched hide apron and little else, came from the rear of the shed to lower a heavy sigil-covered pot on another chain so that it nestled among the scrap.

'That pot looks like it's iron but it's not. It can get hot enough to melt all the other metals in there without melting itself.'

'So . . . how did you make it?' Quina asked.

Arka frowned. 'That happened before my time. But I guess we'd be in trouble if we lost it.' She frowned again. 'Though we do occasionally find metal it can't melt.'

The woman with the skull-like face took a pole with a scoop on it and began to move stars from a box to one side, dropping them one by one into the grey pot. As she added them each ceased its shining and instead the sigils on the pot began to emit a redder glow along with a fierce heat.

Yaz backed off, not wanting to cause the stars to burn too bright and drive the sigils to incinerate them all.

'It's the heat,' she said as Arka looked her way. 'I can't take it.'

Yaz retreated outside the shed and Arka followed to stand in the doorway.

'I've seen it all before, many times, but I never get tired of watching the molten metal being tipped out. It's like liquid fire. Ixen makes ingots and also pours various shapes for the other smiths. Almost all of it goes to the priests.'

Yaz wiped the chilling sweat from her brow. 'If you can make that much heat why do you need miners? Surely you can just melt the stars from the ice and make any tunnels you need just like the coal-worms do?'

'I thought Quina would be the first one to ask that question.' Arka rubbed at the scars running down her cheek. 'It's a question of profit and loss. When the stars are used to drive sigils they're eaten away by it, the star you take out is smaller than the one you put in. It's rapid for small stars – a pot will consume handfuls of dust just to make a little heat. And slow for bigger ones. But even with our largest stars we would find less of value in what ice we melted than the pot had consumed in order to melt it. It's like life up top. Every decision is about what you gain and what it costs you.' She glanced back. 'He'll be pouring soon. Come and watch if you're not going to faint.'

Yaz stayed outside after Arka returned to the furnace heat of the interior. She walked slowly to the shore of the lake, wondering. She knew what her decision to throw herself down the pit had cost her. She had less idea about any gains, but if she didn't find Zeen then it was all loss. The Ictha had cast him aside but to her he was still clan, still valued, and she would find him irrespective of loss and gain. It seemed to Yaz that if she had allowed them to throw her brother away without protest, as if he were worthless, or indeed if she had stood by and watched any child be thrown into that hole and said nothing, then something of herself would have been thrown away too, something more valuable than what she had lost by acting.

Thurin had said that the stars could split away the worst parts of a person and give them new voice. Yaz knew that watching the regulator toss children into the pit split away something good within those who watched and confined it to a place every bit as dark and silent as the hole into which those children vanished. She couldn't say how she knew this or how she held to it in the face of the harsh arithmetic that governed life upon the ice. But she did know it, blood to bone, however much she might long for the blissful ignorance that seemed to enfold the rest who had watched that day.

With a start Yaz realized that she had reached the shore of the lake and wet her toes in the shallows. It grew rapidly more deep, lit from beneath by stardust drifting against ridges in the rock, but the constant rain of meltwater from above rippled the surface too much for a clear view of the depths. Even so, it held a beauty and a peace: black rock, ice in every shade of pearl between white and clarity, the marbled seams of stardust glowing in all the colours that can be broken from the light. Beneath the many-tongued voice of falling water lay a distant glacial groaning, as timeless in its way as that of the wind. Yaz let the wonder of the place enfold her. The serenity—

Bang. Bang. Bang.

Yaz started forward in surprise and stepped farther into the shallows, soaking one foot in near-freezing water.

Bang. Bang. Bang.

The hammering came from one of the other sheds and

Yaz, irritated at the intrusion, stalked over, every other step a squelch, to see what warranted such a din. With her hands at her ears she leaned in through an open doorway.

A young man stood surrounded by tools and pieces of metalwork hanging from the rafters. He held a small but heavy hammer in one hand and the other steadied the sword blade he was working on. The glow from a small furnace pot picked out the topography of his well-muscled chest and arms. But the angles of his jaw and cheekbones beneath a half-wild mop of lustrous red-black hair were what stole the breath from Yaz's lungs. She understood that the arrangement of some men's features were more pleasing to the eye than others. Quell had been her friend first before any other attraction grew between them, but when working with the clan on the ice his face drew not just her eye but those of the other young Ictha women. Her mother called Quell handsome. The beauty of the man before her, however, had a magic to it that reached inside and made her ache.

The hammering stopped. Yaz had been spotted. The man offered her a smile, half shy, half amused, and beckoned her forward.

'You're from the drop-group.' Not a question. How else could she be here?

'Yes.'

'Arka's showing you around?' He looked past Yaz to the door as if expecting more company. 'Sorry. Am I shouting?' He lowered his voice. 'After the hammer everything seems too quiet.'

Yaz grinned. 'We Ictha say after the north everything seems too warm.'

The man frowned. 'Ictha? Oh, is that your clan?'

'Yes.' Yaz tried not to let her surprise show. Everyone knew of the Ictha.

'Ah, don't look like that.' His smile erased the offence she'd taken, making her answer it with one of her own. 'I'm Kaylal. I've been here since I was a baby. The Ictha must not get thrown down the pit very often!'

Kaylal turned to face her and in a poorly disguised moment of shock Yaz saw that both Kaylal's legs ended in stumps not far from the hips. Rather than standing as she had assumed he was seated on a high stool.

'You've noticed.' Kaylal smiled but pain ran behind it. 'You don't find men like me up there, do you?'

'I . . .' Yaz couldn't look away. Physical deformity was almost unknown among the Ictha and always the result of injury. 'Did it hurt?' She could hardly imagine the creature that had taken his legs. An outsized dagger-fish? A blue shark maybe, or a pavvine risen from the black depths? Harder still to imagine how he had survived the blood loss.

Kaylal laughed. 'I was born this way. My parents threw me down the pit when I was a baby. I've no memory of it.' His laughter ended and he met her gaze with deep blue eyes. 'We're not all broken the same way, but the Broken look after whoever comes to us. Eular tells me that my parents lived hard lives and made a hard choice. Beneath the ice we make different choices. There are some prices we won't pay, not even to survive, because the life that demands those prices for continuing loses its value in the paying.'

'I keep hearing about this Eular . . .'

'You'll meet him soon enough.' Kaylal smiled past her as someone entered the shed.

Another young man joined them, also dark and handsome but lacking Kaylal's unearthly beauty. He set down his clanking burden and came to stand by the smith, the hand he set to Kaylal's bare shoulder possessive, his smile guarded. 'One of Arka's group? Well, you've met our finest craftsman.

Kaylal can fashion an iron snowflake with a ten-pound hammer.'

'This is Exxar,' Kaylal said, reaching to touch the hand on his shoulder. 'The best of us. You can trust what he makes and what he says.'

A call from outside broke a moment's silence. 'Yaz?' Arka's voice.

'I . . . uh . . . better go. It was nice to meet you both.' Yaz made a clumsy retreat, knocking into several of the hanging workpieces and setting them clanking together.

The others had joined Arka outside and with them stood the familiar figures of Pome, holding his star-torch, and Petrick, the hunska boy who had distracted Hetta while Yaz climbed to safety. Petrick pushed aside the unruly black weight of his fringe and grinned at her as she crossed over to them. Pome just watched her from narrow eyes. He didn't have the size of a gerant or the dark hair of a hunska so Yaz guessed he must be a marjal, hiding some elemental talent or one of the rarer powers. Perhaps as Thurin had suggested his magic was in his voice, for many of the Broken had listened to him after the hunter came although he had only harsh things to say.

'Eular only asked to see these two.' Pome jerked a thumb towards Thurin and nodded towards Yaz.

'Take them all,' Arka said. 'He'll want to see them soon enough and I'll only have to repeat myself if you break the drop-group.'

'Not my problem, *drop-leader*.' Pome put an edge on Arka's title, clearly still stung by the loss of whatever prestige it carried.

'Take them. Or I will bring them myself.' Arka turned away. 'You'll find me here when you're done.' She started to hop out among the rocks that studded the lake edge. Yaz wondered if there might be fish to catch.

'Come.' Pome began to walk away, leaving it unclear as to who should follow.

Quina shrugged and set off after him, the whole group followed. Yaz stayed at the back with Thurin, not wanting to spark Pome's star-torch to greater brightness.

'You met Kaylal then?' Thurin smiled knowingly.

'I did.'

'He's a fine-looking fellow.'

'Yes.' Yaz felt the heat rising in her cheeks.

'A word to the wise: don't go making eyes at him. Exxar is very jealous of competition. Though he has no need to be.'

'Oh . . .' Yaz saw Quina flash a quick grin at her from further ahead where she walked beside Petrick. A little flustered she asked the next question in her head, 'Who is Eular?' She spoke in a low voice but it was Petrick rather than Thurin who answered.

'The man who wants to see you.' He left a pause as if he thought he'd made a joke then added: 'The eldest elder we have. Tarko leads us but he takes advice from Eular just as those before him have, and those who come after will.'

'And why does he want to see just me and Thurin?' Yaz hoped the splashing of their feet in the narrow worm tunnel would keep their conversation from the others.

'Because Thurin was tainted and we need to know if he can be trusted again,' said Petrick with brutal honesty. 'And you make the stars burn brighter.' The boy glanced back at her, his face lost in darkness, head silhouetted against the glow of Pome's light.

'You know?' Yaz hadn't been sure if they did or not.

'Of course. It's why Arka told me to draw Hetta off you.

111

That was quite a risk. It's never safe to tangle with that one, however fast you are.' Petrick shuddered. 'When you were fleeing from her in the outer caverns I could see each band of stars light up as you ran past. It's harder to notice close up. But from a distance . . . I saw it before I saw you. Arka said we had to have you then.'

'What does it mean?' Yaz asked.

'Don't know.' This time Yaz caught the gleam of the boy's grin. 'But it's not something we've seen before. Pome's the only one of us who can get close to the bigger stars and even he doesn't like to touch them. Seems like you're something new!'

At the front of their line Pome led the way through a series of low caverns. In places the slope of the rock reached the ice and gouged patterns in the roof as the flow moved on. Gravel and small round stones formed drifts here and there, giving off an eerie light from stardust caught in the voids among them. Once again Yaz wondered that all this beauty could have existed for so many years beneath her people's feet without their knowledge. She wondered: what else she might find and what other marvels lay silent, miles down, never to be discovered? Did beauty need an observer to matter? Was anything beautiful without someone to think it so? She found herself wondering – in this world of different eyes, different hair, different faces – how others saw her. Did Thurin think her ugly? Again she felt guilty. All her thoughts should be bent on saving Zeen, not on childish worries.

The group walked on unspeaking for a while, just the splash of feet, the dripping of meltwater, and the groan of the ice echoing in the caverns. And then a distant roar that froze them in their tracks.

'What was that?' It had seemed to come from behind them.

'Another hunter? From the city?'

'I know what it was,' Petrick muttered.

'Black gods damn it!' Pome started off again, hurrying now.

'What? What *was* that?' Yaz hissed at Petrick's back.

'Hetta.'

Yaz went cold, remembering those teeth. 'She's far away though, and we're close to the settlement?'

'She's cunning. If you know this place well enough you can use the tunnels to make it sound as—'

A huge shape burst from behind the cover of a rock ridge, diving into their midst. Quina and Petrick moved before Yaz even knew what was happening, both diving clear. Hetta bundled through the rest of them, shouldering Kao aside as though he were nothing, her great hand reaching for Yaz.

'No!'

Thick fingers grazed Yaz's ribs, catching hold of her coat in a grip that with a better aim could have snagged flesh and bone, crumpling them up as easily as skins.

Yaz threw herself back, twisting. If she'd buttoned and fastened the coat there would have been no escape, but in the heat she wore it loose and open, and now writhed free of it even as Hetta lifted her to slam her against the ice overhead.

She ran then, gasping, outpacing the others around her, panic driving them all.

The sounds of Hetta's raging fell away behind them and Yaz came to a halt, panting, leaning against the cavern wall. The darkness around them was almost unbroken.

'Why . . . why isn't she following?' Yaz asked, looking round. 'Where's Pome?'

'Still running.' Petrick raised his arm towards a point of light bobbing away in the distance.

Thurin spat, wiped his mouth, then started to call names. Kao, Yaz, Petrick, and Quina answered when he spoke. 'Maya?'

'Is she with Pome?' Yaz asked.

'She couldn't have run that fast.' Quina shook her dark head. 'She's only little.'

'Hetta has her then,' Kao said.

'If Hetta has Maya, why is she still hunting around back there?' Yaz could see the tainted gerant, the shape of her black against the faint glow of the ice, striding back and forth, kicking through the drifts of stones.

'The girl must be hiding,' Thurin said.

'Well, that won't work for long. Hetta will sniff her out. She can find you in the dark, that one.' Petrick shivered.

Only when Thurin caught her shoulder did Yaz realize she was starting to walk back towards the raging gerant. 'Are you mad? She'll tear you apart!'

'I was afraid to die once, and it killed someone.' Yaz shook Thurin's hand from her arm. If she had owned up to her defect at the first gathering someone stronger would have been beside her youngest brother when he needed help and her parents would have Azad with them on the ice today.

'What can you do against Hetta?' Quina shouted after her.

'Finish what I started.' Yaz kept on walking, breaking into a jog now. Her certainty was fading as the black shape grew larger and memory painted detail onto darkness. She wished she had her knife, or better still one of the iron weapons she'd seen the warriors carrying.

'Slow down.' Thurin came up on her right. 'We need a plan.'

'Keep stabbing her till she falls over?' Petrick caught up on her left, an iron dagger glimmering in his fist. Some might call Petrick ugly, his face too narrow, mouth too wide, nose long and crooked from some old break. But when he smiled, as he often did, the unbalanced collection of his features found its purpose and he became someone Yaz wanted as a friend.

'Good plan,' she said.

More footsteps behind Yaz, Kao's heavy tread and Quina's quick patter. Neither looked eager but perhaps something of her own determination had struck an echo inside them. They had all been thrown away the day before and discarding Maya to her fate wasn't something any of them could swallow, whatever common sense might dictate.

'Can you do that thing with the roof like Tarko did with the hunter?' Yaz asked Thurin.

'No. Well . . . I don't think so.' Doubt creased his pale brow. 'And if I could how would I stop it from crushing Maya? We don't know where she's hiding.'

It was true, and staring ahead Yaz could see very few places Maya could have concealed herself, unless she was just circling to keep the outcrops of rock between Hetta and herself.

'Kao will have to grapple her legs then, get her on the floor, and the rest of us can pound her while Petrick cuts her throat.'

'Hells . . .' Kao, behind her. Hetta had stopped her hunt and now slowly turned her head in the direction of their approaching group. 'She's . . . huge!'

Hetta reached behind her and drew from her belt an iron blade, a stolen sword as big as any Yaz had seen but seeming a mere dagger in the woman's fist. Between the wrist and elbow of her other arm the gerant had bound a great thickness of hides secured by an iron bar twisted into a spiral, a shield of some kind to ward off blows. With a scream of rage Hetta charged and sudden terror turned Yaz's muscles to water.

Hetta came roaring, a band of scarlet across her eyes filling both with blood, and a jet-black stain reaching out like fingers in all directions around her impossibly wide mouth.

The two hunskas, Petrick and Quina, leapt to either side; Petrick, who hardly reached the woman's hip, lashing out with his knife. Thurin and Yaz were knocked aside as Hetta seized her largest opponent. She caught Kao around the neck and slammed him down on the rocky floor, water spraying up from the impact. In the next moment she was turning to follow Petrick, her sword swinging low. Swift as the hunska was he couldn't outrace the leading edge of her sword. Instead, he jumped, clearing the blow by fractions of an inch.

Yaz sat, shaking away the strange lights that filled her vision after Hetta's rancid bulk had hammered into her. She saw immediately that her plan had been suicide. If Kao had managed to get her down they might have had a chance, but Hetta stood head and shoulders above him.

As the hunskas danced out of reach Hetta turned back towards those on the ground. Thurin had almost got to his feet. Hetta could split him in two with that cleaver of hers but she seemed reluctant to grant a quick death. She reached for him instead, and as she did so Thurin threw out both hands in a gesture of rejection. Somehow Hetta's lunge slowed to a crawl. Both of them stood as if locked in a contest of strength though with neither touching the other. Hetta howled and started to advance while Thurin's legs buckled, losing traction on the small ridge he'd braced them against. She drove him back, still not making contact, as though a thickness of glass were interposed between them.

Quina, seeing her moment, rushed in to pummel Hetta's exposed side, her fists a blur. Petrick charged in too, launching himself at the gerant's back, driving his knife in as high as he could and trying to heave himself up with it, or to draw it down carving a great wound. It seemed though that the blade had lodged tight and he lacked the strength for either.

Ignoring both attacks Hetta drove Thurin towards the edge of the cavern. Thurin seemed to be weakening but as the wall loomed behind him he drew back one arm and thrust again, this time sending forward jets of fractured ice from the wall. The ice blasted around Hetta's face, blinding her and allowing Thurin to twist away.

'Run! Run, Maya!' Thurin took off back the way they had come, Petrick and Quina at his heels.

Yaz, on her feet now, made to run too. There was still no sign of Maya but the girl had had time to make her escape.

It wasn't until she passed by Kao, out cold . . . or dead, that Yaz came to a stumbling halt. Behind her Hetta had cleared her eyes, still framed by that band of scarlet skin, and now came forward, howling murder and scything her sword before her.

Yaz turned. Even as she did it she was asking herself why. The boy was immature and too full of himself. And yet the answer came to her even more quickly than Hetta did. Throw any single life away as if it holds no meaning and how will your own life be valued thereafter? Everyone she had ever known had stood and watched her brother be thrown down the Pit of the Missing. Abandoning Kao now would say that they were right.

The river that runs through all things had first revealed itself to Yaz in a moment of great calm when her mind lay serene, clear as slow-ice. She had been watching the new sun rise over the white plains, and the reaching redness of its rays had become a multitude twisting in her mind, flowing and joining, and the river had been before her and in her and through her.

To see the river again so soon after touching its power was not easy. To do it in the grip of terror as death rushes howling upon you, impossible. But Yaz had set aside her fear and stepped forward, accepting the likelihood of her own end. She reached out into that calm and found the river, rushing at her more swiftly than her enemy. Where before Yaz had only dared a finger or the palm of her hand, this time she thrust both hands into the flood and immediately the power of the current came roaring into her.

Yaz tried to pull free before the river's surge carried her away or the force of it swirling through her tore the flesh from her bones. She found herself flying backwards, jolted by the separation, drunk on the strange energies she'd taken, overfull, bursting. The world around her seemed uncertain, fracturing into dozens of possibilities, each drawing Yaz along a different path into the future.

Kao lay helpless before Hetta but she carried on past the boy, aimed squarely at Yaz.

It took the singular threat of Hetta's continuing charge to nail Yaz to the moment. For several heartbeats it had seemed to Yaz that she would simply fall apart into different fragments of who she might be. Instead she rose, blazing with barely contained power incandescent in her hands, trails of magic scintillating down past her elbows as if it were a liquid drawn by gravity's pull.

Yaz raised her arm against the swing of Hetta's sword and with a bright retort the blade shattered. The other hand, driven flat-palmed at Hetta's chest, slammed her backwards, both feet leaving the ground. The force of the blow threw the cannibal for yards, sending her hammering into the ridge of rock that she had previously hidden behind. She collapsed against its base in a broken heap, her chest smoking.

'Yaz!' Thurin was the first to reach her. He gazed at the fallen gerant. 'What happened?'

Yaz folded her arms under each other, trying and failing to hide the light still shining from her hands and well past her wrists. 'Kao didn't get up. I couldn't leave him.' She willed the remaining energies she'd taken to sink deeper into her flesh but they were slow to obey.

Thurin knelt beside the boy, checking the back of his head. 'I made the water in the puddle cushion his fall. He seems to be in one—'

Kao let out a groan and his eyes fluttered open. Quina and Petrick were approaching Hetta now, Maya with them, trailing at the back, her eyes full of watchfulness rather than fear. All of them glanced Yaz's way. It's next to impossible to hide a light source in a dimly lit cavern and although the power in her was fading it was not yet gone.

'We need to tie her,' Yaz called out and moved to join them.

'We need to cut her throat before she wakes up,' Petrick said, knife in hand. Already Hetta's limbs had begun to twitch and she made a low groan of her own. A purple stain had begun to reach up across her thick neck from beneath her furs.

'No.' Yaz drew level with Petrick. The boy had slowed as the distance between him and Hetta shrank to little more than a yard.

Petrick shot her an incredulous look. 'She ate your friend. Killed and ate him. What do the Ictha do to murderers? Tie them up?'

Yaz hadn't forgotten Jaysin and she didn't know what the Ictha did to murderers. She wasn't sure murder had ever happened among them. But she knew the Ictha had watched an old man push children into a miles-deep hole and done nothing. 'Hetta was one of the Broken once, wasn't she? Like Thurin. Was Thurin responsible for what he did while tainted?'

'It's a madness. The demons take control.' Thurin joined them. 'She has three in her at least. It's worse when there are more than one, and even more so when they are different breeds.' He indicated the purple, black, and red stains moving across the gerant's brutal face, the changes as slow as the writhing of the dragons' tail lights in the northern sky.

'Can't we save her?' Yaz knew Hetta as a monster but Zeen was a monster now and she wouldn't allow this fate for him. 'Like you were saved?'

Doubt clouded Thurin's face. He stared at Hetta as if he was remembering her in the years before she was taken. 'I don't—'

Hetta drew in a great shuddering breath, startling them all, though her eyes stayed shut. Maya let out a brief scream then stifled the rest of it. The Axit girl was back to being her scared little self, Yaz thought.

'There's no time for this.' Petrick started forward. Something in the way his knife trembled made Yaz sure the boy hadn't taken a life before.

'Where do you think I'll find a home when she dies?' The voice came from Hetta's night-black lips but sounded too calm for the howling monster that had attacked them. Hetta lay motionless, eyes still closed, only her mouth moved and the inky stain seemed to flow into it from all sides. Hetta's pointed teeth gleamed blackly. 'Thurin son of Gatha has already shown himself cracked and open to my kind. He'll make an acceptable replacement. Will you try to kill him too when I take him?'

'If you're going to kill her, do it quickly!' Thurin moved

behind Petrick. 'I won't let them in my head.' His voice had a quaver in it though and he stepped away as if eager to put distance between himself and the deed.

Petrick gritted his teeth and reached his blade towards the gerant's neck. His arm steady now. All of him tensed to spring aside should she wake and lunge for him.

'Hear me, Yaz of the Ictha.'

Petrick paused. 'How does a demon know your name already?'

The demon working Hetta's mouth seemed untroubled by the knife so close to her throat. 'Did you not think it strange that no Ictha has fallen here in twenty years and then three take the plunge *in a row*?' Within the scarlet stain one of Hetta's eyes opened, wholly red like the skin around it, save for the black point of the pupil.

Yaz had no answer.

'I spoke to the child before we tore his head off,' the demon whispered, inviting Yaz to lean in closer. 'Jaysin, he called himself. He was very keen to let us know he shouldn't have been down here.' A black tongue licked black lips. 'Shouldn't have been down here. Even the regulator said so, little Jaysin told us.'

'What do you mean?' Yaz snarled.

'Don't listen,' Thurin called out from behind her. 'The demons always lie. They cast a spell on you with their voice.'

The black mouth spoke again. 'Regulator Kazik pushed little Jaysin down the pit to bring you a message. He promises to send more innocents down to repeat it if you don't follow his instructions.'

'What message?' Yaz shouted.

Hetta's other eye snapped open, scarlet and demon-filled. Her body remained slumped against the rock, a trickle of blood running out from behind her head. Close up the size of her continually shocked Yaz and the idea that she had thrown the woman back with such force seemed hard for even her to believe.

'Ah . . .' Hetta or the demon exhaled slowly. 'I could tell you. But then you would have to swear by all your gods to let me go.'

'We can't do that.' Petrick brandished his knife, though his voice lacked conviction.

'Kill this woman then,' Hetta said. 'Though she was once one of your people and has no control over the things we make her do. Condemn more children to the pit to carry Kazak's message to Yaz of the Ictha. And see what happens to your friend Thurin when you make us homeless.' A grin showing pointed teeth. 'But whatever you do, do it swiftly for she is waking and when she does the time for talking will be over.'

'Why were you hunting me?' Yaz demanded.

The black mouth only smiled.

'What was the message?'

'Do you swear to our bargain?'

Yaz spat. She didn't want to let the cannibal go but she didn't want Petrick to slit the woman's throat either. Especially not if Hetta was simply a victim of these monsters living under her skin.

'I swear by the Gods in the Sky and by the Gods in the Sea that if you answer my questions I will let you leave this cavern unharmed.'

'The others too?'

'By Eon of the Ice,' Thurin muttered. Petrick echoed him in a whisper.

'By the White-Hope-That-Burns-Above.' Quina named some southern deity unknown to Yaz.

'There,' said Yaz. 'Now—'

'And the tiny one who wrapped the shadows around her,' Hetta said. 'The fierce one.'

'By the Seven Gods of the Wind,' Maya said.

Hetta's head turned to stare past Yaz. 'And the gerant who is pretending to be unconscious.'

'By Eon of the Ice.' Kao sat with a groan, rubbing the back of his head.

'Ask your questions,' Hetta said. The purple stain now wrapped her neck like a strangling hand.

'Why were you hunting me?' Yaz asked.

'We weren't hunting you. We were hunting the new one.'

'New one?' Yaz wondered if Kazik had already thrown down another child.

'Most unusual. Seemed to be a grown man, not built like a gerant. Has a spear. Not tainted. Spying on the Broken. Cunning too. But we'll catch him.'

'What was the regulator's message?' Thurin asked, still keeping his distance. It was the question Yaz wanted to ask but one she wanted answered for her alone, not spoken in front of an audience.

'The regulator wants you back, little Ictha. You weren't supposed to jump! If you come back soon he will allow you to bring Jaysin with you . . . oh . . . well, we still have his skull in our collection . . . you could take that maybe.'

'What else did he say?'

'Most of it was screaming. Some begging.'

Yaz ground her teeth together, regretting her oath. Hetta's death might be a price worth paying if it destroyed the monstrosity speaking with her mouth. 'About the regulator. What else did he say about the regulator or his message?'

'Nothing.'

'Go.' Yaz pointed. 'Take her away before we forget our vows.'

Hetta got slowly to her feet, joints cracking, more blood sheeting down the side of her neck. She stayed hunched, growling as some awareness returned to her eyes, then lumbered off, moving as if nursing some great pain.

'We should leave too.' Yaz glanced around her. The others were all staring at her, making no move to go. 'What?'

Quina stepped in close, quicker than quick, her face too near Yaz's, staring.

'You jumped?'

CHAPTER 10

Pome intercepted the group before Petrick could take them to Eular.

'Here comes the light-bearer to save us,' Thurin muttered.

'Does he carry that star everywhere?' Yaz eyed the approaching glow.

'It's his way of reminding us all that he can tolerate having one so close to him,' Petrick said. 'He thinks it makes him special. But they don't shine any brighter for him than for the rest of us.' He shot Yaz a narrow glance.

Pome strode up to them, flanked by two warriors carrying spears. Behind him loomed Bexen, the gerant who had stood with him when he challenged Tarko's authority the previous day. The gerant scowled at them all, one eye milky as if the frost had got into it somehow. He was nearly as large as Hetta, his face brutal. Most of the gerants had that look, as if their bones were too eager to grow, broadening their brows, making their jaws jut forward.

'Where's Hetta?' Pome demanded, scanning their ranks for losses.

'Don't know,' Petrick answered. 'We ran for it. Just not as fast as you. Or as far.'

Pome moved his star to light Petrick's face, eyes narrow, searching for any hint of mockery. The boy flinched away and Pome sneered. 'Bexen, patrol the ridge caverns. If you find Hetta bring me her corpse.'

The gerant grunted his assent and led the two spearmen away. Pome raised his star. 'Come on then. Eular's waiting!'

Pome made sure to walk beside Yaz, holding his star out ahead of him as if concerned for her comfort. 'You're very new here, Yaz. This must all seem very strange. I remember it took me a while to adjust after my drop.'

Behind them Thurin suppressed a snort.

'You're getting a view of things down here through Arka's eyes. Be sure to use your own too though. She'll draw you a picture that misses out the bad. The matters I'm planning to change. But you'll see them, and if you're wise you'll know who to line up behind when things come to a head.' The more Pome spoke the more reasonable he seemed. His words scratched at Yaz's mind, trying to burrow their way in.

With an effort Yaz clenched her brain and held it tight, imagining it as two fists held together. She listened to Pome but tried not to allow him in. And in time he fell silent, as if somehow sensing his efforts were being wasted. 'Kao, isn't it?' He turned to the gerant.

Pome led them through a series of steadily darker, smaller, and colder caverns. The constant dripping slowed, then stopped. The ground underfoot began to crunch as puddles became iced over. The ceiling grew lower.

'Why do we have to come out here?' Yaz whispered to Thurin as they walked. 'Doesn't he live in the settlement with the rest of you?'

'Us. The rest of "us". It's just us now.' Thurin gave a tight grin. 'And no. He spends a lot of time meditating in the margins. They say it clears his thoughts. Often we don't see him for weeks. It seems longer than that since I last saw him, now I think of it.'

Yaz had more questions but ahead of them Pome had stopped. They'd reached their destination.

'You with me.' He singled Yaz out. 'The rest wait here. Petrick, see they don't stray.'

Pome took Yaz along what might have been a worm tunnel, now ancient and distorted by the glacial flow. They emerged into a cavern so low that a gerant would have to stoop. Even Yaz might graze her head. Curtains of icicles ran here and there, catching the blue light of Pome's star and returning it in ghostly echoes.

'Watch your tongue here, girl.' Pome moved his star to light her face as he had with Petrick. As it came close it began to blaze, lighting the cavern from wall to wall, unchaining its beauty. Yaz heard the star's whisper swell to a song and smiled even as she closed her eyes against its brightness. Something in her answered the song, calling on the star to sing louder and burn brighter still. Pome, caught off-guard by the sudden change, shrank back from the blazing star. His hand began to shake and with a sharp oath he dropped both rod and star. The impact with the rock broke the star free and it rolled away from them across the floor, dimming to its original level.

'Thank you, Pome.' A kindly voice, cracked with age, the speaker hidden on the far side of the cavern. 'I will talk with the young lady. She will return with your star-stone when we are finished.'

Pome seemed unwilling to leave. 'But—'

'Thank you, Pome.' A little firmer this time.

Pome looked at Yaz with murder in his eyes, scowled, then stalked back along the inky tunnel.

Eular waited until Pome had retreated into the distance. 'Join me.'

Yaz moved forward, weaving around the icicles, her breath billowing in clouds before her. The star's light revealed an old man, white-haired and bony, facing away from her, kneeling on a roll of skins just before a perfectly round pool. Yaz was surprised to see the water unfrozen. Eular turned to face her. The star's stark illumination, slanting upwards, threw his face into a confusion of shadow and light, so much so that it took Yaz a few moments to understand that where his eyes should be Eular had only scarred pits.

'Hello.' Eular smiled.

Yaz found herself shocked once again, just as she had been by Kaylal's lack of legs. Physical deformity was so rare among the Ictha that just seeing it made her uncomfortable, a twisting in her stomach, followed by guilt and shame, and a knowledge in her bones that such a reaction lessened her.

'It's all right to stare,' Eular said. 'I have been told that I'm quite a sight. Pome should have warned you.'

'You were thrown into the pit as a baby?'

'No. I was a grown man. My clan, the Hjak, tried to hide me. My mother was the clan-mother.'

'Hjak?' Yaz had thought she knew all the clans who gathered.

'I am the last of them.' Eular bowed his head. 'That was the justice of the priests. A lesson for the other clans. Their lives were forfeit.'

Yaz opened her mouth and said nothing. She had heard of the power of the priesthood but not that they slaughtered whole clans.

Eular waved his hand as if dispelling thoughts of the past.

'So here I am. None of the old bloods show in these veins. My magical power is . . . that I can't see.'

'But you knew Pome had dropped his star.'

'I can't see, but I can listen. What I hear paints a picture. The words, the way they are spoken, what is left unspoken, the sounds of the chamber. And what I have heard about you wraps you in a fire that I could see through the walls long before you arrived here in my little cave.'

'Oh.' Yaz could think of nothing else to say.

'Can you see this pool before me?'

'I can.'

'The Broken made it and several others like it. Long ago. Few remain who remember their making. Each is a basin, polished to a high shine. In such a receptacle water, if it is kept very still, can stay liquid long after we might expect that it would freeze.'

Yaz stepped forward, her shadow swinging across the pool. 'It should be frozen.'

'Most of them are. But as the ice ebbs and flows the paths taken by the heat shift, and sometimes – not often – one of the pools reaches this state. It wants to change but every change must start somewhere and in this pool the change has nowhere to start.'

Yaz frowned. 'That . . . doesn't make sense.'

'And yet it is true,' Eular said without offence. He reached out to hand her a small piece of stone, a gritty fragment smaller than a baby's first tooth. 'Touch it to the water. Drop it in.'

Yaz knelt beside the old man, the rock biting into her knees. She reached out with the piece of grit pinched between the tips of finger and thumb. She touched it to the unrippled surface before her, and in an instant, like the opening of a white wing, traceries of frost spread from the point of contact, infinitely complex, breathtaking, an expanding symmetry. With a gasp of surprise she let the fragment drop. The rapid freeze followed in the stone's wake, penetrating the depth of the water now as well as spreading across the surface. Before her eyes the thickness of the pool became solid, the clarity of new ice filling with ghostly flaws, fractures frozen into the moment. Within a handful of heartbeats half the pool lay solid, creaking as it expanded, the effect still spreading towards the far shores. Yaz pulled her hand back to her chest.

'Sometimes the introduction of some new thing can change everything, Yaz.' Eular reached out and rapped his knuckles on the new ice. 'Regulator Kazik did not throw you down the Pit of the Missing, I think.'

'Why do you say that?' Yaz wondered at how much this old man with no eyes could see. There had been no time for Hetta's revelations to reach him even if Petrick or someone in the drop-group had wanted to give her away.

'There are many ways to be broken but only four of them arise from the old bloods showing again in a new child—'

'Thurin said there were three: gerant, hunska, and marjal.'

'Four tribes of men beached their ships on Abeth when this world was still green. The Missing had already left, knowing that the sun would continue to wane, but in those days Abeth was still a kindness after the black seas our ancestors had sailed for so long.

'The tribes mixed their blood to breed a people who would thrive in this new place. The gerants with their size and strength, the hunskas with their swiftness that can stretch a moment into an age, the marjals with their mastery of a myriad lesser magics . . . and the quantals who see the one true Path that joins and separates all things, and who may take from it as much power as they are able to own.'

Yaz looked away from Eular's eyeless face and gazed upon

the marbled beauty of the frozen pool. 'Why didn't Thurin mention these quantals then?'

'Because none are cast down among us. The priests of the Black Rock keep them. The quantals *are* the priesthood. So Kazik would not have thrown you down the pit. Which leaves me to ask were you so clumsy as to slip, so hated as to be pushed or pulled by some other of your clan, or . . . did you cast yourself among us? All would seem remarkably unlikely, but one among them must I think be true.'

'I jumped.' It sounded silly when she said it now.

'After a friend?' Eular asked. 'There's nothing like friendship for pulling someone down a hole. Or out of it.' He smiled and turned his head, and though his sockets held no eyes Yaz could tell that the old man's gaze was a distant one. 'My first friends are dead now, all of them, taken by the years. It's one of the prices paid in the process of becoming old. But I remember them. Oh yes. Every day. The games we played, the fun we had, the tears shed. We are victims of our first friendships. They are the foundations of us. Each anchors us to our past. The blows that drive those nails home are randomly struck, but they echo down all our days even so.'

'It was my brother. I jumped after my brother. To protect him.'

'To protect him? You thought he would survive the fall?'

'I . . .'

'Aim for honesty with others, girl. But never, ever lie to yourself.'

'He did survive. I came to save—'

'Only the truth, child. Your life will run that much smoother if there are no untruths between your heart and your head.' Eular rubbed both hands across his face, slowly, and ran gnarled fingers up among the white tufts of his hair. 'I have been young and now I am old and it amazes me how long the journey was and how swift. Everything every elder has ever said to you about getting old is true . . . and none of it will mean anything to you until you have made the journey for yourself.'

'The pit has a pull to it . . .' Yaz remembered the dark gullet, endlessly patient, endlessly deep. A threat, a challenge, an invitation. 'When the regulator didn't push me . . .'

'Part of you felt robbed?'

'Most of me felt relieved.' Yaz shook her head. There had been regret as well as relief, though she could only understand the latter. 'But then he pushed Zeen.'

'And your brother is with the Tainted now.'

'Yes.'

'And has Kazik tried to get you back yet?'

'He sent me a message. He told me to come back by myself.'

'Those messages will become more urgent and insistent if he discovers that you have a power over the star-stones.'

'But you said the priests are all quantals . . .' Yaz frowned. 'Why would he be so eager for one more?'

'Many of the priests have some quantal blood in them, but for most of them it's just a touch. Even Pome may have a small touch of it. One of the reasons he so resents his life down here. He feels he should be up there, living in the Black Rock, a lord of the ice!

'A few of the priesthood are half-blood quantals. I don't know if any of them are full-bloods. And even among full-bloods any level of mastery with the star-stones is rare.'

'What are the stars?' Yaz asked, wondering what the priests did with them, and why the tribes had never seen even their dust.

'Things of the Missing. The heart of their civilization,' said Eular. 'Our ancestors made similar stones. The largest of them sat deep within the ships that sailed between the stars and brought us to Abeth. Shiphearts, they are known as. The Missing also used these star-stones, heart-stones, core-stones – call them what you will – to power their cities, before those cities were abandoned. And as the ice ground over what was left behind, it scattered the stones. Most were broken into many pieces, but a star-stone is always a sphere: break one in half and you have two spheres; grind it to dust and you have many tiny spheres. The flow of the ice has long since carried away anything from the city that was above ground, but the stones' heat means the ice can't carry them far. They sink and are caught amid the bedrock's folds. This is why we are here. This – iron and star-stones – is why the priests give us what little they do to keep us from dying too swiftly.' He sighed. 'If you want to return to the ice then speak with Tarko. Tell him about the regulator's message.'

'I'm not going back without my brother.' The words burst out without permission. Even with Zeen at her side Yaz wasn't sure she could go back. Not now. Not after seeing all this. And how would Zeen live up there in the wind if what they said about being broken was true? 'I mean it.'

Eular chuckled at the defiance in her voice. 'Did I ask you to?'

'But the regulator wants—'

'What do I care for what the regulator wants?' Eular rapped his knuckles on the frozen pool again. 'All of the Broken are like this water, child. Long overdue for change and yet unable to change. And now you have fallen among us and I think that the change will come swiftly and that nothing will ever be the same again. That includes you, Yaz. You have the potential for greatness, but first you need to change yourself. Not by degrees, but all at once, like the pool. Dangerous, maybe, but it's something that couldn't happen up there in the monotony of your old life.'

CHAPTER 11

'What is it you want me to do?' Yaz had lived her whole life taking direction. From Mother Mazai, who led the clan from one sea that was closing to the next that would open. From her parents. From the wind and ice themselves. To survive as part of a people all working together was hard. To survive alone, impossible. In the darkness of his cave the blind man seemed to offer direction and something within Yaz yearned to take it.

'What should you do? Who should you be? Everyone wants answers to those questions. Life isn't that simple though. There's no one thing we should do, no guiding quest, just as there's no one person we should be. I'm full of different voices, pulled in a dozen different directions. Aren't you? If I'd had the chance I might be a dozen different men. Perhaps a fisher on the Hot Sea, perhaps I'd lead a dog-team in the south, or . . .' He stretched out his hands as if grasping for ideas. 'I'd rule the Black Rock.' He laughed. 'Or be a priest of whatever strange faith they have in the green belt of the world.' He shook his head. 'The point is that you don't have to choose, you never choose. You follow whichever of your voices is loudest and make the best of it. The pit – that was a choice that's hard to back out of, but what to do, who to be? Those you can try out for size. See what fits. Given enough time you can be all of them, do everything . . .

'I'm an old man rambling. Don't listen to me. I've advised Tarko and those that came before him. And here we are. The Tainted grow in number and the Broken diminish. Soon all who are dropped from above will fall into their hands.' Eular pursed his lips. 'But as to what to do . . . it was my advice and the actions of our leaders that brought us here. What we need is an agent of change. Someone with new thinking that follows their own direction. Who told you to jump into the pit?'

'Nobody.'

'Keep listening to nobody.'

'And what do the priests tell you about the Tainted?' Yaz asked.

'The priests have not communicated with us for generations,' Eular said. 'Not since the hunters woke in the city.'

'Woke?'

'Maybe our scavengers dug too deep. We don't really know what returned them to life. All we know is that one day they were there, roaming the city, hunting any that ventured in the abandoned chambers. And today I hear that another one has passed the gateposts and attacked us in our own caverns.'

Yaz frowned. 'What is it that you want though? Freedom? To climb out into the open?'

'Gods no!' Eular laughed. 'It has been a very long time since my fall. Longer than most here have lived. But I remember that the surface is a cruel place, that the air is never still and is full of teeth, that the only food is to be found in bottomless depths of water. I will never return there. But some here might. They should at least have the choice, no? What we need is change.' He turned to face her and smiled. 'Your eyes are fresh. Your mind unchained by our struggles. What do you think we need?'

Yaz frowned and thought. 'For the priesthood to speak with us, to aid us against the Tainted and the hunters, to let our families know we still live and to tell them of the service we render to the tribes. To be treated as human, not some waste thrown into a hole, gone and forgotten.'

'Well and good.' Eular nodded.

'So . . .' Yaz stopped herself from saying, *what should I do?*

'Go back to Arka. Do what you feel you must. Maybe nothing will come of it. Maybe the regulator will claw you back to the surface and nothing will change here, and we will continue to die. But' – and he smiled – 'the star-stones sing louder when you are near, and that is a thing so rare that it is not in the memory of the Broken. So . . . we shall see. Sometimes even the blind must wait and see.'

'Thank you.' There seemed little else to say.

'Before you go: tell me about the others in the drop-group.'

'They're all outside with Pome and Petrick,' Yaz said. 'You can speak with them yourself . . .'

'Humour me.'

'Well, you know Thurin.'

'I'm not sure I do. That's why he is here. It has been a very long time since anyone was reclaimed from the taint. Many of the Broken do not believe it to be something that can be truly cleansed. They worry that the evil is still inside him, deep in his bones, waiting for its moment to return. They think him vulnerable to the demons in others and will not place their trust in him.'

'I trust him.'

Eular nodded. 'But then again you need to. You need to believe Thurin has been saved so that you can believe your brother can also be saved.'

Yaz clenched her teeth against a hot reply and before the tension in her jaw eased she found herself wondering if Eular were not simply using her description of others to shine a light on herself. 'Maya is the youngest, perhaps thirteen. She seems kind and timid. A gentle soul. But sometimes I find her watching me and I wonder if there's more to her . . .' Yaz remembered that Maya hadn't seemed scared of Hetta, not until the end. 'I think she must be marjal. She can pull the shadows around her and hide.'

'She would make an excellent spy, would she not?'

'I . . .' Yaz hadn't thought of Maya in those terms. 'I guess so.'

'And the others?'

'Quina is hunska. I've never seen anyone move so fast. She's clever too. And hard. I like her though.' Yaz hadn't realized it until she said so but she did. There was something in the girl that reminded her of her brothers. 'Her clan come from very far south. They have different stars!'

'I have heard that if you go far enough to the south you will find that Abeth still wears a green girdle, a belt around the world where the ice has yet to reach.' Eular smiled. 'I don't know what green is. But still, I should like to touch it.'

Yaz hid a smirk before realizing she didn't have to hide it. For one so old to believe cradle tales amused her. 'We can touch the rocks here. I'm not sure what would be gained by touching them and seeing the sky at the same time . . . or why they would be green.' Green was a colour she had seen only on the belly of rainbow fish and the fins of emeraldine.

It never lasted long after the fish were taken from the sea but it was pretty enough.

'And the last of them, the boy?'

'Kao,' Yaz said. 'He's bigger than any man among the Ictha but there's no strength inside him.'

Eular pursed his lips. 'Give him time. I'm told he has seen only twelve winters.'

'He's twelve?' Yaz found her mouth still open and closed it. 'That would explain a lot. I thought . . .'

'Eyes are all well and good.' Eular nodded. 'But it never pays to put too much faith in what they tell us. Listen too. Form slower judgements.' He nodded again, perhaps to her, perhaps to himself. 'I will speak with Thurin next.'

'Wait! I need to know how to save Zeen. Arka says the cleansing hardly ever works.'

Eular nodded. 'That is true, it often fails, and the tainted one is killed. Burned inside by the star-stones.'

'So—'

'I don't know. But I do know that a quick, strong exposure leaving nowhere for the devils to hide works best. The process is most successful when the largest stones are used. The dust never works. For Thurin his mother managed to get five stones the size of the one Pome dropped just now. Those are rare. As is the influence to get the Broken to agree on their possible destruction in such a ceremony.'

'And where could I find the biggest stars?'

'The city or the ice. Though a month hunting the deep places of the city will sometimes yield as much as ten years mining the ice. And of course . . . each hunter has a star-stone at its heart, some so big you could hardly get both hands to meet around them.'

Yaz stood slowly, trying to assemble the many pieces of information into some coherent structure in her mind. She had questions, most half formed, and no idea if she would be allowed to return to ask them. Instead she asked an entirely new one. 'You said the quantals see the . . . Path . . . was it?'

'I did.'

'But I see a river . . .'

'You've lived your whole life in a place without rivers or paths. The mind imposes its own will on such things. But if it is a river, then my advice is not to let it carry you away. The quantal magics are not gentle and many with such power are consumed by it before they learn their own limits.'

Yaz nodded, but then realized the gesture would go unseen. 'Yes.' She bent to pick up Pome's fallen star and the rod that had held it, seeing now the thin strands that had held the star in place. Metal wires rather than the sinew that the Ictha would use. 'Thank you.'

Yaz left the chamber, ducking beneath the icicles and entering the tunnel. The star blazed in her hand, too bright, glaring from the curving surfaces of the ice. She felt its rapid pulsing in her fingers, beating behind the star's wordless, ethereal song. Blinking, Yaz raised the star to her mouth and whispered to it so that the light retreated leaving a blue glow. The stone became a ball in which bright shades of sky marbled shades of sea, all in slow and rolling motion. Still blinking away after-images she emerged into the chamber where the others waited.

Pome stood closest at hand, watching Quina with predatory eyes. His look made Yaz remember what Arka thought of the disappearances of those that opposed the man. Yaz could believe it. She could see him trailing someone into the less walked caverns, knifing them in the back, pitching the corpse into a ravine, or leaving it for Hetta.

Pome turned as Yaz came into view. 'What have you done?'

He stared in horror at the muted blue glow in Yaz's right hand and the rod in her other. 'You've broken it. You stupid child.'

'I'm not a child. I passed the regulator's inspection. Twice.'

Pome looked up from the star, startled and sneering. 'Everyone who drops is a child. And you're still wet from the fall.'

Behind him Petrick and Thurin looked worried, Petrick spreading his hands and gesturing down in a motion that told her to leave it, that this was a dangerous man she did not want to make an enemy of. She was a day old in a new world and Pome held sway among gerants who would twist off her head at his order.

Yaz drew in a deep, slow breath. 'I wasn't dropped. I jumped. I am Yaz of the Ictha and you will treat me with some measure of respect or there will be a reckoning between us.' Before the astonishment of her drop-group Yaz strode across to stand in front of Pome, just feet between them, his face not so far above hers. 'Your star.' She held it out to him, making it blaze.

Pome ground his teeth together, cheek twitching at the star's proximity. 'It must have broken when it fell. It's no use to me now.' He turned away. 'I have duties to attend. Petrick, you can escort the other children back to Arka when Eular is done with them.'

They watched Pome stalk away and nobody spoke until he was gone, then all of them tried to speak together.

'Why would you do that?' Thurin asked.

'Not clever.' Petrick shook his head. 'Pome deserved it but a lot of the Broken listen to him, especially the warriors. He speaks of times when they will be more important than the other castes. So watch him. He holds grudges, that one.'

Yaz studied the star in her hand, returning it to its sleeping state. The blue glow bled around her fingers. 'He wants to kill the Taints, doesn't he?'

'Yes.' Thurin nodded.

'That makes him my enemy.'

While Thurin went in to speak with Eular Yaz crouched and examined the star that Pome had abandoned into her keeping. It felt cold in her hand and yet the stars sank through the ice. But slowly. The heat given out must be a very small amount. She rolled it idly across the rock then brought it back. It seemed that trails were left in the air where it had passed, lines thinner than the finest hair, perhaps invisible to someone without the talent to see them, but there even so.

'Why doesn't it shine any more?' Maya had come away from the others, who were still muttering together.

'I asked it not to,' Yaz said.

'Do they speak?'

'No . . . maybe . . . like the wind and the ice maybe. They speak but we're not meant to understand it.' She rolled the star towards Maya but the girl shied away.

'I can't.' Maya shook her head. 'When I get too close to them I get voices in my head. It scares me.'

'So they do speak?' Yaz was intrigued.

'No . . . I don't think so. It's like the voices are parts of me. As if the star were . . . breaking me apart.'

Yaz bit her lip, thinking. She reached to retrieve the star, and finding it just out of reach she made to shift position. But before she could move, the star somehow answered her desire and rolled to meet her fingers. No one but Maya saw and the girl looked at her wide-eyed. 'What?' hissed Yaz. 'You can pick up shadows and make a cloak out of them!'

A grin escaped Maya at that and she shrugged her accept-ance. 'Everyone has some trick they can do. My sister's friend could balance three fish bones end to end in a tower on the tip of his finger. I would rather have had a trick like that, one that meant I could have stayed with my family.' The grin faded once more.

Yaz picked up the star again, the strange tingle of it buzzing beneath her skin. The whole thing was no bigger than an eyeball.

'What else can you do?' Maya whispered.

Yaz wasn't sure. Staring at the star she began to see hints of the river again. To her it had always seemed to be the reality behind the world. Eular had named it the source of the quantals' power. She had never been able to see it again so soon after touching it. Always it hid from her, sometimes for days. But just around the margins of her hand she saw it, running into the star as if it were a hole. With an effort of concentration she pushed on the star without moving her hand. For a heartbeat it wobbled then slowly it rose. Just an inch or two before something in her mind slipped and the stone dropped back into her hand.

'Still playing with that thing?'

Yaz looked up and tried to refocus her blurred eyes. She realized that it was Thurin speaking and that she had a splitting headache.

'What . . .'

'I said, still—'

'You went in to see Eular.'

'I know.' Thurin crouched beside her. 'Maya's in with him now. Are you all right?'

'I . . . think so.' Yaz frowned and rubbed her brow. 'Wasn't Maya just here . . .?' Time seemed to slip by in chunks when she looked at the star. The Ictha made all their hides with plenty of small pockets. She slipped the star into one and stood, finding her legs full of protests. 'I'm fine. Just some cramp.'

'Well, stamp it out!' Thurin stood with her. 'Petrick thinks Arka might take us to the city today.'

Yaz didn't try to hide her surprise. 'So soon? Isn't the city supposed to be dangerous?'

'I thought you would have realized by now.' Thurin shot her a dark-eyed look, half sad, half amused. 'Everything is dangerous down here.'

CHAPTER 12

Speaking with Eular left each of the drop-group quiet, their thoughts turned inwards. Even Kao seemed subdued and Quina without her usual quickness that turned every motion into a twitch. She knelt beside Yaz and muttered, 'He told me that "we are all victims of our childhood, even good ones, for they made us what we are, and it's a rare person who isn't disappointed with that". What gave that old man the right to speak to me as if he knows me?' She seemed angry but distracted, as if the words did hold some special meaning for her.

Yaz shrugged. 'People get like that if they live long enough to turn grey. They think they've seen it all and have answers for everyone. But they're so distant from living life that they forget that we all have different paths.' She met Quina's eyes. 'Maybe . . . or perhaps he does have a power after all, and we should listen.'

Quina nodded, and half turned to move away, still troubled. 'I thought I was dead when the regulator gave me the push. I knew it was coming. I was too fast. Different. Feeling the cold every night no matter how many furs I scrounged.

I thought I was going to die. Even after the drop for a while I thought I must be dead and this is what the hells are.'

'What changed your mind?' Yaz grinned. 'Could you make a better hell?'

Quina echoed the smile. 'I guess the Tainted are like a hell on our doorstep. But this . . .' She waved at the starlit cavern. 'It's *interesting* down here. I had expectations about my life with the clan but one thing I never expected to see was anything different. I expected to spend my whole life looking at the ice. The same thing, every day. A long white view to a white-on-white horizon. And that's gone. The wind is gone. Predictability gone.'

'Safety gone,' Yaz said.

'True. But I've been given something I never knew I wanted. Not these caves, but the possibility of change. The idea that I have no idea what my life will be tomorrow, or next year.'

'You'd go back though,' Yaz asked, examining her own mind for any trace of doubt.

'Hells yes. In a heartbeat.' Quina snorted. 'But it would be a different me who went back. Already, even after just a day.' She walked away, aiming herself at Petrick. The two were of an age and Yaz had already noticed them spending time in each other's company.

Yaz returned to her own thoughts. The regulator wanted her back but his message didn't tell her how to leave. Or perhaps it did and Hetta had chosen not to pass that part of the message on. Did she truly want to return? If she managed to recover Zeen, and if the regulator allowed him back too . . . wouldn't the ice kill him? And life for her would be in service to the priesthood, part of their number, caged within the confines of the Black Rock, her clan forgotten. Was it better to be imprisoned in the priesthood, part of the system that discarded children into the Pit of the Missing? Or to have the freedom of the caves along with all the hardship and danger that came with them?

Eventually Petrick led them back to Forge Lake and, following his report of recent events, stayed at Arka's request.

Yaz joined the others in the smiths' shed to observe the beautiful Kaylal and his friend Exxar tease iron into chain links with their hammers. Later the drop-group provided an audience while silent Ixen and the bony woman sorted newly scavenged metal by type. And finally they watched a gerant smith and several apprentices beating steel plates into pieces of armour.

At last, with their ears ringing and sweat running inside their furs, Yaz and the others followed Arka from the cavern. Yaz found herself eager to leave. To free Zeen from the taint she would need stars of a size the Broken were unlikely to risk using up for someone who had never been part of their community. The city held such stars. Eular had said as much.

Arka lined them up and cast a critical eye over their short rank. 'We will be going down to the city. I fear you may find it somewhat quiet after your recent . . . excitement. On my last dozen trips to the city I saw no Taints and only once glimpsed a hunter. So you already have me beaten with just today! In any event, we shall not be going deep. Just far enough to give you an idea of the place.' She led off, waving for them to follow. 'Keep your eyes open. They say bad luck comes in threes.'

Yaz walked near the back with Thurin. Petrick brought up the rear.

'How is it', she asked, 'that Hetta was hunting someone through the tunnels and ready to attack us all when only the day before I put my knife through her foot and hand?

I know she's tough and . . . well . . . insane, but I've seen Ictha take weeks to recover from smaller injuries.'

'Maybe the Ictha heal slowly.' Thurin offered that half-grin of his. 'There has to be a price to pay for not feeling the cold, surely? And for being ridiculously strong.'

Petrick spoke up from behind. 'The Tainted are full of demons. And some of those demons bring gifts as well as curses. Hetta's been left for dead before and killed someone a week later. We have orders to remove her head next time. Just to be sure.'

Yaz walked on, thinking about Hetta, the size of her, the ferocity, and how she'd eaten Jaysin. Thurin said it was the devils under her skin that made her do it, but it was difficult to hate a black stain rather than the woman who has tried to kill you.

Several times Yaz had the strong feeling she was being watched – followed through the caverns. But glancing back over Petrick's head all she saw were gloom and shadows divided by the distant glow of stardust. She found it hard to imagine Hetta as a stealthy tracker even if she had managed to surprise them earlier.

Arka led the group through chambers thick with fungi, great swathes of the stuff growing silently in the light and relative warmth of broad bands of stardust. It seemed to Yaz that the fungi mimicked in beige, browns, purples, and pinks the striations of colour in the ice above them, their muted palette echoing the stars' glow.

In several places harvesters could be seen working alone or in close pairs among the groves of fungi. Yaz picked her way between the growths, some as round as wind-carved ice balls, some open with feathery fronds, and yet others taller, thinner, and blunt-ended. Kao made some remark about these last ones and sniggered but Yaz missed what he said.

As the air grew colder and the caves darker the fungi groves began to thin and vanish. Tending one of the last of them was a gerant so huge that all of the drop-group stopped to stare. Arka called the man over and he came shambling across with his sack on his shoulder, his patchworked furs hanging loose around him, big enough to serve as a tent for all the rest of them.

'This is Jerrig,' Arka said, 'a long-serving harvester. When you eat tonight it will likely be something Jerrig has tended and picked.'

Jerrig smiled at them. Despite the brutality of his forehead and jawline something timid lay behind them, and the eyes that peered from beneath those brows looked half shy. The man stood perhaps ten feet tall and slabbed with muscle albeit softened by a layer of fat, and yet he seemed nervous of children half his height and fresh from their drop. Without speaking he opened his sack to show them his collection. Scores of the round fungi, none smaller than two fists, and all blushing either reddish-brown or purple-grey.

'Thank you, Jerrig.' Arka touched his arm and the man smiled again before returning to his duties.

'Can't he speak?' Kao snorted.

'He can,' Arka said. 'But he is a wise man and chooses often to be silent.'

She led them on, leaving the growing chambers far behind.

The caverns grew darker, the stars either mined out or absent due to the whims of the ice. Their footsteps rang in the frosty air and the darkness returned no echoes. Arka slowed her advance, leading by memory. Yaz strained to see in the deepening gloom. Someone was following them, following her, she felt sure of it, something creeping behind them. The sudden groaning of the ice made her flinch. The others started at the sound too, all of them on edge.

'Something is wrong here . . .' Arka came to a halt.

Something *was* wrong. The darkness sat around them, hungry and waiting. The ice, Yaz's companion all the years of her life, felt wrong. It had always been uncaring, unforgiving, as brutal as the wind . . . but this was different. A cold malice.

'I . . . I could make some light.' Yaz's voice seemed thin and cracked, even to her, a feeble challenge to the silence that had grown among them.

Nobody answered her. Beside Yaz Maya shuddered and hunched in on herself. Yaz reached for the pocket where she had placed Pome's star. Everything resisted her, as if the sense of hopelessness that had enfolded them had thickened the air itself into ropes that bound her arms. Even so she forced her hand forwards, ever more slowly, sinking into the depths of the pocket, fingers questing, certain now that they would find nothing. Nothing good at least.

When Yaz's hand closed about the star it was as if a clean wind blew through her, clearing her mind. She drew it out into the open, reminding it of how it once shone, and in an instant the marbled blue glow became a fierce, unforgiving light.

On the surface, the true stars that lit the long night for the Ictha offered no warmth but their red glow came softly through the darkness, whispering away details, hiding wrinkle and blemish. Yaz's starlight carried a harsh edge, throwing each face into sharp relief, accentuating any defect, edging Arka's scars in black, making something grotesque of Thurin's mask of horror.

'Brighter,' Yaz murmured, and the darkness slunk away, retreating down tunnels and into adjoining caverns.

The others shook themselves, throwing off the malaise that had ensnared them.

Where Kao, Maya, Quina, and the rest of them looked about themselves in confusion Thurin stared upwards, hunting.

'There!' He pointed, hand trembling.

'No?' Arka saw it too.

It seemed like a shadow to Yaz. A shadow on the ice above them. Only there was nothing to cast such a shadow. 'The ice is . . . grey?' It took her a moment to understand. 'The ice is grey!'

Following the stain back across the cavern roof she saw that it thickened and darkened until it vanished into the gloom of the next chamber – where it might even be black.

'Back!' Arka turned, arms spread, ushering them towards another cavern.

'What is it?' Quina asked, staring but backing away.

'The taint,' Thurin said.

'You didn't know it was here?' Kao asked Arka, pale in Yaz's light. 'You led us into it?'

'Theus is behind this. I know it.' Thurin backed away slowly as if holding every part of himself tight. 'The taint can spread. It can move. Not fast, but faster than the ice moves.'

'It's followed some fault in the ice or a shift in the heat flow,' Arka said. 'I don't think Theus—'

'You don't *know* what he's capable of!' Thurin was nearly shouting.

'You're right. I don't.' Arka held up her hands, peace-making. 'All I know is that it can spread.' She ushered them into a tunnel leading away. Standing to count them past her. 'But it almost never does . . .'

Thurin followed Yaz away from the cave with a last glance over his shoulder and a shudder. 'A lot of things that never happen have happened today.'

Even as she left, something tugged at Yaz, the feeling that she was being watched an unbearable itch on the back of her neck. She swung about, shaping the star's light into a beam. It took an effort, a small shard of pain made itself known deep in her head . . . but the star shone as she asked it to, and she sent its radiance lancing into the chamber from which the taint had spread.

'Arka!' There, exposed in the distance, darkness's black sheet whipped from them, stood a handful of ragged figures, grime-stained, frozen by the light's sudden interrogation.

'Tainted!' Thurin cried the warning. But the Tainted were already in full retreat, running for the security of the shadows.

The smallest of them lingered, just a moment, casting a malevolent glance over his shoulder, black eyes gleaming, mouth twisted in a rictus of hate. And in that heartbeat before he looked away and sprinted after the rest of the Tainted, Yaz recognized her brother.

'Zeen!' She gave chase with no thought for her safety, knowing she could never catch her brother in a footrace.

Thurin brought her crashing to the ground and they struggled briefly before she flung him away, slamming against the nearest ice wall. Yaz found her feet but Zeen was gone, even the sound of his footsteps had faded into the distance, and into the momentary silence came Thurin's groaning.

'You stopped me!' She helped him up, her anger warring with concern that she might have done him some serious injury.

'It's how they trap you!' Thurin rose, clutching his side.

'That was my brother!' Yaz shouted.

'That was a demon wearing your brother like you wear

a hide.' Thurin winced and straightened. 'They would have trapped you in the black ice and tainted you.'

Arka joined them, the others following. 'It's true. At least you know he's alive.' She gave an apologetic shrug. 'Though it might be better for him if he weren't.'

Yaz shook off the hand Quina reached tentatively towards her. Her anger still smouldered even though she knew they were right. Zeen was alive and she wasn't able to drive the taint from him. Not yet. 'Come on.' She headed back the way Arka had been leading them, eager now to reach this city.

Even in the tunnel Yaz felt followed, as though the taint might be snaking after them through the ice, and the Tainted following in its wake. Zeen's hate-twisted face returned to her mind whenever she rested her eyes on any patch of shadow. Thurin, limping beside her without complaint, was her only proof that her brother remained behind those demon-tainted eyes, whole and restorable.

The sensation of being watched returned so strongly when they came into a wider chamber and crossed it that Yaz turned back, asking her star to shine once more, shaping its light into a beam that reached out to where they had entered. Three figures became visible and immediately drew back. Two with spears and behind them someone huge. They lacked the ragged twitchiness of the Tainted.

Arka turned just in time to catch a glimpse. Her face tightened in shock. She spoke quickly and quietly as the others stared at the dark mouth of the tunnel into which the trio had retreated. 'That was Pome, I'm sure of it. Was there a gerant? Yes? That would be Bexen, his enforcer. The other one was probably Jalla, a hunska warrior in his faction.'

'What are they doing?' Yaz asked. 'Why would they follow us?'

'Quickly!' Arka was already moving. 'If they're following us, way out here near the city, then whatever they want is nothing good. They're not here to protect us from the Tainted. That's for damn sure!' She had them jogging now. 'Pome has always had a brittle pride. You were wrong to push him, Yaz. He knows how to talk, that one. He has many who listen, and he wants Tarko's position. If you make him look weak then he has to do something to take that strength back again.' She hurried them through a narrow, twisted tunnel, the close confines carrying her voice back to Yaz. 'The day he makes his move there will be blood. Pome's the sort who would rather break something and own the pieces than see another hold it whole. And I don't mean to let him start with us!'

Yaz hurried on with only Petrick between her and any pursuit. At every moment she expected a spear to come winging out of the darkness. She had seen something in Pome's eyes, an emptiness that reminded her of the wind and made her think him capable of anything if he thought he held the upper hand. She hoped that Zeen would keep clear of him. Something told her Pome might not be much of a warrior but she was certain he enjoyed killing when the odds were heavily enough in his favour.

Arka led them at a stiff pace, all of them watchful, no longer trusting the ice until at last they came to the long slope.

'Here,' Arka said. 'The taint can never come here. That at least is for certain. And this is scavenger ground. No warrior would choose to face us here. Warriors they might be but they still fear the hunters.' Even so, she glanced back to where Pome and the others might appear.

'What is it?' Maya seemed more awed by the slope than scared of pursuit.

Arka smiled and gestured ahead of them. 'You're looking at something the Missing walked on.'

It was obvious that the slope couldn't be the work of nature, but how men or any other could have made so long, broad and even a surface Yaz couldn't say. Neither could she explain why the ice hadn't simply scoured it away.

The ice-free slope led down across a rocky hillside at an even gradient, sometimes cutting into the bedrock, sometimes rising above it on a different kind of stone. About halfway down two black pillars flanked the ramp-way, each taller than a man. Yaz could only imagine they held their own heat and that the advancing ice that had erased the city simply melted around them, leaving them unscathed in their own bubbles.

To either side of the descent ice walls glittered, glowing with stardust, the occasional brighter star twinkling amid the constellations. The cavern that the slope led down into was vast, a hundred times larger than the largest Arka had yet shown them. The glow came most strongly on the west side where the walls stood shining with the spoils of the ice's theft, the glittering remnants of a city full of stars. Clearly the ice had once ground its way across the city of the Missing which had been standing here long before the original four tribes of man beached their ships on this world. All that remained now was scraped rock and strange scars.

'It's beautiful,' Maya breathed beside Yaz.

'It is.' The ice glowed in a million shades. The air was frosty here, as cold as it had been in Eular's small cave out on the margins on the far side of the Broken's territory. The constant sound of dripping had faded then gone, and Yaz hadn't noticed it leave. For a moment even the ice itself was quiet, no distant groans, no creaking, just a frozen silence. Yaz found the stillness more beautiful in its rarity than even the swirling wonders her gaze tracked across the walls. A peace that held the breath in her lungs. Holy perhaps. After a life lived leaning into the wind she could imagine that silence housed its own gods.

In that moment, standing beneath the vast ethereal ceiling of the city cavern, Yaz decided that this would be her new life. She and Zeen would remain with the Broken. She would refuse the regulator's claim on her.

'Why've we stopped?' Kao glanced over his shoulder then pushed to the front. He looked as though he might be about to whistle for the echo, but a dark look from Arka diverted him into another question. 'Where's the city?'

'What remains is under the ground in tunnels and chambers carved through the rock.' Arka pointed towards the middle of the chamber. 'There are a great number of ways into it in that area.'

'What about the hunters?' Quina asked.

'They are generally deep in the complex, roaming the regions where there is still material to be scavenged, which is where they will find scavengers to hunt. If they try guarding some of the entrances we just use an alternative. But one hunter did come out today so we will go carefully.' As they descended the long slope Arka began to point to locations on the cavern floor. 'At the first sign of a hunter we run and we hide. We do not all hide in the same place. To hide you want to get deep. You've already seen what kind of reach they have. The best spots are marked with purple splodges. These are the ones I'm pointing out to you. But any hiding place is better than none.'

'Hunters are made of metal,' Yaz said. 'Why do they chase us? Can they eat flesh?'

Arka paused before answering. 'Nobody knows. They carry their victims away and we don't see them again. Not even their bones.' She drew in a deep breath. 'It's overconfidence that gets you captured. They take the best of us. Those who delve deepest and have been scavenging the longest. Those who start to think they're too good at scavenging to ever get caught. Those who oppose them when they roam into our caverns.' She frowned as if assailed by a painful memory. 'But hunters are certainly not the only danger down in the city. I've known scavengers lost to cave-ins, to strange machinery, gas, explosions . . . or just plain lost and unable to find their way back. It's big down there. Much bigger than what you see up here. A world below ours just like we are a world below the ice clans.'

As they drew nearer to the two gateposts a pressure began to exert itself on Yaz. At first a mental pressure, a reluctance to advance, and then a physical one where the air itself pushed against her. None of the others appeared to feel it.

Yaz pressed on even as the two black posts swallowed her vision, driving everything around them into insignificance until only they and she remained. Both seemed a hundred feet tall, a thousand, taller than the Black Rock itself, and as they grew the space between them diminished, stealing away the possibility of progress.

'Are you all right?' Quina asked beside her. The girl reached out to set a hand on Yaz's arm, bird-quick, tentative, the contact broken as soon as it was made.

'Y-yes,' Yaz lied. She found herself at the back of the group, stumbling. Grinding her teeth together she set her gaze firmly on the floor before her feet and focused on taking the next step. She couldn't let them leave her here for Pome to find. And what she needed to save Zeen lay down there, in the city under the city.

Even with her head down she could see the gateposts in her mind, huge with forbidding. 'I can . . .' Each step came harder, the pressure building along with a vibration in the marrow of her bones that quickly turned into pain. Yaz didn't even know why she was fighting it, and hiding the fight. She felt that she must be bleeding, from her eyes, her nose, blood sweating from her skin. You couldn't battle so hard and not bleed.

Zeen! The city held the stars that would save him. In that instant she saw him falling, felt herself jumping, and knew why she was fighting. For her brother, but not just for him. It was more than that. She was fighting against . . . against everything, against the system that saw children thrown away, against the thinking behind it, against the ice itself. And suddenly the pain and pressure were gone and she was falling.

CHAPTER 13

'Yaz?'

Yaz opened her eyes to find Thurin trying to lift her into a sitting position. Behind him a line of backs presented themselves as the others stared at the gateposts to either side of the long slope. A purple fire filled both posts, as though they were glass rather than the black iron they had seemed to be. For a moment she felt very conscious of how close Thurin was to her, his arms around her. The dark eyes locked to hers were full of concern. She felt the nearness of him, the warmth of him.

By the time Yaz got to her feet, refusing Thurin's arm, the effect within the posts had died to flickers within the blackness.

'I tripped. I'm fine.' Yaz brushed at her knees and elbows.

Thurin looked back along the smooth ramp then returned his gaze to her, saying nothing.

'Perhaps it's to do with the hunter escaping,' Arka was saying. 'I've seen a hunter chase a scavenger right to the posts then stop as if they've hit an invisible wall. It's very difficult for a hunter to leave the city and when they do they return to it quickly. But if the gateposts are broken and won't hold any more . . .' She shuddered. 'Things will be very different.'

Arka carried on, sparing only a frown for Yaz and seeming to accept that she had simply fallen. Instructions on hiding places came thick and fast now, with special mention for the gerant-sized ones, though Kao could likely still squeeze into those used by people of more regular size.

At last they came to the more level ground. Here the bedrock had been scraped by the ice's teeth for aeons as it moved slowly towards the Frequent Sea many miles to the west. Despite this toothed erosion having carried on for untold millennia the rock still bore testimony to the vanished city. Everywhere it lay scarred with shafts of different rock revealed as depressions or prominences depending on the hardness of their composition, some like worn teeth jutting a yard or more into the air. In other places there were holes rimmed with rust, or metal columns reaching down into the rock, the exposed lengths torn and bent in the direction of the ice. All of it fringed with frost.

'What kind of buildings must they have been to have had foundations like these?' Thurin asked. 'I've seen it before and it still amazes me.'

'Foundations?' Yaz looked away from the stone 'tooth' she had been examining.

Thurin tilted his head. 'Your tents are held to the ice with pegs, so I'm told.'

'Yes, or the wind would take them.'

'Well.' He gestured around. 'These are the city's pegs. The Missing just drove them deeper than the Ictha do.'

Yaz opened her mouth but found no reply. Instead she gazed up at the distant ceiling, trying to imagine what the dwelling places of the Missing must have been like.

'What about the Missing themselves? Do we know how they looked?' Yaz had always been fascinated with the figures that some of the elders would carve from whalebone and whale teeth. In the darkness of the tent on the long night Mother Karrak could whittle away at a bone to reveal men and women inside, kettan figures, so detailed that come the dawn the Ictha would gather and laugh, recognizing themselves and their family among those freed from the ivory. Perhaps the Missing had left a similar record. 'Did they leave images?'

'Nothing.' Arka shook her head. 'Nothing that lasted. But their lives were very different from ours. Eular thinks many of their possessions and their art may have been temporary and changeable, and their records locked away in ways we can't understand. We do know, though, that they were of a similar size to us.'

'How?'

'Many of their chambers were of a size that would suit us. Their stairs also fit our stride.' Arka looked around. She had not stopped looking around since they stepped out onto the flatter ground. 'Stay vigilant. Allow a wonder to seduce your eye and a hunter may take that moment to pounce.' She waved them on, pointing out holes to hide in as they advanced.

Finally they reached the fractured edge of a large hole leading down into a darkness punctuated with individual points of starlight. A warm draught rose from the void, the first wind Yaz had felt on her face since her fall down the pit.

'The heat tells us that there are still many stars down in the city,' Arka said. 'And the cavern tells us that our efforts have had minimal impact on that total.'

'How?' Quina scowled, clearly hating not to be able to work it out for herself.

'It isn't dripping,' Arka said. 'Only the east wall runs, where the advancing ice melts away at exactly the rate it advances. A stream carries the water off. The rest of the cavern is in equilibrium. The warmth is just enough to sustain it.'

The rising air carried a stale smell along with muted undercurrents as alien as those of the forge huts. Yaz sniffed it with suspicion while trying to concentrate on what Arka was saying about minding their heads on the low ceilings.

'You wets are all terrible at climbing, and there's really nowhere safe for you to practise, so this is it. *Think* about what you're doing, where your hands are, where your feet are. This isn't the ice.'

Arka carried on talking. Hulking beside Yaz Kao muttered, 'I should be on the ice. Not in a hole going into a deeper hole.'

Quina on his other side snapped back, 'Seriously? How was any of this a surprise for you? Did you not notice that you were twice the size of your playmates? Your parents should have been preparing you for the gathering long before you came to the pit.'

'Perhaps his clan thought it a kindness not to tell him,' Yaz muttered. 'Maybe all the adults knew and none of the children.' She had lived with the burden of the knowledge since her first gathering and it had soured the years left to her among her people. Ignorance might have been less cruel.

Arka took out an iron rod, longer than the one Pome had used to hold his star, and scooped a star from a small depression near the entrance. With its light to guide them she slipped easily down past the stone jaws and began to climb the slope of broken rock beneath.

Yaz let Kao go first. If he fell she wanted to be above him not below. Maya followed, nimble-footed.

When it came to her turn to climb Yaz found herself in

immediate difficulty. She had lived her life on the level with nothing in her path but pressure ridges in the ice. The descents to the Hot Sea and the others that opened periodically when upwellings of warm water melted through the glacial sheet were treacherous things but the Ictha lowered themselves on hide ropes. Here she had no rope, only a complex, ever-changing surface to negotiate. By the time she reached flat ground again every limb trembled and sweat ran in trickles inside her hides.

'Gods in the Sea! I'm glad that's over.' Yaz clambered down to join Thurin.

'Over?'

She saw that they were crowded on a ledge and that the steep slant of the tunnel continued, considerably closer to vertical than to horizontal. She peered over into the darkness. 'How deep does it go?'

'Nobody knows. Scavengers say they've been as deep as the ice is tall, but I'm not sure how they could tell that.' Thurin offered a crooked smile. 'It's hard work. I've been down before and I'm glad of it, but I wouldn't want to do it every day.'

The next stage of the climb brought them through narrow sections which Yaz found it impossible to believe that a hunter could have fitted along. The rock seemed to press on her from all directions, constricting her chest even when not touching it. She felt the weight of all that silent stone, stretching above her for hundreds of yards.

'How could a hunter get out of here?' Quina asked the question for her.

'They can reshape and rebuild their bodies.' Arka squeezed between two great blocks of stone. 'It takes them a long time. But they can do it. Which is one of the reasons we need to draw them away when they have someone cornered in a hole. Because given enough time they will reach you.' She vanished through and called from the other side. 'Also some of the ways in and out are wider than this one. We're using this one to avoid hunters.'

During the descent the character of the rock began to change, from some kind of natural fissure, broken open by the action of water and ice, to the strange stone of the long slope. They began to pass other openings, some square, some just new fractures and faults. Arka led them down into a ravine onto which rooms and chambers faced like open mouths, as if the bedrock had split wide and revealed them trapped in stone as bubbles are trapped in ice.

'Many of these chambers may have been where the Missing lived.' Arka lifted her star to reveal one as they descended past it. 'Others were meeting places perhaps, or storage rooms, or housed markets or workers. We really don't know. But what *we* are here for is metal, star-stones, and anything else that can be carried away. There is very little here that you can pick up that will not be of use to us.'

'There's very little here that we can pick up,' muttered Yaz. The chambers she had seen were echoingly empty.

'The Broken have been at this for generations,' Thurin said. 'You have to go deep to find anything. Really deep. Some scavengers are gone for many days at a time.'

'Careful here,' Arka called, leading the way across a stone beam that bridged the ravine down whose side they had been working their way.

Even as Arka said it Yaz began to fall. She hadn't even reached the beam but something snagged her foot and without it the rest of her started to tumble towards the yawning chasm.

'Got you.' Quina's hand fastened around Yaz's wrist. She didn't seem to have bothered with all the usual business of moving the hand through the space between where it had been before and where it now gripped her. Her speed was a kind of magic. She braced herself and hauled on Yaz so that she swung back into the rock face.

'Ooof!' Yaz pushed away from the rocks. 'Thank you.'

A small smile broke out on Quina's narrow face, as quick as the rest of her, then gone, but in that moment it lit her up, the pinched look vanishing, replaced by something unguarded and happy. 'It's nothing. Watch your feet.'

'But then I'll walk into a wall.' Yaz grinned.

'Which will hurt less than falling into a hole!' Another flash of a smile and then Quina was herself again, moving on.

Yaz crossed the chasm, trying to ignore the dark pull of the fall to either side, and hurried on into the gaping chamber ahead. She paused to stare about. The space was nothing more than scarred grey walls joining at right angles, but she found herself snared by the idea that untold years ago the Missing themselves had walked here, spoken, lived, loved – if the Missing loved – and above them a city had towered, the sunlight falling on its people, the ice a distant threat . . .

'Yaz!' Kao shouted. 'Come on!'

Yaz shook away remnants of the images that had filled her mind and hurried after the boy, last out of the room.

Arka led them on and on. Each echoingly empty chamber or dusty corridor led to another empty room or passage. As the dozens of chambers mounted through scores towards hundreds Yaz became increasingly aware that the place was a labyrinth and if she lost Arka she would never find her way back. Many of the chambers had three or more exits. Cave-ins blocked their advance at frequent turns, rubble piled to the ceiling. Everything looked much the same and Yaz had no idea how Arka could remember the way.

As if reading Yaz's mind Arka drew their attention to the floor. 'Don't forget, these arrows will guide you out.' She scuffed away some dust with her foot.

Now that Yaz knew to look for them she could see the faint scratches.

'These ones are very old. They need redoing. The real danger though is deep down. If you reach an unexplored area and don't make your marks, or you get chased into unknown corridors, then you might find that getting out again is . . . difficult.' Arka rubbed her scarred cheek. 'I spent seventeen days lost in the deep city once. My food ran out after ten. I'd been a day and a half without water when I finally crawled up the long slope.'

Yaz nodded and made a special effort to stay close after that. The feeling of being followed had returned despite Arka's assurance that Pome and the warriors with him would not dare to come against them in the city. The silence that had seemed so mystical in the cavern above felt oppressive in the dry emptiness of the undercity, swallowing every noise they made and giving nothing back, just as the darkness took their light.

'It's waiting,' Yaz murmured.

'What?' Thurin looked back at her.

'The whole city. It's like it's waiting for something. Holding its breath . . .'

The next chamber was domed, a change from the depressing regularity of right angles and flat surfaces. On the far wall three symbols glowed, each a yard tall. They reminded Yaz of the sigils that turned a star's light to heat.

'We'll see more of these as we go,' Arka said. 'We don't know their purpose.' She pointed to areas of textured colour spattering the stone around the symbols, patches of brownish yellow and pale blue-green. 'That's lichen. Another kind of plant, but not good to eat. It grows down here anywhere that there's light.'

The drop-group moved over to inspect, and as Yaz drew closer the same forbidding that had opposed her at the gateposts flared, though with less force. She ground her teeth and stopped her advance, hoping that nobody would notice. The symbols, however, had grown brighter and Maya turned to stare at Yaz. 'Are they shining because of you?'

Yaz forced a laugh and shook her head. She could see that where the wall was pitted the symbols persisted as if they were written through the thickness of the stone. 'No.'

'Come closer then,' Quina said, running her fingers across the lines of the central symbol.

'I . . .' Yaz turned away and went to sit against the opposite wall. 'I'll just rest here.'

'They faded as you walked away,' Arka said, lifting her star towards Yaz. It too burned brighter as it approached her, underlining Arka's point. 'Can you read them?'

'Of course I can't read them!' Yaz snapped. Then, forcing herself to calm: 'I can't read anything.' But she knew what the symbols said though. They told her to *leave*. They told her she was not permitted here.

Arka stared without comment then led them from the chamber. The symbols flared as Yaz passed them and she felt that stab of pain, the compulsion to go back, but pushed on through.

They came to a great dusty space where the low ceiling rested on innumerable pillars. Here and there a shaft would vanish into the floor, large enough to swallow a boat and with no bottom to it. Other shafts led upwards, shrouded in darkness.

'What *is* that noise?' Yaz pressed her fingers to her ears but it made no difference: the sound was in her head, a discordant rhythm, faint but wild. 'It's like . . .' It was like the heartbeat of a star, only wrong. It seemed familiar somehow.

'Yaz?' Ahead of her Arka stopped and turned, the others bunching around her.

'Run.' Yaz wanted to say more, needed to say more, but that was the only word to escape her lips.

'Yaz?' Arka repeated, tilting her head.

'Run!' A shout now. 'Hunter!'

The screech of metal on stone, growing louder, coming closer. Quina and Petrick were already running back. The hunter dropped from the nearest vertical shaft, scraping sparks from the walls then absorbing the impact of its landing on five articulated legs. A nightmare creature built from scraps such as the Broken hunted: iron plates, springs and coils, chains, wheels, and wires, its core a black fist from which a hot red light leaked, escaping through every chink in the monster's armour.

The thing lunged for Arka's group with one of several arms, none of them the same. Although too short to reach across the intervening gap the arm proved versatile, the three-fingered grabber at the end detached and flew out to hit Thurin in the back, flooring him. Yaz started forward as the others ran towards her. The long metal fingers of the grabber were closing on Thurin even as the chain attaching it to the hunter's arm began to haul it back. Before Yaz had crossed half the gap Thurin had twisted free and was up, sprinting for freedom, large pieces of his coat dangling from the iron fingers that had so nearly trapped him.

'Run!' Arka shouted Yaz's own instruction back at her.

The hunter scrabbled across the stone floor, claws seeking purchase, accelerating slowly but with the promise of great speed.

Yaz and Thurin were last through the doorway Arka

selected, and before they were ten yards along the corridor the hunter slammed into the entrance behind them, a host of black metal limbs reaching for them while mechanical legs thrashed to try and cram the monster's bulk in after its prey. Yaz heard the hunter's talons snapping closed on the air just behind her. She ran on, taking a corner at speed and crashing into the wall. Behind her the hunter released a long scream of rage, a noise like a metal file being scraped across a rough edge, only magnified a million-fold, vibrating through Yaz's bones and setting her teeth on edge.

'Wait!' Arka caught them as they came around the turn. 'It can't follow. It will look for other routes to overtake us.' She drew a deep breath, pale-faced in the light of the star she held above them.

The scream came again, discordant and making Yaz's stomach want to empty itself.

'Sounds like we made it angry.' Thurin tried to smile. His furs hung around him in tatters, his exposed body lean and muscular.

Arka did not return the smile. 'It's calling for other hunters.' She turned away, shaking her head. 'We need to go slow. Be vigilant. Take the narrow ways. Too many scavengers are lost when they run from one hunter into the jaws of another.'

Arka led them at a cautious pace, muttering to herself from time to time.

'I thought she said you hardly ever see a hunter,' Maya whispered.

'Normally you wouldn't,' Thurin said. One of the metal fingers had scored a red line across his exposed back, beaded with blood.

'Only since the drop . . . there's been no normal.' Petrick glanced towards Yaz.

'I . . .' Yaz hung her head. She couldn't argue. The jump

that had upended her life seemed to be turning the Broken's expectations upside down too. As if the waves from her impact hadn't died to ripples and vanished against that stony shore but instead had passed on through the ice, growing and growing all the time.

Less than half an hour later they saw the hunter again, charging at impossible speed the length of a shadow-haunted hall, betrayed by its clatter as Arka ushered them into a narrow passage. And a short while after that a long thin arm lunged out from some narrow pipe at foot level, scything talons that narrowly missed Quina who leapt above them with inhuman swiftness. The rest of them edged around the blindly reaching hand, just beyond the reach of its iron claws.

After that Arka seemed to have lost the creature, though she showed no signs of relaxing.

The deeper Arka led them the warmer it got. They encountered more symbols, glowing quietly through the stone in rooms bearded with so much lichen that the walls looked diseased. Most stood a couple of feet tall, some a little larger, some that could be covered with a hand. All were varied, flowing, and complex. Even the smaller ones hinted at largeness, as though they might be the shadows cast by something infinitely more profound and dwelling in more dimensions than a human mind could fathom.

Most of the symbols offered Yaz no resistance, others she had to battle past, but all of them shone brighter as she drew near.

Some of the descents required the navigation of rocky slopes, elsewhere there were stairs. In two places they went down vertical shafts using ropes of an unknown material that had been left hanging there by scavengers. Cables, Arka called them. Kao slipped on the second climb, fell the last two yards, and hurt his ankle.

'When you can't run it's time to head back.' Arka looked up the long shaft above them, a hundred feet and more, vanishing into the gloom. 'I'll take us by a different route with more stairs and less climbing.'

Kao muttered that it was time to head back when the hunter first saw them. Arka stiffened but didn't turn to rebuke him. Yaz felt a certain sympathy for Kao on this one. Whatever his size he remained a child in a maze full of horrors, and now he lacked even the option to run from them. On the other hand it seemed that nothing beneath the ice was safe, and perhaps harsh lessons were all that could be offered. They would learn to survive, or die trying. And much as Yaz wanted to leave this place, she had come here for stars large enough to give Zeen a chance of surviving the cleansing he needed. She hadn't seen so much as stardust yet . . .

Arka led them through a series of long galleries, echoingly empty, burdened with a sadness that the rooms before held only whispers of. Yaz saw that this time the others felt it too. Maya had tears cutting tracks through the dirt on her cheeks.

'We call them the Crying Halls,' Arka said, her face held tight. 'Parts of the city will play tricks on you like th—' She stopped dead, spreading her arms to keep the others from passing her.

'What is it?' Yaz tensed, ready to run from a hunter.

'Those were not there before.' Arka pointed at a string of symbols on the wall just ahead of them, smaller than those before and so faint they could be easily missed, almost hidden by the light of the star she held above her.

'Maybe Yaz is just making them brighter so you can see them, but they were always there,' Quina offered.

'Maybe.' Arka frowned but carried on. Behind her Yaz

imagined the Missing who had walked the hallway before them in the long ago and wondered what sorrow might have happened here to linger so many centuries.

More strings of symbols came into view: some small enough to circle with a finger and thumb, some more visible than the ones Arka had thought new, but all seeming to alarm her. As Yaz passed by the lines a brighter pulse followed along them and a whispering filled her ears as if the text were being read aloud, the words just beyond hearing but laden with meaning.

Arka quickened her pace, bringing them into a vaulted chamber from which a broad flight of stairs led upwards. Four large symbols blazed on the floor and Arka came to another halt. 'These are definitely new!'

'Does it matter?' Thurin asked, worry and confusion edging his voice.

'I've come back and forth through these halls for twenty years. I've never seen a new symbol appear or an old one change.' The fear in Arka's voice infected the rest of them, the sorrow at their backs turning to foreboding. Even from the rear of the group Yaz could feel the pressure the symbols exerted, like a strong wind opposing her together with the promise of good things if she just turned aside.

SCCCCCREEEEEEEE!

A hunter's scream, worryingly close, ricocheting from the archway to the left.

'Quick!' Arka skirted around the walls, avoiding the symbols burning on the floor. Kao hobbled after her, then Quina and Petrick, then Maya. Thurin beckoned Yaz on and she tried to follow, straining against the forbidding that lay written out before her. The symbols blazed as she defied them. The light became so fierce that it seemed a brilliant world waited beneath the stone and that the curves of the symbols were just gaps through which it shone. Wisps of pale fire started to dance above the lines. Each of the symbols shouted at Yaz, roaring, adding its voice to a wordless four-part harmony.

SCCCCCREEEEEEEEEEE!

Even louder this time, setting Yaz's teeth buzzing in their sockets. In the distance the clatter of metal claws on stone.

Yaz came to a halt with her back pressed to the wall, seeking to distance herself from the source of her pain.

'What are you doing?' Thurin reached out towards her. She read the words from his lips, his face pale, dark eyes wide. 'We need to run!'

'I . . .' She coughed and spat blood on the floor, her head about to split open. The symbols' song filled her, ringing in her bones.

'Come on!'

Gathering the same determination with which she faced the wind as the long night closed in, Yaz forced herself on. Something had to break. For a moment it seemed it must be her. And then, with a last flash and flare, the symbols released their hold.

'This is all wrong,' Arka muttered to herself, starting on the steps. She glanced back into the room as if expecting the hunter to burst in any moment. 'All wrong.'

They climbed at speed, held back only by Kao and his ankle. More symbols appeared along the walls of the stairway while Arka led the group up the square spiral of steps. Strings of text ignited as the drop-group passed them. More and more. Lines of symbols so small each could be covered with a finger, and so bright that they wrote themselves across Yaz's hides as she passed, whispering to her all the while, their voices filled with reproach. She felt them burn on her skin, a searing that she thought must leave a mark. The others, though, showed no discomfort as symbols slid across them.

The stairs gave onto a large rectangular chamber with many exits. Rubble scattered the floor from old roof falls. Huge single symbols decorated the walls opposite and to either side, lighting the chamber. The lack of any lichen told Yaz immediately that these too were new.

Even as Arka led them in, more symbols appeared, not revealing themselves by growing brighter but scrolling down from above the ceiling or as strings of text running in through the doorways. Thurin and the rest looked wildly around, the script writing itself across their faces in light, flowing over their bodies. For a moment they reminded Yaz of the regulator and the complex burn scars all across his skin. When they reached her she gasped in pain at their fierce heat.

Behind them on the stairs a sudden crashing and thrashing, metal on stone, approaching fast, loud enough and close enough for Yaz to hear it over the cacophony of symbol song that none of the others seemed to notice.

'Run!' Arka shouted. In moments all of them were chasing her through a brightness that was almost blinding. Where the others ran straight paths, symbols of forbidding forced Yaz to twist and turn. More came, moving, shifting, almost as though they were herding her.

Without warning all the symbols vanished, leaving total darkness. Behind her Yaz heard the hunter take the last turn of the stairs, whirring and clanking, the angry pulse of its core-stone echoing in her head. She took two more steps blind then tumbled as the ground beneath her feet gave way. And for the second time in two days Yaz was dropped into empty space, screaming into the depths of a fall that no person should expect to survive.

CHAPTER 14

Green. A carpet of green. Innumerable green blades, like the swords of an army pointing at the sky. Yaz could find no sense of scale. She lifted her head and found that the blades were no longer than her fingers and marched in from the distance, running beneath her splayed hands and on behind her. The stuff bent beneath her palms, it stirred in a breath of wind. It seemed to grow from the ground itself, and that ground, hidden beneath a thickness of the greenery, was soft, like nothing she had ever felt before. Not yielding to her weight but lacking the rigidity of ice or rock. And the heat. Heat suffused her. Not with the fierceness of a flame, but soaking into flesh, warming bones.

The city! She had been falling! In sudden panic Yaz got to her feet, spinning around, overwhelmed by a view so open and yet so complex, nothing in it familiar, nothing that made sense save the sky and the red eye of the sun. Even the clouds were strange. Great puffy white clouds, moving lazily, seeming so close she might touch them. She tensed to run, but where to? There was no ice. None. The ground swelled and dipped and rose towards distant hills. Green everywhere.

Beneath her feet. Rising in lumps. Crowning tall structures, a million waving, fluttering pieces. Yaz found herself able to do nothing but stare, overwhelmed.

'Hello.'

Yaz turned to find a young man walking towards her. It didn't seem possible that she could have missed him. His smile broadened.

'I'm Erris.' He was taller than her, broad-shouldered, his skin as dark as Tarko's, the leader of the Broken. Yaz had never seen its like on the ice. The clothes he wore were like nothing she had seen before. Impossibly colourful, and from no beast she had ever seen or heard of. They didn't hang like hides or furs. 'Lestal Erris Crow, actually. But call me Erris.'

'Where are we?' Yaz glanced around, her gaze returning to the man.

'Not far from where you fell.' Erris pointed behind her. 'Above those trees you can see the ruins of the city.'

'Trees?' Yaz turned. The things her eyes had refused to understand. They were trees. So tall, like vast tent-poles, splitting, branching into an infinitely complex storm of green. And where Erris had pointed so many of them stood that there seemed no space between them, just a vastness of them. Objects reached above the treetops, hazy in the distance, buildings. Ruins, Erris had called them, but Yaz had no idea what they would look like if not ruined. They gave an impression of height, making the trees, which must surely tower above her, seem tiny in comparison. 'I don't understand.'

'It was like this when I first came here.'

'You . . . Are you one of the Missing?' Yaz stared, trying to see past his disguise.

'Ha! No. The Missing were gone long before I came to their city. Before our people even came to Abeth.'

'But . . . there's no ice.' Yaz shivered despite the pervading heat. 'And no wind.'

Erris pursed his lips, seeming gently amused. He watched her with dark eyes. His black hair held close to his head in tight, tiny curls. Yaz had never seen anyone like him.

'I came to the city a very long time ago. The ice followed me a while later.' Another smile. Yaz guessed him to be around Thurin's age. Handsome. Strong features. 'I wasn't supposed to, of course. All our laws forbade it. For our own safety, they said. But how many our age are going to ignore a city of wonders on our doorstep "for our own safety", I ask you? It wasn't just that law keeping fools and dreamers away though. The city had its own defences. Much stronger back then. The script would turn anyone away in those days, although it was most effective against quantals like you.'

Yaz tried to hide her surprise in a question. 'Why didn't it stop you then?'

Erris shrugged. 'That was my talent. You quantals might get all the fire and the glory, but we marjals sometimes manifest curious talents. Nobody ever stopped me going anywhere. Not locks and doors. Not ship-tech security. Not even a Missing script-wall.'

'Eular said the marjals had lesser magics . . .'

Erris's smile showed all his teeth. 'There's no such thing as magic. If a thing is part of the world, part of how it works, then it's real and obeys laws just like gravity and electricity do.'

'I . . . don't know these words.' Yaz shook her head. 'And magic is real!'

Erris held up his hands, a placatory gesture. 'You win.' He looked around, a sadness entering his eyes. 'I loved it here. Out in the countryside. I never knew it at the time. It was the kind of love that you grow into, familiar, taken for granted. Like a mother's love. You feel it most when it's gone.'

'But it's not gone.' Yaz saw something white and yellow among the green at her feet and crouched, fascinated, finding more of the small wonders. 'What are these?'

'The grass? Oh, you mean the daisies. They're flowers. A type of plant. Have you really not seen . . . No, well, I suppose it's all ice and snow now.'

From the treeline black dots rose, a swirling cluster of them. 'Gulls?' Yaz ventured.

'Birds. Gulls are a type of bird. Those are starlings, I think.'

The starlings swooped over, shoaling like fish, sharp calls piercing the air. In their wake Yaz became aware of a world of other sounds that her overwhelmed mind had paid no attention to. A myriad of birdsong, some raucous, some lilting, some rising in breathtaking complexity, the notes a shower of liquid joy.

The beauty and strangeness of the place reached into Yaz and twisted something deep within her chest. She found her eyes misting, ridiculously close to tears. She gritted her teeth against it. 'I don't understand. How can this be here?'

'It's not.' Erris walked past her to stare at the distant ruins. 'I made it for you.'

'I was falling!' The assault on her senses had somehow driven that fact to the back of her mind. She got hurriedly to her feet.

'Would you like to go back?' Erris asked. 'It's nicer here. We could stay. I could show you the world that was. It's as missing now as the ones who built those towers over there.'

'I want to stay.' Something fluttered past her, like a bird that was all wings, no bigger than her palm, bright and filled with colours. 'But I need to go. My brother is in danger.'

'Those others are safe enough. It was only you the city took against.'

'Zeen wasn't with them. He's somewhere else. Somewhere worse.' Yaz frowned. 'And why me? Why did those symbols come? What did I do that was so wrong?'

'The city is very old, very damaged. It mostly sleeps. When it acts it's instinctual more than anything. The script is its voice. Once it was enough to keep away anything – people, rats, even flies and ants and things too small to see. But all that's faded away, gone by the by. Just the headlines remain, the most important directives, and those were always to keep away whatever was most like the Missing, whatever might be capable of following them.'

'I'm like the Missing?' Yaz looked down at herself just to check she hadn't changed in this strange place. 'And why would they want to keep themselves away?'

'The ones most like them have the most potential to abuse the power left in the cities. For humanity that means quantals. The city tried to keep you out because you're a quantal. It should have worked, too. The real question is why didn't it?'

'I want to go back now.' Yaz was far from sure that she did, but duty led her tongue. She knelt again, running her fingers through the grass, touching the complexity of the daisies, pressing the warm soil beneath. Now that her eyes had begun to accept the sights, and her ears the strangeness of the sounds, her nose started to register the scents of Erris's world, rich and varied, a melody in themselves, as varied as the birdsong. 'I have to go back.'

Erris turned to look at her, lips pressed against regret. 'I don't know if I will ever be able to bring you here again.'

Yaz bowed her head. The sun warmed her neck. Something black and orange and no bigger than her thumbnail buzzed lazily past. 'I can't stay.' She couldn't explain it to him. It was more than Zeen. She had been a part of something her whole life and now she was a broken piece, unable to go back, unable to move on. She wanted to ask him why he had done this to her, offering her a happiness she didn't deserve. She didn't know how to dream on her own, she had never allowed herself to. Dreams were selfish, a luxury the Ictha couldn't afford. And yet here she was, in the middle of one so golden she could never have imagined it. She would give it back if she could. It was too beautiful. A poison that would sit in her heart, aching through the years. 'I have to go back.'

In the next moment Yaz's hands were against dusty stone, the same stone that pressed against her knees. Her fingers remembered the grass. The green world still filled her mind. She lifted her head and stood. A chamber of the Missing, lit by a light that cast no shadows. Unlike the rooms Arka had led her through this one was crowded with objects, all of them unfamiliar, all grey with dust. Scores of . . . things . . . some larger than the largest man, some smaller than a child, many of them complicated with dozens of parts: wheels, rope-like attachments, glassy panels . . . many of them looked broken, though quite what made her think that Yaz couldn't say. She found herself standing in a clear area at the centre of the room with the chaos heaped towards the four corners. Set in one wall were three rectangular windows spaced evenly in a row between floor and ceiling, each giving a view into a blackness so complete that it seemed to suck at the light.

'Erris?'

Yaz. The word pulsed through the chamber.

'Erris?' She turned, trying to identify the source of the voice.

I'm here. In the void.

The answer emanated from all directions but something turned her around to face the three dark windows. 'I never told you my name.'

I watched you with your friends.

'Where are you?'

In the void. Which is another way of saying that I don't know. A sigh. *This is why I wanted to talk to you where we were.*

'I don't understand. Why don't you just come out?' Something about the darkness scared Yaz. The way it drew her eyes and made her forget about time. It shared a lot with the stars, which often seemed to be holes into a world of light. The windows seemed to be holes into a darkness that existed outside the world. 'Are you trapped?'

The sigh came again and Yaz could picture the dark youth standing in grass, bathed in sunshine, a crooked smile on his lips.

I fell too, Yaz. A long time ago. I became lost beneath the city and it hardly knew I was here. I fell into the void. I think it was the city's heart when the Missing were here. Now . . . it's something different. I can make worlds in here. But I can't leave. Sometimes . . . sometimes I think that I'm not really alive any more, that I haven't been alive since I fell, that I'm just a memory of me. A memory the city keeps.

Yaz stepped slowly towards the lowest window and crouched before it. The dark seemed like the surface of a pool. How deep it might be and what might reach out of it to seize her she couldn't say. Gathering her courage she set her hands on the sill and leaned in towards the blackness. It had a song to it, like the stars in the ice and the script on the walls. A slower song, wordless and discordant. A song full of sorrow and loss. 'What do you do in there, Erris?'

At first I did everything. I watched stars being born. I

watched them die. I walked the world, but it was always an empty one. I saw the ice come . . . These days I sleep mainly. Just like the city does. I sleep and wait for something to happen. For there to be an end.

'Then I came,' Yaz whispered.

Then you came. And the city woke me up. I think it wanted me to speak to you. I don't think it knows how any more. Maybe it never did. Perhaps that's why it kept me . . . or remembered me. To speak with you.

'What does it want you to say?'

Ah, well, there my theory breaks down. The city doesn't speak to me so I don't know for sure. I can sense its moods, though, and it's still angry about the last time.

'The last time?' Yaz turned from the unnerving darkness.

Another, like you. Another quantal came and defied the wards. He didn't get far before he was driven off, script-burned. Not nearly as far as you, but he found core-stones that earlier scavengers had missed. Whole ones, not fragments. And he used them to build entities slaved to him and not to the city.

'Entities?'

The constructs. The things that stalk and trap your people.

'The hunters?' Yaz glanced around as if one of the monstrosities might be concealed among all the broken parts crowding the chamber. The idea that they had been constructed by a man rather than by the Missing amazed and horrified her. Who would do it, and why? And what did script-burned mean? The only person she'd ever seen with burns was the regulator himself. 'When did this happen?'

Recently. Very recently. Let me check . . . Oh.

'What?'

Two hundred and seven years ago. I hadn't meant to sleep for that long.

'Two hundred years ago? And the city is still angry?'
Yes. With you.

'With me? But that was before I was born! Years before.'
I'm sorry about that. Erris did sound sorry. *But the city
. . . well, it's not rational. Not in the way we are anyway.
It's damaged, confused, angry.*

'You're talking as if the city is a person.' He sounded as
if he cared for it too.

*She is. A broken person. Older than she was ever meant
to be.* He paused. *I think she loves me in her way. We've
been together a long time. So many of the other cities have
gone dark and they can't talk to each other any more.*

'The cities talked to each other?' Yaz clamped her jaw,
aware she was just questioning everything he said.

*Once they did. Something haunts the ways now. A bad
thing.* Another pause. *Anyway, she couldn't stop you coming
in so instead . . .*

'Instead what?'

She doesn't mean to let you leave.

CHAPTER 15

'I need to get out!' Yaz spun around, too fast to see if there were any exits, then turned again, this time slowly enough to see that there were none. Or if there were any that they must be hidden behind all the artefacts. Remembering her fall she looked up, expecting to see some kind of shaft above but found only a ceiling of plain stone. 'Where's the door?'

There's no door.

'Where did I fall through?'

Things work differently in the deep city, Yaz. Some of the Missing liked to live simply, they had houses, places to walk, doors . . . Some even rejected all the wonders of their technology and lived on the ice far to the north, much as your people do now. But they didn't hunt because they needed to. They didn't need food and shelter like we do. Like you do anyway. They only used doors because it reminded them of who they once were. The Missing didn't walk away from Abeth; they didn't set sail into the heavens. They left in a different kind of way—

'I need an exit, Erris, not a history lesson.'

To leave this room you would have to walk through the wall. Without the city helping you.

Yaz moved to the wall beside the windows, one of the few places she could reach it. She ran her hands against the stone. 'There's a hidden door?'

No.

'But you said . . .' Yaz tried to remember what Erris had said. 'Oh . . .'

She began to consider the . . . things . . . littering the room, moving slowly from one to another. The Broken would consider it a treasure, a great weight of metal to be melted down and given to the priests of the Black Rock in return for the necessities of life. Fish, salt, hides. It seemed a poor trade knowing how the clans prized even the smallest iron tool, but when you're in a miles-deep hole perhaps any trade is a good one.

'What is all this stuff? How did it get here?'

I brought it here. Saved it from the scavengers. Most of it is broken, but there are useful parts . . .

'But you said you're stuck in there.' Yaz looked at the windows.

I have my ways.

'What's this?' Yaz pulled aside some dusty boards made of nothing she recognized to reveal a black cube, its sides maybe eighteen inches. As she looked at it the black surfaces turned to white and then to a vibrant green.

A thing.

The green shaded into brown. The same dark shade as Erris's skin. A moment later Erris watched her from the cube as if each surface were a window onto the world of grass and trees and buzzing beasts that he had taken her to. 'Hello, Yaz.'

Yaz found that she had taken several steps back. 'Hello

. . . How are you in that box? How are you so small? And what is *that*?'

'A butterfly.' Erris laughed and with a sweep of his hand the brilliant blue wings took flight from his shoulder. 'The real question is how are we going to get you out of here?'

'We?' Yaz felt a moment of hope. 'You're going to help me?'

'Of course. I told you, I have a talent for getting into places, and out of them. Admittedly I've been stuck in the void for thousands of years, which may cast some doubt on my claim. But the void is something else again. Walking through walls, however, is mere child's play!'

Yaz knelt and reached out to touch the green world she could see once again. But her hands met a barrier, as if the cube were still there, walling her off from the warm breeze and the softness of grass. 'How can you help me through the walls? Do you have a hammer?'

'I'm coming out to join you. Well . . . in a manner of speaking. Don't be scared.'

Yaz gave the small Erris a sideways look that dared him to suggest one more time that she might be scared.

'All right!' He held up his hands in a placatory gesture. 'Then don't laugh either.' The cube turned black again.

'Laugh?' Yaz glanced about, her gaze coming to rest on the windows to the void.

Something moved behind her. A grating noise. A shifting among the heaped detritus that Erris had somehow gathered.

Yaz spun around. Pieces fell aside as the something rose, toppling cabinets, shedding layers of flexible sheeting, raising dust. The thing kept rising. A head? Some dark shape atop two shoulders . . . a metal arm reaching.

Yaz stepped back sharply. 'What . . .'

A hunter was lifting itself from the chaos. Only it wasn't

quite a hunter. It had more of a man's shape to it than those multi-legged horrors, and although large, Yaz had seen bigger gerants.

'Hello, Yaz.' The voice buzzed around the edges but it sounded like Erris. In place of a head was a black sphere returning no light; the body beneath was formed of gleaming steel with complex moving parts exposed, the arms mismatched, one of jointed steel tubes, the other a flexible set of overlapping rings like the armour of an eel-shark. Both ended in hands sporting blunt digits rather than a hunter's claws.

Yaz gaped, open-mouthed.

'Well . . . laughing would be better than whatever this is.'

Yaz realized she had backed against the wall and had a metal bar gripped in both hands, ready to swing. She didn't even remember picking it up.

'Erris?' She peered at the thing before her.

'At your service.' Joints squealed and the not-Erris made a short bow. 'This is how I escape the void. I built it myself and it took a long, long time.' Even with the buzz and the crackle Yaz could sense in his voice an echo of the years spent. 'I have a better one in another part of the city but that is far from here and I'm keeping it for a special occasion.'

'We still don't have a door.' Yaz put the metal bar down and stepped towards Erris, trying to see if there were eyes hiding in the black sphere of his head.

'No, but we have you and you can walk through walls.'

'I can't.'

'You can walk the Path, can't you?'

'The Path?' Yaz frowned. 'Oh. You mean the river?' Eular had called it the Path, the source of the power that only those with quantal blood could reach.

'The names are important, though you will have forgotten why on the ice where you have neither. A path or a river . . . both of them take you somewhere. There's more to it than touching the Path. The trick is to walk it.'

Yaz shook her head. 'I touched the river today. And the day before. Normally I have to wait days before I can see it again. A week if I want to be safe touching it. Safe-ish.' Another shake of the head as she remembered how the power had nearly broken her apart when she faced Hetta. 'There's no way that I could—'

'You haven't noticed it yet.'

'Noticed what?'

The body that Erris had built himself owned none of the casual movement that a person had. It moved only when he willed it and stood statue still between. Now its stillness took on a new character, as if perhaps Erris had retreated to the void.

'Noticed what? Are you even there?' Yaz resisted rapping her knuckles on the construct's chest. 'What am I supposed—'

Listen!

Yaz listened. Silence. No wind complaining. No drip of water. Not even the groan of ice. The song of Pome's star whispered in the back of her mind, its heartbeat swift as drumming fingers. 'I can't . . .'

It's very deep.

'I . . .' And there it was, the restless song of a star. Star-stones, Arka had called them. Eular had also called them core-stones and heart-stones. Whatever they were, they sang, and this one sang so deep that the notes reverberated through the longest bones in her body then sank deeper still, beyond sensing. Rising here and there like a whale breaking the surface before plunging into the endless fathoms of the sea.

BOOM.

A shudder ran through the stone beneath Yaz's feet, so deep that she would not have noticed it except for Erris. It was as if something the size of a mountain had fallen far away.

'What was that?' Yaz almost knew but the answer felt wrong.

Its heartbeat.

'Oh.' Her answer had been right. Every star had its own heartbeat, the small ones racing so fast that they became a buzzing that rose beyond hearing as their star's size descended towards dust. The large star that she and Thurin had taken from the ice by the settlement had a heartbeat swift as a running child. But the star that Erris had made her listen to had given just one beat and even as the breath she held became painful in her lungs there was no second beat.

'How big is—'

BOOM.

That is the star that feeds the void.

Yaz could feel it now and was amazed that she had not before. She felt it tugging at the boundaries of who she was, washing against her mind in waves, setting voices whispering inside her head. 'How big is it?'

Large.

The metal body in front of Yaz shifted as Erris returned to it. The arms flexed. 'This is why your people scavenge from the city. Surely you know this? Even a small star brings the Path closer to the world. When close to a star of good size even a half-blood quantal can reach the Path and work wonders with the power they can take from it.'

'They're not my people. And there are no quantals among the Broken.' Yaz frowned.

'But they hunt the stars for quantals to use. They trade them, do they not?'

'That's why they throw children down here,' Yaz breathed. 'The priests of the Black Rock. They might want the stars even more than they want the iron.'

Erris shrugged: an odd thing to see, metal grating on metal. 'There may be other reasons. It doesn't seem an . . . efficient . . . solution. But yes, those are reasons too. Any star should be worth a billion times its weight in metal, but I concede that the realities of life in a frozen wasteland might change that balance, especially if the ability to exploit them is rare.'

Yaz looked around. Her stomach growled, she licked dry lips with a dry tongue, her head ached and her body felt sore. 'How does this help me leave?'

'You should be dead, Yaz. Being this close to the void star would drive almost anyone else mad, their brain would bleed, they would die. Even most full-blood quantals couldn't get within a hundred yards without their personality being torn apart. The human mind wasn't built to withstand this power. It's like fire. From a distance it lights the way. Closer up it warms us. Too close and we burn. With the stars it's similar. At a distance there is light. Closer to us they open the Path to those who can find its power. Too close and they split our minds apart. The piece of you that longs to murder becomes its own creature. The part that is jealous, the part that lusts, your anger . . . all of them break away and find their own voice.'

Yaz nodded. 'I can feel that. Voices in my head. A splitting pain.'

'It's good you can feel something! I was starting to think you weren't human at all.' Erris raised a metal hand. 'Don't be offended. It's just that the city brought you here to die. It's as if you had been thrown into a furnace and were standing there in the white heat only now just beginning to sweat. It shouldn't be. And yet it is.' He set his steel fingers to her shoulder and Yaz kept herself from flinching. 'And I am glad of it. Truly.' He looked around and pointed at a section of the wall no different from any other. 'That's where we need to go. Look for the Path. This river of yours.'

Rather than argue that it was too soon Yaz let her eyes defocus, ignored the pain lancing through her skull, and looked beyond the world.

If the river were visible at all so close to her last touch then it should have been a gossamer thread far beyond reach. Instead the river roared all around her, a torrent rushing through the world's impossible angles with a speed that might strip flesh from bone. The shock of it threw Yaz back against the wall and left her trembling.

'I saw it!'

Erris bent his dark head. 'I noticed.'

'What do I do?'

Erris turned away and began clearing a path to the opposite wall, pushing aside heavy blocks from which black ropes emerged, metal casings, parts of . . . things. 'You're the expert, not me. But it shouldn't be hard. Remember that the Missing have made this route for you. All you need to do is follow it. And take me with you.'

Yaz advanced along the cleared path towards the wall, kicking away small objects Erris had missed. One whirred alarmingly and scuttled away on pin-like legs to hide among the heaped debris to one side. She came to the wall as Erris hauled aside the last obstacle, metal squealing on stone.

'So, I just . . .' Yaz set her palms to the stone, finding it warm to touch – warmer than ice anyhow. She gathered herself for the effort.

'You don't need to pound your way through. Use the Path to take us, let it show you the way.' He reached out to tap the stone with a steel finger. 'We should probably hurry.' Another tap.

'Hurry?' Yaz looked back over her shoulder and favoured the impenetrable darkness where Erris's face should be with her hardest stare. 'Through a wall?'

'Yes.'

'Yesterday I was on the ice, where I had always lived. And now I'm miles below the rocks that are miles below the ice in a city built by the Missing, and I am being instructed on walking through walls by a man who might have died thousands of years ago and is talking to me from inside a body made of metal and . . . and I don't know what else. All of which is to say: Give me a godsdamned moment here.'

Erris had the wisdom to say nothing.

Yaz returned her attention to the wall. She could feel the pressure of the void star, feel it eroding who she was, prising apart the constituents of her mind. She leaned in and set her forehead to the stone. 'How dangerous is this?'

'Less dangerous than staying here.'

'Will I get stuck? Lost in the rock?' When someone became separated from their clan the wind would lie them down in time. The snow would cover them. The ice would take them into itself, locked forever in its depth. 'Will I die?'

Erris's voice came soft now, almost free of distortion, almost how he had sounded under the warmth of the sun, standing with the grass waving around his feet. 'I don't know.'

'Thank you for showing me the trees,' Yaz said, a bittersweet pain around her heart as she remembered how they had looked. 'At the end of the long night the Ictha take any oil that remains and melt ice. We build a windbreak and our elders dribble the water out . . . it freezes at once, but the skill is to build sculptures as it flows and freezes. They call it the garden.' The shapes had always reminded Yaz of veins, spreading and branching. They were tall and fragile and beautiful, built only for the wind to tear down. A rare Icthan extravagance. But for a while they lasted, and overhead the dragons' tails lashed in the last of the night sky, the aurora, shifting, ghostly veils of colour. And when the light turned green and echoed within the branches of the ice garden the elders would sing a song without words, holding only loss. The burning of the oil was the only time, save for leaving the dead to the wind, that any Ictha ever wasted anything. Yaz had never understood it, or known what lay behind the sorrow in the garden-song. 'If I die here . . . well . . . I still will have seen trees. You taught me something. And for that I am grateful.' Perhaps it was the void star's song eroding her barriers, or the accumulation of weariness since dropping into the pit, or just the fear that she would die, but Yaz found herself trembling, her eyes prickling, the breath threatening to catch in her throat. 'Thank you for the flutterby too. And the grass.'

'Butterfly.' Erris bowed his head. 'I'm sorry this has happened to you. You were thrown from the only life you knew. Maybe the only life you could imagine.' His metal hand rested beside hers against the wall. 'I fell and lost my future too. The things I had wanted and hoped for. Small things maybe, foolish things, but they were mine and it still burns me even though all those times are gone and forgotten. It still hurts. Both of us . . . we've fallen into lives we don't understand and didn't ask for.'

Erris's ancient pain echoed in Yaz, bringing with it an image of aurora light shivering through ice trees before the dawn. Her face twitched, eyes stung. Her fingers moved to touch Erris's without instruction and in that moment, without any sense of movement, she stood once more before the timeless peace of the forest, caressed by a warm breeze, her hand in his, flesh and blood once more, black fingers laced with copper fingers.

'There was a girl I loved. But I fell into the void and never went back to her. I never knew how long she waited for me, what became of her life, or how she died. But I loved her and I was loved, and I keep that with me. It makes me think that I must still be alive . . . some kind of alive . . . because how could even the Missing capture a thing like that in their machines, something so sweet and fragile and strong as love?'

Yaz lifted her face and found Erris watching her, a tear on his cheek. She could have held onto her own misery forever maybe. The Ictha have strong walls. But that tear cracked her and a sob shuddered through her. Then another. And for a long time they stood, caught in each other's arms and in their own sorrow, with the trees swaying and butterflies rising from the grass all around them, until their tears were spent.

The warmth of that day, lost in the centuries, covered by the tide of the ice but somehow preserved for her here and now, melted something in Yaz. A coldness, the frozen core that she had been wrapped about all her life, surrendered to an ancient summer. The resolution that she would do her duty, play her role as the Ictha needed and demanded, set aside her own hopes and imagination in the grim service of mere survival, all these ran from her. Under the light of a brighter sun long-forgotten dreams began to unfurl with the caution of budding flowers.

Yaz's presence of mind returned all at once rather than by degrees, in much the same way the enormity of recent events had suddenly overwhelmed her. She found herself in Erris's arms, her face buried between his neck and shoulder. Shocked, she broke free, and in the next moment she was standing in the dusty junk-filled room once more, the metal construct looming above her.

'I . . . I thought we had to hurry.' She found her voice shaky, her body remembering the shape of his. The scent of him still seemed to linger on her.

'We do. Time passes differently in the void though.' He sounded uncertain too, hesitant, and that pleased her for some reason that she couldn't squeeze into sentences. 'Are you ready?'

Yaz looked beyond the wall to the endless river of power that flowed about her, there for the taking but so fierce that the slightest error would overfill her and the stolen energies would shred both flesh and bone. She didn't have to break through the wall – Erris had told her that. She just had to travel. Yaz didn't reach to touch the river as she always had before. Instead she strained some unsuspected muscle in her mind, trying to let the river touch her. Almost instantly she felt the currents of it flowing through her as they flow through all things, but now they seemed to notice her, to pluck at her flesh, to sweep her along. The effect was immediately alarming and swiftly became painful. The river flows in every direction the human mind can imagine and in far more that cannot be imagined. Before the competing forces could tear her apart Yaz pushed against the wall. She felt the weight of Erris's steel hand descending upon her shoulder. At the wall the currents began to converge until, when pressed against it, Yaz could feel the dominant tug of one current in one direction. With a sigh of relief she let go her hold on the world and allowed the flow to carry her away.

CHAPTER 16

'Are you there?' Yaz could see nothing, feel nothing save that there was ground beneath her feet.

Only silence. Silence and a cold light, very faint, starting to grow to one side of her. This at least reintroduced direction into her world. A confusion of stark black lines began to make themselves known against the diffuse light, a thousand of them, rising, dividing, reaching, growing thinner. A wind blew. Not the sharp, fierce wind of the ice, but chill and insistent. The black lines swayed and Yaz knew them for the innumerable branches of trees, stripped of their fluttering green, left bare and black to greet the dawn.

'Erris?'

But it seemed that she had failed to bring Erris through to wherever this was. A dead forest deep below the ice? But there was a lightening sky and a wind.

'This isn't real.' Yaz turned slowly, twigs snapping beneath her feet.

Another light burned not far off, just visible between the black multitude of trunks, this one a flame, a warm, flickering glow. A lamp. She began to move towards it, weaving her way between the trees, warding off their scratching fingers, stumbling as the ground itself tried to snare her with gnarled roots that looped and twisted before plunging into black soil.

The wind at Yaz's back slackened and turned colder, the air becoming brittle with frost as the temperature fell. Swaying branches stilled. Traceries of ice began to wrap the trunks and still the lamp's light seemed to get no closer.

It grew colder still, not a breath of wind now. The ground's softness turned to iron. Branches shattered as Yaz knocked them aside, running now and not knowing why. Slanting shadows painted the forest. Behind her a sun rose, its light whiter than the sun she knew, and where it should give heat it took it instead. The white light saturated the forest, enveloping dead trees in ice. This was a cold even an Ictha could respect. Far behind her came a loud retort, then closer at hand, much louder, a thick tree cracked open with shocking violence, spitting fragments of frozen bark, surrendering to the pressures of the ice expanding within it.

Suddenly the hut was there before her, the single lamp hanging before a wooden door that opened as she drew near.

'Hurry.' A thin, dark-haired man waved her in. He glanced about at the trees, a nervous quickness to him.

The interior of the hut seemed smaller than the building in all dimensions, as if the plank walls of the rough shack were a yard thick. The man heaved the door closed as though it weighed many times what he did, and joined her at a tiny table before a small but fierce fire.

'You made it then.' He seemed surprised, watching her from dark, intelligent eyes set in a face pinched up into a prominent nose. His age was hard to determine. Not young. Maybe not old. Well preserved. His eyes were old though.

'Who are you?' Yaz dispensed with manners. She was having too strange a day for politeness.

'A drink?' He glanced around, disappointed. 'Well, maybe. I'm sure I had some absinthe here a moment ago . . .'

'Who are you?'

The man leaned in over the table, both elbows on the boards. 'My name is Elias. At least, that's part of my name, but then I am only part of myself, which seems to be a common problem these days.'

'I have no idea what you're talking about.' Yaz looked towards the door. 'Where's Erris? He said I had to hurry and now instead of running away I'm . . . here.'

'Ah yes, young Erris. A good-hearted boy, to be sure. I apologize for hijacking your escape, but there'll still be time enough for all that running and screaming. It's just that we don't get many visitors down here and—'

A screech reached in through the shuttered windows, at once huge and yet far away. A scream like nothing Yaz had heard before or even imagined. Nothing human. A roar so laden with threats of violence and pain that Yaz immediately wanted nothing more than to cower beneath the table and hope for it to end. Instead she fought to keep the quiver from her voice as she asked, 'What was that?'

'That?' Elias flashed her a dark look. 'That's what the end of the world sounds like.'

'It's after me?' Panic clawed at Yaz's heart. She shoved it down, ashamed at her weakness. The scream seemed to echo in her skull.

'It's after us all, dear. By definition.' Elias allowed himself a small smile. 'But yes, today it's after you. But only because I showed an interest.' He went to the window. 'Care to take a look?'

'Is this a test?' Yaz stood, warily. Her head brushed the ceiling.

'Everything is a test.' Elias set a thin, long-fingered hand

197

to the shutter. 'Quickly, though. Look at him too long and he'll look at you.'

Yaz crouched to peer out as Elias eased the shutter back, opening it a crack.

The cold cut at her with the fierceness of the polar night. The forest lay thick with snow beneath a blazing white sky, all the trees had burst asunder, an army of bare, broken trunks, their branches fallen. And above it all with the frozen light bleeding around it, some great dark . . . thing, a creature as large as the sky, like a hand but not, a creature of spindly legs reaching out to encompass the world, supporting a knotted body the colour of venom and despair. The thing hypnotized the eye, drawing on the mind behind. Yaz felt her thoughts leaking from her.

'That's Seus.' Elias pulled her back.

'What is it?'

'In this place it's what you see it as. A monster that wishes to destroy you. Out in the world it's a city. The heart and mind of a great city.'

'That thing is the city?' Yaz was horrified to think it already held her in its clutches.

'What? No! This city is Vesta. A cracked and broken thing. Seus is far to the south, its mind much more intact, though sadly still afflicted with a kind of madness. Seus has poisoned a great many cities and closed the paths between them. Once upon a time I could travel from city to city in the space between two heartbeats. What I need—'

The light of the fire dimmed and Yaz's breath plumed in the air between them.

'He's found us.' Elias's voice took on a note of urgency. 'Listen to me, this is important.' A white tracery of frost began to form across the walls, tendrils of ice reaching out across the planks. 'Whatever bad thing is chasing you out there – Seus is worse. Whatever plot you find, dig deep enough, scratch away enough layers, and you'll find Seus at the bottom.' The hut began to groan as if a great weight were being loaded upon it. Yaz found herself shivering, truly cold for the first time since leaving the north. 'He's closed all the ways. I can't reach him. You need to take me to him, Yaz.'

'He's right outside . . .' As if to underscore her point some large timber surrendered to mounting pressure and the hut shook, ice scattering across them as it broke from the low ceiling. The fire was nothing now, hardly an ember clinging to its glow.

'You need to take me to where he lives. To the city. And not this me. There's too little of me here.' He handed her something. A small silvery needle not more than an inch long.

'I don't understand.'

Elias went to the door. He glanced back at her with a narrow smile. 'I'm a man of many parts, Yaz. I've been many things. Juggled many rings at once.'

'Juggled?' Yaz was finding it hard to talk, her face a frozen mask, the air so cold she could feel it fraying her lungs with each breath.

'My first-ever job was to find out how the world worked . . .' Seeing her blank and pained expression he waved the matter aside. 'Never mind.' He set his hand to the icy door. 'If you live long enough to understand the battle you're in – the big one, not the little one – then use the needle and find me.'

'Where are you going?' Yaz asked it through chattering teeth.

'Outside. Seus needs something to kill while you escape.'

'You can't just—'

'Watch me.' And in the next moment he was through the door, outlined for a moment in the cold blaze of a day like no other. The door shut. An awful scream rang out and then everything was darkness and silence.

'Are you there?' Yaz could see nothing, feel nothing save that there was ground beneath her feet and that the incredible cold had left, leaving only the memory of a shiver.

'I am.' As Erris spoke beside her a faint glow started somewhere within the complexity of his chest where things Yaz could only think of as metal bones and metal teeth pumped and threshed.

'I was somewhere strange! There was a man called Elias and—'

'You arrived at the same time I did,' Erris said. 'And we still need to hurry.'

'Where are we?' The increasing glow outlined a small cubic chamber, wholly empty. Another place to die? The new reality overwrote images of frozen forests and sky monsters. Yaz turned to inspect the stonework behind her. 'I can walk through walls!' It came out half laugh, half gasp.

'You can walk along paths the Missing provide for you, even if they happen to lead through walls, yes. I wouldn't try it on other walls, or too far from a sizable star-stone.'

'So, where are we?' Yaz returned her gaze to the room.

'A junction. We need to leave . . . this way.' Erris crossed the room in three strides and set a hand to the wall. 'And quickly, before the city realizes what we're doing and starts to make things difficult.'

'Vesta?' Yaz asked.

Erris frowned. 'Yes. How did you know that name?'

'I told you, there was this man and—'

'You were intercepted. It's a danger when you travel this

way without proper understanding, and there are powers that watch for strays. Come on. We need to go.' He beckoned her to him.

Yaz joined Erris and then pressed her forehead to the stone below the point where his fingers touched the wall. She noticed a gleam in her hand and found she held a silver needle, clutched tight between finger and thumb. Without comment she stuck it through the hides over her collarbone.

'Quickly would be better . . .'

Yaz bit back a retort and once more she opened herself to the currents of the hidden river. A moment later they swept her away.

There were no more interceptions. No gaps at all between pressing against one wall and stumbling away from another.

Erris led them through a series of junction chambers. He said he was threading their way through holes in a network that was supposed to keep them in. The fourth, fifth, and sixth transitions became progressively more difficult, Yaz having to let the current tear at her before the stone would surrender, and having to battle to win free of the wall at the end of their journeys. Each time they emerged the song of the void star sounded more distant, a host of competing voices beginning to rise above the depth of its refrain.

'From here we walk.' Erris pointed across the large hall, now lit by the light that Yaz had woken from Pome's star. 'The main thing we have to worry about is—'

Yaz found herself shoved from behind as if by a strong gust of wind.

'Ah, hell.' The wind that was not a wind even set Erris staggering forward.

'The main thing we have to worry about is?' Yaz prompted.

'Right behind us.' Erris turned to face the wall they had

just emerged from. 'I can slow it down. But not for long. You have to run.'

'I'm not running.' Yaz stepped beside him, staring at the blackness where his face should be. She wanted to see those dark eyes of his, both young and old, with a thousand years and more behind them. 'I can help!'

'No, you can't.' Erris swept her back with one arm, his strength alarming. 'Run!' He shouted the word loud enough to leave her ears ringing. The wall was fuzzy now, like the last ice before the sea shows itself.

'But . . .'

'This pile of junk isn't me, Yaz.' Erris slapped a hand to his silver chest. 'When it's destroyed I'll go back to the void. Just run. Please. And don't come back.'

Something within the stone roared. A black shape began to press into being in the space between Erris and the wall. With a sudden rat-a-tat-tat black spikes hammered out of nowhere, piercing Erris's steel skin. The shape, becoming more definite, reached out for him. Yaz began to run, the squeal of tearing metal chasing her across the hall.

She reached the far doorway and turned into it just as half a dozen black spikes hammered into the wall behind her.

Yaz ran on, pursued by what sounded like an avalanche of metal. A hideous scraping noise underwrote the thunder behind her, as if somehow whatever was left of Erris continued to cling to the monster, trying to anchor it.

For a long time Yaz focused only on speed, always taking the smallest exit, always heading upwards when presented with a choice. Soon the sounds of her own panic, the rasp of her breath, and the pounding of her heart, drowned out any other noise. Finally she tripped and fell, too exhausted to rise from the floor. She lay, hunting for breath, and when she found it there was nothing to be heard but her breathing. She was alone in the vast labyrinth of the city, with neither Erris nor Arka to help her.

Yaz sat, rubbing her ankle. By starlight she saw that at some point the rock had moved and created an unexpected step across a room. This had been what tripped her. The pain in her ankle made her remember Kao hobbling along after his fall. She hoped Arka had led him and the others to safety.

After a time Yaz got to her feet and limped on. She wondered how far the others might have got. It didn't seem that she had been delayed very long. If she knew the way to go she might even beat them out. First out or last, though, she knew it would be a different Yaz that hauled herself back beneath the ice sky of the great cavern. She had seen a thing that she had never thought to see, and something amid the gentle swaying of those trees had found its way into her heart. Her imagination burned and every wild thought seemed edged with possibility.

For now though, the floor held most of Yaz's attention as she walked, and her ears strained for any hint of hunters or the black monster that had chased her. In these endless halls the only thing that would save her from death by thirst or a violent end in a hunter's claws would be the marks left by scavengers to show the way.

When she came to the first decision point and saw the scratches at the base of the wall Yaz gave a broken gasp. She shocked herself by nearly breaking into tears for the second time in a day. Until she saw the small arrow she hadn't allowed herself to acknowledge how much the thought of being lost here had terrified her. The scratches looked quite fresh, not scuffed and almost worn away like those

Arka had shown them. It meant she was still deep in the city, almost at the limits of the scavengers' explorations.

Following the markings led Yaz by efficient routes to a series of stairs, natural fissures, and vertical shafts hung with ropes. With cables, to be more accurate. Steel cables, some with plastic coatings. Yaz wondered how these words came to be in her head. They belonged to Erris. She frowned and moved on.

This deep there were no concessions to trainee scavengers and the climbs demanded both a level of skill and a tolerance for heights that Yaz didn't possess.

'I'm not scared of heights. I'm scared of drops.' Yaz pushed the words out past gritted teeth as she hauled herself over the lip of a shaft taller than ten trees stacked one atop the next. Sore-handed, arms aching, she lay with a dry mouth and wondered for the hundredth time just how deep she was. Only her Ictha strength was keeping her alive, her grip compensating to some degree for her lack of talent when it came to scaling natural rock or tackling a hundred yards of dangling cable. It definitely helped that she could draw up the whole of her bodyweight with one arm.

Yaz pulled herself away from the mouth of the shaft then got to her hands and knees, groaning. She had come to the city in the hopes of securing a star large enough to safely drive the taint from her brother. She was leaving empty-handed and half alive, knowing that the city while still a city was also a being that would use all its resources to prevent her returning. More than that, her efforts to escape had somehow bound her into a conflict between unknown gods that lived beyond reality. And now, in that strange somewhere, a being called Seus, which was both the mind of a distant city and – from what Yaz could see – also a dark god, had marked her for destruction.

'These things too the wind shall take.' Yaz found comfort in the old saying. Cursing at herself to muster the required strength, she stood and moved on.

A dozen more rooms, sections of corridor, and she started up another square spiral of steps, seemingly endless. Her legs ached now, the repetition of unfamiliar action melting the endurance from her thighs. She hoped she was returning to sanity, to clarity, and something more familiar. It seemed that the deeper into the world you fell the more unreal things became.

The only thing to take comfort in was a lack of the glowing symbols that had opposed her on the way in and finally driven her to fall. She hadn't seen a single one in all her wandering.

Yaz rested on the stairs, half dozing, haunted by dreams of water. Eventually, feeling little better, she carried on, stumbling from time to time. Exhaustion had her mumbling to herself, promises and threats. The faces of her family came to her, distant, as if it had been years since she had seen them. She thought of Quell, then of Thurin, then of Erris. She wondered where Zeen was now, how the Taints passed their time; she worried for him, for little Maya who she hardly knew, for Kao who she hardly liked, limping his way from the city.

And with a start she discovered that without realizing it she had stopped climbing stairs and shuffled into a corridor pierced on one side by small windows through which a faint light was bleeding. Yaz stopped at the first, too narrow to climb through, and looked out onto a rocky cavern lit from above by faint shafts of starlight. The illumination reached down through two square holes in the ceiling. The 'sky' of the great city chamber must be above those exits. The air was colder here, fresher. Hope rose in her, a fire licking up along her bones. The far wall of the cavern was a steep, rocky slope that led almost to the smaller of the two exits and in the uneven floor a shadow-filled pit reached back down towards the depths.

Relief floated away her exhaustion. After so long in the dead and dusty halls of the Missing Yaz had begun to think that she might never emerge, that the signs were a lie to deceive her, and that she would die, choking on her thirst, without ever seeing the ice again.

Yaz heard the noise as she turned her head from the window shaft. Something scraping stone. A foot? She turned swiftly, sending the light of her star lancing down the corridor behind her. Nothing but retreating shadows and dark doorways. The passage was surely too narrow for a hunter to move along at speed, but Arka had said they could reshape themselves to squeeze through unexpectedly small gaps . . .

Silence. An old silence. Yaz's breath plumed before her. She dimmed her star to a glimmer, not wanting to advertise her movements, and advanced on soft feet. One pace, five, ten. There it came again, the slightest scrape. Somewhere ahead of her now . . . A prickling ran down her spine, sweat in her palms although she had thought herself too dried out for that. A hunter was stalking her. With freedom so close, with the voice of the ice whispering to her. To be caught here after so long climbing from the depths would be too cruel. Yaz wished she had kept the iron bar from Erris's room of broken wonders.

She moved on, all her senses tingling, sure that unseen eyes watched her progress. She stopped, listened . . . nothing. A sigh emptied her lungs. She was being foolish. She began to walk again.

The attack came from behind. From a doorway she had already passed. The room beyond had been empty! Yaz found herself caught and hauled back with implacable power. She yelled despite herself and fought to escape. The thing that held her exceeded her Ictha strength. Even so she tore free, sacrificing hides and loosing a scream as another appendage reached for her mouth.

With an energy that she thought long exhausted, she opened her stride to run. For a moment she thought she'd won clear. Hunters have a long reach though. Yaz made it ten paces before something closed around both legs and brought her to the floor. She twisted and fought, pounding at the shape that reached over to pin her down. Somewhere in all that thrashing struggle two realizations managed to find space amid the panic crowding her mind. Firstly that not all the yelling was coming from her, and secondly that whatever she was fighting was not made of metal.

'Yaz?' A male voice.

'W-who . . .' Yaz stopped thumping the fur-laden shape. 'Thurin?' It felt too solid for Thurin, but not huge enough for Kao. She groped for her star only to see that it had rolled to the wall and lay there glimmering, its light breaking out softly here and there like foam on the ocean.

'It's me, Yaz.' As if that would be enough.

Yaz stretched her arm towards the star and her mind reached further. It started to roll towards her open hand and as it rolled the light broke from it, bright enough now to show her attacker's face. Black hair, straight and thick, reddish skin across broad cheekbones. Strong, even features, eyes as pale as her own, the irises like sea ice.

'Quell . . .' Pome's star rolled into her open hand and she closed her fingers around it.

Quell grinned, a white smile, and wiped the blood from his nose where her fist must have caught him. 'I came to save you.'

'How . . . Why . . . You attacked me!'

Quell got off her and offered his hand to help her up, glancing over his shoulder as he did so. 'There's something down here with us. I wanted to pull you aside and stop you shouting. Keep you quiet until you understood.' He kept hold of her hand as she found her feet. 'But we seem to have ended up with the exact opposite.' He winced. 'You pack quite a punch!'

'But *how* are you here?' Quell didn't fit in the world of the Missing or the Broken any more than a shark belonged on the ice. Everything was wrong, and everything was right at the same time. He smelled of home. Of the Ictha. Of the life she had fallen from. Of seas and ice and sled oil and noisy tents. A world away from dry and ruined cities with broken minds.

'Come!' Quell pulled her back towards the doorway he'd lunged out of and she let him take her. Quell took his spear from its place leaning against the wall on the other side of the doorway. The length of hide-bound whalebone looked fragile compared to the iron spears of the Broken, but she knew Quell could skewer a submerged lungfish at fifty yards and haul it back to his boat on the attached line. Even so, against the beasts that haunted these passages neither kind of spear offered much protection. 'We should get out of here.' He seemed nervous but not so nervous that he didn't notice how weak she looked. He stopped suddenly and took her shoulders in his hands, studying her face. 'Are you . . . You're too dry.' He shrugged off his pack and dug into it, cursing. 'Everything melts in this damned heat.' He pulled out an empty-looking waterskin and a small lump of ice that Yaz guessed had been a lot bigger recently. 'Here.' He handed her both.

'Thank you.' From its weight the skin might still have a

mouthful left inside. Yaz held it in trembling hands, terrified she might spill some. She set the bone spout between parched lips and drank. The water tasted wondrous, like life pouring into her. She took it in three small swallows then bit off a piece of ice to suck. The Ictha knew about thirst. The wind killed those lost on the ice, but they died thirsty. Without whale oil and a tent there was no way to melt enough to drink. 'Gods, I needed that.'

Quell grinned. 'Good to go?'

Yaz nodded. She had questions. A thousand of them. But getting to the surface beat them all. Even so she couldn't take her eyes off him. Although he was alone Quell brought the Ictha with him. The world that saw her and Zeen as broken, the world she had fallen from, now stood before her, hale, hearty. Had he come to lead her back to her life? A life that Quell had stood at the midst of like the centre pole of a tent from which all else depended. Before her drop he had said that he loved her, that he wanted to build a future with her. He brought that sense of calm with him, that sense of security that she had somehow thought was throttling her only to miss it from the moment they parted. How was he here? And why was her joy at his arrival tempered by shades of regret she could neither name nor explain? She answered his grin with a smile of her own. 'Let's go.'

'I didn't come in this way, but it looks as safe as any.' Quell took the lead, spear levelled before him. 'There are signs on the floor to show—'

'I know.'

He glanced back at her, flashing that smile she'd known all her life, white teeth pinked with blood from her punches. 'Of course you do. Sorry.'

Within a hundred yards they reached a turning into the

cavern that Yaz had seen from the corridor windows. Quell breathed a sigh of relief and stepped out, waving her to join him. The water from Quell and the starlight reaching down through the square holes above combined to squeeze a last turn of speed from her and she shuffled forward almost at a jog. She could smell the ice, scent her freedom from the long dry nightmare of the Missing's city.

'Come on.' Quell bent low and hurried across the chamber towards the ramp of broken stone that would take them to the edge of the more distant hole.

Yaz followed, her mind crowding with the questions to be asked. How could Quell have possibly found her in such a maze of rooms? How did he even get below the ice?

The silence seemed larger in the vaulted space, their footsteps an intrusion. They passed beneath the larger, inaccessible hole, both of them bathed in starlight, and skirted the pit before approaching the slope. One last scramble and they would be free of this place.

When the hunter rose from the slope ahead of them, shouldering aside small boulders, debris streaming from its black carapace, Yaz stumbled to a halt, choking down a sob at the unfairness of it all. This one looked a lot smaller than the hunter that had left the city, but its armoured body was still as large as three men. It moved cautiously over the uneven gradient on half a dozen many-jointed legs. Something about it reminded Yaz of the crabs that Clan Zennik take from the Infrequent Sea, the serrated pincers on its two reaching arms perhaps. The thing glowed from within, red light escaping the chinks in its armour and illuminating the base of each leg where it joined the body. The crash of tumbling rocks and the clatter of metal on metal sounded shockingly loud after so long in the city's endless peace.

Quell looked tiny standing between Yaz and the hunter,

his bone spear clutched in both hands, but he stood there unflinching even so. Yaz moved to join him, empty-handed, she couldn't run, not again, and not without Quell. She hoped the end would be quick.

Yaz covered half the ground between her and Quell before something caught her foot and she went sprawling. She twisted to free herself and saw with horror another, far larger, hunter rising from the pit, a nightmare of waving arms reaching out over a behemoth's body of black iron plates and other makeshift armour. A fierce red light lanced through every gap. A metal tentacle had snared her leg from her foot most of the way to her knee. The appendage was disturbingly reminiscent of the right arm that Erris had built himself but dark.

'Get off me!' Yaz caught up a loose stone and hammered at the coils about her leg.

The hunter jerked her across the rock towards the pit it was still rising from. A scream tore its way from Yaz's lungs as she slid towards the edge of the hole where huge claws now gouged the stone, seeking purchase. She braced her feet against the nearest claws, determined not to go over without a fight. These hunters weren't like the soldier that the city had sent chasing her through walls, firing its spikes. She had only glimpsed that one before it destroyed Erris but it was not like this creature. Erris had said these were the work of the thief who had stolen significant stars from the depths of the city and so enraged it. An image of the regulator flashed across her mind even as the hunter hauled on her. Erris had said the thief who took the stars generations before was script-burned. The regulator bore scars that looked like letters; Yaz saw the burn marks with her mind's eye. Script had been seared across the man's scalp and face. The regulator was old too, old beyond the memory of any elder, and unchanging with the years. Regulator Kazik had stolen the stars that the city mourned and made these monsters around them . . .

Yaz reached out for the star hidden inside the huge hunter, seeking it with her mind. She knew it would be big but she had commanded Pome's star to dull its light. She had even made it float above her hand. Maybe she could– the fierceness of the hunter's star took her by surprise. It was like a fire. Not the flame of a lamp but the savage roar of fire let loose as she had once seen it when old Vallak and his wife had set their tent alight in the long night.

'No!' The shock of that rage from the star loosened her grip for a moment and now she found herself among those iron claws, clinging to them, her legs over the drop as the tentacle tried to tug her free.

Yaz strained to keep her place and reached out with her mind, struggling to influence the star burning deep within the hunter's makeshift bulk. She could see it there, hear its heartbeat, slow and powerful like that of a resting man, but she could no more touch it than she could pick up ingots red with heat in the forge, no more oppose it than she could turn the ice winds with her own breath. Hope escaped her and her grip on the claws to either side of her began to fail.

Quell came into view, shouting and flailing with his spear. It was not the rescue Yaz had hoped for. He came backwards, dragged like her by a tentacle of many overlapping iron rings that bound both his legs. The hunter lifted him from the ground and he dangled head-down before it, caught in a beam of red light that lanced out from where something like an eye opened in the main body. Yaz now heard not only the heartbeat of the star inside but its song also, wordless, violent, broken.

'Yaz!' Quell spotted her. Twisting, he lifted his body and somehow drove his spear into the hunter's eye. A metal shutter slammed across the opening, shattering the spear. Broken pieces dropped away, trailing their bindings.

In one smooth motion the hunter swung Quell against the rocks as an Ictha might brain a fish, the impact brutal and crunching. Yaz craned her head back to see where he lay. The world turned around her, that slow rotation, as old as the night. Zeen had fallen into the pit and guilt had pulled Yaz after him. That had been a moment like no other. Quell lay with his arms and face to the rock, blood leaking beneath him. This was her second moment. All her anger, all her frustration, all her outrage twisted together in a white heat pinning her to the instant. She reached towards the intolerable fire dwelling within the hunter's armour and took hold even though it burned her. She found no give in the hunter's star, no possibility of overcoming the stone that bound and animated it, and yet she refused to let go.

Quell! It had killed Quell!

The world retreated. Yaz no longer knew or cared if she were still clinging at the edge or being hauled away into the depths.

It had killed Quell!

Quell who knew the secrets of her life and whose calm stitched together the pieces of her, those she liked and those she did not, into something worthy of his devotion.

It had killed Quell!

Something broke within her. Something that was not meant to break. And with it came new strength and new weakness. Suddenly the balance of the struggle shifted, and with a vast effort that brought blood running from her mouth and from her eyes, she struck the hunter's heart a blow.

The hunter fell with the slow inevitability of ice cliffs calving into the sea, its heart stunned, limbs slack as the beat sought to re-emerge from a confusion of irregular fluttering. Yaz came back to herself with the claws tearing gouges into the rock on either side of her while the beast fell away. She was falling too. Her hands caught the craggy edge as she jolted over it. A shake and a twist of her leg and the slack metal coils around her shin released their grip. Her own hold proved firmer and with a scream of effort she hauled herself back onto level ground.

The second, much smaller hunter stood over Quell's inert form, one jagged pincer reaching down for his neck.

'No.'

Yaz reached out for the hunter's star, smaller and less fierce than the other one's, its heartbeat that of a child. She reached out and twisted, ignoring the broken pain that flooded through her. Between one moment and the next the hunter fell apart, lurching back as it did. All that remained were its constituents, a pile of ill-matched junk, more than a scavenger might show for a year's work. The star-stone rested amid the pieces, a dull red with darker patches drifting over it – clouds across the face of a dying sun.

Slowly, spitting blood, Yaz crawled to Quell's side. Pieces of the hunter lay scattered around him, toothed wheels, iron plates, black wires, all of it sharp with an unnatural stink that clawed at her throat.

Too weak to move him she lay down at his side.

Once when she had fallen ill Quell had stolen cubes of harp-fish from Mother Mazai's tent. They had eaten them together in his boat, rocking amid the mists of the Hot Sea with the water steaming all around them.

Yaz closed her eyes. There had been a time, before she was old enough to go out and fish, that she had thought of water only as molten ice. But the vastness of the sea changed all that. The largest of them, the Hot Sea, stood ten miles and more across in some seasons. Her father had once told

her the waters of the sea ran beneath more ice than the rock
did. How he knew that she didn't know, but her father spoke
very seldom and when he did it was never to give voice to
a lie.

Her weakness felt like a sea now, and she sank into it,
even her thirst not enough to keep her afloat. But when she
heard the groan beside her Yaz opened her eyes again and
rolled her head to the side. 'Quell?'

'D-did . . . did I get him?'

'Yes.' She couldn't help smiling.

'Good.' Quell levered himself up, his face bloody. 'Don't
think I could take more than two or three others though.'
He moved with caution as though every part of him hurt.
He should be dead but the toughness of the Ictha was a
thing of legend.

'Just need to . . . rest a while yet.' He lowered himself
back to the rock with a gasp and a wince. 'Are you okay?'

Yaz considered the question. Something inside her had
broken and she didn't know what. She did know that she
had begun to shiver though. For the first time since she had
jumped into the pit and escaped the wind the Broken's
caverns felt cold.

CHAPTER 17

'Here!' Quell reached a hand down to pull Yaz from the undercity.

Yaz grabbed hold and in a moment stood beside him in the great starlit cavern. Quell immediately recoiled, a confused horror etched across his face. He ended up sprawled on his backside, yards away, trying not to retch.

'Sorry. I'm so sorry.' In her other hand Yaz held the smouldering star-stone that she had taken from the destroyed hunter. 'I forgot. I—'

'It's fine.' Quell shuddered. 'Just give me a moment.'

She moved away from the hole and crouched, shivering in her torn furs. Even a star the size of the one she'd taken from Pome made most people uneasy close up. This star had driven the hunter, supplied its energy, bound the pieces of it into some semblance of life. It weighed twenty times what Pome's did. Calmed by her will the hunter's star glowed a sullen red with patches of darkness moving slowly across its surface.

'I don't understand how you can touch that thing . . .' Quell winced and returned to the side of the hole. 'I get the horrors if I go anywhere near it. Like my thoughts are breaking.'

'I don't know.' She did know. It was in her blood. If she cupped the star in both hands she could almost completely surround it. Its song filled her then, clearer than ever before, as if there might be words to it, as if they might reveal their meaning were she only to take the time to listen. She felt its fire burning at the edge of her mind, giving whispering voice to parts of her that normally held their tongue. But even touching this star was nothing like as bad as being however many tens of yards she'd been from the void star. 'I don't know how I can stand it. I just can.'

Yaz huddled, clutching the star to her in both hands. It had a warmth to it and she was colder now than she had ever been save in the long night.

'It seems a shame to leave all that.' Quell was peering down at the scattered ruins of the hunter. To the Broken it was a scavenger's dream but to the Ictha it was a greater wealth in metal than the entire clan owned. More than they could trade for over three generations.

'You'll find they value things down here differently. A lot of things. Not just iron.' Yaz set the hunter's star down in a hollow in the rock and came to stand beside Quell where he crouched at the edge. 'Mother Mazai says we're never free until we can walk away from what we want carrying only what we need.'

'That old woman is too wise for her own good.' Quell looked up with a forced grin. 'Perhaps we could just take a—'

'Quell! What are you even doing here? I mean, how did—'

'I told you.' He got to his feet, half a head taller than her, wider. He smelled good. Like home. 'I came to save you.'

'You didn't jump into the Pit of the Missing? Not for me. That's madness.'

'Of course not. Jumping in would be crazy!' He offered her a wry smile. 'I stole just about every rope the Ictha have. And a dozen sets of dog harnesses from the Quinx and the Axit.'

'Quell!' The Ictha never stole.

'Well, I borrowed them. Quietly. While everyone was sleeping after the final night of the gathering, drunk on ferment. They can have them back. Well . . . most of them can, I expect.' Quell pursed his lips. 'I tied them all into one long rope. You should have seen it, Yaz. It would have reached from the top of the ice cliffs to the bottom of the sea!'

'You climbed down the pit?'

'It started that way, yes.' A frown. 'I tied the rope to an iron stake and let it down, then started climbing. And climbing. And climbing. That is one *deep* hole! So, about three lifetimes later I'm hanging there in total darkness, my arms are half dead, everything is soaking wet . . . And suddenly one of my knots gives way and I'm falling.'

'Splash.' Yaz remembered the shock of it.

'Exactly. And it seemed like I was falling, or sliding, forever. I don't think that rope would have reached anywhere near the bottom even if it hadn't come apart.'

'And nobody found you?' Yaz imagined that so long after the regulator stopped his cull the pools would not be well guarded.

'I decided to watch and wait. I've seen others in the caves, but they didn't see me. Everyone seems very busy down here, like something important is going on.'

Yaz stepped back to take Quell in. So familiar and yet so out of place. It seemed extraordinary. All of it. Not least that he would be so reckless, and for her.

'Why would—' But she didn't want to ask that question.

Not now. She wasn't sure that she was ready for the answer. She had asked her mother about love once, and her mother, a practical woman not given to sentiment, had pushed back her long hair, streaked with grey, with both hands and said that love was like a storm in the night. 'You wake up in the morning to find that the world has changed. There's a new landscape beyond the doors of your tent, everything familiar yet different.' Yaz had wondered about that. With Quell there had been no storm. They had grown together, comfortable in each other's company.

'We can't stay here.' Quell took a last look at the wealth of metal scattered on the rocky slope below the hole.

'It might be better to stay,' Yaz said. 'I'm not sure I remember the way back to the settlement. But the Broken come here every day, I think.'

'Yes, but we don't want them to find us.' Quell flexed his hands as if missing his spear.

'We don't?'

'No.'

'The Broken are our future now.' Immediately Yaz felt guilty. Quell had come for her, thrown away the life he loved. And for what? She was broken: there was no life on the ice for her. Maybe it was the star setting the point of its wedge to her mind but two voices spoke to her, equally loud. One told her she was a burden on the Ictha, her sacrifice necessary for the survival of the whole. Her weakness hadn't only dragged her down but had now brought Quell low too. She didn't deserve happiness. She could not be saved. It was her own voice and she believed it. The other voice was also hers and it told her that a whole which survived at the expense of its children did not deserve to continue. This voice told her that maybe, just maybe, she could be saved but that she could not be saved alone. If she deserved more than this then so did every child cast into the pit. She drew a deep breath. 'The Broken are our future. There aren't any other choices down here.'

'Well, we can escape. That's a choice.'

'You think you can climb back out of the pit.' It wasn't a question. Nobody could climb that. Not even Thurin with his ice-working. Not even Tarko, though their leader would be the least inclined to try.

Quell's old smile returned. He nodded at the hole beside them. 'I think it's pretty clear now that the priests don't mine their iron from the roots of the Black Rock. And we both know that if you consider all the clan, the priests trade a *lot* of metal over the year.'

Yaz nodded.

'So they must have a way of hauling it from these caverns to the surface, and it won't be up that twisting slanting shaft from the pit. The loads would snag and get caught. And it's too exposed, half a dozen local clans come to pray there at different times across the year. The secret would never have kept so long. All we have to do is find out where and when the next load goes up, and we go up with it!'

Yaz's eyes widened. She had only been away from the surface for a short while but already it felt like a lifetime. The idea that she might return was a dream. Part of her didn't even want to step back out into the wind. That part of her had kept quiet until this moment, but it spoke now, surprising her. 'I can't go back.'

'Of course you can. The regulator passed you. You weren't pushed into the pit, you . . . fell.'

'I can't go back without Zeen.' But it wasn't just about Zeen, not now, maybe not even when she jumped. Something was wrong with the world, with everything, when being less than perfect, less than the tribes' idea of perfect, just meant giving up on people, throwing children into a hole in the ice. Yaz knew that in her core, felt it blood to bone. Bringing Zeen back with her would mean something larger than just saving one child. Like a crack spreading across a cliff face it would be the start of something. The start of something larger beginning to fall. 'He's my brother.'

Quell rolled his eyes upwards as if about to appeal to the Gods in the Sky, but finding only ice above him he sighed. 'Kazik rejected him. There's no life for him with the Ictha, Yaz. The wind—'

'The wind might kill him, yes. But do you think the priests don't lie? They certainly keep some pretty big secrets!' She swung an arm to encompass the chamber and the scars of the Missing city all around them. 'Zeen needs to be given the choice. He might choose to stay or to come with us and see whether the wind really will kill him.'

Quell shook his head. 'Fine . . . But I'm going to advise him to stay here. And it ends with Zeen. I've seen you with your friends. We can't bring them all back. They'll probably try to stop the whole thing anyway.'

'Oh.' Yaz hadn't realized that Quell had already watched her. Something in the way he said *friends* hinted at a jealousy she wouldn't have suspected he had in him. She appreciated his reluctance to approach them though. The gerants especially looked very intimidating. Yaz's first encounter with Hetta wasn't something that would ever fade from her memory.

'So, where is he?' Quell asked.

'With the Tainted.'

'The who?' A raised eyebrow.

'The Tainted. They live in the black ice. It drives them mad.' Said out loud it sounded as impossible as reaching the surface.

221

'And they've taken Zeen?'

'He's one of them – probably.' Yaz walked back to the hunter's star. 'If we get him back then this will drive the taint out of him. But we're going to need help.'

Quell blinked. He drew a deep breath, and then gave a nod that made Yaz wonder if there had to be a storm or if sometimes love just stole up on you. 'All right. Let's do it.'

Yaz hid the hunter's star in an ice-filled hollow close to the cavern wall. They watched as its warmth began to melt a path down. The water would refreeze above it, and with the glow dimmed by Yaz's will, there would be nothing to betray it save the aura. According to Quell, at its edges that aura felt more like a suggestion to keep away. The sort of feeling that might unconsciously slip into a man's mind and turn him along a different path.

Quell led the way back up the long slope, past the gate-posts, which remained silent, and into the chamber beyond. Yaz took out Pome's star for additional light. She paused and raised it level with her head. The blue of it reminded her of the brittle blue of Pome's eyes and it struck her that despite his slight build and relative youth he was perhaps the most dangerous of those beneath the ice with her. Even the largest of the gerants presented a knowable threat but Pome, with his faction and politics and ambition, could be capable of anything. She hardly knew him but it was clear he had generous measures of both pride and cruelty, a dangerous combination. He clearly had the skill to sway others with his words. A power that was both small and large at the same time. But what other magic he might hold from the corruption of blood that had seen him thrown down eight years before she didn't know. Shadow-weaving? Ice-working? Or something more deadly and held secret?

'You made that star roll to your hand,' Quell said. 'Back in the city, when I was failing to keep you quiet.'

'I was going to brain you with it.' Yaz exerted a little pressure and the star's song changed ever so slightly. She held the star between thumb and finger. *Stay*. She lifted the finger, lowered the thumb, withdrew her hand. And the star remained, though it started to rotate slowly.

Quell's eyebrows rose. 'They do that?'

'Apparently.'

Yaz took a step back and the star followed, as if its instructions were relative to her rather than the world. She laughed. Slowly the star began to move around her on an orbit she could almost see, as if it were following a thread so fine that it dwelt just beyond the edge of vision. Yaz pursed her lips then shrugged. It would keep her hands free.

'The man I took this star from might want it back. He doesn't like me very much. He could be trouble if we meet him out here.' Yaz remembered the look on Pome's face when her light had found him, stalking Arka's band in the shadows, others with him. Pome hated her, she was sure of that. How much danger that might put her in she was less sure of. 'We'll be fine once we're with the others back at the settlement.'

They moved on together, the star winding its way about her and lighting their surroundings where the ice grew dark. Even there though she kept the star dim, not wanting to draw unfriendly eyes their way. They drank from standing pools, the water delicious after their long dry time in the city. Yaz tried raw fungi, choosing only those she remembered as safe. They tasted better cooked but her stomach was too hungry to care about her mouth's opinions. She felt she was already losing weight, as if the bulk that sustained the Ictha on the ice was deserting her as other changes came fast and furious. Soon she would be a skinny wretch, too narrow to withstand the wind. She chomped at another tough fungus cap with focused dedication. Quell waited impatiently and hurried her on at the first opportunity.

Quell crossed each cavern as if he were still stalking the Broken, moving around the edge in a crouch, pausing frequently to listen, staying out of the light. Yaz followed in his footsteps, aiming for stealth. None among the ice tribes were hunters though. Nothing lived on the ice save the rare predators that, like the humans, moved from one temporary sea to the next. Should even one of the main seas stay closed for a season people would start to die. If it remained closed for two seasons whole clans might vanish.

Quell paused at a turning in a coal-worm tunnel, listening. 'I miss my spear.'

'They're good people, Quell. They're just children from the tribes.'

'I saw one of your "children" who must have been ten feet tall and looked like he could wrestle a hoola.' He moved on.

'Well, some of them are grown-up children. The Broken have been living down here for generations.'

'Some of them didn't know when to stop growing up,' Quell murmured. He raised a hand to halt her and caution silence.

'What is it?' Yaz tried to whisper but the tunnel made hissing echoes of it.

Quell said nothing, only sniffed.

Yaz breathed in deeply through her nose. There it was, a familiar scent reminding her of her arrival on the Broken's shores. Blood.

CHAPTER 18

The body lay sprawled in a grove of blue-grey fungi, broken stalks and crowns scattered all around it. Somehow it was this desecration, this waste of something edible in a land of hunger, which drew Yaz's eye first. The anger and horror about *that* she could fit inside her mind. A dead person though, someone she had spoken to not long before, that was something more difficult to wrap her thoughts around. She had seen the dagger-fish take her youngest brother, Azad. She had fought to keep him in the boat, and had lost, but she had not seen him die, his body never came back from the sea. She had yet to come to terms with the image of Jaysin's head swinging from Hetta's belt. And now this.

'He's huge . . .' Quell walked around the gerant, trampling more fungi.

The spear that had killed him remained, the haft jutting from his back. Yaz imagined that whoever had driven it through him had lacked the courage to recover it before the man was truly dead, and lacked the time to wait for it to happen. Jerrig was dead now though. The harvester lay in a pool of his own blood, half across the sack he had been filling. His massive ten-foot frame curled around his wound.

Quell set a hand to the iron spear.

'Quell!'

'What? You don't think we'll need it?'

'I think some of the Broken are warriors who've trained with weapons for years. They're less likely to stick something sharp through us if we seem unthreatening.' Her voice carried less conviction than she hoped it would. If Pome found them with the body he might well have them killed whether they were armed or not. 'Besides, we should let him lie.'

Quell shook his head. 'Dead is dead. The ice will take him to the sea, and the gods will take care of him.' He hauled on the spear, using it as a lever to turn the corpse. The point emerged a hand span beneath Jerrig's ribs. 'He's smaller than a tonnerfin. Shouldn't be . . .' A grunt of effort as he drove the spear through the gerant's body.

'Quell!' Yaz winced and put a hand to her eyes. She had seen butchery before, enough blood to turn the sea red, but Jerrig . . . he wasn't meat from the sea.

'Done.' Quell hauled the bloody length of iron from the corpse and held it in crimson hands. His lack of concern surprised her, but perhaps to him this was a nest of dangers and Jerrig's remains were no more a cause for sentiment than those of the hunter were.

'When they see that in your hands there will be no end of questions . . .' Yaz frowned. 'At least wash it.'

'I will.' Quell nodded. 'But now I'll have an answer if whoever did this comes after us.'

The pair of them moved on with greater caution, every shadowed tunnel and dim-lit chamber seeming full of threat now. A spear could come winging out of the darkness at any moment. Yaz tried not to imagine Quell transfixed as Jerrig had been but the image kept returning.

Chamber after silent chamber wore at Yaz's alertness. When the ice groaned and creaked she would start and turn, nerves jangling. They picked paths through more groves of fungi, including some where Yaz remembered harvesters had been at work.

In two places they smelled smoke, which was odd as Yaz had seen no fire at all since coming beneath the ice.

'Where is everyone?' The whisper escaped her. It must have been one of the Tainted who killed Jerrig. Had they mounted an attack and driven the Broken back to some defensive line?

Quell opened his mouth to reply but a distant scream pre-empted him. He exchanged glances with Yaz and led off in the direction of the cry. Sound carried strangely in the chambers and tunnels beneath the ice and the scream was not repeated. Soon Yaz found herself lost, or more lost than she had been before.

'Did you see the black ice?' she asked. 'When you were searching for me.' On the return from the city Yaz had found a route that avoided the taint which Arka had led them through, but she wondered now if the blackness might be spreading elsewhere, fingering into the Broken's territory like frost reaching across still water, drawing the Tainted with it, perhaps Hetta with them, the heads of Yaz's friends swinging from her belt, their blood on her sharpened teeth.

'I saw black ice, grey ice, red, green, all the shades of the icebow. But I couldn't go in. There is no light in those places.'

Yaz blinked but didn't question the truth of the statement. The taint didn't spread where there were stars, so beyond the fringes there would be no light to see it by. 'We should go back. I can find the way to the settlement from where we found Jerrig.'

Quell shook his head. 'I know how to reach your friends from here. I spent a lot of days scouting this place, looking for you.' He led on.

Yaz followed, her brow furrowed. Days? It was easy to lose track of time so far from the sun . . . but *days*? Unconsciously her fingers returned to the needle at her collar, physical proof of what she would otherwise consider a fever dream. Had Elias and Seus stolen days from her while they fought their secret battle?

'What happened here?' The chamber before them lay strewn with broken ice, much of it glowing with stardust.

Yaz looked up at the ceiling, no longer smooth but pitted and cratered, crisscrossed with ridges hanging like shattered teeth. 'Ice-work.'

Quell led the way around the edge of the cavern, the dimness and soft glow confusing to the eye. Frost hung in the still air. This wasn't mining. There had been fighting here. An ice-worker had brought the ceiling down. Maybe Tarko had done it, or Thurin, or others among the Broken.

Yaz placed her feet as carefully as she could but still the broken ice announced her, *crunch, crunch, crunch*. Everything else remained silent. The glaciers held their tongue. No screams. Just Yaz and Quell, their slow advance betrayed with each step.

'Wait . . .'

Quell stopped and turned his head slowly to look back at her, a question in his eyes.

Yaz held herself motionless, listening hard. She was sure she had heard something, an echo almost, like the soft crunch of a footstep that was not her own and not Quell's. She reached out with her mind to the tiny stars in the ice heaped all around her, its glow so faint it lit her to the knee and no further. Quell they lit only to the ankles.

Though they were like dust, each star was a perfect sphere and sang its own song, dipping only now and then into the register in which her brain could detect it. Their heartbeats were a faint whining. Yaz spoke to them and with one voice they answered, their glow elevating to a fiercer light that lit the chamber, throwing strange diffuse shadows in all directions.

In one spot the shadows held on, a mist of darkness shifting reluctantly before the light that should have dispelled them. Quell turned and in the same motion drew back his spear arm for the throw.

'No!' A voice from the thinning shadow.

Yaz threw herself to the side and brought Quell down into the crushed ice, throwing glowing crystals into the air. Both of them rose together, spitting the stuff from their lips.

A small figure stood where Quell would have thrown his spear. Darkness still clung to her but streamed away as they watched. 'Yaz! Where have you been?'

And in the next moment little Maya rushed to hug her, the last of the shadows trailing from her long brown hair.

CHAPTER 19

Yaz let the girl hug her until the questions each had for the other forced some space between them.

'Where have you been?' Maya got in before Yaz.

'In the city. I . . . fell . . . I had to come back up before I could escape. It took hours.'

'Hours?' Maya tilted her head and studied Yaz's face. 'You've been gone three days.'

Yaz turned to look at Quell. He shrugged. 'I would have said a week, but I lost count of time. I ran out of food. I ended up eating those . . . things . . . off the ground.' He made a disgusted face.

'How—' But Erris had said something about time running differently in the void. 'What's happening? We found Jerrig dead. Are the Tainted attacking?'

'Jerrig?' Maya's face crumpled. She looked down to hide her tears. 'He was only good.'

'Who did it?' Yaz asked. 'Maya, we need to know!'

Maya looked up, her eyes drawn to Quell as if noticing him for the first time. 'Who's he?'

'That's Quell. He's a friend.' Yaz waved Maya's attention back to her. 'What is go—'

'How is it doing that?' Maya's mouth stayed open, her eyes tracking the dim blue glow of the eyeball-sized star as it continued its slow upwards spiral around Yaz's shoulders.

'It just does. They do that.' Yaz snatched the star from the air and tucked it into a pocket. 'What is going on?'

'It's Pome,' Maya said. 'He's killed Tarko and he's trying to take over.'

Yaz tried to say something but found her mouth too dry. Eular had said she was like the stone he'd told her to drop into the pool. One touch and the whole body of water had begun to freeze before her eyes, ice spreading out in all directions from the point of contact. An agent of change. The blind man had called her that. She'd dropped into the Broken's world and now everything was changing around her whether she wanted it to or not. 'Is Thurin safe? Are the others safe?'

'Thurin?' Quell asked.

'The others,' Yaz said. 'Are they all safe?'

'Nobody is safe!' Maya suddenly spun around, checking the entrances. 'It's too bright here. We have to go.'

Yaz dimmed the stardust, returning the chamber to its previous gloom, mottled with the faint, coloured glow of the dust bands. 'Not until I know what's happening. Where is everyone?'

Maya drew a deep breath. 'It's war. They're fighting among themselves. Pome and his people are based around the forge pool. Arka and Eular are holding out against them at the ravine where the drying cave is.'

'That's not very big! How many of them are there? And what about the settlement?'

'There's about thirty of us. The settlement is empty except for maybe some old folk and sick. There was a lot of fighting there.'

Quell stepped up beside Yaz. 'And what were you doing out here, child?' He frowned, studying Maya closely. 'Clan Axit, aren't you?'

The bands tattooed on the outer edge of her left ear gave it away. Yaz had always thought it funny that this timid girl belonged to the famously warlike Axit. Perhaps among their tents being kind and gentle was all it took to count as broken.

'I was spying,' Maya said. 'Arka needs to know the disposition of the enemy.'

Quell blinked. 'The what?'

'What Pome is up to,' Maya explained. It seemed that even the Axit children knew more of the language of war than Ictha men.

'We should go to Arka,' Yaz said. 'Will you take us?'

'I know the way.' Quell gestured back the way they had come.

'But Maya knows the way *and* how to stop us getting filled with spears by some overexcited guards before we can explain ourselves.'

Maya seemed doubtful for a moment, looking Quell up and down with mistrustful eyes. She was still a few years shy of the time when she might be swayed by handsome young men.

'He's my friend,' Yaz said. 'He came down the pit on a rope. To save me.'

Maya's doubt seemed to deepen still further, but at last she nodded. 'Follow me then. But be quiet. I heard you two coming from a mile off.'

Maya led them through a series of narrow tunnels made by coal-worms and squeezed by glacial flow over the intervening years. No gerant could have used them. At several points Quell struggled to fit through. He made no complaint but Yaz could see her own fear echoed on his face. They had both lived a life on the vast open of the ice and tight confines held a horror all their own.

As she followed, Yaz found herself wondering about the time she had spent in the city. *Days?* How long had she been in the void, dreaming strange dreams? Erris had spent a hundred lifetimes and more in its dark heart. Just a little longer in his green world and Yaz might have woken like Jekka Ixo from the old tales, emerging from his nap in the witch's cave to find the world had moved on without him, his people changed, his children forgotten, and like Jekka she would have walked the ice beneath a burden of years that had imparted only age and no wisdom.

Crossing a wider chamber Quell drew level with Yaz. 'If these people are fighting a war among themselves they aren't going to be interested in helping rescue your brother.'

Yaz had been thinking the same thing herself. 'There are other kinds of help. We have no idea what we're up against with the Tainted. Arka knows things we need to know. And Thurin was living among them until recently.'

'Thurin? You mentioned him before. He was tainted?'

'Yes.'

Quell shuddered. 'I've seen them, you know? Not just the giant woman—'

'Gerant.'

'I've seen others wandering outside the changed ice. Especially by the big pool. I thought they were sick, or driven mad by being down here too long, but those must have been Taints too. I knew there was something wrong as soon as I saw the first one. I'm no coward, you know that, but I just turned and ran the other way first chance I got. I—'

'Quiet!' Maya hissed. She motioned for them to stay and moved on alone. As she went the shadows dragged around her like a cloak. A moment later she was gone, hidden by the curve of the wall and by gathering darkness.

'Can you trust her?' Quell asked.

'Yes.' With the word out of her mouth Yaz wondered where that judgement came from.

They waited and the silence built around the creak of the ice and the drip of meltwater. Quell began to shuffle that way he did when he wanted to ask something. He had shuffled just the same for two days before he first asked to kiss her when she was eleven and he was twelve. Now Yaz found herself on the point of telling him to spit it out when he finally spoke.

'I don't know why just saying a handful of words is harder than letting myself down into an endless hole on fifty thin ropes knotted together . . . I want you, Yaz. I want us to share a tent, raise children. One day you'll be clan-mother. Everyone knew that. Come back to us, yes, but come back to *me*. I came here for you.'

'And Zeen.' Yaz's cheeks burned and she couldn't meet Quell's eyes.

'For you. You weren't pushed. You jumped. And it made me think you were running from something. There's no curse on your blood . . . But Zeen too. I said I'd get him back and I will if that's what it takes.'

Yaz nodded. He hadn't said he loved her again. Maybe that was too hard a word to repeat. Or maybe he only needed her, like a piece of his life that left its own hole when taken. She tried to find an answer, but Quell was right, words can be hard to say. And there *was* a curse on her blood. The regulator hadn't meant her for the pit, but he did mean her for the Black Rock. He'd decided for her. Decided on a life spent in mountain caves praying to the Hidden God that only the priests knew. A few brief excursions to the clans maybe, but as a stranger, an outsider to all she knew, dispensing law and cheating precious food from them in exchange for what must be a tiny fraction of the iron they took from the Broken.

They waited, the silence still thick about them, aching for an answer but now at least free of Quell's shuffling. Yaz grew tired and she crouched. She took Elias's needle from her collar and studied it. In tales the gods gave more impressive gifts. With difficulty she tied a hair about it and let it hang from thumb and forefinger. She could feel Quell's gaze on her. Mother Mazai had an iron needle that would always point to the north. As Yaz had half expected, Elias's needle turned slowly then stopped.

'Is that north?' Quell asked.

'I don't know.' At least that was now an acceptable answer. 'This place has me all turned around.' This was also the answer she had been unable to give to what he had said before.

She returned the needle to its place and set her hand to the dark grey stone beside her. Her fingers traced the scrapes and grooves left by the endless flow of ice. For a moment she saw trees about her, grass beneath her fingers, warm and springy, the chatter of birds in her ears, so different from gull cry. A gentle breeze that caressed rather than bit.

'Yaz?' Quell tilted his head in question, then helped her up. 'She's back.'

Maya stood a short way off in the tunnel's gloom. She waved them on. 'The guards know we're coming now.'

Yaz saw nobody watching for them on their approach to the ravine. It unsettled her to think she had missed them even knowing that they were there.

Along the near side of the ravine half a dozen cave mouths glowed with starlight, isolated islands of illumination below which the rock face steepened towards vertical and plunged away to the hidden torrent roaring in the distance. Yaz still felt unsafe on the narrow path down, which was really just a series of grit-strewn ledges crudely joined together.

Not far from the top they approached a cave mouth that Yaz hadn't noticed on her earlier visits, now lit from within and crowded with Arka's faction. The handsome, legless smith, Kaylal, sat near the entrance and waved a greeting. 'Yaz! They found you!'

Yaz smiled back. Beauty aside, something good shone out of Kaylal, she'd seen it the first time she laid eyes on him. The other young smith, Exxar, moved up behind him and set both hands on his shoulders, arms sliding out from the thickness of his rat-skin cloak. His was a different kind of handsome, solid and clear-cut, but lacking the unearthly quality Kaylal possessed. And his gaze was less friendly. *This is mine,* it told her, *keep walking.* Kaylal grinned at her and lifted a tolerant hand to cover one of Exxar's.

'Arka's in here.' Maya led them on past the cave, down to the door of the drying hut. She knocked twice then stood aside for them to enter.

This time Yaz found the warmth of the drying hut a welcome change from the cold outside. Whatever had broken inside her when she'd torn that hunter apart, it had left her still less of an Ictha than she had been before. Behind her Quell muttered an oath as he entered. He would have never felt such heat before.

'Yaz.' Arka spoke from a chair towards the rear of the cave. She was flanked on one side by Ixen from the forge and Madeen the cook. On her other side stood an older gerant, one thick arm heavily bandaged with bloodstained furs, and beside him an armoured man with a shaved head, a sword ready in his hand. Eular stood closer at hand beside the wall with Thurin next to him, perhaps as his guide. Thurin gave her a smile but he looked troubled. The old man favoured Yaz with his eyeless regard. 'Remarkable,' he said. 'The hunters didn't get you after all.'

Arka beckoned them closer. 'We thought we'd lost you down in the city. But you found your way out *and* found a friend. This would be the elusive spearman who knocked down Goxx in the Pillar Cavern?'

Yaz glanced back at Quell in surprise.

'I did knock someone down.' Quell came to stand beside her. 'They were in my way and others were chasing me.'

'You seem to have exchanged spears too. Where did you get that one?' Arka eyed the bloodstained iron.

'We found it with Jerrig's body.' Yaz spoke before Quell could answer.

'Jerrig!' That brought Arka out of her chair. They all asked their questions at once, shock on every face. Were there others with him? Had he fought? Which cavern? How long ago?

Arka and the four around her soon fell to arguing loudly among themselves. Even Ixen found his voice.

'You said they would leave the others alone. My mother is still in the settlement!'

Yaz led Quell across to Thurin and Eular. Small as it might be, Arka's faction were clearly not of a single mind. On the ice the Ictha had no problem choosing their direction in a featureless waste. Down here many directions beckoned, and every mouth held a new opinion.

'Yaz.' Thurin stepped towards her as if he were going to take her hands, then faltered. 'We thought you were dead! We thought the hunters had you.'

'It takes more than one of those to stop an Ictha!' Quell moved forward, almost between them. 'We dealt with—'

'Are Quina and Kao all right?' Yaz interrupted. She didn't want everyone there to know about the hunter she had undone. Not yet. Not before she had a better understanding of what was going on. Also she was worried about Quina. And Kao.

Thurin nodded. 'A lot of others aren't, though. Enza and Herro were killed. Jecca and her brother badly hurt.'

Yaz couldn't put faces to those names. It reminded her though that Thurin had been born here. This conflict meant far more to him than to the rest of the drop-group. She reached out a hand to his arm, midway between shoulder and elbow, the way the Ictha offered sympathy.

'Even when you're not here you cause change, Yaz.' Eular sounded neither sad nor happy, as though what had happened had been as inevitable as the ice.

This was all on her? Blood and death and friend against friend? The sudden weight of events left Yaz staggering beneath the burden of weariness she already carried, almost unable to keep her eyes from closing. She looked from Quell to Thurin, both of them drawn up to their full height, facing each other like boys playing at warriors. Quell stood shorter, broader, the strength of him in his face, his pale eyes normally so calm now tinged with something more fierce. Thurin, taller, thinner, more delicate. As ever, Thurin looked haunted, carrying his tragedy like a wound, dark eyes narrow above sharp cheekbones, his hair as black as Quell's though wild, a standing shock where Quell's fell long and even. She let herself stumble to distract them from releasing whatever pointed exchanges queued behind their lips.

'Yaz!' They both came to her. She mumbled that she just needed sleep and together they helped her from the cave.

Maya guided them further down the ravine to a place she might rest.

Yaz hardly saw the chamber that Maya led her into or the faces of those already there. Instead she sank onto the thin pile of hides they set for her and plunged into sleep.

The dreams that rose to catch her were green and growing, and somewhere in them a dead boy waited for her.

CHAPTER 20

'I'm dreaming.' Yaz stops her wandering and stands, bare-footed, on the cold stone. The ice sky arches above, no more than a spear's length beyond the reach of her fingers. The chambers of the Broken, like bubbles beneath sea ice, open on every side from this one, stretching all the way from the Missing's city to the pit.

All around her the space reverberates with the same glacial song that has been sung since long before the gods of sky and sea made the first man and the first woman. Yaz wonders if the great whales, those behemoths who swim to unknowable depths and know the secrets of the ocean, learned their own songs from that of the eternal ice, for both have much in common. A refrain of old sorrow, immeasurable memory, a language of loss in which the true names of all things are known and spoken.

Yaz crouches to touch the bedrock. Once a rich dark soil blanketed this place, deep enough for the roots of trees, warm enough for flowers. Around her fingers grass grows, tickling against her palm, ghostly green, many-bladed, struggling for the sun. She looks and all about her a memory of pine and oak is building, a memory of beech and elm, rising high above, up into the ice as though it were the phantom and the trees simple fact, here and now and always true.

'How do I know your names?' Yaz stands and the wood has become the world, a blueness waits high above, glimpsed in whispers through myriad leaves and reaching arms.

She walks with the warmth and complication of twigs and leaves and fallen acorns beneath her feet. 'I'm dreaming.' But the bark beneath her hands feels rough and gnarled, detailed beyond her ability to imagine, too solid for any dream where sleeping hands might close on air.

In a glade a fallen tree several seasons down lies reaching for the sky, branches stark against puffy clouds. On the far side in the treeline's shade a doe nibbles fresh shoots.

Yaz stares at the doe, amazed at its strangeness and just as amazed that it is somehow familiar to her. As if the time that escaped her in the void were not truly lost but had been filled with experience and somehow that knowledge, those memories, have begun to bleed into her dream.

'It's beautiful, isn't it?' Erris stands beside her. Across the glade the doe looks up with liquid eyes and darts off among the trees, so fleet of foot that Yaz's heart almost chases it.

'I don't have words for what I've seen here.' Yaz's gaze remains captured by the space where the doe had stood. She has lived a life in the jaws of the wind, her eyes trained to find meaning within a hundred shades of white and grey. She has lived as a singular mote of warmth upon a vast and lifeless wilderness. 'It's too much. There's too much . . . of it.'

Erris's hand is on her shoulder. How so light a contact can be so heavy with meaning she has no idea.

'Are there no other people here?' Yaz asks.

'None that the void remembers.'

'So . . . we're like Zin and Mokka.' She feels the blood in her cheeks.

'Who?'

'Zin and Mokka.' Yaz blinks at him. 'The first man and woman.'

Erris grins. 'Not all myth is true.'

She scowls at him, suddenly conscious of his weight of years, more than all the elders she has known put together. 'Next you will tell me that the Gods in the Sea are a lie, and the Gods in the Sky.'

He laughs now, a thing as warm as the forest about them. 'No, Yaz, there are definitely gods in the sea, and if so small a thing can hold gods then the sky must also.'

Yaz gazes at the sky. It is not her sky, neither the star-scattered ceilings of caverns nor the merciless vault above the ice, scarred at its utmost heights with ribbons of frost. It is not her sky and she is not here.

Somewhere her body is lying on a cold stone floor in a cave. When she wakes it will be to a war she wants no part of, murder in closed spaces, friend against friend. And her escape, her impossible escape, would take her into the black ice then up through untold miles to the white hostility of a land that wants to kill all of them, clanless, tentless, and even if they had both tent and clan . . . hopeless.

'You could stay here with me,' Erris says, and Yaz doesn't know if she is remembering this, dreaming it, or if the offer is really here and now and that somehow Erris can reclaim her to the void to live a green eternity in the memory of a vanished world.

'When you're lost on the ice they say that you reach a point where the wind ceases to feel cold. They say a warmth enfolds you, a sleepiness, and that all you want to do is to lie down, just for a bit, to lie down and coil around the wonderful warmness that is your death. And they say what makes the Ictha who we are is that we never do. We never surrender to that illusion. They say that we are found frozen on our feet.' She turns to meet his gaze, his serious eyes. 'I don't know if that's true or not but the point of the story is true. It's not in us to give up. And this . . .' She waves her hand at all of it. '. . . this wonderful, miraculous place, and . . .' *And you*, she wants to say. 'All this is the warm death. This is giving up.'

Erris's smile is a sad one. 'I can't argue with that. Much as I would like to. The void is a miracle. It offers everything. But it is not life. And I could never tell you that it was.' The hand on her shoulder steers her to where he now points, a darker place beneath the arms of a great yew, its boughs laden with dark green needles and berries like drops of pale blood. 'The way back, my lady.'

'Thank you.' Yaz begins to walk. She looks only forward, eyes on the blackness amid the tangled bracken. Grim steps, teeth gritted against the need to look around. If she does that, if she looks again . . . how will she leave? Birdsong fills her ears. She knows the skylark dropping its notes in a silver chain, warblers and finches peppering the air with heartbreak. Still she walks.

'Be careful of Theus. He is so much more than he seems. And so much less.'

Theus, ruler of the Tainted, and perhaps even of the taint itself. She's scared of what lies ahead. Scared of finding him in her path. She would be stupid not to be. But if this Theus stands between her and her brother then he should worry too.

'Wait!' Erris calls. Then, softer, 'Wait?'

Yaz nearly turns but the blackness before her is diminishing, burning away in the day's heat. Now or never. She has to leave.

She's walking into the dark's margins now. It rises to greet her. A cold mist promising nothing good. The chill sinks immediately into her bones. Already she's shivering. The sky above her is a cold whiteness now and a dark stain spreads across it like the claws of a reaching hand. Seus has come bringing another war, a greater one that lies beyond her understanding. But one thing she does know is that she wants no part of it, any more than she wants any part of the Broken's war.

'Run, Yaz!' Erris's voice, distant and panicked. 'Run and don't look b—'

But Erris is gone. There is only darkness and freezing air and hard stone biting through the thin furs beneath her cheek.

CHAPTER 21

'Yaz! Wake up!'

Someone was shaking her. 'Thurin?'

'You have to get up now.' Thurin gripped her arm and hauled her to a sitting position. 'Pome's coming.'

'Pome?' Sleep cluttered her mind, fragments of her fading dream still fluttered through. Was this it: the final battle? The cave was small, crowded, lit by a few small stars on high ledges. Everyone else was on their feet, some readying weapons. Others were already leaving, filing out onto the narrow path leading up the side of the ravine. 'Pome?' she repeated, still searching for focus.

'Yes, Pome. Mean little man with an uncanny ability to get gerants to do what he wants them to.'

'All except Jerrig.' Yaz shook the image of the fallen harvester from her mind. What would he have made of trees and grass and all that tangle of living things? 'Why? Why is Pome coming?' She knew what Pome wanted: power, all of it. He was more than ready to kill for it. But those around her lacked the quiet panic that an attack would bring.

The cave was emptying quickly. Maya and Quina were there too now, standing beside Thurin.

'They're saying he's come to talk. Arka is meeting him in the Icicle Cavern.'

Yaz got to her feet. She still felt tired, bruised from the floor, and cold. 'Where's Quell?' It should have been her first question. He had come by himself to save her.

'He's in Arka's council of war,' Thurin said.

'War? I thought you said Pome had come to talk.'

'No, I said that's what he said he's come to do.'

'And why aren't you at this council?'

Thurin gave a wry smile. 'They don't trust me yet.'

Yaz frowned. 'Come to think of it, if Quell is there why aren't all of the drop-group? He came here *after* we did!'

Thurin shook his head. 'He's an adult. You're all children. And besides, he knocked one of our handful of grown gerants on his arse, and that counts for something . . . apparently.'

Thurin made to leave but Yaz reached for his arm, holding him back.

'This is madness, this fighting. Arka said the Broken were already losing ground to the Tainted and now you're killing each other.' She hunted his eyes. 'You can't not see that?'

'So we should let Pome have his way? Let him rule us like a king from the stories? That will be his reward for killing a good man? And make no mistake, Tarko was a good man.'

'Yes,' Yaz said simply. 'If that's what it takes, then yes. What else is there? Do you think Pome has come to talk so Arka can convince him of the error of his ways? He's here to negotiate your surrender.'

Maya and Quina looked to Thurin for his answer. He had known these people all his life.

'Gods damn it!' Thurin pulled free of her grasp, fists balled. 'That can't be the only choice.'

'It's the only sane one,' Yaz said. 'Unless . . .' She waited until all three of them had their eyes on her. 'Unless you come with me and Quell to rescue my brother.'

'How will that help?' Thurin let out a frustrated breath.

'Because once we've got the taint out of him we're escaping. Going back to the ice.'

A snort then a sigh. 'Even if that were possible. Which it isn't. And even if you stood a chance against the Tainted. Which you don't. And even if you could get the taint out of your brother. Which you can't. It would still be an insane plan because THE ICE WILL KILL YOU.'

Yaz opened her mouth but found no reply on her tongue. Before she had worked her will to destroy the hunter a part of her could still believe that she might survive up there. Could believe that the claim which saw the regulator throw her brother into the Pit of the Missing was a lie. Though even before her change it was only a small part of her that had believed all this to be a lie. The idea that so many people would do such harm on the basis of an easily disproved untruth was hard to accept. But she had needed very much to believe that she and Zeen could return.

Now, however, with the cold nipping at her heels even here, far from the wind's teeth, she knew it for a cruel truth. None of them could live their old lives again.

'I . . .' She felt the weight of their gaze upon her. Quina, Maya, and now Kao lurking at the doorway, they wanted her to have an answer. It came to her in a sudden vision – trees reaching for a warm sky. 'We go south, always south, and find the gods' belt.'

'You said that was a myth,' Kao rumbled from the exit.

'You'll want us to search for Zin and Mokka next.' Maya

squeaked a pained laugh. Even the youngest of them, a child, was no more able to believe in Yaz than in tales of the first man and first woman.

'My clan journeyed north for a month to reach the pit,' Quina said. 'The ice goes on forever and it is scarcely less cold where the Kac-Kantor roam.'

Yaz grasped the offered straw. 'But it *is* less cold! And a month further south, warmer still.'

'But—'

'Eular believes it.' Let them trust in Eular's wisdom if not hers. 'Eular told me there is a green place far to the south. He had heard stories. Stories! Not myths . . .' She looked around at the others, their faces held tight, closed against hope.

Quina met her eyes. The girl held out her clenched hand between them, reluctant, a tremble in it. Slowly fingers unfolded to reveal a small brownish bead, polished by touch, swirled with lines of darker and lighter brown, beautiful in its way.

'Our clan-mother has a necklace of such beads,' Yaz said. Mother Mazai's polished stones were an heirloom, as prized as iron. A reminder that there were things other than ice in the world. A reminder that under the ice there is sea or stone.

'It isn't stone.' With great reluctance Quina placed the bead in Yaz's palm. 'I stole it from our clan-father. When I knew I wasn't coming back from this journey to the pit. I wanted it so I took it.' Her cheek twitched, guilt warring with defiance.

'It's hardly weighs anything.' Yaz took her star and made more light, studying the swirls. 'What kind of stone is it?'

'Wood,' Quina said. 'It floats on water.'

'Wood?' Thurin frowned.

'Is it a . . . gem?' Kao said the word as if dragging it from memory.

'Wood. From a tree.' Yaz gave the bead back and folded Quina's hand about it.

'Once, very long ago, there was a winter that lasted a year and the Kac-Kantor fled further south than they had ever been. A traveller came to our tents, bitten by the frost and dying. He said he had been travelling northwards in search of a witch known in his people's legends. His food had run out. He had eaten his dogs. And still he travelled north. In all that time we were the first people he had seen. The bead was his gift for the witch. He hoped for wisdom in return. He said that in his southern rangings he had looked down upon the trees from the heights of the ice.

'My clan-father's grandfather's grandfather offered the traveller ten iron stakes for the bead but the stranger would not part with it. When the man died three days later the bead passed into the clan-father's line.' Quina looked down, voice trembling. 'I thought . . . I don't know what I thought . . . maybe that if I took something valuable enough then my people would come and get it back . . . I don't know.' She shook her head.

'It's wood. From a tree,' Yaz said with conviction. 'A tree that stands in the green belt around the world.'

Thurin walked away. He paused by the door. 'Even if a green belt *was* there it's too far. A year of travel maybe. The cold would kill us in a night. We have no tents. Thirst would kill us in days. Our water would freeze. Hunger would kill us in a week. We don't know where the seas are and we have no boats or nets.'

This time when Yaz opened her mouth the answers came quickly. 'We can line our furs with stardust for added warmth. We can tow boards from the settlement and make shelters each night. We can warm them with heat pots from the drying cave and the forge. We can make a sled and pile it with fungi from the groves. We can do all this. Or die trying. Either way it's better to die trying for a life we can take for ourselves than to die fighting each other in the dark for an existence we were condemned to.'

The others were filing out through the doorway now and Yaz followed. None of them spoke as they made their way up along the side of the ravine. Yaz had said her piece. Scattered her ideas on the water. Sometimes it took a while before something rose from the depths to bite. And sometimes such ideas just sank without trace.

Most of the caverns had icicles and in most of them they were regularly knocked down by harvesters or by other Broken just passing to and fro. In the Icicle Cavern, however, some source of meltwater high above combined with the chamber's coldness and lack of stars to generate icicles at such a rate that the Broken had long since abandoned the fight. The cavern was large enough to hold all the Broken even before bloodshed had reduced their numbers and all but a central corridor was festooned with icicles, some hanging ceiling to floor, some scarcely longer than fingers, a myriad of them, some clear, some milky, curtains of them, veils, frozen torrents. They caught the light of the stars that Arka's folk brought with them, glowing with it, casting strange shadows.

Yaz had never imagined such places might exist. She had spent a lifetime on the surface of things, tramping the ice, and beneath her feet, miles deep, how many wonders had she passed over, places no one had ever seen, places no one would ever see? Kaylal, who saw the amazement on her face as she passed him, offered a grin that said he understood the feeling.

Quell stood with her now, iron spear in hand, free at last of Jerrig's blood. A single bruise covered much of the left side of his face, a memento from the hunter slamming him into the ground. For a moment he almost looked like one of the Tainted. Petrick stood to Quell's right. Thurin stood on Yaz's other side, Quina, Maya, and Kao to his left, the gerant boy showing nervous determination, eyes narrowed beneath the pale curls of his fringe. Eular had told Yaz that Kao was only twelve but those were just words standing in the shadow of his great size. Seeing him there among the gleaming icicles and alien shadows Yaz understood properly for the first time that Kao was the same age as Zeen, a child, lost, alone and in a bad place. In fact, in the face of the events that had swept everyone up, all of them, young or old, might be considered lost children, helpless as any boat in a storm.

Arka stood with her inner circle. There was no sign of Eular.

Pome entered the Icicle Cavern from the other side, flanked by gerants bearing iron swords. Dozens of his followers came behind him, knocking aside the longer icicles to make room. Despite their numbers they looked nervous. A curious mix of nervous and excited.

In one hand Pome held an iron rod shorter and thicker than the one he used to carry, and in it a star larger than the one he had ceded to Yaz. The new star burned a deep crimson, not unlike the hunters' stars, and filled the chamber with bloody light, making red and dripping spears of the icicles about him.

A fault in the rock split the cavern floor, a gap of a yard or more yawning between the two factions, ice-clad on either side. It could be spanned easily enough but it stood as a barrier to keep them apart, a physical representation of the solemn oaths of truce sworn by Pome and Arka.

Pome came forward. To either side of him a gerant with a great square shield stood ready to deflect possible spears, and crouched before him a hunska with shaved head and ugly scar, as if he thought he might knock aside any missile from the air. Yaz paid more attention to the star Pome held. Its heartbeat was much louder and deeper than she had expected it to be.

'Does my word mean so little, Pome?' Arka approached the opposite edge of the chasm without any guards to hand.

'We'll see what it's worth.' The crimson light of his star pinked Pome's teeth as though he might have bitten his tongue.

'You requested this meeting . . .' Arka spread her hands as if granting the man permission to speak.

'I demanded it.' Pome's smile was a savage thing. 'This farce is coming to an end, Arka. I have the forge, the settlement, most of the groves. And you have . . . a huddle of caves. Tarko is gone. The Tainted are coming; they must know of our weakness. Who will lead us against them? You, Arka? If you were fit for such duty then you would be winning. You wouldn't be hiding in the drying cave with a handful of children and dreamers.'

Yaz felt his voice pull at her even as the words themselves grated across her. If Pome had ever mastered wisdom or kindness, or even some semblance of the two, then he would have been unstoppable. Fortunately his unpleasant nature shone through sufficiently to weaken the glamour of his voice.

'What do you want, Pome?' Arka sounded weary. 'If all it took to make you king were talking then you would have been on your throne long ago.'

'The Tainted *will* attack. You know this. Theus has waited years for this moment. Decades.'

'And you have given it to him, Pome. Should we praise you for that? Are you proud?

'Are *you* so proud, Arka, that rather than standing with me, united with the Broken, you would keep up this resistance against a thing that has already happened and let the Tainted claim us all?'

Arka shook her head, striding along her side of the divide. 'How then would King Pome defend us? He has killed our best ice-worker, left some of our finest warriors dead or injured. All for what? So we can engage in open warfare with the Tainted when we stand at our weakest.'

Pome looked past Arka to those who stood behind her. 'I'm told that the girl you thought you'd lost in the city has returned . . .' His eyes hunted Yaz in the gloom.

'Yaz?' Arka's voice betrayed surprise. Pome had a spy in her camp. 'What does this—'

'Give her to me. Give her to me and return to the fold. Those above have demanded her!'

Arka barked a laugh. 'You don't talk to the priests, Pome! And what would they want with Yaz?'

'The regulator demands her. And in exchange he has worked a miracle that will see the Tainted laid in ruin!' Pome's grin was a huge and bloody thing now.

Somewhere behind him came a rumbling, a grinding of metal and stone. Icicles began to fall in droves, tinkling as they broke against each other, crashing on the floor below. A shape larger than any gerant hulked into view behind Pome's followers and they parted before it, more scared than exultant. The heartbeat that Yaz had thought to be from Pome's new star grew louder still.

'Pome . . .' Arka stepped back, horrified. All around her the Broken retreated, weapons raised.

As the hunter stepped into clear view Yaz's friends drew

back, only Quell and Thurin standing their ground beside her. The thing stood taller than the one she had destroyed, its iron-scaled head scraping the ice ceiling, broader too, its limbs an irregular array of steel and iron, some ending in serrated blades, one with a sharp spike longer than her arm, yet another with an articulated hand that looked disturbingly human though far larger. Yaz understood now. She had been listening to the heartbeat of the star within the hunter, fierce and strong and deep. If she could redis-cover the strength she had used in the city she might stun the monster but there would be no ripping this one apart, it was just too powerful; her mind ached already just at the thought of reaching into it.

The hunter took another step, a clawed foot striking sparks from the stone.

'Stop!' Pome held up his arm and the hunter halted a yard from him, red starlight glowing from its joints.

Arka rallied herself, the scars on her face deathly pale. 'You can't trust in that thing! We've spent our lives running from them. How many of us have they killed? I don't know how the regulator has bound that monstrosity to his will but even if it serves him now I still don't trust it because I don't trust that old man, not one jot. He personally threw all of us down here, for gods' sake!'

'I don't trust anyone, Arka.' Pome brought his new star closer to him on its iron rod and, to gasps from the opposite side of the fissure, he reached out, closing his other hand about it. His face twisted as if he were holding his palm above a lamp flame but with a snarl he pulled the shining red stone free of the clasps holding it. His fingers couldn't quite meet his thumb around the surface and the crimson light turned his whole hand bloody. 'I trust this!'

Pome made a violent gesture towards the hunter with the

star and the massive metal body slammed back across the chamber as if struck by some invisible hammer that only a god could wield.

The thing clattered to a halt yards back, having narrowly missed crushing several of Pome's followers. The hunter picked itself up as the men and women who had thrown themselves aside got to their own feet.

'I trust this!' Pome held the star aloft, twitching with effort. 'The hunter has a star like this at its heart and as I control this one I control it too.'

The hunter began to advance again. When it reached the fissure it would be over in one stride.

Yaz stepped to meet it, shaking off Quell and Thurin who both reached to stop her.

'Bring her to me.' Pome clutched his star as if it burned him and gestured the hunter towards her.

Yaz extended her will across the ice-rimmed fissure. Her mind skimmed across the blaze inside the hunter's iron casing and settled instead on the rapid pulsing of the star-stone in Pome's fist. Something had been done to the star, some subtle alterations to its patterns. Pome had called the hunter the regulator's gift, his miracle, and Yaz sensed the old priest's hand in these changes. And behind the priest stood the Black Rock's Hidden God. And behind the Hidden God? Just like the Pit of the Missing, there was no telling how deep it all went.

Undoing the priest's changes to the star was beyond Yaz's ability, certainly at a distance and in a hurry, but she had an alternative. At the last moment Pome sensed what she intended but his opposition was clumsy, as weak as a toddler wrestling a full-grown man. She dimmed his star's fire, reducing it to a molten glow.

Immediately the hunter slowed then stopped. It lost direction, casting about for its target. The crimson glare from its eye slits slid across the Broken on both sides of the cavern.

'Bring her!' Pome roared, extending the star towards the hunter as it teetered on the fissure's edge.

But Yaz had hushed the voice of Pome's star and instead the monster painted him with the fierce glow of its eyes as if considering him prey. And in that moment, with the light of Pome's star no longer streaming between his fingers, Yaz noticed it. Two stains retreating to regain the shelter of the sleeve that had been pulled back when Pome reached his star towards the hunter. A black stain and a scarlet one, both moving like oil on water. Evidence that the star he now struggled to hold had already broken free parts of his mind.

'Pome's tainted!' Yaz shouted, pointing. 'Look! Devils under his skin!'

As she shouted her accusation the hunter seized Pome in its over-sized metal hand and at the same time jabbed its killing-spike at his closest guard, Bexen. The gerant, with his unsettling stare, one eye savage, the other milky, looked small for once. The spike's tip punctured the great shield he was holding and tore it from his grasp, sending him sliding perilously close to the fissure.

On all sides the Broken began to run. Nerves, already stretched to breaking point, now snapped. The instinct to run from hunters was strong, and they ran. Yaz ran too, straight for Quell. 'This is it. We need to leave now. We get Zeen and then get out of here.'

They sprinted from the cavern with the last of the stragglers, the floor behind them thick with broken icicles. Turning the corner into the next smaller cavern Yaz found Thurin waiting for them. Quina had stayed with him, Kao hulking at the back. Petrick hung uncertainly at the opposite exit.

'Where's Maya?' Yaz looked around, half expecting to find the girl stepping from a cloak of shadows.

The rest shook their heads.

'She's good at hiding, that one. She'll be with Arka or the others.' Thurin looked worried despite his easy words.

Quell shrugged. 'If we're going to get Zeen then let's do it.'

'And after that?' Quina asked. 'All those things you said, Yaz? Do you think we really can escape?' Screams came from the Icicle Cavern.

'I think we should try.' Yaz didn't want to lie to them. 'I think the dangers won't be worse than what we have to deal with down here. Just different.'

'Is it true though?' Quina asked. 'About the green place? Somewhere we can live?'

'I just want to go back,' Kao rumbled from behind Thurin, his voice a man's, his tone a child's. A great crash made them all glance towards the tunnel they'd fled down.

'I can't go back. I've never been.' Thurin pressed his lips into a worried line. 'All my life is here. My ancestors. Leaving it would . . .'

'Would be like being thrown down the pit,' Yaz said. 'You'll survive it and find a new world. Just like we all did. But we need you, Thurin. *I* need you. Without your understanding of the Tainted and this Theus who leads them I don't know if we can find Zeen, let alone save him.'

Thurin's dark eyes found hers. He took her hands as if there were no one watching. 'The surface sounds terrifying but I would rather go there naked than return to the black ice. We will all die there. Those they can't inhabit become their sport. They torture them to death. Think on it again, Yaz. Think again.'

'Did your mother think again when she came after you?' Yaz squeezed his hands and felt the fear there, trembling in his bones.

Thurin hung his head and for a time he said nothing. The sounds reaching them down the tunnel sounded like the hunter's iron footsteps. Still no one spoke.

'You'll go whether I come or not,' Thurin muttered. He met her gaze briefly. 'I can't let you do that.'

'You've said yourself that the Tainted will come for the survivors when this war is over,' Yaz said. 'In days they'll wash over the Broken and the nightmare won't just be lurking in the black ice, it will be everywhere. Face it now and we can still escape.'

The battle raging inside Thurin dragged on. Finally, with the hunter's glow colouring the tunnel ice and warning of its imminent arrival, Thurin looked up again, his eyes bright, his determination rekindled. 'All right then. Let's go.'

CHAPTER 22

Thurin led the way to the Tainted's caves. He took them through coal-worm tunnels too narrow for Pome's rogue hunter to pursue them along. Yaz followed Thurin, Quell close behind her. Quina and Kao coming next, with Petrick bringing up the rear. The hunska boy had followed when Quina beckoned him to join them. He carried a slender sword over his shoulder, the hilt and the pale hand holding it nearly lost in the dark mats of his hair. Normally only the warriors were allowed swords and spears but normal had made itself scarce of late.

This time the taint didn't appear as a questing tendril of blackness spreading through the ice but as a slow greying. The air had been growing colder, the stars thinning, winking out until there was no light but the blue glow from the star slowly orbiting Yaz. She drew her skins closer about her, shivering, though more from the pervading air of malice and threat than from the dropping temperature. Ahead madmen haunted the darkness in thrall to demons, all bound to the will of this Theus. And Zeen, if he still lived, was one of them.

The darkness seemed to press in on all sides, squeezing

the light of Yaz's star, speeding up its heartbeat. Whispers haunted the shadows and they all felt watched. Thurin continued to find his way with the same surety he showed in the Broken's territory.

'Demons live within this ice.' Thurin spoke loudly enough to be heard at the back. 'They want nothing more than to find their way under your skin. Let one in and it will fill your mind with its ugly thoughts and you'll lose yourself to its will. The longer we stay in the black ice the more certain that is to happen.'

In the next chamber the ice shaded darker still, save for the opposite wall where Yaz's light showed what seemed to be a bruise, the centre black but ringed with halos of colour, a deep maroon, a sickly yellow, a green that came from a different palette than the one used to paint Erris's world of grass and trees.

'Where demons of one particular sort gather the ice can take on their colour,' Thurin said. 'Red for rage, green for envy, the yellow ones particularly enjoy inflicting pain. You'll find many shades here. Where they come together they are black.'

Yaz moved slowly towards the blackest area where the ice devoured her light and returned not even a glint. The nothingness of it shared the same draw as the void in which Erris lived, the same fascination that dwelt in the jaws of the Pit of the Missing itself. This darkness held more than that though. The malice there, the ancient evil, the sense that it was waiting with endless patience for her touch, all of these turned that initial pull into a push. Even so, she pressed on, closing the gap still further.

'Yaz!' Thurin turned back. 'Don't!'

Yaz held her star before her and moved forward, pouring its light into the ice, sure that she must see something of the surface if she only got close enough. 'We're going into this stuff. It's going to be on all sides, under us, dripping on us. Better to find out about it here than a mile inside the Tainted's territory.'

'What's to find out?' Kao wrapped his thick arms around himself. 'It's evil and it hates us. I can tell that from here.'

Yaz pushed forward, the radiating malice almost a physical thing. The star in her hand blazed with blue-white light, and slowly, as the distance narrowed from feet to inches, the ice began to grey, revealing itself in glistening ridges. The effect was far from uniform, the blackness pushed back in a ragged circle but some patches of darkness proved more resistant than others, as dirt will cling here and there beneath a flow of water that has carried the bulk of it away.

One persistent black spot remained amid almost clear ice and Yaz nearly had to touch the star to it before with great reluctance it began to retreat into the thickness of the wall.

'The demons don't like stars. We know that,' said Petrick, unimpressed. 'It's all that's kept the black ice from spreading into our caverns.'

Yaz shrugged and retreated towards the group, not trusting the blackness not to leap out at her if she showed it her back. 'The Ictha find very little that is new to them, and when we do we like to look into it.'

'We have a much bigger star,' Quell said. 'Maybe we should—'

'No.' Thurin said it so fast that Yaz almost thought he might have voiced his objection just to disagree with Quell. 'Carrying something like that in there will alert all of them.'

Without waiting to argue he led them on into the next chamber. Yaz glanced at Quell, shrugged, and followed Thurin out.

He caught up with her swiftly, putting a hand to her arm and hissing just for her ears, 'I don't trust this one.'

Yaz shook his hand off and walked on, saying nothing. Quell gave everyone his trust until they betrayed him. This wasn't the Quell she knew above the ice or the Thurin she knew beneath it. She wondered for a moment if they were really at odds over her, engaged in some sort of unvoiced competition for her good regard. She pushed the foolish notion away. They couldn't be jealous of each other, surely? And besides, if they were competing for her respect then all they were achieving was to let it slip through their fingers.

A short way along the next tunnel Yaz reached an area of red ice that looked as if someone had dealt the wall a huge wound leaving old blood frozen in with the water. Passing it, she felt an echo of the anger stored there. Not anger at her in particular, just a bubbling rage of the sort that can lash out in any direction. It proved infectious, blowing at the embers of her own discontent, the fire of resentment she had started to bank even before the Ictha first had sight of the Black Rock. A fury at a world so set against giving her a place in it. She gritted her teeth, hastened her stride, and tried not to let the demons' anger become one with her own.

'Will we find the Tainted wandering alone?' Quina hissed as they advanced along a long tunnel through faintly grey ice. 'Because if they stay in a big group then what chance have we got?'

'I saw two,' Quell said. 'Both on their own.'

'What do they even do?' rumbled Kao. 'I mean, they're crazed, yes? They don't forge or scavenge or tend the fungi. Do they just wander around being mad?' He paused and his stomach chose the moment to growl. 'What do they eat?'

'They eat the fungi from the ground, or better still they eat the rats that eat the fungi.'

'Raw?' Quina wrinkled her nose, though until her drop Yaz was sure the girl had never eaten a cooked meal.

'Raw.' Thurin nodded. 'As for the rest, they stalk the Broken, looking for anyone they can steal without open conflict. But mostly they search the ice. Mining it. Melting it. Drinking it.'

Ahead of them the cavern they were crossing opened onto a much larger space and the roar of rushing water made itself known.

'Search for what?' Yaz asked.

'Once you're tainted you don't think to ask questions like that.' Thurin slowed as he approached the opening. 'Theus tells them they'll know when they find it. He tells them to mine the ice and bring it to the melting pools. Always digging, melting, drinking. The Tainted are full of demons, so it takes a strong new fiend to force its way into them. If they find one it normally ejects one of their weaker passengers. Sometimes, though, the tainted person's mind breaks entirely and demons flood into them until they contain a multitude. We call those eidolons. Very dangerous. Even Theus can't control those. They just wander off beneath the ice. Some say they find their way to the surface and haunt the world above.'

Thurin took them out into a space too large for Yaz to light. Before them a ravine ran through the rock, possibly an extension of the same cleft in the stone that the drying cave looked out over. Far below a hidden river churned the darkness, and reaching out to span the chasm was an ice bridge, ten yards long, a yard wide.

'Be watchful. The Tainted's territory properly begins on the far side.' Thurin waved them to gather around him. 'We used to maintain this bridge. I remember it being three times this wide.'

'We?' Quell asked.

'The Broken.' Thurin scowled.

'Is it safe?' Quina sounded worried.

'I doubt it's stood here all these years waiting for you to cross it so it can collapse.' Thurin smiled. 'Besides, if it's going to break when one of us crosses it then it's going to be for Kao not you. He weighs as much as the rest of us put together. We'll send him first.'

'Hey!' Kao actually took a step back.

'You've got to cross sometime. Why not first?' Thurin stretched out a hand to wave Kao on.

The boy blanched but with all eyes on him his pride wouldn't let him back down and he began a reluctant advance. Without saying anything Quell went after him, overtook, and stepped out onto the fragile span of ice.

Yaz made to follow him but Thurin took her arm. 'One at a time.'

She started to pull away but in the end surrendered to his logic rather than his strength. Instead she sent a beam of starlight lancing out across the chasm to interrogate the nearest of the dark tunnel mouths on the far side.

'Why don't they guard it?' Quina asked.

'Why would they?' Thurin looked grim. 'They want us to go in there.'

Kao crossed next, protesting that Quell had stolen his chance to test the bridge properly. Thurin followed. When Yaz's turn came she focused on ignoring the drop to either side, so reminiscent of the pit. She wondered if there was ever an end to 'down' in this world that she had for all her life explored almost entirely on one level. Did everywhere you might drop to have another fall waiting, another pit that might plunge you into a wholly new life if you survived the landing?

Quell's hands received her almost possessively as she reached the end of the bridge. Thurin, beaten to her side by Quell, stepped back to encourage Petrick on. Yaz watched the boy's awkward progress. His speed wouldn't save him if he lost his balance. It seemed odd to her that either faction in the conflict, the Tainted or the Broken, suffered the existence of the bridge. It wouldn't take a couple of gerants with hammers long to bring it crashing down. Perhaps in its way the bridge was a symbol of hope for both groups. The hope that they would prevail and claim what lay on the far side. Destroying the bridge would be an irrevocable act, an admission of failure, a statement that neither side seemed prepared to make.

'So the plan is just to wander around and hope that we bump into Zeen?' Quell directed the barbed question at Thurin, as if coming here had been his idea.

'I didn't know we had a plan,' Thurin replied. 'This is all madness. But we're running from madness too.' He looked tired, dark circles beneath his eyes, as though sleep had evaded him for several nights.

'We're going to find someone eventually,' Yaz said. 'And if it's not Zeen then we either don't show ourselves—'

Petrick snorted. 'We are carrying a light. Which we need. And the Tainted can see in the dark. They'll see us long before we see them.' He set the point of his sword against the icy rock and rested his hands on the pommel. 'I'll tell you how this will go down. We'll be advancing along and suddenly one or more of the Tainted will come howling at us out of the night. Others will hear them, and if we're not out of there fast then we'll have the whole lot on us. At that point being killed is the best we can hope for.'

'What in the hells are we doing here then?' asked Kao.

'It's a good question.' Petrick twirled his sword on its point. 'I just followed you. All I know is that Yaz wants her brother back and is scarily determined to do it. And since I just saw her turn Pome's own personal priest-given hunter against him, she's someone I want to stay close to. But marching straight in there is crazy. Unless Zeen happens to be the first of the Tainted to rush us then we've got no chance.'

'So how did Thurin get rescued if this is all so impossible?' Quina asked.

'His mother, Arka, and some of the warriors spent a long time stalking Tainted through the margins, the edge of their territory where there are areas with just about enough light to see in. Eventually they got lucky and found him on his own. And they still didn't manage to get clear without a fight.'

'We don't have time for that . . .' Yaz felt the beginnings of despair. She was risking all their lives and the chances of success seemed slim to none.

'I know a way.' Thurin started off along the tunnel into the darkness. Yaz could hear strain in his voice, as though he were fighting some internal battle. 'I can get us to the melting pools. There are places to hide, and the Tainted come there on their own mostly, dragging ice.'

'But the light,' Petrick said. 'They'll see us before—'

'I don't need to see to get us there.' Thurin stared down at his hands as if the admission shamed him. 'I was one of them for more than a year. And most of the Tainted can hardly see in the dark. They feel their way. Only the ones with really strong demons are able to see far without light, and then only if the demon moves into their eyes.'

Yaz set off after Thurin, dogged by guilt at expecting the others to follow, and knowing that if she paused too long to think things through she would retreat into indecision. Quell followed, and one by one so did the rest, drawn into the darkness by the bonds between them, the desire not to be alone, and the lack of options.

'Hide the star.' Thurin's voice came to Yaz from the gloom ahead, harsh with strain.

She quieted the star until it gave nothing but a glimmer of the sea at evening, then concealed it in her skins. 'Everyone take hold of the person ahead of you,' she hissed, and reached out to find Thurin even as Quell took a firm grip on her belt.

'Stay calm,' Petrick hissed as he followed the others. 'The demons find their way in most easily when you're angry. Any flaw can be exploited: cruelty, jealousy, hate. But anger's the hardest to avoid.'

Without talking now they walked blind into the Tainted's caverns. Of all of them, Thurin at the front and Petrick at the rear must have known the most fear: Thurin in particular, for he was returning to a nightmare already experienced, but Petrick too, having lived for years with this threat and tales of the waiting horrors. All of them were scared, however. No one walks blind into a night haunted by creatures like Hetta without fear.

Imagination turned every drip of meltwater and every groan of the ice into the approach of a monster. Yaz tried to dispel the feeling that Zeen was watching her, a twisted thing now, infested by demons that had wrung his flesh into new forms. The noise of the others behind her, their muffled footsteps, the breath drawn into their lungs, all of it combined to give the impression that the Tainted were gathering around them, corralling them, an awful hunger on their grinning faces.

The Tainted's territory seemed quite extensive. They stumbled on for what might have been a mile. Yaz tried not to brush against the ice. She could feel the hate emanating from it. Sometimes there were bands of anger, lust, or greed, but an ancient malice ran beneath all of these, the only constant. The menace of it wore at her and stray thoughts that were not her own crept across her mind. Given time she knew that this place would wear her down, get inside her.

'We're here.' Thurin's voice sounded different when he whispered. His breath tickled at Yaz's ear, making her shiver. 'Pass it on.'

The space felt like many they had passed through, open and cold, with ice-scraped rock beneath her feet.

She felt behind her and patted her way up Quell's bare arm to find his head. 'We're here.' She felt him nod. Solid, dependable.

The faint whisper travelled down the crouching line.

Thurin's hand discovered Yaz's in the blind darkness, his fingertips stroking between her fingers from knuckle to knuckle where her fist was knotted in his skins. A complicated shiver ran along her arm and into the core of her. Bare hands had been a revelation for her. The intimacy of this touch was too much. Almost. And here, in this place, with evil on every side and Quell at her back. She didn't understand.

Thurin did it again, more slowly this time, more intimate. Her grip loosened. Part of her wanted to hit him, strike him to the floor for being so forward, for presuming. The rest of her didn't know what she wanted. His palm brushed her wrist, pushing back her sleeve. She bit her lip against any sound she might make and pulled away.

In that instant he was gone. The faint sound of skins brushing skins and he left, moving away as he rose to his feet.

'. . .' Yaz opened her mouth but made no sound. She daren't hiss after him.

Without warning cries rang out. Quell twisted and lost his grip on her. Iron clattered across rock. More shouts and cursing, real terror in the mix.

A voice rang from the blackness of the cave, not close at hand but not too distant. 'You can bring that star out again, Yaz of the Ictha.'

Yaz had already been fumbling for it among her furs, hunting for the right pocket. Whoever had spoken it was not one of those who had entered with her. Her hand trembled around the star's blue glow. She opened her fingers and bid the light pour out.

Through slitted eyes she saw that Quell and the other four members of their group were crouched on the open floor, Quell with a bloody nose and without his iron spear. At the outer limits of the star's illumination well over a dozen figures stood in a loose circle around them, at least three of them gerant, many almost naked. Fear flooded through Yaz so swiftly it threatened to drown her. The Tainted watched with broad grins full of malice, just as her imagination had painted it.

'Zeen!' She saw her brother beside a barrel-chested gerant. Zeen wore only leggings, reduced to tatters below the knees, and across his neck and ribs black stains spread. She wanted to believe them bruises, but no bruises ever looked like these and his grin was as hate-filled as the rest. He stared at her with no sign of recognition.

Thurin stood just a few yards from her. A black stain covered much of his face and filled his eyes. The stain returned no light, so that against the background of darkness and black ice it looked almost as if that part of him had been bloodlessly taken, sliced away by some great knife.

Of all of them Thurin was the only one not to smile. He opened his mouth, white teeth framing a black tongue, and spoke again with a stranger's voice. 'You may call me Theus. I command here and have done so since long before your kind began to arrive beneath the ice.'

269

CHAPTER 23

Yaz stared in horror, unable to find words. Thurin had betrayed her. Her hand tingled where the monster had so recently stroked her flesh.

'Were you always in him?' It was Petrick who spoke, bleak-eyed, rising to his feet. One of the gerants had wrenched his sword from him in the dark, but he had his knife in hand now and pointed at Theus with it. 'Or did you catch him while he led us?'

Now Theus did smile. 'Oh, I never left the boy. I wrapped myself around his bones and came to have a look-see around your settlement.'

'Did he . . . did he know?' Yaz asked. A calm had descended on her. She would die before she let any demon enter her. This was the end she had fallen to. She was prepared to accept her death. She only hoped that she could take Zeen with her. 'Did he know he was carrying you?'

'Young Thurin?' Theus licked his lips with a black tongue, Thurin's lips. 'No. He thought the stars burned us out. And they did burn the others. They couldn't sink as deep as I did. But of course, I could be lying. I do like to lie. Honesty is one of the pieces of myself that I am still missing. One that I won't find here of course.' He waved a hand at the surrounding cavern. And in that moment Petrick lunged, faster than blinking, throwing himself across the gap between them, knife in hand. He almost made it, but some invisible force yanked him from the ground and held him just beyond reach of Theus.

'That was rather predictable.' Theus frowned, possibly with effort, and Petrick's feet lifted still further above the rock. He hung there, snarling, unable to drive himself forward. 'The human body is almost all water. You do understand this? And your friend Thurin has considerable influence over the stuff. Especially when it's me doing it and not caring if I break anything in here while I do.' Theus tapped Thurin's head with a finger.

Petrick drew back his hand to throw his knife but the same force wrapped him and his thin arm remained raised, trembling with effort.

Theus shook his head. 'If I let you throw that blade would you do it? Kill your friend? It would be no great inconvenience to me. I have many bodies. I'll have yours too if I like, and attacking me just makes it easier for me to find a way under your skin.'

In a blindingly fast advance Zeen shot from the shadowy margins to tackle Petrick, bringing him to the ground. Another of the Tainted came forward and set a foot to pin Petrick's wrist to the rock, immobilizing the knife.

'Now,' said Theus in a louder voice, a current of anger rippling beneath it. 'It happens to be very hard for me to be so reasonable for so long. Please don't try my patience. It's something else that I misplaced long ago.

'You are going to be inducted into our ranks and then, since obviously I know all about your domestic troubles with young Pome, we are going to conquer what remains of your territory. Adding you to my collection will make an already fairly uneven contest still more one-sided. Murder, bloodshed, oh my!

'The truth is that my friends here are an unruly lot and need to be allowed to indulge their baser instincts once in a while. In fact base instinct is all most of them are.' Gasps, wicked chuckles, and unhinged laughter rang around the circle at that. 'So I propose to let you go one at a time and hunt you. Some of you might even escape. Who knows?'

Yaz looked along the line of her companions: Quell, tensed and ready with murder in his eyes, Quina coiled and poised to strike, her hand on an iron knife at her hip. Kao scared but dangerous even so.

'We came here together and we'll fight you together,' she said, wondering if Thurin was still looking out at her from those wholly black eyes. 'We're ready to make you bleed.'

'Me?' asked Theus. 'Poor Thurin will do the bleeding. I will be fine. It's not my blood.' He pointed at one of the exits. 'Run, Yaz!' All around them the Tainted started to hiss and call, the largest gerant began to roar, a thunderous noise, and a crimson-eyed child, frothing at the mouth, screamed as if she had been set on fire.

Yaz forced more light from the star, setting its heartbeat racing. The thing vibrated in her hand and the Tainted fell back to the walls of the cavern, their shouting dying away. Zeen and the other Tainted abandoned Petrick but not before kicking the knife away. Only Theus stood his ground, though he squinted against the light and set his mouth in a grimace of pain.

'What a talented child you are,' he snarled through Thurin's teeth. 'But that fragment will burn out before it starts to do more than irritate me.' He looked at Kao and took a sudden step towards the boy, making him flinch. 'You should run. A big one like you might win free!'

'None of us are running,' Yaz said, afraid that if the Tainted started screaming and roaring again her nerve would break. She steadied her voice, coaxing still more light from the star. 'Why don't you tell us what you really want? It can't be just to capture the last handful of the Broken.' That didn't seem a particularly grand ambition for Theus to have nurtured for so long. 'What are you hunting for out here?'

Theus raised a hand and peered at her from behind the shadow it cast across his face. He rested his black gaze on Yaz and where the others among the Tainted radiated only hate and rage, she sensed something more complex in his stare. He shook his head slowly, seemingly in admiration, and clapped his hands together. 'Quina, you're the clever one. Why don't you tell Yaz what I'm doing in these miserable caves?'

Quina gave him a suspicious look. 'How would I know? Drinking demon-juice?'

'Hunting for something you've lost,' Kao said.

Theus smiled a black smile. 'Young Kao has it. Just drinking demon-juice, Quina? You've got to credit your enemy with some intelligence if you want to beat him. The Golin clan know that, so Kao knows it too. I've ridden many Golin over the years. Good workers. Don't ever think your enemy is just wasting their time.' He waved a hand at the black ice above them. 'The stars, as you call them, are said to purify. Their effect on my people, the ones who made them, is similar to their effect on your kind. They give voice to different parts of who we are and split them away. The Missing . . . let's call my people the Missing . . . the Missing purged themselves of anger, greed, malice, and all the other traits they considered to be impurities. What you call demons, the creatures like me that saturate the black ice, these are all unwanted elements of the Missing. They wanted to be gods: sublime, spiritual beings who could ascend to a new level of existence. They felt the more basic of their instincts pinned them to the dirt, imprisoned them in their flesh. And so they shed these things, carving them away with stars of which you have seen only fragments. They trapped these unwanted pieces of themselves in impregnable vaults, and they moved on.' Theus seemed to relish an audience and looking at the Tainted Yaz could understand why. All of them, even Zeen, seemed barely restrained, not really listening to what was being said, just a heartbeat from violence, as if each of them were the fragments Theus described, too shallow to hold onto much interest in the world beyond the exercise of their singular passions. In many ways the title that the Broken had taken for themselves would sit better with Theus and his fellow demons, so broken that they could act only when infecting someone else like a disease beneath the skin.

'The vaults weren't so impregnable as they thought though?' Yaz gazed at the snarling faces of the Tainted. She avoided looking at Zeen. It hurt too much to see the madness in him. 'You got out.'

Theus made a mock bow. 'Time is a digger, time scratches and claws its way into any prison sooner or later. Time is not a healer – it's a destroyer. Time is ruin. Time opens old wounds. The ice scraped away the cities that the Missing had abandoned, and one by one the ancient vaults failed. We spilled out into that ice. Creatures like me. Broken pieces, overpowered by our nature.

'Over years, however – decades, centuries – I did what my fellow escapees seem unable to do and set my will to regathering myself. I did not agree to being torn apart and discarded. When I have reunited all that was shriven from the original me I plan to seek out the rest among the golden halls of the Missing and make myself whole once more. A person rather than a thing.

'So the truth is simple. Those that you call the Tainted are hunting something, and what they're hunting is me. Pieces of who I was, scattered amid a multitude, lost among screaming millions. And very shortly you will be joining them in that search. So, I—'

'It's not going very well, is it?' Yaz didn't know where her courage was coming from. Perhaps it was just the certainty that her chances had fled and that the death she had expected at the end of her fall had arrived. 'It sounds as if you've been looking for years. Generations? What do you have them do? Chip at the ice, melt it, drink it, hoping to randomly find the other little demons that together make whatever monstrosity you are?'

Theus stalked towards her. She felt Thurin's ice-work like a giant hand squeezing around her, trying to compel the blood inside her to move at his command, attempting to lift her from her feet. She ground her teeth together and struggled to find some muscle in her mind that could resist him. Quell stepped between them with the same hard and determined look she had first seen when he faced the hunter in the city. A moment later the invisible force of Thurin's magic tossed him aside, seeming to find it easier to get a grip on Quell than on her.

'I won't ever let one of your kind control me.' Yaz clenched the star burning in her hand. The room dimmed, and as she focused on her glowing fist her full weight rested once more on the rock. She had said they wouldn't run, so she stood her ground. She opened her hand to let the light out once more. 'You can't own me.'

'You know,' said Theus, drawing ever closer, 'I believe you.' He held her gaze with his unreadable black eyes, the stain moving slowly across his face, pouring into his mouth, coiling about his neck, Thurin's neck, like a serpent.

Suddenly there were hands on her arms, the star shaken from her fingers to roll across the rock. A gerant had her from behind. Quina leapt to attack, Kao bellowed and charged. All at once it was chaos and Theus had the cold blade of a knife against her neck. Quell found his feet, his roar almost as loud as the screams and howls of the Tainted. He took the eight-foot gerant trying to wrestle him and slung the man across the room with undiminished Ictha strength.

Yaz ignored the knife and fought to free herself but the gerant's strength overmatched her. She had expected to die. She hadn't thought it would be Thurin's knife that killed her though, or that they would be face to face at the moment her life ended. His eyes cleared, a desperate horror filling them as the darkness drained away. Still, the hand holding the blade to her neck did not retreat. All around them were the sounds of struggle, cries of pain and rage, but even now she couldn't look away from Thurin.

'I believe you,' Theus repeated with his impossibly black tongue. 'And if you can't be tamed . . . what use are you?'

'The stars!' Yaz blurted. 'The stars can help you!'

'The stars *did* this. The stars broke us apart. Even now, like this, they hurt us.'

The sounds of struggle diminished around Yaz as the Tainted brought her friends down. Only Quell remained on his feet, his bruised face running crimson from a scalp wound. He wrestled with a gerant while a woman, her face almost as red but from demon-stain rather than blood, beat at his shoulders and head with a large thighbone. The unaccustomed fury on Quell's face made Yaz fear that the demons were already in him. Surely they would be soon.

'I know the stars hurt you! I've seen it!' Yaz fought to keep her voice steady and loud. The knife pressed at her throat, a cold, hard line. 'The stars drive demons back through the ice, but the strongest are last to retreat. Couldn't that help your search? If a star drives back the tide, pushes away the multitude, wouldn't the last to go be most likely to be fragments of you?'

Theus stood back to regard her. Close by another Tainted threw himself at the back of Quell's knees and he finally went down beneath the gerant still grappling with him.

'That's . . . not entirely stupid.' Theus seemed taken aback. He took the knife from her neck and toyed with the blade. 'It would take a big star though, to have much of an effect.'

'I have one. From a hunter.' Yaz shook her arms free of the gerant's grip.

'A star that large would break you,' Theus said. 'Not that I care but it would let the many in the black ice flood into you and you'd be useless to me.'

'No, I can resist it.' Yaz reached towards her fallen star and it shot back into her hand. 'You've already seen what I can do.'

Theus's face twitched, a snarl on his lips, wild anger, raw hatred, and something else holding them back but just barely. He answered through his teeth. 'I will think on it.' He took a coil of hide rope from Thurin's pack, forcing his face to calmness. 'For now give me your wrists.'

Yaz shrank back. 'No.'

Theus looked meaningfully across to where Quina stood, stretched between two Tainted, each holding a wrist in two hands. Both of the men were bleeding from gashes that she had apparently cut into them. A third Tainted, this one a young girl, had recovered Quina's knife and came to stand in front of the trapped hunska.

'Present your wrists or the little one there will show us all what you people keep inside your bellies. It's actually quite surprising, though rather disgusting. You wouldn't believe the length of intestine that can be pulled—'

'Here.' Yaz raised her crossed wrists. 'Just do it.'

CHAPTER 24

'Where's Kao?' Yaz could see nothing. The cave to which they had been dragged was cold, dry, and utterly dark.

'They must have taken him a different way.' Yaz hardly recognized Quina's voice and realized the girl must be trying not to cry.

'This is bad.' Petrick sounded utterly dispirited.

'How are we going to escape?' Quell asked at her side. From the strain running through his words Yaz guessed he was trying to break his bonds again.

No one answered and even though she couldn't see them Yaz felt that each of the others was looking her way. She'd never asked to be the leader but it seemed that that was what happened when you convinced people to follow your ideas. She had brought them here, hunting her brother, and somehow she'd acquired responsibility for all their lives.

'I don't know.' They'd made her leave her star, reduced to a faint glow. None of her friends had weapons. They were all tied, and blind once more in the dark. Lost. She wanted to ask their forgiveness but knew that she didn't deserve it and that asking would remove the last strand of their hope.

'I think my offer was a good one. I hope Theus agrees to it.' But whether the creature inside Thurin was sufficiently rational to see where its best interests lay, Yaz was far from sure.

They lapsed into silence. Yaz found herself shivering, the cold having as much to do with it as her fears did. Working with the stars really had removed the last traces of Ictha resilience from her. She shuddered to think what havoc the winds above the ice would wreak upon her weakened body.

She thought about how shockingly thin Zeen had looked. Yaz had never seen starvation before she threw herself into the Pit of the Missing. The wind up above wouldn't allow anyone to grow thin. The cold would kill a person long before their ribs began to show.

Time passed in its slow way. None of them had much to say and the ice spoke into the silence between them, its groans seeming a lament.

Yaz wriggled her way to Quina and found her shivering. They huddled together for warmth, saying nothing. Quina's silence heightened Yaz's sense of guilt. She liked Quina. She liked her quick mind and her humour though it often came with a sharp edge. Given more time they could have been close friends. Quina who had saved her from falling to her death in the city. Quina who despite her toughness had stolen that wooden bead and kept it close to her heart, hoping that those who valued the trinket more than they did her might recover them both. Quina who always had something to say . . .

Quell worked at his bonds but without light, a weapon, and direction there seemed little to be gained in freeing hands and feet save some modicum of pride and a little comfort.

Whispers spoke in Yaz's head, hate-filled, mocking, urging

violence, telling her that she had killed her friends. Sometimes it was hard to tell which voices were her own. She had led her friends to their death. The black ice pressed on her though no part of her body touched it. Soon it would find a way inside her and her companions. Petrick was already muttering as though he were responding to voices inside his head.

'Stay quiet!' A new voice hissed at Yaz's ear, and for a long moment she was unsure if it was inside her or just very close by. A blade began to saw at the hide strips around her wrists. 'And be quick when I tell you to move.'

'Maya?' It seemed beyond reason that little Maya should be here.

'Ssssssh!' The girl moved on to the bonds around Yaz's ankles. 'We don't have much time. I had to kill one of them.'

Kill? For a moment Yaz wondered if Maya had been taken by a demon. She sounded very different to the timid child who hardly seemed to have stopped trembling from her drop.

Yaz rubbed her wrists and waited for Maya to free the others. 'How can we get out?' she whispered as the girl returned to her.

'I can see in the dark,' Maya murmured. 'And you have this.'

Something soft swung against Yaz's hands. A wrap of rat skin on the end of a long cord. She fumbled with it, already sensing the quiescent star inside. Pome's star, recovered from the chamber where they had been captured. Maya had dragged it behind her to avoid its effects.

'Keep it hidden until we need it,' Maya said. 'Take hold of me. I'll lead you out.'

Quell's hand patted for Yaz's belt, the others shifting positions to form a line.

'Wait!' Yaz hissed. 'What about Zeen, and Kao . . . and Thurin?'

'They're lost. Finished.' Iron ran through Maya's voice. 'In war you have to learn to let go.'

Yaz suddenly understood that this was Maya's clan speaking through her. The Axit remembered their days of war and taught the arts of it with a fervour, as though it were as important as knowing how to fish or how to pitch a tent against the wind. 'I can't let go of them.' Yaz reached for the girl, finding her small frame in the dark and taking hold. 'You didn't let go of us.'

'I need you to complete my mission. Come on. Quickly. No talking.' She moved off, tugging Yaz along.

Mission? Yaz bit back on her questions and moved as quietly as she could. The others weren't lost. She couldn't allow that. But she did need to escape if she was ever going to be able to help them.

Maya led them, making no sound herself. Yaz tried to emulate the girl's stealth. Quell, Quina, and Petrick managed to avoid stumbling or scuffing their feet behind her. They hadn't gone far before Yaz smelled the blood and stink of whoever Maya had murdered on her way in. She prayed that it wasn't Zeen, but didn't ask.

Yaz wondered why the demons from the corpse hadn't invaded Maya, but maybe they required the killing to be done in a rage or motivated by malice in order to make the cracks the demons needed to find their way into someone. Yaz wasn't sure that dispassionate murder was better. If you were going to take someone's life, shouldn't it matter? Yaz didn't know how to feel about this new Maya any more than she knew how to feel about the new Thurin. Both of them had revealed a hidden aspect that – even though it left what she had known of them before unchanged – still changed who they were.

Fifty yards further on Maya stopped and reached round to unhook Yaz's fingers from her furs. 'Wait.'

She moved off ahead. Moments later a sharp sigh broke the darkness and something heavy slumped to the ground. Maya returned, smelling of blood. 'Hurry.'

It seemed to Yaz that rather than the gerants with their seven-foot iron greatswords, it might be a small girl with murder in her heart and impressive marjal shadow-work that was the deadliest thing under the ice. At least the deadliest thing with a pulse.

Maya called another halt. 'Pome's hunter is still rampaging,' she hissed. 'It was on the edge of the Taints' territory not long ago. That might be why you were tied and left. So they could try to deal with it.'

Far off Yaz began to hear the clash of metal on metal, perhaps a hunter running. It grew a little louder then slowly faded.

Maya led off again. They moved faster now. At one point Yaz banged her head on the low ice ceiling and filled the darkness with her own personal stars. She carried on, cursing silently.

The malice-soaked darkness clawed at them as they moved from chamber to chamber. Sometimes Maya doubled back, sometimes she had them squeezing through tunnels almost too tight for Yaz and Quell. On two more occasions Maya left them to scout ahead. Whether any more killing occurred on these trips, Yaz didn't know. Twice, when Maya was with them, unearthly screams rang out close at hand, shattering the silence. And always the black ice was heaping doubt upon their shoulders, filling them with the certainty that escape was as far away as it had ever been. Yaz even found herself half convinced that Maya was deliberately leading them in circles.

In some of the warmer chambers the ice was melting. The first splat of black water hit the back of Yaz's neck and ran beneath her hides, freezing and yet burning at the same time. Whispers filled her mind, the words almost loud enough to hear. She ignored them, worried that to pay them attention might be to invite the demons under her skin.

With Maya looking out for them Yaz worried less about Tainted rushing unseen upon them and more that it might be Quina or Petrick who turned on them, driven mad by demons just as Zeen had been. Quell she didn't worry about. He hadn't succumbed even when fighting for his freedom in the heart of the black ice and her worry that he might have been now shamed her. The idea that Quell could be turned seemed as crazed as the thoughts that the demons tried to ignite within her skull. Her life stood on several pillars, and Quell's steadfast loyalty had proven more sturdy than the devotion of her parents or the solidity of the ice.

They moved on and it seemed to Yaz that some grey hint of light had insinuated itself about them. Even the malice of the ice felt blunted. Behind them, distant but not distant enough, a roar of primal rage echoed through the caverns. A moment later another howl rang out, louder and closer.

'We need light and speed,' Maya hissed.

Yaz tore her star from its pouch and woke its light, keeping it at a level that wouldn't blind them after so long without sight. The ice had greyed to the point that it returned enough of a glimmer for them to avoid running into walls. They raced on with Maya in the lead, her sense of direction seemingly unerring even under the stress of pursuit.

Another hundred yards of panting and sprinting and they came blinking into the twilight of the ravine. The ice bridge stood only a short way off, the hidden river churning far below.

Maya led the way along the narrow rock ledge between the ice and the ravine. Yaz found herself wanting to shout at the girl to hurry while at the same time not wanting to move so swiftly across wet rock with the terrifying drop to one side and the dull malice of the grey ice wall to the other.

Maya reached the bridge and started to cross just as the Tainted began to boil out from tunnels and cavern mouths all along the dark side of the ravine.

'Run!' Maya shouted and followed her own advice, almost slipping from the bridge before she reached the relative safety of the far side.

Yaz released her fear in a wild scream and ran across the narrow span of wet ice. Quell pounded along after her.

'Yaz of the Ictha!' Theus's voice boomed out, somehow louder than the roar of the hidden waters below them. 'We have a deal!'

Yaz turned to see Theus standing at the place they had emerged from only a few moments earlier while the Tainted rushed past him. A couple of yards ahead of him a lean man in ragged skins paused to fling Quell's iron spear, arching his whole body into the throw like an Ictha whaling on the Hot Sea. The length of iron arced over the heads of the Tainted in front of him, passing by the ear of a gerant closer to the bridge. Yaz saw the whole of the weapon's trajectory in a frozen moment, lacking any time to move or even scream.

Petrick, at the start of the bridge and just yards ahead of those leading the chase, saw the spear, as did Quina ahead of him. Both of them, having hunska blood, rotated with inhuman speed, twisting their bodies since the ice wouldn't give them the traction to turn.

The gleaming spearhead cut through the air towards Petrick's chest. He found himself unable to move out of its way but somehow in a blur of motion he managed to deflect its flight so that it merely scored his ribs, passing beneath his armpit.

For a moment Yaz thought Petrick had won clear of the danger. His momentum carried him on towards the middle of the bridge but the shove he'd given the spear to turn its course had unbalanced him too. Again a heartbeat stretched into a paralysed age as Yaz watched the boy begin to fall with painful slowness, one foot slipping over the edge, arms pin-wheeling.

Incredibly, Quina had turned and was running with fierce determination towards both Petrick and the Tainted. It seemed impossible that she would reach him though. The dark-haired girl ran faster than Yaz thought any human could, her feet sliding on the ice, lungeing for Petrick's outstretched hand.

Suddenly the moment released Yaz and ripped her scream from her.

Petrick fell, the horror on his face swallowed by the black mats of his hair rising around his face. The gap between his fingertips and Quina's narrowed to inches, then suddenly yawned wide and he was gone.

Quina, unable to halt her advance on the ice bridge, leapt at the leading Tainted, a broad-shouldered woman, and kicked off from her chest. The action sent the woman back into her fellows, spilling one into the ravine, and sent Quina sliding back across the bridge onto the safety of Yaz's side.

Yaz made her star a blaze of light and threw it into the cavern mouth behind her to block the way against the Tainted as Quina raced through. After that they ran, all of them flat out, Quina vanishing ahead, Maya falling behind, until at last, after many caverns and hundreds of yards, Yaz found her resolve and came to a halt. Quell pulled up alongside her, composed and ready where she was a breathless mess.

'We shouldn't stop,' he said.

'But Maya!'

'She does things to the shadows. They won't find her.'

The shouts of the Tainted were very distant now. The star had either held them back until it burned itself into nothing or they had managed to bypass it but been delayed.

'We should go,' Quell said.

'Wait. She can't be far behind.' Part of Yaz wanted to keep running, and not just to put distance between her and the Tainted, but to stop the truth of Petrick's death catching up with her. Quina would feel it badly too: she had liked Petrick and had sought time in his company. Perhaps she was still running from her grief somewhere far ahead of them.

'Let's at least move to the wall then.' Quell stepped away from the centre of the chamber. 'Can you dim the light in here?'

'Petrick fell!'

'I saw.' Quell nodded grimly, black against the bands of stardust running through the ice chamber.

'We should—'

'We need to get out of this place, back onto the ice where we belong.'

'I need to go back for Zeen. And the others. I need to save—'

'You can't save everyone, Yaz. You just can't. I don't like that this place exists any more than you do. But it's here for a reason. Nobody down here would survive on the ice. There's nowhere for them to go. Even if the ice does run out thousands of miles to the south . . . none of them could ever get there.' Quell raised his open hands, muscles straining against each other as if trying to claw the truth from the air itself and make her see it. 'We can save ourselves. I thought we could save Zeen. We tried and we failed. The rest of them we were never going to be able to help.'

Yaz shook her head. 'I don't accept that. I can't accept it.'

'We need to forget this hole. Everything will be all right again once we're out. The regulator said—'

Yaz looked at him sharply. 'The regulator said what?'

Quell frowned and rubbed his forehead as if it pained him. He shook the question away and beckoned her to join him by the ice. 'Make it darker!'

Yaz stayed where she stood out in the open. 'Quell—'

The sound of running feet interrupted her. One person with a light footfall. 'Maya?'

As though summoned by her name Maya came hurrying out of the gloom, trailing shadows into the chamber, her knife in her fist, the blade bloody.

'We should go,' she said.

CHAPTER 25

They couldn't find Quina. For Yaz that was the last load that made the ice break beneath her. Something snapped deep in her chest, the loss of Thurin and Kao and Petrick hit her like a hammer and sobs broke from her. She found herself calling for Quina, careless of who or what else might hear. Quell had to wrestle her to the floor and all the walls pulsed and blazed as the stars echoed with her grief.

Maya spoke into the silence that followed. 'We need to get to the city.'

Yaz allowed herself to be led, Quell at her side, Maya ahead, scouting for danger. Maya seemed to be a new person, as though the timid child had been shrugged away like a cloak to reveal something hard and full of purpose.

They saw no one, heard nothing save the groan and drip of the ice. Yaz's resolve returned by degrees. The magnitude of her failure had frozen her thoughts but a slow thaw was setting in. She felt ashamed. She was Ictha and the Ictha endured no matter what was heaped upon them. The world above had been taken away from her, and now piece by piece the world below was being stolen too. Yaz knew she had been foolish to try to dream new dreams. She didn't deserve happiness. But even so, she would fight to the end, just as all her clan did, even if their eyes were no longer turned her way, even if none of them ever knew what end she fell to. She would not surrender, not go gentle into her fate.

In one of the brighter chambers Yaz turned and went to the wall while Quell watched, keeping any question to himself. She reached into the ice with her mind, listening to the song of the stars, filtering through the beats of their many tiny hearts. Then with both palms to the cold surface she sent out a slow rhythm, the heartbeat of a star as large as the ones inside hunters. She sped the beat, sped it again, and once more, until finally she found an answering resonance. Deep within the ice one star now burned far brighter than all the rest, the largest within many yards of her. She spoke to it, trying to picture the complex sigil set into the iron of the forging pot. The star dimmed, and almost imperceptibly it began to sink as the extra heat it now radiated melted a path through the ice. Yaz drew it to her. It took time and the blades of a headache began to cut their way inwards from behind her eyes, but before too long the star popped from the ice wall and dropped into her hand amid a rush of lukewarm water. A greenish star about half the size of Pome's. It reminded her of Erris among the trees, and for a moment she stood staring at it in her palm, lost in its song.

'Yaz.' Quell set a hand to her shoulder.

'We can go now,' she said, and let the star slip from her fingers into a slow orbit around her head and shoulders.

'What was Thurin saying, before they left us, about searching for himself?' Quell asked. 'It made no sense. Is he just mad?' Maya had gone ahead again to scout the way and they crouched together in a dim cavern.

'That wasn't Thurin. The monster in him—'

'A man is what he has inside him,' Quell said, brooking no argument.

Yaz made no reply. She was thinking about Elias and the needle that he had told her would show the way to another part of him. She wasn't sure what Elias was but he seemed a very different creature to Theus. He'd seemed whole and balanced, just weak, where Theus was strong but clearly the collection of fractured pieces that he claimed to be. And Theus lived out here in the muck and blood of the real world whereas Elias dwelt in the strange dreamworld that Erris had shown her.

Yaz shook her head and took hold of her new star again. She was just a girl from the ice. The wars of gods and demons lay beyond her understanding. 'All I know is that we need a star. One much bigger than this one.'

In one of the harvest caves they found bloodstains and trampled fungi, and further on an encroaching tendril of black ice, killing all the fungi around it, leaving just grey husks. Once Quell knelt to examine strange scratches on the rock. 'Pome's hunter has been here.'

'Or some other.' Yaz kept her eyes on the cavern's exits.

It wasn't until they finally reached the long slope and reunited with Maya that Yaz dug her heels in and stopped allowing herself to be led.

'What are we going to do?' she asked.

'We're going to escape,' Quell said.

'How do you propose that we do that?'

'You were the one convincing us all that we could survive on the ice, head south, find the green land,' Maya said. 'You must have an idea.' The look on Maya's face suggested she already suspected that Yaz didn't.

'Well . . .' Yaz felt fresh guilt at the reminder of her role in taking their friends to the taint. Now that she had to say it out loud her plan sounded too thin to have ever rested their hopes on. 'All this iron the scavengers collect and the forgers work. It has to go to the priests. So someone must know when—'

'The next collection is soon, a day or two at most. Maybe less than that,' Quell said with confidence.

'No,' Maya said. 'The next collection is in twenty-three days.'

Quell snorted. 'You're wrong.' He set a hand to Yaz's shoulder. 'Wait here with me. The collection will be soon. We can escape with—'

'Twenty-three days.' Maya narrowed her eyes at Quell. 'I know this one is your clan, Yaz, but he has been here less time than us and alone for most of it. How would he know?'

'How would *you* know, child?' Quell retorted, an unusual anger flaring in him.

Confused as to how everyone seemed to know more than her, Yaz turned to face Maya. 'Back there in the black ice. You said something about a mission.'

'She said she needed you to complete her mission.' Quell frowned and looked uncomfortable. Most un-Quell-like.

'Iron is power.' Maya met Yaz's eyes with a bold stare. The soft lines of her face had hardened into something fierce over the days since her drop. 'The priesthood use that power to dominate the tribes. The Axit do not live that way. We fight for our freedom!'

'But you need iron like the rest of us,' Yaz said. 'So you accept their laws.'

'No. We fight.' Anger flashed in her brown eyes. 'But the first part of any fight is to understand the enemy. The priests say they mine and smelt iron from the heart of the Black Rock. They say there is coal and ore to be had. But the Axit have long watched them and the smokes that escape that mountain are not sufficient. For days to either side of the gathering the Black Rock pours smoke but in the months when the priests believe the clans are chasing seas the chimneys barely trickle.'

Quell smiled. 'And yet there is a great pit melted through the thickness of the ice just a few miles from their mountain.'

Maya nodded. 'And so every Axit child is told that if they are ever thrown into the pit it is their duty to discover the secrets of the iron and escape with that knowledge.'

'And what then?' Yaz asked. 'They say thank you very much and throw you back in?'

Maya scowled but Yaz could tell that her question had hit the mark.

'Do you know how they get the iron out?' Yaz asked.

Maya nodded. 'They put stars in two sigil pots and lower them on wires to rapidly melt two narrow holes all the way through the ice. The water pours out through the roof of the city cavern. They pour coal down one of the holes and clog it up. Then they call a coal-worm somehow and it follows the line of coal, melting a big wide hole, with all the water draining through the other narrow hole they made.

'The worm veers off before it falls through the ceiling but they can melt through the last bit themselves. And then they lower a cage for the iron loads and haul them up. When it's all finished ice-workers at this end seal the hole so a new pit doesn't start, and the flow of the ice squeezes the rest shut after a while. When the Pit of the Missing moves too far away from the city they start a new one here. They do that about every thirty years or so.'

Yaz and Quell looked at Maya in astonishment.

'You did not hear all that just eavesdropping for a few days!' Yaz said.

'And no elder would have laid all their secrets bare to someone so new, surely?' Quell frowned.

'I asked Petrick,' Maya said. 'Made him feel awkward for not knowing. Then I spied on him during the sleep periods until he went and demanded that Arka give him the answers.' She shrugged. 'You just have to know how people work. Petrick didn't care about not knowing until it put him in the same basket as a girl still wet from her drop. Then he *had* to know. The next collection is in twenty-three days.'

Yaz's mind plagued her with images of Petrick's slow, inevitable fall from the bridge. He'd been the one to save her from Hetta when she was still dripping from the pools. She shook the thoughts away. 'You're thinking we should ride up in the cage?'

Maya nodded. 'I am.'

'In twenty-three days? Theus will have taken all the caverns by then, unless Pome regains control of his hunter. And if that happens Pome will have all of the caverns and we won't be much better off than we would with Theus. That new star of Pome's has tainted him . . . as if he weren't bad enough before.'

'We could hide in the city.' Even Maya sounded doubtful, and she could hide herself in shadow.

'There are things down there that would kill us quicker than Pome or Theus would,' Quell said.

'You have a better idea?' Maya asked, her expression growing fierce again.

Quell turned away, his hands in fists at his sides. He started to walk down the long slope towards the city cavern, kicking at the ground as he went. Yaz had never seen him like this, angry, unsure of himself.

She was on the point of starting to follow when he spun

around and marched back, his face dark. 'Yaz . . .' He faltered before her stare.

'What is it?'

He reached into his furs and brought out a small yellow star, no bigger than the nail on his little finger. Holding it seemed to pain him and he held it out to her, gesturing for her to take it.

Yaz lifted it from between Quell's finger and thumb without touching it, and let it hang in the air between them alongside the as-yet-unasked questions about its existence. The star shone a sour yellow light and its song seemed out of key. Something about it made her think of black strips of skin fluttering in a breeze.

'He said I could save you,' Quell said helplessly. 'But I had to lie to you. If you knew he was behind it then—'

'But *you* were behind it . . . *you* came to save me.' Yaz had never understood when the stories spoke of heartbreak but something was breaking in her chest now. 'Quell?' She drew in a shuddering breath to steady her voice. 'You stole the harness ropes to—'

'They gave the ropes to me because the regulator told them to.' Quell hung his head. 'I didn't even need the ropes. The priest told me I would be safe if I leapt in. But I was too scared to jump . . .'

Yaz snatched the yellow star from the air. Instantly she had flashes of scars seared across face and scalp, the sigil shapes familiar from the walls of the Missing's city. The gaunt and sour lines of the priest's face. The Icthan whiteness of his irises. She released it as if bitten. 'You used this to schedule an early collection of iron?'

Quell nodded. 'I can't talk to him but he said if I held it and thought hard about you he would know I was ready and would arrange the collection.'

'So he knows we're coming. They'll all be waiting for us out on the ice when they haul us up? Ready to capture us.' Yaz shook her head. 'Quell, how could you?'

'How could I what?' He sounded angry now. 'How could I want to bring you home? You just threw yourself into the hole. You didn't have to. You left us. You left me! And now you're cross with me because I needed help to save you?'

'You should have told me you were working with the regulator.'

'I was scared you wouldn't come back with me. I didn't understand what had happened to you. To your mind.' He took a breath and spread his hands in incomprehension. 'You threw yourself down the pit, Yaz!'

'Zeen—'

'Yes, Zeen! I know. It was bad. But a score of children go down the pit every gathering. Nobody throws themselves after them. Nobody. Not even the mothers. Certainly not a sister!'

'Well, maybe they should!' Yaz practically screamed the words and the sound echoed back from the roof above the long slope, fading into silence as the two of them stood facing each other, fists balled, breathing hard as if they'd been wrestling.

That she had jumped. That was what stood at the heart of it. What had pushed her and what had pulled her. Theus had said that everyone was searching for themselves, and evil as he was Yaz saw a certain truth in his words. She had always been a mystery to herself, a battle between the pieces that Theus said the Missing cut away and discarded. Had she been escaping her life? Saving Zeen? Railing against the injustice that she had been saved from only by a hair's breadth? Quell stared at her, his eyes demanding an answer. Yaz could only shake her head.

Maya was the first to speak again. 'Then we wait here a day or two and ride the collection cage up.' She began to walk down the long slope and, after a short pause, Quell turned to follow her.

Yaz watched them go, past the warding pillars and into the glow of the city cavern. She held the regulator's star between finger and thumb, willing its light down to a whisper and then down again until she held nothing but a translucent yellow globe. She found a pocket for it, and released a long, slow sigh. Then, still deep in her thoughts, she followed the other two into the ruined city.

Quell made slow progress, pausing to watch for any signs of hunters before darting on to the next cover. Yaz caught up with him amid a small forest of metal girders, bent by some ancient flow of ice that had defied the upwelling heat, yet unrusted by the years, subject only to a slow powdery corrosion.

The collective song of the stars overhead, tiny and numberless, pervaded the whole cavern. Yaz hadn't noticed it on her previous visit but her sense for such things had sharpened. The ancient refrain filled the silences between the groaning of the ice. Amid the girders it seemed closer to a dirge than Yaz had ever heard it. The unvoiced chorus somehow sketched the city that had once towered here, suggesting form and shapes, eulogizing lost beauty.

'What I don't understand' – Quell cut across her contemplations – 'is if the regulator made the hunters – and the fact that he gave one to Pome seems to back up what you learned in the city – then why on Abeth would he set them to guarding the city and killing the Broken? They're attacking the very people trying to gather the iron the priests need for trade.'

Quell made a good point. So good in fact that it overcame Yaz's resolve not to talk to him. 'They take them.'

'What?'

'The hunters take the Broken that they get hold of. Nobody knows what they do to them. The bodies aren't found.'

Quell pressed his lips into a flat line – it was the way he looked in the tent. Lamp-lit, considering a difficult move in the game of eight. 'Well, it still doesn't make sense.'

Maya waited for them at the crack through which Arka had first led them down into the city chambers. She stood staring down into the darkness below. 'We don't have any food.'

'Or water,' Quell replied.

'It doesn't matter.' Yaz took the regulator's star from her pocket, held it out over the edge of the chasm, and let it fall. She looked slowly from Quell to Maya. 'You both turned out to be different from the person I thought you were.'

Quell winced. 'Yaz—'

'I haven't changed though. Somewhere in all that escaping and running away I forgot who I was.' She looked out over the ice-scoured rock, scarred by the city's foundations. 'I threw myself down here after Zeen and I'm not going anywhere without him. Or', she said, 'any of the others. I'm taking them all back.'

'That's madness, Yaz.' Quell reached for her, but thought better of it and let his arm fall.

'It would take a miracle to get them out of Theus's clutches,' Maya said.

'Yes, it will.' Yaz gazed back at the long slope. 'But while I was down in the city I met someone who knows all about miracles.'

CHAPTER 26

'I'm going down into the city to find my friend.' Yaz looked at the others, daring them to object. 'Maya, you're going to the settlement to scavenge water flasks, heat pots, salt, and anything else that could come in handy on the ice. Quell, you're going harvesting. Bring as many fungi as you can find and pile them up somewhere discreet. When you've got a really big heap team up with Maya and start bringing material for shelters and sleds. Lightweight boards and the means to join them together. The settlement must have plenty to spare.'

'If you're going into the city, I'm coming with you,' Quell said.

'No. You're going to do what I said.' Yaz turned and looked behind her, stretching out a hand. 'This is coming with me.' The hunter's star rolled from the distant hollow she had placed it in after freeing it from the ice. It looked like a ball of iron still cooling from the forge, glowing a dull red in places, a darker red elsewhere, almost black. Maya and Quell backed away along the chasm edge as it approached, a little smaller than Yaz's fist, its heartbeat the pitter-patter of a child's.

'I still don't see how this Edris—'

'Erris,' Yaz said.

Quell scowled. 'Erris. I don't see how one man is going to—'

'You'll understand when you see him.'

'He's like a hunter but friendly?' Maya asked.

'It's more complicated than that. But yes.'

Maya frowned. 'Couldn't you just . . . build your own hunter with that?' She nodded to the red star that had rolled to a stop at Yaz's feet. 'I mean, you seem so good with the stars and you say the regulator built them . . .'

'I don't know how long that took him,' Yaz said. 'It's not something I know how to do.' And besides, she didn't want to build monsters like the regulator had. She wanted friends beside her. If she could get Erris to come with her the Tainted would be powerless against him.

'This is madness,' Quell said. 'We don't need to do it. We can just go back.'

'Doing what you ask would put my mission at risk,' Maya said.

Yaz picked up the hunter's star and let it glow more brightly. She narrowed her eyes at Maya. 'You said you came after us in the black ice because you needed us to complete your mission. Or did you just need me? Were you hoping to trade me to the priests if you couldn't escape to tell your discoveries to the Axit? Hoping if they had me they might not care about letting you run off to die on the ice?' Yaz felt another weight settle on her already heavy heart. She'd thought Maya came back for them all out of loyalty and friendship. 'Well, the priests *will* be waiting. And I'm not coming without the rest of us.'

Maya at least had the grace to look shamed and studied her feet for a moment.

'Just do what I asked,' Yaz said. 'You both know it's the right thing.' She set the hunter star orbiting her and lowered herself over the edge of the chasm onto the narrow path Arka had shown them.

She met their eyes one last time, Maya's then Quell's, before stepping out of sight. She descended slowly, trying to focus on the climb as the path soon vanished and she had to clamber down over fractured rock. Stray thoughts kept intruding though: Quina reaching out to save her from a fall, Kao wolfing down his first hot meal, pausing only to complain about his burned mouth and shovel in more food, Petrick dancing around Hetta as he led her away, Thurin's smile as he lifted water from a puddle to show her his magic, the rippled light moving across his face. One day she wanted to see him work fire.

She thought of Zeen too, so proud of his knowledge about the Black Rock. Knowledge that now seemed like tiny grains of grit on an endless gravel bank. Even little Azad visited her thoughts, happy and laughing in the boat on the day before the dagger-fish took him.

Yaz reached the stone beam that crossed the gap and would take her to the first of the Missing's chambers. The hunter star slowly swung into her vision, following its orbit, and she became aware of its unearthly song, a wordless refrain that had been there all along, unmooring her thoughts and letting them drift.

She fought for focus and crossed into the exposed chamber on the other side, a dusty rectangular box of poured stone, older than the ice caves but lacking their ever-changing beauty.

Yaz made her way steadily, alert for hunters, descending at every opportunity. She didn't know where Erris would be but she knew he would be deep. She just hoped she'd find him before she found the creature that the city had fashioned to destroy her. Its assassin. It made the regulator's hunters look like finger-fish next to a shark – and not just any shark, one of the black kind that rarely surfaced but when they did drove all the whales from the Hot Sea.

She knew the undercity to be vast and her search hopeless, but for one thing. If she went deep enough she believed that Erris would find her. The star she held would act as a beacon for the watching minds that lurked in the depths of the undercity. Erris would find her. Or something else would.

The monotony of stairs and shafts and endless dusty halls nibbled at her vigilance and once again her thoughts began to drift with the red star's song. Her resolve came and went in waves, iron at the peaks, rotten with self-doubt in the troughs. Quell's desire that she return to the surface might lie in parallel with the priests' but it was also his own, born of love. And here alone in the empty home of the Missing she could call Quell's motivation what it was. He loved her and in the name of that love had dared a world unknown and undreamed-of and full of danger.

The thought brought a smile to her lips but did not turn her around. It brought a question as well. Did she return that love? Did an answering passion burn inside her too? Did she even know what love was? Once Quell had been everything she wanted. Everything she could imagine. Her everything . . . but that was also the crack through which a cold wind blew. She had known so little. Her options had been so few. The course of her life had run before her with a frightening certainty. The inevitability of it had appalled her. And yet when anything had happened to threaten that surety – Azad's death showing how thin the ice beneath your feet could be; her growing strangeness reeling her towards the pit like a fish on a hook of its own making – when those things had challenged her certainty it too had terrified her.

Yaz wondered at her refusal to return to the regulator, a man whose wisdom her clan respected, a man whose judgement held such sway that her own parents had watched him topple their son into the black throat of the pit and had done nothing. Yaz had no regrets at following Zeen, though she didn't fully understand why. But then does anyone fully understand themselves, or even want to? Wouldn't that be very dull?

'No,' she breathed, finding herself at a four-way fork with no memory of the choices that brought her there. 'No.' She did have a regret about following Zeen. She regretted not hauling the regulator down with her.

'No.' She spoke the word again. Louder this time, marvelling at the roundness of it in her mouth, the taste of its defiance. 'No.'

Was she refusing to leave her friends just for that desire to reject . . . everything? Everything from the cruelty of a society that threw their broken children away to the harshness of existence in the caverns where Broken and Tainted were locked in struggle, battling for different masters. Was she saying no to the inarguable necessities of life in a world of ice and brief seas? But you can't just say no time and again. You need an alternative. Another answer.

Erris had shown her the green world. She had been the first Ictha to see anything like it; her parents had seen nothing even close, nor theirs, nor any along a long chain extending untold generations into an unchanging past. She had seen it and although she had never imagined such a thing she knew within moments that it was right. It was where she belonged. Where they all belonged. She knew that it was her answer, even though it was an answer that made no sense. It had continued to make no sense right up to the point that Quina had put into her hand a small wooden bead and with it a story of a man travelling an unimaginable distance from the south. The green world stood against the world of ice and all its cruelties, just as she now stood against the options offered to her.

Yaz found that she had come to a halt before a great glowing symbol on the rear lichen-covered wall of an arched hall. The lichen almost obscured the symbol like a thick, rough skin, scaled with disease. The script wall had opposed her on her first journey into the city, its defences becoming ever stronger as she travelled deeper. This time she'd seen only symbols like this one, heavy with lichen, indicating they were part of the city's normal complement rather than freshly generated to oppose her.

'It's easier this time.' She wondered if the city had now accepted her, or was perhaps luring her in deep before closing its jaws around her. Either way she needed to be noticed because the Broken had searched the city for generations without uncovering even half of it, and so the chances of her finding Erris were vanishingly small. He would definitely have to find her instead.

Yaz knew that on her previous visit it had been the city's opposition to her that had drawn Erris's attention. That meant she had to wake the city again. She would have to prod the bear in its lair, and hope that she could cope with what came next.

Lacking instructions Yaz decided to experiment. She took the red star in her hand and began to trace the symbol with it, reaching up above her head to start at the outermost coiling line. She scored the star's smooth surface through the shaggy lichen along the faintly glowing lines of the symbol.

Everywhere her hand went the symbol blazed more brightly behind it, until at last the whole thing shone with enough light to illuminate the chamber. Other smaller symbols began to show, as if the light had leaked from the larger one into their dry channels. A host of tiny script now shone weakly from the rear wall and Yaz heard music. Not the wordless song of the stars that seemed to belong to a voice, but a complex spiralling melody, at turns sad then joyous, the sounds of instruments though none that Yaz had ever heard before.

Ghosts filled the room, phantoms that she almost saw, like words spoken just beneath the threshold of comprehension. An impression of dance. Graceful whispers haunting the emptiness of the air. Fading then gone.

Yaz found herself in the darkening hall with a tear on her cheek and a profound sense of loss. This had been a place of music and light and movement once, unimaginably long ago, and now only the sorrow of the vast city's crumbling mind remained.

She moved on, hoping to encounter some other way of drawing Erris's attention.

The first sign of the hunter was a variation in the song of the star in orbit around her. Yaz heard a harmonizing, as though a second voice had joined the first. And then, as she focused her thoughts on the problem, she became aware of its heartbeat, very faint but growing stronger. With the heartbeat came an idea of direction and, as she strained her senses, she became aware of other hearts still fainter and more distant. She wondered how she and Quell had wandered into two hunters as they tried to leave the city. All she'd had to do was listen and it was there for the hearing.

The hunter drew closer, moving at speed, an urgency in

its heart-song. Yaz took a narrow turn and followed a long stair upwards even though her destination lay far below. The hunter continued to close, its direction swinging around her in a manner that indicated it to be racing through the empty rooms at reckless speed.

A wide shaft, down which scavengers had hung cables, offered her a quick descent of two hundred yards. She reached the bottom with her arms limp and trembling. The strength of the Ictha had left her and she wondered at how the other tribes survived with such weakness in them.

A metallic clatter echoed down the shaft after her, the hunter growing ever closer. With a curse Yaz began to run, bathing the corridor ahead of her with red light, alert for any narrow passage or crack through the foundations of the city by which she might escape.

She reached another shaft, narrower and deeper than the first, hung with a single thin cable, secured by an iron peg hammered into the poured stone floor.

'Gods in the Sky!' Yaz's arms felt like jelly. She wasn't ready for another long climb.

A crash far back along the corridor told her that the hunter had reached the bottom of the earlier shaft.

Seized by a sudden idea Yaz snatched the red star from the air and held it in both hands. She willed it to rise and let it do so until her arms were stretched out above her. She could feel the pressure of it against her interlocked fingers. Grinding her teeth she commanded the star to rise and at the same time hauled down on it. The thing nearly escaped her to go hammering into the ceiling, but she held it back, just barely, standing on tiptoes.

A red glow insinuated itself into the far end of the corridor, growing brighter until the black bulk of the hunter emerged, hooking its claws all around the edge of a doorway to haul itself through. The star inside it shone in bright crimson lines through every joint and chink in its iron armour. The heartbeat of this hunter was slower than that of the one she had shattered to gain the star currently trying to lift her from her feet. A bigger star, a bigger hunter, a more deadly threat.

Yaz snarled in frustration and stepped to the lip of the shaft. 'Gods save me.'

Ignoring the cable at her feet she stepped off, trying to force the star in her hands upwards. For a moment she hung there, feet dangling in space, her body suspended below the star as its light pulsed bloodily through her hands. Then, slowly at first, she began to fall.

About fifty yards from the ground Yaz understood that she was travelling down too fast. The stone floor rushed towards her at ankle-breaking speed. Grunting with effort she tried to force the star upwards more strongly. She slowed but not enough. With twenty yards remaining she reached out in desperation, trying to grab the cable flashing by her while retaining a hold on the slick ball of light with one hand.

What happened next was too fast for her brain to make sense of it. She caught hold of something, had something ripped from her grasp, turned in the air several times, and hit hard.

Yaz lifted her head slowly – as if it weren't already far too late for such delicacy. Crimson light swamped her vision and the taste of blood filled her mouth. She drew a slow breath into lungs from which all air had been driven at speed, and daggers stabbed her chest from both sides.

The sound of iron clanging on iron got her crawling, blood drooling between mashed lips. She made it through a doorway into the darkness of another room before the awful screeching began, the sound of the hunter's claws as it dropped down the shaft she'd come from, scoring the four walls to tame its descent.

Yaz reached back and her red star rolled after her, coming to a halt in her hand and illuminating the room beyond.

Another dusty chamber, two doorways in the rear wall, a vertical shaft in the middle of the floor. Yaz crawled on. The doorways seemed too far away, the clattering, clanking charge of the hunter too close. She rolled over the lip of the shaft clutching the red star. Gravity reached for her with its implacable strength and yanked her away into the darkness of the fall.

Once again Yaz hung from nothing but her will for the red star to rise. The fear of the drop filled her stomach while the pain of opposing it sliced through her head.

She dropped into a huge chamber, slower than falling, more like a diver plunging into water. The starlight glowing scarlet through her hands made of her something like those strange fish that are sometimes carried from the deepest depths of the ocean by swift upwellings, the ones that hang in darkness carrying their own light before them. The glow partially illuminated the nearest wall as she fell past it, the light painting red stone and black entrances. The chamber seemed to be something of a junction where dozens of shafts met, some opening at various heights along the walls, a similar number piercing floor and ceiling.

Yaz hit the stone with an 'Oooff!' that crumpled her into a ball of hurt and swallowed her vision amid a constellation of spinning lights.

For uncounted time Yaz hung among those lights in a bliss of forgetting. Without memory of destination or recollection of pursuit all urgency left her. She drifted, moved only by an idle curiosity. Stars . . . she floated amid the stars, not the red scatter dying in the black heavens above the ice but marbled giants that swung through the void in slow majesty. Close by, a huge crimson star burned like a banked fire, and just as Yaz could make stars orbit her this great star had smaller ones that orbited it. One among a dozen that spun about the dull heat of the red star caught Yaz's eye, a ball of pearly white on white, all aglitter with the reflected light of the greater star, as if ice were burning. She drifted closer until she began to realize that even this small star was vastly bigger than her, its unending whiteness beginning to fill her vision. And at the last, as its shadow threatened to swallow her and she saw that it was larger than mountains or seas, she was able to make out a thin, dark line about its middle. The shadow deepened, the great red star falling behind the growing bulk of the white star, and in those last moments of light the line about its middle turned from a black thread to something with a hint of thickness and a hint of colour. And that colour was green.

The darkness engulfing the world became the shadow of a hand, and suddenly Elias stood there in a space with no walls, his clothes like Erris's being made of something that was neither hide nor fur.

'Hello.' In his narrow, long-fingered hand he held the white star, barely large enough to cover his palm. He looked at her without recognition. 'Who are you and what do you want?'

'I'm Yaz of the Ictha. We met . . .' She tried to recall how long ago it had been. '. . . before.' A part of her purpose returned to her as she reached for her answer. 'And I'm looking for a star.'

'I can't let you have this one, I'm afraid.' He held up the white ball. 'I'm supposed to protect it.'

'From Seus?'

Elias twitched, worry entering his quick, dark eyes. 'Yes.' He closed his hand around the star. 'Elias Taproot. Pleased to meet you, young lady. But you say we've met before?'

'Yes. Then Seus came and . . .'

'Ah. I must be all that survived. The basic framework, so to speak. Recent memory gone.' He frowned. 'I can't remember anything before . . . Well . . .' He held up the star again and studied it. 'Put it this way.' The thin line broadened slowly into a wide green belt so that nearly a third of the world lay free of ice. 'Since the world looked like this.'

'Is Seus the winter?' Yaz whispered.

Elias shook his head. 'This world was always going to freeze in the end. He's dead set against anyone slowing it down though.'

'What does he want? To destroy the world?'

'Never that.' Elias flashed a nervous smile. 'Just all of your kind.'

Yaz suddenly found her island of the present crowded with returning past and future. She had been falling. She had been hunted and been hunting. 'I need a star to save Zeen and the others!'

'Big picture!' Elias snapped his fingers irritatingly in her face. 'I just told you Seus wants to close the Corridor, ice-over the green zone, and kill well over ninety-nine per cent of all humanity on the surface of this planet.' His eyes flitted to her collar. He reached out to tap a finger to the needle there. 'You need to use this to find me. A better me who can use – who can help you to stop Seus!'

Yaz stepped back and fixed Elias with a hard stare. *Big picture* wasn't a phrase she had ever heard spoken but somehow she understood the sentiment. It was the same mindset that saw children sacrificed to the greater good, that saw awful deeds against the few to preserve the many. Maybe it was right or maybe it was wrong. Yaz left that for the gods to decide. But whatever they decided, her course was fixed, right or wrong. 'I'll care about your fight when I've finished mine. Now send me back!'

'Send you? Dear girl, you brought yourself.'

'Then how do I . . .' But the words were slurring from a mouth whose cheek was pressed to cold stone and a tongue that tasted blood. Her vision blurred and the great red star about which the others had orbited swung back into view out of the darkness.

Time passed and the circle of illumination from her star, now lying just beyond the tips of her outstretched fingers, began to surrender to the growing glow of at first half a dozen large symbols, themselves manifesting like stars from the general darkness of a night sky. Soon there were scores of them, lighting a chamber in which all the peoples of the gathering could have assembled without rubbing elbows.

Yaz got to her feet, groaning and wiping fresh blood from her mouth. She was back in the chamber into which she had fallen while escaping the hunter. The rest of it could just have been the result of banging her skull too hard against the floor. Her head and chest competed to see which could ache the worst.

'Hello?'

The vastness of the chamber swallowed the word. By way of an answer the dark mouth of one of the many side shafts lit from within with crimson light. A hunter emerged moments later, hooking black claws around the exit and hauling itself into the room in a single smooth motion that brought it crashing to the stone floor five yards below. The same hunter that had pursued her down so many falls.

A sigh escaped Yaz's lips. She called her star to her hands

and began to advance on her foe. She had few illusions about her chances of beating the creature, but the time for running had passed.

This hunter resembled a giant black crab with a complexity of many-jointed legs bearing up a body three times as wide as Yaz was tall. One arm massively outweighed two smaller ones on the other side. Where those two had fingers like tentacles the other sported a claw large enough to snatch up a gerant and snip him effortlessly in two.

Whether surprised by her advance or recovering from its drop the hunter remained where it was, close to the base of the wall, its iron carapace backed almost against another of the several dozen identical entrances.

Yaz advanced in a straight line, save where she tracked around one of the shafts that opened in the floor. She held the star out in front of her, smaller cousin to the one she could sense powering the monster ahead. In its light she saw the river that runs through all things, wider and clearer than she had ever seen it before, its power hidden but terrifying even in the hints and rumours it offered to her eyes. The star she had recovered in the city chamber had once more opened the river to her. She feared it more than she feared the hunter though. If she touched it the river could flood through her in half a heartbeat, filling her with energies beyond her capacity to own. She would sooner stick her hand in a forge pot than dare the river like this.

The hunter rose on its legs as Yaz closed the remaining distance between them. It lifted half a yard and raised its huge claw still higher, regarding her with mismatched glass eyes, gleaming darkly at the ends of two small articulated arms.

'You're going to be mine.' Yaz spoke the words through gritted teeth as she exerted her will through the star in her hands, seeking to influence the one pulsing amid the ironwork body looming over her.

The crab advanced in quick, stuttering steps, the weight of it scoring the stone wherever one of its sharp legs set down. The claw, big enough to squash Yaz flat, now hung poised above her head. She felt the creature's heart with her mind, a fiercely defiant fire refusing her command. Yaz ground her teeth and raised a hand towards the claw as it descended.

'No!'

The crab hesitated, the iron bulk of it groaning as its forward momentum was arrested. In the next instant its heart-star flared, deep red light shone from every joint and a bright pain blossomed in Yaz's head. Something brittle fractured in her mind and she fell, blood running from her eyes. The massive claw followed her to the ground.

Before the claw's jagged teeth could close around her the whole of the monster jolted. Yaz heard an awful squealing and a swift series of snapping sounds. Then, with sudden violence, the entire crab burst into pieces. An eye hit the ground close to Yaz's head and shattered, scattering broken shards over her. A section of its carapace bounced just past her, its edges gleaming where the thick iron had been torn. Yaz saw the claw skitter across the ground before toppling down one of the shaft openings, swiftly followed by several lengths of cable and a glowing star almost the size of a newborn's head.

With a groan Yaz rolled over into a sitting position and began to scramble backwards. It looked as if some dark core remained amid the wreckage of the hunter. Even as she watched, it seemed to unfold, shedding iron cables, metal plates, toothed wheels and a great blue-black spring coil. The thing revealed amid the hunter's ruin was something almost human and perhaps only a little taller and wider than

Hetta or Jerrig, though cast in black metal. It followed a careful design rather than the seemingly improvised hunters that the regulator had created. And although Yaz had never had a clear sight of it before she knew exactly what it was: the assassin that the city had sent to stop her escape. On that occasion only Erris's sacrifice of his own iron body had slowed it sufficiently for her to escape.

The assassin had torn into the hunter's back and emerged from its wreckage. The hunters were the regulator's doing and now the city had risen against them. Though it seemed that the avatar the city had sent was focused on Yaz. The hunter had merely been an impediment, stealing its prey.

The assassin raised its hand towards her, fingers extended and tight together. Yaz realized that even if she thought she could master the city's creation where she had failed to master the regulator's, the only star that she could hear was the one in her hand. Whatever powered this killer it was something new, something over which she had no influence.

With a soft click four black points appeared at the ends of the extended fingers. The next two things happened simultaneously. Four black darts shot towards her with the same velocity that had seen them hammer into stone at their last encounter. And Yaz plunged both arms into the river that flows through all things. For a moment she became one with the universal current, the awful power flowing through her with a force that should strip the flesh from her bones. In the next moment the river rejected her and she lay gasping in the same place she had been before though it seemed to her that she had been carried a great distance. The energies still inside Yaz made her feel like a plucked harp string resonating to the note of creation. Her body wanted to break apart, to stride off in a dozen different directions, each part carrying away a different piece of her mind. She stood, shuddering like a flag in the wind, scarcely noticing the four flattened pieces of black metal that slid from her lap. The spent projectiles tumbled down across the shield of golden light that encased her and struck the ground with ringing tones. Yaz and the assassin faced each other, one golden, one dark.

Yaz thought of her friends, of her purpose, of Thurin and Zeen trapped amid the black ice. With a great cry, half rage, half ecstasy, she managed to grab the tatters of her being and drag them back into a unity. She became united, drawn more definitely into the world than she had ever been before, understanding at the same time how very close she had come to dispersing across the surface of her stolen power like oil spilled across the face of the sea.

Yaz spread her hands, cupped, half surprised not to find them full of fire. Something invincible ran through her veins, her lungs didn't need to draw breath, her muscles screamed with a strength that could easily tear her asunder. When she took a swift step forward the black assassin took a swift step back.

Yaz struck. Not with her hands, but with everything that was in her, a blast of something white and black and chaotic and loud. The force of it flung the assassin away like a child's toy, hurling it yards back on a rising line to hit so high up the wall that Yaz couldn't have reached it with her fingertips.

Her opponent fell back to the ground, face forward, hitting with a clang like an iron bell. A rain of fractured stone pieces rattled down around it from the impact crater high above them. Yaz stood, trembling, watching the inert, gently smoking form at the base of the wall. She was glad it was dead. She had, in that one act of violence, discharged herself, shedding everything the river had given her. It would be at least a day before she saw the river again. A week before

315

she could touch it with anything even approaching safety.

Yaz slumped, the fear leaving her body and uncovering all her aches and pains as it retreated. Exhausted, she turned to examine the closest of the downward shafts.

The scrape of iron on stone turned her sharply back around and reversed the tidal flow of her terror. A great metal hand twitched. Joints groaned in protest and the assassin slowly levered itself up, turning its blank face towards her once more. Even in her fear she wondered for a moment if she were looking into the face of the Missing. Had the city crafted its assassin in their image?

The assassin stood and stepped towards her, limping on one leg, grinding metal on metal. It smouldered here and there, the energies she had unleashed on it still sparking across the formerly glossy exterior, now deeply scored and etched in almost geometric scar patterns. It held its hand out and the fingers shuddered, but the black spikes that would have torn through her didn't come. The mechanism that threw them seemed broken.

Part of her wanted to turn and run. To throw herself down yet another shaft. But she didn't want to die with her back to the thing. Exhaustion wanted to put her on her knees, but that wasn't an option. Not for an Ictha. She would meet death standing.

She raised her star, thinking perhaps to throw it. She had felt ready to die before, back there beneath the black ice, but maybe that had been the weight of the demons' malice crushing her spirit. Now she was anything but ready. She had unfinished business. People that only she could save.

Yaz wasn't ready but she understood she had nothing left. Just holding her arms out before her with the star was taking all her strength.

Without warning something struck the ground between

her and the assassin. A something that must have fallen from one of the shaft openings on the ceiling. It hit fast as a thunderbolt but without any sound other than a slap like a palm against stone. Yaz blinked. A figure, a human figure, coiled against the impact, crouched between the towering assassin and Yaz, who realized only now that she was on her knees.

The star fell from Yaz's hands as Erris unfolded from his crouch. Facing her, rather than the metal giant. Not Erris in his body of mismatched parts but Erris as she had seen him in the green memories of his life: tall, calm, his skin the same rich brown she remembered, hair close to his skull in tight black coils. He wore a white linen tunic and leggings. Yaz discovered that she knew the word 'linen' and what cloth was. Something else that had slipped into her mind while wandering Erris's memories with him.

'Yaz. I told you not to come back.' A sad smile played at the corner of his mouth.

Behind Erris the assassin took a step closer, now directly behind him. Erris's head reached only just above its hips.

Erris turned and looked up at the assassin's blank face. 'I can't let you have her.'

'H . . . How are you here?' Yaz struggled to her feet, heavy with exhaustion. 'You said you didn't have a body.'

'Actually, I said I had two. One better built than the other.' Erris kept his back to her.

'But . . . the other one was metal, like a hunter's.'

'And this one has metal in it too.' Erris's gaze remained on the blank plate of the assassin's face where symbols suddenly began to glow, many of them, flowing down over the iron like a slow waterfall.

'No!' Erris said.

The assassin backhanded him. A seemingly lazy blow but

one that sent him flying across the expanse of floor. Yaz cried out as he fell into a shaft, but somehow his fingers caught the edge and heartbeats later he had hauled himself out.

The assassin reached for Yaz and she backed away. With impressive footspeed Erris returned to interpose himself. His face just inches before the iron fingers reaching for Yaz.

'You know how long it took me to build this body,' he said to the assassin. 'How much of myself I put into it. How hard I worked to hide it from you.'

The iron hand closed like a trap around his head, engulfing it. Yaz staggered forward to grab one finger with both hands. She tried to prise it back but found no give in it.

'You don't think breaking this body will break me?' Erris spoke beneath the assassin's wrist. 'You have held me too long. I have lived too long.' He was speaking to the city, to Vesta, not to the work of metal and magic that held him. Addressing the vast but broken mind that had kept him across all these centuries.

The symbols flowing across the assassin's faceplate shone brighter now, painting themselves across Yaz. Every symbol on the walls glowed more strongly and the shadows, with no place left to hide, went scurrying down the nearest shafts.

'This isn't what you were made to do,' Erris said.

The fingers moved fractionally, beginning to squeeze. Erris gasped as if in pain. 'There. I've done it.'

In that instant every one of the thousand symbols on the walls, ceiling, and floor burned red. The assassin opened its hand and released Erris's head. The script continued to flow over its face.

'I've bound myself in here,' Erris said. 'This is all I am. I've finally escaped you. I can live or die but I can't go back.'

A tone like metal being torn screeched out from the assassin's chest and Yaz had to cover her ears. The voice was nothing human and yet the hurt in it, the depth of its sorrow, threatened to carry her away like a wave stripping fishers from their boat.

'I understand that I can't return if I leave.' Erris hung his head. He turned and reached for Yaz's hand. She let him take it and folded her fingers into his. His flesh felt warm. Almost human. But not quite. 'Yaz will come with me.'

The symbols pulsed again.

'She will not return. Will you, Yaz?' He met her eyes.

'I . . .' She found that she didn't want to say so. Even though it was a place of emptiness and death it also held mysteries and answers. The idea that she might never come again, that all these secrets would be locked away from her forever, somehow seemed too much to ask, even though she had been inches from death and didn't stand much further from it now. 'I will go as far away as I can get.'

Erris began to lead her towards the mouth of the nearest horizontal shaft. They walked quickly and quietly beneath the glow of the symbols' scarlet fire.

'What did you do?' Yaz hissed, afraid that if she spoke too loud it might somehow make the city change its mind.

'I used the only currency I had,' Erris said. 'Myself.' He glanced back at the assassin. 'I have been a part of the void so long, even as the city's mind fell apart, that I think it values my existence. A kind of love if you like.'

Behind them a clang rang out and looking back Yaz saw that the assassin was literally falling to pieces, coming apart now that its purpose had been served. A maelstrom of emotions swept over them: sorrow, anger, loss. Yaz's own feelings floated on that tide, leaving her hollow, walking like a dead man, tears running from her eyes, her breath hitching in her chest as she fought against sobbing.

The whirlwind of feelings began to subside as they entered the corridor. Their footsteps echoed before them and, as the entrance receded behind them into a square of red light, the star orbiting Yaz began to provide their illumination. As it circled it sent their shadows in a slow dance, drawing together, merging, parting, sliding across one wall then the next.

Yaz realized that they were still holding hands and self-consciously undid herself from Erris's grasp. 'I still don't understand what you did back there.'

'I did what I used to do best,' Erris said. 'I escaped.'

'What, just like that?' Yaz frowned. 'Why didn't you do it years ago?'

They walked in silence for several paces, circled by their shadows.

'Well, it wasn't "just like that". First I had to build this.' Erris patted his body. 'Which took finding, unlocking, and mastering some of the more complex machinery left by the Missing on the lower levels. That took some time.'

'How long?' Yaz knew it took a woman the best part of a year to make a baby.

'Lifetimes,' Erris said. 'Dozens of them. And then I had to work out how to put myself wholly in it, with no part left to anchor me into the void. It's fortunate that when the city took me it took all of me, including my marjal skills.'

'Even so, you didn't really just figure it all out and get everything ready at the same time I happened to appear, surely?'

Erris stopped walking and turned to face her. 'No.'

'Why then?' Why now, she meant. Why because of me, she wanted to ask. Didn't he know she was broken? Didn't he know she'd already failed those who put their faith in her, time and again?

'Why would I leave? I know what's up there. Ice, ice, and more ice. A dead white world. A world that will sink its teeth into this body and bear down until the power cells are exhausted, and then at last there'll be an end to me.' He paused. 'I was scared to leave. Everyone I ever knew or cared about had gone.'

Yaz met his dark eyes, both reflecting a single red star. 'Why . . .' She found her mouth too dry for her question. 'What changed?'

He smiled a smile with too much uncertainty in it for someone thousands of years old.

'You made me care.'

CHAPTER 27

'Don't look so astonished!' Erris laughed. 'I haven't seen another human in two hundred years, and that was the man who built the hunters. So it's not as if you had a lot of competition. My mother always said I follow the first pretty face I see.'

Yaz found her fingers resting on her own unaccountably hot cheeks and lowered her hands quickly. 'And do you?'

'Well, maybe. But I followed the last pretty face I saw for years and we were to be married. Only I had to go exploring some old ruins . . .' He grinned, showing white teeth. 'Come on. Let's go before we find some other trouble to get into down here.' He started walking again. 'I'm sure there's enough trouble waiting for us up above?'

Yaz didn't know whether Erris was talking about the ice caverns or up on the ice itself. The answer was the same either way. 'Yes. Lots.'

Erris led the way, paying no attention to any scavenger symbols. Where there were hanging cables he climbed them at a remarkable rate using just his arms. Twice Yaz had to call for a rest.

She found herself very thirsty and had to be thankful for the turn of events that had reunited her with Erris so quickly as she wouldn't have lasted long. She made a mental note to check that Maya had stolen enough waterskins before realizing that if she stole a heat pot then they would be able to melt ice as they went once they reached the surface.

'The way the assassin hit you. It would have killed me.' Yaz tried to see any sign of bruising or swelling on Erris's face.

'I'm tough stuff.' Erris thumped his chest jokingly. 'Built of alloys and polymers.'

'Just how strong are you?' Yaz knew that even Quell wouldn't be able to haul himself up two hundred yards of cable without breaking sweat.

'I'm not sure.' Erris shrugged. 'It depends in part on how much power I draw from my reserves and how much risk I want to run of damaging myself.'

'You said you would live until your . . . cells . . . run out? How long is that?'

Erris smiled and widened his eyes at her. 'Nobody wants to know exactly how long they have left in the world. The truth is I don't know. Years rather than months, I think. My cells store a lot of energy, but they last longer in the warm. I would live longer in these chambers than in the ice caves above, and much longer in those caves than up on the surface, out in the wind.'

Yaz's face fell as a sudden guilt overtook her.

Erris shook his head. 'Take it from me though, centuries are overrated. It's what you do with time that makes it matter. I'd rather spend a year making new memories than a thousand wandering around in the same old ones.'

Yaz got to her feet again, still tired but driven more by her thirst than the desire to rest. 'Ready to go?'

'You still haven't told me why you came back.' Erris rose smoothly from his haunches.

'I came to find you. I need your help to get my brother—'

'Zeen.'

'Yes, Zeen. To get him back from the Tainted. And to rescue my friends too.'

'Friends now? You do like to raise the stakes. And what do they need rescuing from?' He resumed climbing the long stairway they had been resting on.

'From the Tainted. There's this . . . man . . . Theus—'

Erris looked back sharply at that. 'Theus? Not Prometheus?'

'I . . . I don't know. I don't think so. I've only ever heard him called Theus.' Yaz let her red star rise above them. 'Who's Prometheus?'

'Someone the city dreams of.' Erris frowned. 'Someone it's scared of.' He shook his head and carried on up the stairs. '*Greatness and torment and fire.*'

'What?'

'I'm not sure . . . Just words that float through me when the city dreams of Prometheus.' Erris shrugged. 'Tell me about this Theus of yours.'

So Yaz did. She told Erris about the Tainted and about her ill-fated raid to rescue Zeen, and about what Theus had said he was doing there in the black ice.

'So what do you think?' It had taken an hour or more to tell it all, and although there were no obvious signs to indicate it Yaz felt that they were close to the surface now. 'Is he lying? Or is this Theus really some cast-off piece of one of the Missing? Is that truly what the black ice is? Purged sins?'

'I really don't know.'

'But you're my expert here!' Yaz exclaimed.

'I don't get out much, you may have noticed.' He reached up and pulled himself into a narrow vent that Yaz hadn't seen. His voice came back muffled as his feet disappeared into the dark hole. 'Whatever else this black ice is, on the scale of the city's lifetime it's a new development.'

Yaz sighed and jumped to catch the edge of the vent. Cursing and panting with effort she managed to drag herself up and in. She advanced on her chest, letting the star roam ahead of her. An irregular dark stain running down the middle of the narrow shaft hinted that water had trickled down here in the not so distant past. Touching her fingertips to the stain Yaz could even imagine that it was damp. She unglued her tongue from the roof of her mouth and hauled herself forward on sore elbows.

Erris found water seeping from a narrow crack in a chamber not long after they escaped the crawl-way and Yaz slaked her thirst impatiently, a quarter-mouthful at a time, marvelling at how good gritty, mineral-heavy water can taste when you've been dried out for too long.

'You said the city dreams of Prometheus. Does the city dream of Seus too?' Yaz asked. 'Or of Elias Taproot?'

Erris's brows lifted in surprise. 'Is this some quantal power of yours? Are no secrets safe from you?'

'You know them then? It was when we were going through the walls. You said I got intercepted and—'

'And I was too busy escaping to ask you more. And then too busy being torn into small pieces.'

'So you know them then? The city dreams of them?'

'It's always a nightmare when Seus is in the dream. Vesta is terrified of him. Sometimes I think it was him that drove her mad.'

Yaz didn't ask how one city could be a he and the other a she. Instead she asked about the one who had seemed human. 'And Elias Taproot. Is he like you?'

Erris shrugged. 'Well, he is much, much older. I think he was old beyond imagining before he came to Abeth.'

'Then how is he like he is? Like you—'

'Whatever happened to him happened somewhere else, long ago. He might have been a man back at the start but now he's a memory, an echo of that man, and he lives in minds like those of the cities. But not just one like me. He's shared between them. Back when all the cities were still connected, when they all spoke together, he would move where he liked. But when those connections broke he was left scattered. Not in pieces, but in copies – some stronger than others though, more detailed, truer to the original, with more of their memories and the power that goes with memory.'

'He told you all this?'

Erris laughed. 'No. I can uncover secrets too. Elias Taproot always had bigger fish to fry. I was beneath his notice. So count yourself honoured!'

Yaz didn't feel honoured, she felt targeted, drawn into a larger war that she had no concept of. Taproot's interest had focused the eyes of a dark god upon her just when she was already in the worst peril she could imagine.

It took maybe another hour before they emerged into the glow of the city cavern from a different hole than the one that Yaz had left it by. Erris reached down to haul her up then stood marvelling at the ice sky high above him.

'It's beautiful.'

'It is.' Yaz came to stand beside him, looking up too but listening with something other than her ears for signs of the hunters. Overhead the bands of stardust held in the ice marbled the ceiling with muted rainbow shades. In time much of the dust would fall with the meltwater and be washed down the gentle gradient to join the oncoming ice that might carry it once again into the heights.

Erris made a slow turn, gazing at the pockmarked rock and occasional twisted beams. "'Look on my works, ye Mighty, and despair!'"

Yaz cocked her head questioningly.

'A line of ancient poetry that dates back to even before the beaching. Did you know that the ships that brought the four original tribes to Abeth were powered by star-stones almost identical to the ones in the city?'

Yaz shook her head; the Ictha had a little mythology about the black oceans between the stars. Mokka, the first woman, had sailed her boat there once when she argued with the Gods in the Sea. There were a few other tales. 'Tell me about the poem.'

Erris smiled. 'It's just a line that stuck in my head long ago. The poem says that however you try to set your mark on the world, time will come and wash it all away.' He reached out a hand towards her. 'Let me show you how it was when I came here.'

Yaz found his smile echoing itself on her lips. She reached out and let him close his hand around hers. 'I don't—'

But then she did. The ruins grew around her, far taller than she had imagined when glimpsing them in the distance of an early visit to Erris's memory. The towers reached up through the ice ceiling of the cavern to daunting neck-craning heights, and yet they were still merely stumps of what had once stood there, the metal skeletons reaching up above the poured stone to challenge the clouds. In the memory Yaz stood on rubble that covered the ground to an unknown depth, great chunks of poured stone, some bigger than whales, and like the carcass of some vast beast their iron bones broke from stone flesh. Bees droned lazily by and a riot of ivy, heavy with white flowers, pursued the ruins up into the air.

Yaz gazed up at the defeated structures, marvelling, awestruck. Even their wounds seemed beautiful, exposing a complexity of floors and chambers inside, high above the ground. The buildings had their own grace, no two the same, and few of the straight lines she had grown so weary of in the chambers below. These were variously fluting, bulbous, slender, as if like the fungi in the caves they had grown rather than been built.

'What—' Yaz felt Erris's hand leave hers, fingers trailing across fingers and the illusion vanished, replaced with the ice cave that now seemed small and dull by comparison to the past glories taken from her. She repeated the line: '"Look on my works, ye Mighty, and despair!"' No more need be said. She understood some of the city's sorrow now. It too had been broken and cast aside. Abandoned by those who made it.

'What's next?' Erris rubbed his hands together and looked about expectantly.

Yaz contemplated the long slope. Taking Quell and Maya back into the black ice would put them both in danger. Maya could prove very useful, but she also had a proclivity for murdering the Tainted, and given that Yaz was going in specifically to reclaim two of the Tainted it felt profoundly wrong to be killing any of the unfortunates that got in the way.

'We're going to go and find Theus, just the two of us, and I'm going to hold him to our agreement.'

Yaz shivered. Just before Petrick had fallen to his death Theus had boomed at her: *Yaz of the Ictha! We have a deal!*

He might have just been saying it because he saw she and the others were going to escape him and it was something that might bring her back. But whether he meant it or not it was something that she was going to hold him to.

Erris extended his arm towards the slope, tilting his head. 'Lead on, dear lady.'

Yaz frowned. 'Sorry?'

'It's what people say. Said. Don't mind me. I'm just . . . well . . . I think I'm nervous. It's been a long time since I felt anything like this. Excited. With the city's avatar I was scared, I guess, but I knew what I was dealing with, what the options were. This, however, this is all new. It's been a very long time since I've done anything this foolish.' He grinned. 'I'm rather enjoying it.'

'Well, don't enjoy it too much. The Tainted are dangerous. And so are the Broken. And the hunters. In fact everything down here is dangerous and I've no idea how easy it is to stick a spear through your chest or what it would do to you.'

'A spear?' Erris wrinkled his nose as if he hadn't considered something as basic as a pointed piece of bone or metal. 'I think it would be very bad news to get one of those stuck through me. So let's avoid that.'

'Stop enjoying yourself then, and stay alert.' Yaz shook her head and led on towards the slope. Her mission had felt daunting before when she thought Theus was 'just' some dark spirit capable of possessing the unwary. Then he was one of the Missing, or at least broken pieces of one of them, an enigmatic and incomprehensibly ancient being, albeit robbed of most of his memory. And now it seemed he might be Prometheus, significant even among the Missing. A figure who troubled the city's dreams and whose relationship with such entities as Taproot and Seus remained unclear.

Despite her instruction Erris followed Yaz through the ice caverns as if the whole place had been constructed just to astonish him. At the first stream they came to he crouched and for an age would do nothing but let water run over his fingers then cup it in both hands and watch it fall as he lifted it. He marvelled at icicles and frost, at heaps of fallen ice and the banks of stones deposited by the glacial flow. He carried a rough, irregular stone in each hand for some distance, turning them over in his fingers.

'Nobody made this. No human hand has ever touched either of these stones before . . .'

'I'm very pleased for you,' Yaz growled.

'It's just that for more than a thousand years I've seen nothing that wasn't made by someone, or something. A simulation just can't—'

'Ssshhh.' Yaz held up a hand to silence him. Another distant cry rang out. Fainter than the first. Fear, pain, anger, or just someone shouting for someone else? She couldn't tell. She dimmed the light of the hunter star still further. 'Come on.' She beckoned.

'Did you know that the star-stone fragments glow more brightly when you're near them?'

Yaz turned to glare at him. 'Quietly!' She led on. 'And yes. And call them stars.'

Two caverns on and they came into a starlit grove of fungi, some of them types that Yaz hadn't yet seen, tall, slim and elegantly spotted with vibrant red and lustrous blue spots. Some of these reached to her elbows and where they grew together thickly they reminded her of Erris's forest. She turned to find him on hands and knees, examining examples of the capped fungi that tasted so good in stew.

'These are marvellous. I'm amazed to find them growing here, but I guess life finds a way . . .'

'We should go,' Yaz muttered. 'It's not safe here.' As she said the words a rattle of falling or thrown ice snapped her attention to the darker of the two exits. 'Erris!' she hissed, turning back to beckon him to her.

Instead of Erris she found herself looking at the point of an iron spear.

'Arka?' The face of the woman behind the spear had been smeared with mud, leaving her almost unrecognizable, but her rangy build and something around her eyes made Yaz think of Arka.

'Yaz!' And as the hunter star slowly rotated into view from behind her: 'Gods in the Ice! That's the biggest fucking star I've ever seen!' Arka fell back, wincing as the star's aura brushed over her.

Yaz looked past Arka to where the grey-haired gerant who had been among the council at headquarters in the drying cave now had both arms wrapped around Erris from behind. A second of the Broken watched him, clutching a spear. Erris was smiling, seeming both amused and very interested by the development. Yaz found herself wondering about the world he had come from before falling into the city. Did they not have violence or was he simply less protective of his body because it wasn't the one was born into? He should be. From his own account he had spent far longer making it than his mother and he had spent on the original.

Arka continued to edge back from the hunter star, still holding her spear towards Yaz. 'Who's this?' She nodded at Erris.

'That's Erris.' Yaz pushed the star behind her. 'He's new to all . . . this.' She waved at their spears. 'So please don't hurt him if he does the wrong thing. He's from the city.'

Arka frowned. 'You've come from the city?'

'We have. But Erris is *from* the city.'

'Nobody is from the city,' the gerant growled.

'I am.' Erris raised both arms in a slow yawning stretch

and in the process broke the old gerant's bear hug with no apparent effort despite the man's scarred arms being thick with slabbed muscle.

The other Broken, a bony older woman – one of the ironworkers, Yaz thought – retreated two steps, the point of her spear trembling.

'This is . . .' Arka gaped, her gaze darting back and forth between Yaz and Erris. '. . . astonishing.'

'I've been astonished every day since I came down the pit.'

Arka fixed her stare on Erris. 'Are you one of the—'

'He's not one of the Missing, no,' Yaz said. 'But Theus is part of one. Several parts of one. And that's where we're going.'

Arka shook her head. 'No. We're going to secure the city. We're making it our new base. If we deny Pome access to the iron then his power won't last long.'

'You're not worried about the hunters?' Erris asked.

'Always. But I've been worried about them for twenty years. And besides, we have Yaz now and something about that star behind her tells me she knows how to handle hunters.'

Yaz shook her head. 'I'm going to get Thurin and Kao and my brother back from the Tainted.'

Arka blinked. 'That's insanity. Two of you? You need to come to the city with us.'

'I can't.'

'I'm still your drop-leader, Yaz.' Arka's face hardened. 'We need to secure the city before the next collection. Once we have the trade goods from the next shipment we'll start to regain control. Pome's faction won't do so well without fish and salt.'

'The next collection isn't for twenty-three days,' Yaz lied. 'Erris and I will be coming to the city once we have the others. There's time.'

Surprise overwrote the resolve on Arka's muddy face at the mention of twenty-three days. 'You don't know as much as you think you do, girl. There's going to be an unscheduled collection very soon. The coal-worms are on the move. That's a sign.'

Yaz was about to ask how Arka knew what the coal-worms were doing when she became aware that Arka was no longer looking at her or even at the hunter star but at some spot to the left on the wall behind her. The ice seemed to be glowing from within but Yaz sensed no star.

'What is—'

A sudden cracking sound heralded a white explosion and the chamber vanished in a tumult of roaring, curiously warm water. Yaz had no time to grab hold of anything, just a brief impression of bodies tumbling amid crimson waters and then an impact with something hard that took the world away.

Yaz came to her senses spluttering and coughing water from raw lungs. She found herself face down in several inches of the stuff and felt as though she had choked the whole lot out from inside her chest. She quickly became aware of a savage heat and a fierce red light that was not her star. She turned her head to stare across the steaming waters still draining from the cavern. On the far side a creature writhed on the wet stone. A creature not unlike the sea-worms that sometimes cling to whales, only this one was too wide for her to wrap her arms around, many yards long, its soft, segmented body a putrid grey streaked with black, and where a seaworm had a complex head of ugly mouthparts ringed with bone hooks, this creature had only a glowing mass the colour of a forge pot melt and twice as hot.

'Hsssssst!'

The thing looked as groggy as she was, swaying its head

back and forth across the water, sending up great clouds of steam each time it dipped too close to the surface. The ice above it was in full thaw, meltwaters raining down to vaporize on the worm's glowing face.

Beyond the creature gaped the tunnel from which it had been ejected at speed by the pressure of meltwater behind it. Water was still pouring out, colder now and less ferocious.

'Hsssst!'

Yaz had thought the worm was making the noise but now she saw Erris lying against the ice wall opposite. He had tucked himself back in the channel made where the flow of warm water had cut into the base. He was waving for her to do the same. Yaz found she'd become snagged on some irregularity in the stone floor but managed to free herself and roll to the side just as the scorching head swung her way.

She huddled back into the ice channel and looked for the others, finding no sign. She guessed Arka and her friends had been swept away in the flood, and if they had any sense they'd keep on running. Judging by the height of the tunnel and what she had been told Yaz guessed that the specimen before her was a baby. It fuelled her resolve never to meet a full-grown coal-worm.

The creature seemed disoriented, perhaps surprised at having been flushed into a void within the ice, not so adept at sensing gaps as an adult. In any event, its head appeared to be cooling as its fright wore off, now glowing only a dull red, shading into black. In a series of disturbing undulations the worm flowed across the chamber and set its head to the ice wall opposite, slowly melting its way in while pushing the meltwater out with ripples that ran the length of it.

Yaz lay shivering as, in the space of a few minutes, the entire length of the worm vanished into the wall, leaving a tunnel from which water gushed in a continuous stream, and would continue to do so, she guessed, until the worm started heading down again.

'Yaz! Are you all right?' Erris came hurrying across to her, the concern that had been absent when facing a spear now written across his face. 'Nothing broken?'

'I'm not sure.' The words came through chattering teeth; she was as weak as the rest of her drop-group had been the day they arrived, shivering and dripping. Yaz had once believed that there was no such thing as cold water. By definition it wasn't cold – it was molten ice. Ice would never melt inside an Ictha tent without flame. 'I think so.'

Erris helped her up. Only the dim radiance of the walls lit the chamber now. 'Where's your star-stone?'

Yaz cocked her head, listening for the star's heartbeat. 'That way.' She pointed at the exit through which most of the water had drained.

They found the star lighting the tunnel joining the next chamber to the one beyond that. Whether Arka and the other two had been washed further away or had been unwilling to pass the star in the tunnel in order to return Yaz didn't know, but they were gone now.

'Better hurry then.' She stooped to collect her star.

'You need to get dry.' Erris took a handful of her skins and made a fist. Water dribbled out between his fingers.

Yaz willed heat from her star, picturing the sigil on the forge pot. 'I'm fine.'

'You're still shivering.' Erris's dark eyes held a warmth of their own.

'I'm fine.' She pulled away and broke into a gentle run. 'We'll get there faster like this and it'll stop me being cold.'

CHAPTER 28

Yaz and Erris hurried across the Broken's territory from the long slope of the city and now approached the bridge over the chasm beyond which the stars vanished and the taint shaded the world into black. As they'd come closer to the Tainted's caverns the familiar sense of menace had reasserted itself. The old malice waiting patiently for her return.

In all that time journeying from the city cavern they saw no one, heard nothing save the groaning and dripping of the ice. It brought home to Yaz how small the space they all had to live in was, and even so how thin on the ground they had grown. Eular had said she would be an agent of change, and he had been right, but she hadn't wanted that change to end lives, ruin others, and destroy a fragile existence on the edge of what was possible.

Yaz realized that her fall had, against all the odds, taught her to hope again, to think for the first time that things might become better. The worst had already happened. The threat that had loomed over her life for years had finally come to pass, and the girl who had forgotten how to dream had, despite her conviction that it was selfish and more than she deserved, begun to hope for the future.

Now, though, with darkness and despair literally reaching out to engulf her, she knew how cruel and fragile a thing hope is, and how sharp the edges of new-forged dreams can be once shattered.

'The ice is changing.' Erris ran his fingers over the greying walls as they approached the bridge.

'Careful.' Yaz moved to pull his hand away then stopped. 'Can those things actually get under your skin? I mean, if it's not real?'

Erris pursed his lips and looked at his wet fingertips. 'My skin is real. It's just not the same as yours. And the answer is that I'm really not sure.' He wiped his hand on his tunic, still wet from the flood. 'I'll avoid touching it.'

'The bridge is just along here.' Yaz led the way, her star's red light glistening on the walls ahead of her. Everywhere she went the star seemed to bleach the ice, swiftly banishing the grey as though it were reluctant shadow.

The sound of the river reached them now, a muffled roar. 'Will they have guards?'

'I hope so. But they didn't last time. It's not a place you can sneak into without light, and if you have light they'll see you coming.'

Yaz dimmed her star to almost nothing and advanced through the last dim chamber as quietly as she could. She set the star behind her and eased out onto the bare rock by the ravine. A slight warmth, rising from some unknown source, perhaps the river itself, had hollowed out a vaulted roof above the chasm and must be behind the slow disintegration of the bridge. The stars burned few and far between out here, just the occasional tiny point of light in the vast

337

bulk of the ice. On the far side the walls shaded still further into grey and the light died entirely. A group of Tainted waited at the opposite end of the bridge, three adults and four children, two so small that Yaz thought they must have been among those the regulator threw down just before the Ictha arrived at the Pit.

All seven were so dirty and shaggy-haired that Yaz couldn't tell which were male or female. Save by height she couldn't tell young from old. They had descended into a kind of savagery that made them indistinguishable, a monolithic knot of rage and hate. The largest of them clutched a sword that could well be Petrick's. Other than that they seemed unarmed. Yaz found herself very relieved not to see a spear among them. A hurled spear would bring her attempt at negotiation to a swift and unfortunate end. But the Tainted lived to capture, not to kill, and weapons seemed rare among their ranks.

Howls rang out as they saw her. They rushed forward together, careless of the bridge's narrowness. One child almost tumbled into the depths but snagged an adult's leg as it fell and hauled itself snarling back onto the ice. As they came Yaz backed along the edge of the ravine. She let her star rotate into view, increasing its radiance as it did so. The star's unvoiced song reached out, seeking harmonies from the few points of light wavering through the ice. The Tainted lifted their arms to shield their eyes. Running feet faltered. Howls became hisses. Only the sword-wielder staggered on, driven more by his own momentum than by any enduring desire.

The swordsman was alone by the time he passed the cavern mouth that Yaz had emerged from. Erris rose behind him, seizing both his arms. The man stood an inch or two taller than Erris and struggled with a wild, unhinged strength, but Erris held him as if controlling an unruly child, drawing him back into the cavern while Yaz retraced her steps.

Once in the cavern Yaz let the hunter star's crimson light flood out, painting the man in Erris's grasp in stark detail. Erris had taken him to a sitting position on the ground, squatting behind him, still holding his arms by the wrists.

The man was lean, close to the point of starvation like all the Tainted. A black stain covered and infected one eye, reaching down across his mouth and chin. Under the filth his hair was perhaps brown rather than the black it seemed, and he had the early Axit tattoos on his neck and wrists, indicating he had received his push relatively late. The design needled into his neck sat against a scarlet background, this one due to a second demon rather than more ink. He still held Petrick's sword, though his grip had slackened beneath the pressure of Erris's hand around his wrist.

As Yaz advanced, the man began to froth and howl, repeatedly ramming his head backwards in an attempt to hurt Erris while bucking like a landed fish to break free.

'I don't know how to do this . . .' Yaz held the star before her while the man writhed. She needed to force the demons out of him without breaking his own personality into fragments. It felt like trying to clean dirt off someone's face using only a lump hammer.

'I'm just the beautiful assistant,' Erris said, using a gap when the man was sucking in breath for more roaring. 'You're the magician.'

Yaz bit her lip and moved the star closer to the man's head. A moment later he went rigid and began to fit, the froth about his mouth starting to colour with blood. Even as he frothed, the black and scarlet stains began to retreat, flowing down his neck. Moments later both had vanished beneath his rags.

'Stand him up, quickly.' Yaz stepped back.

Erris stood the man back on his feet, lifting him with an

ease that made him look somehow pretend, as if the Tainted were made of rags and sticks rather than flesh and bone.

'Who are you?' Yaz sent her star away and stepped in close. Close enough for the man's stench to hit her, and to see the lines of cleaner skin showing where the drool had washed his chin.

'I . . .' The man looked disoriented, as if waking from a long and dream-haunted sleep.

'Your name.'

'Etrix, of the Axit!' He glanced around, taking in the chamber then the hands holding his wrists, stretching out his arms. 'Who are you?' A snarl reached his lips. 'And where's Tarko?'

Yaz could see the red stain starting to finger its way back up, already touching the man's throat. 'Listen to me, Etrix. You've been tainted. The demons will reclaim you soon. I don't know how to drive them out yet. I'm sorry. But I need you to take a message to Theus for me. You know Theus?'

A shadow of memory crossed the man's face, fear replacing fierceness. 'Theus . . .' A nod.

'Tell him that Yaz of the Ictha is waiting for him at the bridge. I've come to fulfil the terms of our agreement.'

'Tell him yourself, bitch!' Suddenly the man was straining to sink his teeth into any part of her he could reach, the scarlet stain running up beneath his ear. 'You're going to die in these caves and I'm going to listen to your screaming.'

Yaz reached behind her and the red star thunked into her open hand. She brought it back towards Etrix's head and his eyes rolled up until only the whites showed. The scarlet stain sank back down his neck. Yaz reached out, tearing the man's patchwork furs open across his chest. She shone an intense beam of starlight at the retreating anger demon, using the light to drive both it and the malice demon down across prominent ribs. It was like chasing a slippery fish across the ice, a fish that kept sliding free, trying to head off in unwanted directions. But she drove them past his belly before he started to bleed from the eyes.

'Let him go.' Yaz backed off.

Rather than just letting the man fall, Erris lowered him gently.

'What's your name?' Yaz demanded.

'Etrix!' The man stayed on his hands and knees, spitting blood.

'And what are you going to do?' Yaz asked.

'I'm going to kill that stinking Theus!'

For a moment Yaz thought the rage had him again, but no, this was Axit pride. She saw it in his eyes as he struggled to his feet, shaking off Erris's attempt to help.

'Tell him that Yaz of the Ictha is waiting for him at the bridge. I've come to fulfil the terms of our agreement.' Yaz brought the star a little closer, making the man wince but keeping the demons on the run. 'The taint is going to claim you again but if you deliver my message I may be able to help you escape it.'

Etrix nodded. He'd clearly lived with the demons riding him long enough to know that they were still in him. 'I'll tell him. But then I'm going to kill him.' He stalked away from Erris, giving Yaz a wide berth.

At the opening leading out onto the ravine's edge he turned, some conflict twitching on his cheeks. 'Help us. Help the children. Help us or kill us.'

He was gone, running into the gloom, before Yaz could respond.

Yaz paced while Erris crouched. Etrix had been gone some time and the Tainted were still gathering at the bridge, dozens now, though none dared to advance into the light of the hunter star. Yaz found herself longing for somewhere soft to sit, somewhere clean and dry and warm and comfortable. She had been cold and wet, hungry and thirsty for too long. Sleeping on hard floors or not at all. Her body ached for kindness and still all that stretched before her was more hardship, more fear, more fighting.

'I hadn't thought it would be like this.' The first words Erris had spoken since Etrix ran off. 'Children?'

'You didn't know they threw children down the pit?' Yaz had been trying to avoid thinking about the little ones.

Erris frowned. 'I didn't see them in the city. And I didn't know they were being . . . infected . . . like this. What sort of lives do they live in this place?'

'I don't know what we can do about it,' Yaz said, feeling helpless. In a single sentence she had become one with those who threw them down the pit in the first place. But she really couldn't see a way to help them. She didn't even know if she could get Zeen, Thurin, and Kao free.

'What if Etrix does what he says and kills this Theus you're trying to bargain with?'

Yaz went to the cavern mouth and peered at the crowd gathered across the chasm. She worried for Thurin if Etrix kept his promise. 'I think if Theus were destroyed it might be even worse. From what I've seen he is the only one that holds them together. Without him they'd all be like Hetta.'

'Hetta?'

'They'd be running loose, just killing the Broken, maybe eating them too. Theus needs them to search the ice for demons that were once part of him. Without their fear of Theus the Tainted would swarm the Broken within days. They have the numbers, and you've seen what they're like.'

CHAPTER 29

When Theus finally arrived the howls and hoots of the Tainted heralded him. Erris and Yaz were standing by the bridge as he emerged from the dark mouth of a black ice cavern further along the ravine. He made his way slowly, seeming to enjoy the adulation of his minions. Clearly pride was one component of himself that had already been rediscovered and added to the whole during the course of the Tainted's searching. He wore Thurin's body. Kao lumbered behind him, his face a vacancy waiting to be filled, and Zeen capered around them both, wild with laughter, too often dangerously close to the edge and a fatal plunge to the waters far below. Etrix followed, as frantic and unfocused as the rest of them once more.

The Tainted by the bridge parted before Theus's advance, from biggest gerant to youngest child. Something about the fragmented soul carried inside Thurin's slender body made those other demons afraid. It made them forget the mindless pursuit of their own singular desires and listen to his will.

The black stain covered much of his face in a broad stripe from his hairline down across his forehead to his chin and trailing off along his neck.

'Yaz.' Theus showed her a wide grin. 'You came back, following a star like some wandering king. And what a star! Has it led you to the birth of something great, I wonder?'

Before Yaz could answer this strange question Theus's gaze fixed on Erris and blackness flowed into both his eyes as if this might offer more information about the newcomer. 'Here's a curio and no mistake. Alive but not alive. Human but not human. And familiar too. Very familiar.' The smile vanished. 'You're something made in the city. A marjal's mind hiding inside the works of my people. It's as if a dog's been given charge of a grand ship. He sits at the helm in the captain's hat and brocade, tongue lolling out, and no clue as to what he has been given.'

Yaz willed her star forward; it rose before her, red as the sun and burning brightly. The Tainted fell back, hissing, and even Theus took one step away, raising an arm to shield his eyes.

'We had a deal. Give me my friends.' She wanted to ask for them all. To free all those enslaved by the black ice. But Theus would never agree to it.

'Find the rest of me and you can have them.' Theus gestured towards the caves behind him. 'Though I am rather fond of this one.' He ran his hands over Thurin's chest and sides. 'As are you from what I've seen.'

Yaz hardened her features against any blush. She imagined that she felt Erris's questioning gaze against the back of her head and wasn't sure how she would feel about such jealousy. 'I don't have time to hunt the whole of the black ice for you. I said I could help you, not do it all for you. Consider what I'm offering as proof of concept. It will be up to you to refine it and make it work.'

'That was not our deal!' Theus snarled, the rage he was holding in check now beginning to slip free.

'Our deal was made with your knife at my throat,' Yaz

growled back. 'Accept this one or I'm going to see just how well you stand up against this star.' She increased the intensity of the light pouring out. Theus backed two more steps. The rest of the Tainted crowded in the gloom now, a good twenty yards further away to either side of the bridge's far end.

She softened her tone. 'How long has it been since a piece of you was discovered down here?'

Furrows lined themselves across Theus's brow. 'Many drops. Long enough for a child to grow old.'

Yaz paused, astonished and horrified in equal measure. Astonished at his tenacity and horrified at how many lives had been lost in this creature's cause. 'If I find another you let them all go, not just my friends.'

'I would promise it if I thought you'd believe me.' Theus shook his head. 'But even you are not that naive. Find a new fragment of me and I will let these three go with you.'

Yaz could feel Erris behind her, judging. 'Agreed.'

Erris said nothing but as he came to stand beside her she thought that she felt the weight of his disapproval settle on her shoulders and she slumped, accepting her guilt. Erris, though, however long he had lived, was new to this world of ice and hardship. Compromise was how life had to be lived. Everyone had to lean against the wind. Yaz would free them all if she could, but she saw no way to reach that goal. Although she hated the idea she began to see the position her parents and the rest of the Ictha were in with the pit and the weakness in their broken children. She didn't know if the priests' poison was starting to infect her or if this was just what growing up was – a series of compromises that twisted a child's idealism into something shameful.

'Stay out of my way.' Yaz advanced across the bridge. 'All of you.' She swept her star's light across the ranks of Tainted. 'But be close enough for my call.'

She stepped onto the far side of the ravine and recalled her star into her hand, striding towards the closest of the yawning cavern mouths, the one that Thurin had first led them into with promises to guide them safely in the dark. She glanced back towards Theus, staring at her hawk-like, and wondered what kind of darkness Thurin was lost in now, helpless in his own flesh while a demon used him to its evil ends. He'd been returned to the nightmare he had so recently escaped, and why? To save her brother, someone he had never met, one of the Tainted that he cared about least. He was here because of her. Another of her victims.

Yaz stepped into the black ice, Erris at her heels, and let the red star float free a yard before her. She strained that unknown muscle somewhere deep at the base of her mind and made the star blaze until its heart began to beat faster and its song became a war chant. Rather than focusing the light into a beam she let it shine before her in a wide arc, and even then the small fraction of it that reached her burned on her cheeks and forehead, dazzling her eyes behind a shielding hand. She moved slowly, letting the star's light reach into the blackness of the ice and purge the foulness there. Malice and hatred turned to terror as the knife that had once cut these demons free of the beings that owned them now returned to cut them once again.

'Enough!' Yaz quieted the hunter's heart and stood there panting, her skin feeling raw, head aching. All around her the sweating ice walls had become clear, the blackness pushed back almost too far to see. Here and there a stubborn black spot hung amid the fractured whiteness, like the opposite of the stars seen in the caverns where the Broken lived.

It stood to reason that if the Tainted had spent generations mining the ice and found only a few pieces of Theus then Yaz was hardly likely to find several more within yards of the first tunnel that she examined. She focused the starlight into a tight beam and shone it into the ice, directing it at the nearest of the more tenacious demons. Within seconds the patch had gone. Yaz wasn't sure if she was destroying the demons. It didn't seem that they could be moving through the ice, certainly not as fast as they were vanishing from it. But Yaz didn't much care if they were escaping to some unknown place or evaporating in the starlight; either way they were gone, and that was a good thing.

Yaz focused her light on each remaining spot in turn, a little at a time, until just one was left.

'It will be hard to reach,' Erris said.

Yaz shrugged. The blackness, an area perhaps smaller than a fist, lay some yards deep in the ice. She couldn't tell if it was an arm's length or two spears' in. But she had seen the coal-worm at work. With one finger she traced onto the surface of her star the best approximation she could of the sigil from the heat pot. It was more than memory that guided her. When she thought of heat it seemed that it had a shape, something complex and many-angled, like some small piece of the river that flows through all things. She tried to project that shape down onto the confining dimensions of a surface.

'Ow!' She pulled her hand back quickly as heat flared from the star. She let it float free and directed it against the ice in a slow spiralling motion so that the hole it made would be slightly larger than the star itself and allow the meltwater a way to escape.

It took some time to reach the trapped demon, and all the while that the star poured out its heat Yaz felt a coldness growing in her bones. But at last a pulse of blackness came out with the water running steadily from the hole.

'Theus!' Yaz recalled her star and slumped back against the clear ice of the nearest wall. 'Theus!'

He came, prowling in as though she and Erris were his prey. He tried and failed to hide his surprise on seeing the cleared ice on all sides. Yaz hoped that seeing how easily it had been returned to its natural state would make Theus more worried about what she might be able to do to him if he reneged on their agreement.

'What have you got for me?' Immediately he finished the question Theus stepped into a hollow where the meltwater had collected. He lifted his foot with a snarl, the skins wrapped about it now dripping.

'Over here.' Yaz pointed to the stain trying to leech itself back into the ice at the base of the wall beneath the hole she had made.

Theus squinted, frowned, and took one step towards it. A moment of recognition pushed his eyebrows back; then he shook his head. 'Quite powerful. An impressive find, but no part of me. Burn it.'

'Destroy it?' Yaz asked.

'Why would I want any competition?' Theus pulled Thurin's lips back to reveal his teeth. 'Burn it.'

Yaz shrugged and called the star's light out in a beam, keeping it focused on the demon until the last part of it relinquished its hold on the world. 'Is it dead now?'

Theus shook his head. 'It's gone to haunt the barrier between life and death. There are ways back from that place. Not many, but some.'

Yaz returned to her work. Theus had retreated from the star's radiance and left them to it, but he could be called back easily enough. The iron collection was due soon whether she was back at the city or not. There would be more, of course, but surviving until the next one could prove to be a problem. The scale of her task daunted her. She might be working a thousand times faster than the Tainted but the odds were still against her finding a part of Theus in the time allowed to her.

Erris followed her dutifully as she drove her star to new efforts, saturating the black ice with its fierce illumination, to leave small constellations of dark stars in the ice, then focusing ever more intense beams on these stubborn spots and melting paths to the toughest of them so that Theus could inspect the run-off.

Hours later Erris took her arm. 'This is hurting you. I can see that. You need to rest. You need to eat.'

Yaz shook him off. 'There's no time.'

'And how will you hold Theus to his bargain if you exhaust yourself fulfilling your part of it?'

Yaz pressed her fingers to her aching forehead and bit back on an angry reply. Erris was right. She'd never been so tired, but there was so much to do. She managed a smile. 'I was rather hoping that if he changes his mind about letting the others go then you could change it back for me.'

Erris frowned. 'It's not just you that this is taking a toll on. The star-stone is diminishing too.'

Yaz widened her eyes in alarm and looked down at the star making its slow revolutions around her. It looked the same but now she wasn't sure. Slow changes, like ice melting, could happen before your eyes without the mind registering them. Much like the way parents don't see their children growing, she supposed. 'Really?'

Erris nodded. 'It's a fragment, already broken. The tasks you demand of it gradually burn it up.'

'But I need it to get the demons out of Zeen and Kao . . .' The idea of losing the star bit at her in other ways too. Ways that should have been as nothing against the desire to free Zeen. But the fact was there, she found it hard to think about the star being gone, leaving her in darkness, leaving her in silence without its song echoing through her bones.

'Let's hope we're lucky then.' Erris smiled but it didn't take the worry from his face.

More hours passed without result. Yaz had cleared the ice many yards deep along the length of one tunnel and around the edges of two small chambers. The star felt noticeably smaller when she took it in her hands now and its heartbeat had sped up, even when at rest. Despite the speed she worked at it would still take weeks if not months to make a sizable impact. The black ice covered dozens of chambers much larger than the ones she had cleared, and there was no telling how far it extended beyond the regions where the heat had melted gaps between ice and rock.

'That one has been watching us a lot,' Erris said.

'Huh?' Yaz started, jerking her head up. She was shocked to discover that she had been dozing, chin on chest. She'd only sat down, at Erris's insistence, to rest her eyes for a moment. She wiped at her mouth, hoping she hadn't drooled. Erris watched her, a question remaining in the dark calm of his eyes. He turned towards the far end of the cavern, and there, lurking in the gloom, a gerant stood, watching her with wholly black eyes. 'That's Kao, one of my friends.'

The Tainted had long since retreated beyond sight, unable or unwilling to endure the star's light. Yaz supposed Theus might have set Kao to watching them but it seemed a strange choice given that the boy was one of the hostages against her success. She wondered what else might be drawing him closer than the rest. 'If you can hold him for me we could speak to him like we did with Etrix.'

Yaz dimmed her star to a molten glow and began to circle towards Kao while Erris slid the other way around the cavern wall. Kao watched her, baring his teeth in threat, thick arms raised but whether to attack or defend she couldn't tell. Erris moved through the darkness, swift and surefooted. The quiescent star held Kao's attention, allowing Erris to come up behind him unseen. He nodded and Yaz increased the star's glow. With a snarl Kao backed and started to turn. He stumbled over a crouching Erris and fell.

'Quick!' Erris grabbed the fallen boy, dwarfed by his broad frame.

Yaz let the star blaze and ran forward to hold it close to Kao's head as he howled and struggled against Erris's implacable strength. Further back in the adjoining cavern the darkness seethed with motion, but none of the Tainted lurking there dared the star's light to aid their fallen brother.

Just as the ice had cleared before the red glare, Kao's face returned to that of a scared boy. The only difference was the star's much greater potential to damage Kao during the process. Yaz had to force the demons from his head while leaving his mind in one piece. The boy screwed his eyes closed against the brightness, screaming for Yaz to take it away.

She drew the star back as far as she dared to without letting the demons that had claimed Kao surge back into his mind. 'Listen to me. We've come to get you out of here. But first I have to do something for Theus.'

'You're searching for him.' Kao stopped struggling against Erris's hold on him. The city man had him gripped at both wrists with his legs scissored around his waist. 'You're searching for Theus just like we all do.'

'Yes, but when I find a piece of him he is going to let you and Thurin and Zeen go free. I just need to get on with it. You need to be patient, Kao. I'm sorry.'

Kao started to pant and choke, as if he were gulping air

in the gaps between the waves of a rising tide. 'I . . . I know what . . . what you're doing.'

'Let him go, Erris.' Yaz stood and backed away. She couldn't know what Kao was suffering but she hoped her words offered him some hope, a little comfort.

'Wait! Wait . . .' Kao twisted on the wet rock as Erris released him and rolled away. 'The furthest cavern . . . search there . . . They . . . they're all scared of it . . . They don't tell him . . . Theus.'

'Scared of what?' Yaz asked, starting to find her hope.

'The great . . . great darkness . . . My demon saw—' His lips darkened, shading into black and twisting into a savage grin. 'You'll never have this one back, girl.' He rolled onto all fours, panting, reminding Yaz of the Quinx's dogs. One eye turned crimson. He snarled and scampered off, only reaching his feet as the darkness took him.

Erris stood, wiping at the grime on his pale clothes in mild disgust. 'Can we believe him?'

Yaz frowned. 'Kao must have been pushing at his demons to get them to come close enough for us to notice him. He might not have much control but he used what little he could.'

'Why would the "demons" be hiding things from Theus?'

'You've seen what they're like. Why wouldn't they be cruel, treacherous, and untruthful to their own kind as well? Besides, Theus rules over them, forces them to work. I can understand them not being keen to make him stronger. I'm not eager to do that myself.' Yaz repressed a shudder.

'The furthest cavern?' Erris made a slow rotation with his arms spread. 'Furthest from where?'

'I think furthest from the centre,' Yaz said.

'And how would we find that?' Erris widened his eyes at her. Of all of him it was his eyes that were most alien to her, so different from the pale glances she had known all her life with the Ictha.

'Furthest from the heat. So the coldest caverns in the black ice. Out on the edge of the Tainted's territory.' She turned and pointed in the opposite direction to the slow flow of the ice. 'That way.'

Together they abandoned the work so far and walked off towards the black heart of the Tainted's territory.

By the red light of her star Yaz saw the horrors that she had missed during the merciful blindness of her first visit. The bones of scores, possibly hundreds, had been pressed into the ice as macabre decoration, many of them clearly children. Yaz had never seen human bones before, only those of fish. On the ice something had to eat the flesh for the bones to be revealed. Clearly while the Tainted could not sustain themselves by cannibalism they all shared Hetta's instinct for it and would not waste the dead.

In the larger chambers debris from raids on the Broken lay scattered. Precious iron and other building material scavenged at great cost from the city had been strewn carelessly. Twice they encountered some sort of construction: boards, one standing vertically, the other horizontal like a table, with chains at the corners or strong wire. Both of these were bloodstained and about them knives, broken glass, and other jagged pieces of metal sat close at hand. Yaz looked away and hurried by, trying to force her imagination to silence.

It took longer than they had to spare to find the furthest cavern and convince themselves that no other extended further into the flow of the ice. The chamber was dry and the low roof creaked constantly as hair's width by hair's width the unimaginable weight of ice advanced towards the city. A black frost clung to every wall like the fuzz of hair on a baby's head. Clearly enough heat found its way to the chamber to periodically melt the ice back just enough to fight its advance, but it had to be a battle that ebbed and flowed. Currently the ice seemed to be winning, crushing the chamber ever smaller.

The unfocused hatred that infused all of the black ice was fiercer here, a wild anger bubbled all around her despite the presence of her star. Yaz could feel it trying to get in under her skin. And more than that, she felt watched, as if the demons here were more intensely aware of her presence than anywhere else.

'How could Kao have seen anything in here?' Erris wondered. If he felt the weight of evil he showed no sign of it.

'The demons see more than we do.' Yaz urged more light from her star. Even as she did so the frost began to bleach, catching the starlight and turning crimson.

Erris went to the rear where the ice sloped to the ground and he had to crouch to advance. 'The blackness likes to go against the flow. It should have been swept a hundred miles from the city by now.'

The cold had a bite to it here at the limits of the caves and Yaz enjoyed the star's warmth in her hands though her weakness shamed her.

'I can see something . . .' Erris said, setting his brown hands to the jet-black ice, seemingly untroubled by the malice frozen there.

'You can?' Yaz wondered quite how much his eyes could see and what other gifts the Missing had given him. 'What is it?'

Suddenly Erris lurched backwards, sprawling on the floor, and when he spoke it was with a trembling voice.

'Big.'

CHAPTER 30

'"Big"?' Yaz asked. She went to help Erris to his feet, all the time keeping her eyes on the black sloping wall of ice. Something in there had scared Erris. That was something she'd not seen before. 'Just "big"?'

'Yes.' Erris shrugged free of her grip, a little embarrassed perhaps. 'Very big.'

Yaz stretched her aching body and pressed her hands to her forehead, hoping somehow to push back the pain that would soon blossom behind it. She forced a confidence she didn't feel into her voice. 'Let's have a better look then.'

Once more she pushed the star into incandescence, driving its heartbeat ever faster, its song more shrill. She hid her face behind her arm and directed the light forward. Even so she saw the black bar of her arm bone through closed eyes. The pain that had taken root behind her forehead sent thorned tendrils deeper, as though trying to split her brain in half. At last she broke off with a gasp, willing the star to stillness and finding that she had to fight it this time, as if it had gone into panic and wanted nothing but to run and run until it destroyed itself.

When Yaz opened her eyes she saw that the frost had melted from the walls, leaving them slick with running water, and that on two sides she had driven the blackness back many yards, leaving clear ice marbled with ghostly white fractures and flaws. Directly in front of her, however, the ice had cleared little more than a spear's length and a great intrusion of blackness remained, resisting the light. The sight of it carried a new weight of terror that had been absent when all the ice lay black.

'I said it was big.' Erris spoke from behind her.

The blackness reminded Yaz of a great thumb pushing towards her, several feet clear of the rock, rising to many times her height, wider than the entire chamber it was aimed at.

'That thing can't be part of Theus?' Yaz couldn't keep the horror from her voice. If it truly was part of him she wasn't sure she dared reunite him with it.

Erris said nothing; he only came to stand at her shoulder, tilting his head in curiosity.

With a sigh Yaz drove a beam of intense light from her star, feeling a corresponding spike of pain being driven back into her head. Her brain already felt as though a ravine were opening inside it like the one in the bedrock dividing the Broken from the Tainted. She aimed the beam at the centre of the black mass, expecting to clear it piece by piece, but the crimson circle merely burned across the surface.

'Try the edge,' Erris suggested.

Yaz played the beam slowly across the blackness, moving first to one edge then scanning to the other. Here and there it would nibble away a touch of the blackness before encountering the huge and resilient core. As she moved the light she began to get a sense of shape, an idea of the fearsome contours of the thing. The darkness was vast, ten thousand times larger than any of the demons she had freed before, and ten thousand times more resistant to the star's light. What the thing might do to her when released didn't bear thinking about. With such power added to his being Theus would have no reason to hold to their agreement.

Suddenly she began to laugh.

'What?' Erris looked at her as if she'd gone crazy.

'Don't you see it?' She played the light across a steep slope and into a gaping chasm at the front of the blackness.

'I saw it before you did . . .' Erris frowned. 'But why is it funny?'

'It's a whale,' she said simply.

Erris's frown deepened, rucking furrows into the smoothness of his brow. Then, eyes widening, he saw it. 'That's a mouth?'

'Yes.' The mouth in question was large enough to swallow a boat. One of the city's hunters would make a mouthful. Quite how such a creature had come to be taken up by the ice, or what forces had lifted it from the sea to be carried across the rock Yaz had no idea. 'It's one of the great whales, the largest that visit the Hot Sea.' Yaz had only ever seen the back of a great whale as it broke the surface for air. The flowing, rolling surge of the creature had taken her breath. She'd thought it must stretch fifty yards or more. Her father said that once, in his youth, such a whale had leapt from the sea, half of its body clearing the waves and towering over his boat as if it were the Black Rock itself.

'What a thing . . .' Erris sounded awed despite having lived a thousand years amid the wonders of the Missing. 'Does it have teeth?'

'I don't know.' The Ictha had never landed so great a beast. Like ice storms they were a force of nature that you merely let pass and hoped to survive. Yaz tried to shine her light in search of some sign of teeth. But exhaustion rose in her like a wave, carrying her to the floor.

'Yaz!' Erris nearly caught her but her weakness had taken him by surprise. Instead he helped her to sit with her back against the cleared ice, and crouched beside her, his face a mask of concern. 'Are you sick?'

'I . . . I just need a short rest.' Embarrassed, Yaz tried to turn the conversation in another direction. She looked towards the frozen whale. 'It's said that Zin, the first man, was swallowed by a great whale and lived for forty days and forty nights in its belly before his escape.'

'Who?' Erris gave her a curious look.

She met his look with surprise. 'Zin!' Erris might have been born long ago but not before the first man. She told the tale.

Hua, least of all the Gods in the Sea, made Zin, the first man, from salt water, the bones of a tuark, and the skin of a whale. While Aiiki, least of all the Gods in the Sky, made Mokka, the first woman, from ice, clouds, the whispers of four lost winds, and a colour stolen from the dragons' tails.

Zin and Mokka lived upon the ice in a tent twice as tall as a man and as wide as a harpoon throw. They pitched it for years at a time, for in those days Hua concerned himself with the affairs of men and kept a hot sea open even during the fiercest of winters, and Aiiki sang her songs so that the winds sheathed their claws and kept their fangs hidden.

When their food ran low Zin and Mokka would take it in turns to go out upon the sea in their white boat while the other stayed to carve kettan from the teeth of lesser whales, cutting out the forms of the children they would have, children who would carry the story of their lives far across the ice, to be told until the last star burned red and faded from the sky.

Zin and Mokka waited for their children for untold years: long enough for the touch of fingers to wear the first of their kettan smooth once more, erasing the story that the knife had set there; long enough for stars to turn from white to red and fade like embers into nothing. But still no child came to their tent.

Zin set out upon the sea and he called to Hua who had made him and asked why he had been given no son. Mokka went bare-armed upon the ice and she called to Aiiki who had made her and sang her lament for the daughter who had never come.

But it was not Hua who answered Zin upon the waves. Instead, the greatest God in the Sea rose from unknown depths: Hoonumu, he who dwells beneath the light. Hoonumu rose in the form of a great whale, black as night and twice as vast. And the whale swallowed Zin without answer, taking him and his white boat into the void that was its belly.

And it was not Aiiki who answered Mokka but Allatha, the greatest God in the Sky, she who first sets the stars aflame and who snuffs each of them out when their time has been spent. Allatha descended in the form of a snow hawk with wings of ice and flame. She told Mokka that she had asked for a gift larger than the world, for birth is a kind of fire, and there is no gift more precious than fire. It cannot be given back, it can spread unchecked, it grows without limit, able to destroy worlds and leap the black chasms between them. Hua and Aiiki had made between them one man and one woman. But if Hoonumu and Allatha gave Mokka children then there could be more men and more women than fish in the sea or birds in the sky.

Mokka said only that she would pay the price, for the ice had always been lonely even with two. And the Gods in the Sky and the Gods in the Sea said that if she could bring her man from the belly of a whale then ever after she could bring a child from her own belly.

It took her forty days, and how she did it is another story in and of itself, but Mokka succeeded, and in saving Zin she opened her womb and became the mother of us all.

'I can stand now.' Yaz pushed away the hand Erris offered. He might have the strength of the Missing in his arms but she would not allow him to think her weak. Mokka had brought Zin from the belly of the beast and Yaz too had saved a man, bringing Erris from the depths of the void star at the city's heart and out from far beneath the surface. One day she would show him to the Gods in the Sky. She caught herself thinking of them in the roles of Mokka and Zin and pushed a foolish smile from her face.

'We should go,' Erris said. 'There's nothing here.'

'Apart from enough meat to feed a clan, and just yards away from people so starved their ribs look as if they are trying to escape.' She stood looking at the bulk trapped within the ice before her. 'With this the Broken wouldn't need what the priests send them. They could go for months, years even, without scavenging, without sending iron to the Black Rock. They could make new bargains from a position of strength.'

Erris raised his brows, smiling. 'Quite the politician, aren't you?'

Yaz didn't know the word but somehow she had a sense

of it, presumably from the strangely drawn-out time she spent in the void with Erris. 'There's something else.'

'Yes?'

Yaz approached the ice and the behemoth it held. That sense of being watched remained, along with an intense hunger, almost jealousy, as if what watched her envied everything she had, from her star to her skin, and wanted to tear all of it from her. 'I didn't clear them all.'

Erris glanced around. 'The ice is clear. And if that whale is a "demon" . . . well, we could be in trouble.'

'It's not a demon but it's the perfect place for one to hide.' Yaz summoned the dazzling beam of starlight once more and scanned the whale methodically, straining to see any irregularities. Her strength had started to wane and the agony in her head had built to a crescendo when, as the beam slid yet again through the black-on-black openness of the whale's toothless mouth, it seemed as though there were something there: a dark star floating as if in the act of being swallowed.

'Found you.' She let the beam linger, seeing in the midst of it a black sphere resisting the light.

'It's Theus?' Erris asked.

'It's already lasted longer than any of the others we've discovered so far.'

'Shouldn't you call him then?'

Despite her pain and exhaustion Yaz continued to focus the star's light on the demon in the whale's mouth. Part of her wanted to see just how much the thing could take. Another part feared uniting something so powerful with the creature that dwelt inside Thurin. 'Is this a good idea, Erris?'

'You're asking me?' He spread his hands. 'This is all new to me. I don't know any of the people involved. When I was last here' – he swung his arm at the rock and ice – 'all this was fields.'

Yaz grudgingly took his point. She went to where the cavern roof lowered before rising into a larger chamber and shouted Theus's name. Returning to the rear wall of the cave she set her star to melting a path to the demon.

By the time Theus prowled in, with other Tainted haunting the shadows behind him, Yaz had almost reached the resistant clot of darkness and the floor was awash with meltwater. He looked in astonishment at the whale, now lit by the star that had almost entered its mouth.

He recovered himself swiftly. 'Another candidate?'

'The strongest so far.' Yaz watched him warily, remembering how swiftly he had set his knife to her throat the first time he showed himself.

'A veritable Jonah,' Theus breathed.

'Who?' Yaz asked.

Theus waved the question away.

Yaz coaxed the star to radiate more heat then had it rise to let the pulse of black water pass beneath it. She had the star follow the water out quickly while Theus strode forwards with ill-concealed eagerness to plant both palms into the pooling darkness.

The effect was immediate: Theus stiffened, raising his head to show a strained but rapt expression, the tendons in his neck standing out like cables. He began to suck in an enormous breath, accompanied by a disturbing moan, and the veins in his wrists mottled a greenish black, the colour flowing up towards his elbows before being lost beneath his skins. His body shook and it seemed that even the rock beneath him trembled as if in premonition of some seismic shift.

Yaz's star burned in her hand now, still uncomfortably hot, and for a mad moment she thought of bringing it down on the back of Theus's head in an overarm swing. But however terrifying the creature before her might be it was also Thurin, and it would be Thurin's skull that shattered.

Something was coming. Something big. Racing towards them as if the fields that Erris remembered were all that surrounded them. Yaz found herself needing to breathe yet unable to fill her lungs until the tension, building like a storm cloud piled miles high, finally peaked and broke.

Theus leapt to his feet with arms wide and a scream so loud it seemed it must splinter something vital inside his chest. A shockwave threw Yaz off her feet and made Erris stagger. All around them the ice shattered and fell, a white rain turned bloody in the starlight. Yaz found herself on her back with chunks of broken ice hammering all around her. For a moment she thought that the cavern had collapsed and she would lie buried beneath an unknown tonnage of glacier. But the deluge stopped, leaving the rock covered six inches deep. Some part of whatever energies had been released inside Theus during his reunion must have escaped through Thurin's ice-work. He stood now, frost in the black of his hair, staring at the hands he had raised before him, as if marvelling at himself, or perhaps just at the new perspective offered to him now that he was one piece closer to something whole.

Yaz got to her feet, shedding sheets of ice fractured from the ceiling. 'You got what you wanted. Now give me what you promised.'

Theus raised his head to reveal a face the colour of an old bruise with wholly black eyes and a dangerous grin. 'Find another piece of me and then I'll let them go.'

Yaz woke the star in her hand. 'Now!'

Theus flinched but didn't retreat. 'You want this boy that much?' he sneered.

'I want my friends. I want my brother. I want to leave this place and go back up to the ice.' With each 'I want' she pushed more light from the star until its heart pounded, close to breaking free.

Theus raised an arm to shield his face and backed a few paces. 'Life is easier down here. I was on the ice once.' He sounded surprised to hear himself say it.

'You're lying. This was all fields and forest. I've seen it.'

Theus shook his head, continuing to back away from the light. 'Each time I add to myself I recover fragments of memory, and some of the things that once seemed nonsense become comprehensible. I've been many places. All across this world. But I started my journey in the north. My parents . . . I had parents . . . they were of a sect that turned its back on technology. They lived in the far north. As a baby they took me to see . . .' He paused, fingers moving as if trying to assemble some lost truth from thin air. '. . . a wise woman . . . a witch! As a baby they took me to see a witch!' He shook his head again. 'So many broken pieces . . .'

'I don't care about that. Give me what you promised!' Yaz shouted. She narrowed the star's light into a single brilliant beam that struck Theus in the chest, driving him back, pinning him to the cavern wall. 'Now!'

Theus twisted, trying to struggle free, his breath escaping him in gasps and snarls. They fought, Yaz forcing herself to keep the star working at an intensity that didn't allow the creature inside Thurin to turn his ice-work against her. At last, sucking his breath over red teeth, Theus raised his face and fixed Yaz with a black stare. 'The time will come when you realize what you need is here. You'll want me back, Yaz of the Ictha, and you'll find this boy to have been a poor exchange.' He snarled, trying to break free. 'You don't even know what you're looking for. Some remnant of the green world? Nonsense. All of us are looking for ourselves. That's how we spend our lives. At least I'm honest about it.'

Yaz's pain had escaped the confines of her skull. She hurt in places she didn't own. She was certain that blood must be running from her eyes, her nose, her mouth. It wasn't possible to contain so much hurt. Even so, she forced herself to brighten the star and to speak, grating the words out past her teeth. 'What. You. Promised.'

With a howl part rage and part exasperation Theus called out to the Tainted thronging in the next cavern. Yaz didn't understand the language he used. Mother Mazai said that in distant parts of the ice other tongues were used, but Yaz had only half believed her and had never expected to hear with her own ears words that weren't words.

Three figures came reluctantly into the chamber, hunched against the light, feet shuffling on the wet rock. Kao, Zeen, and one other, even larger than Kao, an older gerant with a dirty shock of red hair, blank-eyed and scarred around the neck and face.

The gerant crossed the chamber, reaching out towards Theus, though reluctantly, as if Theus were on fire and the gerant lacked the courage to dare the heat. Theus lunged, stretching to clasp his hand around the gerant's. In that moment of connection something dark flowed from the sleeve of Theus's skins, a mottled stain moving swiftly across his wrist, a trailing darkness in the veins. It seemed to pass between them, blooming across the back of the gerant's hand and rippling up through the meat of his forearm.

'A poor exchange. One you will regret.' The gerant rumbled the words, Theus's words falling from a new mouth as Thurin collapsed to the floor, a puppet whose strings had failed him. The gerant's eyes darkened, the whites shading through greys into black. In three strides he had both Kao and Zeen gripped from behind by the neck. 'These two you will have to empty by yourself. I have nowhere for their fragments to go.' Without warning he smacked their heads together, lifting Zeen from the ground in order to do so; then, dropping Zeen, he clubbed Kao to his knees with one massive fist.

The gerant snarled, turned, and strode away, ducking to leave the chamber. 'Go die on the ice.'

CHAPTER 31

Erris dragged Zeen and Kao from the black ice caverns. They screamed and roared and issued threats that Yaz knew could never have sprung from the minds of either one. She closed her ears to their sickness and kept her star burning, a defence against any change of mind on Theus's part or disobedience among the Tainted's ranks. The light would be no defence against a spear thrown from the dark though, and Yaz kept their pace as fast as Thurin, still stumbling and disoriented, could manage. He had yet to speak though he had retched several times, spitting filth onto the floor. A cold suspicion still ran through Yaz that Theus had broken Thurin's mind on his way out of him, leaving her just a shambling ruin to care for.

At last they heard the muffled roar from the ravine and then finally emerged onto its flanks, all of them exhausted and speckled with the black meltwater that dripped constantly in the warmer caverns. And still they weren't safe. The ice bridge lay to their left just thirty yards away. To reach it they had to negotiate the narrow span of rock between the black ice on one side and the chasm yawning on the other.

'Be careful.' Yaz steered Thurin ahead of her. 'We're getting out of here, just focus on what you're doing.' A vision of Petrick falling from the bridge flashed across her mind. If the Tainted meant to stop them it would be here that the spears flew.

Thurin grunted and shambled ahead, still hunched as he had been in the low tunnels leading to the ravine. Behind her Erris manhandled Kao and Zeen along the ledge, the gerant before him, arm twisted behind his back, Zeen behind him, more or less dragged along, both of them struggling and howling.

Kao and Zeen's protests were echoed by screams and roars from further back in the black ice. The wild cacophony seemed to be getting louder and closer very swiftly, as if the din were racing ahead of a Tainted mob. The black throats of the nearest cave mouths redoubled the sounds before throwing them out into the ravine, drowning out the complaints of the hidden waters. Yaz worried that it wouldn't be long before they vomited forth the demon-possessed horde responsible for the noise.

Thurin stumbled and slipped. Yaz caught his arm, holding him from the fall. Flinching, he shook her off and staggered forward, reaching the ice bridge in ten more steps, each of them looking to be the last before he pitched into the chasm. He stood now at the start of the bridge fighting half-heartedly for balance like a lone tent pole victimized by the wind.

Another scream tore the air behind Yaz. Something in the swiftly diminishing wail dragged her attention away from Thurin. She turned to see with horror that where Erris had been holding Kao and her brother he now held only the gerant and a handful of torn skins. As the shock held Yaz paralysed, the first of the pursuing Tainted began to leap, whooping, from the nearest cave mouths.

'No!' Yaz stood locked in place. It was as though the regulator had pushed Zeen into the pit all over again. '*No!*'

'Yaz! Move!' Erris shoved Kao ahead of him. The gerant came forward, grinning hugely as if her anguish were the sweetest feast, laid out for him to savour. 'Hurry!'

Behind Erris the first of the Tainted were running along the ledge, careless of their safety.

'Yaz!' Erris shouted again, more desperately. He got close enough for Kao to lunge at her and try to knock her into the ravine.

With a scream wholly unequal to the task of expressing what she felt Yaz turned and hurried to the bridge. Thurin was still standing on the ice just at the start of the arc that spanned the ravine. He stood with his feet inches from the edge, hunched and leaning forward, staring into the nothingness beneath him. Yaz reached him and tried to bundle him forward without knocking him over or unbalancing him into the fall. She found his body as stiff as if it had been frozen, every muscle rigid.

Zeen was gone. Zeen! Vanished like Petrick into the dark fall. She tried to force it from her mind but the image of Erris's hand clutching only torn skins refused to leave her.

Over the whooping of the Tainted rapidly closing on the bridge Yaz imagined she could hear Theus's mocking laughter. She'd lost her brother despite all her efforts. Thurin was a broken-minded ruin who probably couldn't feed or clean himself, and all she had was Kao, who she felt bound to only by a grudging sense of duty.

'Yaz!' Erris had caught her up again, forcing Kao ahead of him onto the bridge that they had once worried might not support them singly and now held four of them.

A spear sliced the air between them, shockingly fast, swallowed by the chasm. Yaz hadn't seen it coming, hadn't even seen any of the Tainted carrying it. She shouted again, a mix of rage, fear, and frustration, then grabbed Thurin to bodily manhandle him along the bridge. At the same time she willed her orbiting star to blaze, hoping to drive back any Tainted who might join them on the bridge. Behind her, panicked or hurt by the starlight, Kao redoubled his efforts to break free, even if it meant leaping from the bridge.

Thurin remained as if frozen, just a deep moan escaping him as she tried to carry him forward. He seemed unreasonably heavy and her efforts to move him slackened the light that she could drive from the star. With a grunt she managed to shift him a few inches across the slick ice. She saw something at the corner of her eye, a pale something where nothing should be. Expecting a spear to impale her at any moment she allowed herself a glance.

'Zeen!'

There, yards below them in the darkness, Zeen was rising. He fought it, twisting and spitting with fury, but foot by inexorable foot he was rising from the chasm. Suddenly Yaz understood. Thurin had hold of him. Thurin had reached out with his ice-work as Zeen fell and had taken hold of the water that makes up most of any person. What it had cost him Yaz couldn't know but she did know better than to break his concentration. Instead she turned her focus to the star and flared its light back at those Tainted just gaining the bridge. Erris, lacking any space to get past her and Thurin, waited with Kao, all of them exposed to the next spear to come hissing from the dark.

Fortunately weapons of any kind were rare among the Tainted and if there were spears being held back in the gloom then the owners proved loath to throw them out over the chasm. In battle with the Broken it seemed that the Tainted had to rely on the reluctance of former friends and family to skewer loved ones. That and the fact that they knew no one would follow them into the black ice.

To a rising chorus of howls Zeen came level with the bridge. Yaz knelt and hauled him up, getting a tight grip on his shoulder despite his clawing hands. A moment later he had his teeth in the meat of her forearm. She yelled in surprise. The pain was astonishing, and the fear that he would actually tear free and devour a chunk of her flesh overwhelmed her. She struck out in panic, pounding his head. Teeth slipped from blood-slick flesh and Zeen went limp, sliding soundlessly from the icy bridge.

'No!' But somehow Thurin had the boy's wrist and was dragging him onwards.

Quickly they followed Thurin across and within twenty paces were back in the cavern where they had questioned Etrix seemingly an age ago but in reality less than a day earlier.

'Is he all right?' Yaz hurried to Thurin's side to inspect Zeen. He hung bonelessly in Thurin's grasp with blood running from his nose. A deep pang of guilt skewered her but as she reached towards him his eyes flickered open, showing not the near-white irises of the Ictha but crimson discs, and he lunged for her, jaw snapping shut just shy of her fingertips.

Yaz pulled her arm back, seeing for the first time the dark blood welling from the set of tooth-shaped holes Zeen had put there.

'If you can drive the demons out then do it quickly.' Thurin spoke with a rusty voice as if words had become strangers to him in just the short while since his capture. 'They're both dangerous until you do it.'

Yaz nodded. This was the part she had been dreading. If she failed here what would she do with them? Could she leave, and abandon her brother to the hell he had been enduring since his drop? Would death be cleaner? Or would she die trying and still leave him demon-ridden?

Thurin pinned Zeen to the rock while Yaz approached

with her star in hand. The orb had grown noticeably smaller, her fist almost encompassing it. 'How did they cure you?' Yaz asked Thurin, hesitating over 'cure' since they had left Theus wrapped around his bones.

'They staked me out on a bed of stardust and showered more on me. I felt the demons burn and die inside me. But it took days. We need something quicker if Pome and his hunter are still after us. Is Arka still fighting them?'

'I don't know.' Yaz shook her head, shamed that she had given Arka no thought in an age. 'How can I do it faster?'

'My mother said the demons could be driven into an extremity and cut out . . . or off.'

'Cut off?' Yaz's blood ran cold.

'A finger . . . or a hand.' Thurin didn't meet her gaze. Held in his grip Zeen stirred and started to howl while Kao began to roar and to struggle against Erris once more.

'Here.' Erris tossed something down beside her. 'Tie them.'

Yaz picked up the rope. A cable of some kind, smooth and shiny like old leather, something from the city. She bound Kao's hands and patted her hip for a knife.

'Let me.' Erris released Kao briefly and broke the rope between his hands. 'There.'

Yaz took it, blinking. She saw that the rope had a metal core, an orangey-red, her mind supplied the word 'copper', one of Erris's. She tied Kao's ankles as Erris held him on his knees, then she bound her brother similarly. He fell silent once she'd secured his hands, watching her instead with baleful eyes. She stood back to consider him.

'I didn't rescue my brother to maim him!' The idea of cutting Zeen's hand off turned Yaz's stomach. 'There has to be a better way.'

'Sometimes a clean cut is the kindest way.' Thurin let go of Zeen's head and got to his feet. 'Some cankers have to be carved out before they spread.' He led Yaz closer to the ravine where her starlight would keep the Tainted at bay.

'But there may be another way.' Thurin spoke in a hushed tone so the others wouldn't hear. 'Eular told my mother that if you could get the demons to stay still and then hit them with a massive star they would be destroyed.' His voice lacked certainty. 'She didn't really know what he meant at the time. She didn't have a star anything like the one you've got and she couldn't have held it if she had. But *you* could do it.'

He frowned. 'It would be difficult though. If you're using the star to drive them and trap them in an extremity they'd slide away while you were readying yourself for the final strike . . .'

Yaz bit her lip, pondering. 'Where do the demons like to stay?'

'In the head.' Thurin furrowed his brow, remembering the invasion.

Yaz knew what damage even a small star could do to someone's soul. Pome had some resistance to them and yet a star considerably smaller than the one in her hand had broken his mind, splitting away some of his darker side into a demon not so different from the ones haunting the black ice. 'And if not in the head?'

'The heart,' Thurin said without hesitation. 'Sometimes they go there to let you understand your plight. They return your senses to you and let you think clearly while they sit in your heart to savour your despair. If you try to run or to destroy yourself they do . . . something . . . to your heart, and all you can do is lie there in agony gasping for breath. And sometimes even that's better than standing thinking about what they've made you do.'

'The heart. That could work . . .' Yaz tried not to think about Thurin's suffering. She hoped Zeen's demons had been less interested in torturing him. Either way she would take pleasure in their annihilation.

'I don't know anything else,' Thurin cautioned. 'It's probably a lot harder than it sounds. And if you damage the heart . . .'

'I'll try it on Kao first.'

Thurin glanced at her, a hint of reproach in those dark, haunted eyes of his.

'What?' Yaz felt instantly guilty. 'He obviously has the strongest heart. If it doesn't work on Zeen I won't know if it will work on Kao. But if I start with Kao and he doesn't survive I'll know there is no point trying that approach with Zeen.'

Thurin raised his brows a fraction but said nothing. Instead he gestured back at the cavern where Kao lay bound. He nodded towards Erris. 'You'll have to tell me later who that man is and how he seems so much stronger than an Ictha.'

At Yaz's request Erris laid Kao on the rock beside Zeen and held him steady. Thurin knelt beside Erris, holding Zeen's head to keep him from dashing it on the ground.

Yaz approached Kao, who twisted and turned in Erris's grip, roaring threats. Thurin shrank back as the blazing star came nearer to him, as if the thing were as hot as it looked, but he kept hold of Zeen.

Yaz focused as much of the light as she dared onto Kao's face. He screwed his eyes tight shut and turned his head as far away as he could. Within a few heartbeats he began to quieten, and shortly after the stains left him, moving down his neck. She waited a moment, ignoring the boy's plaintive questions. Where was he? Was that Yaz? Had they escaped? She had no answers for him and only one hope. When she was sure that the demons had had sufficient time to reach his heart and coil there, hiding from the star's glare, she raised it overhead and focused all of its light, and song, and anger, into a tight core at its centre.

With a scream that contained all her fears she brought the star slamming down onto Kao's muscular chest right over his heart and released all that she had stored within the star in a single hammer blow.

There was a crack as though she had split the world and the star vibrated in her hand like a ringing bell, hurting her fingers. Kao convulsed with such force that Erris was thrown back. Silence followed that one moment of violence. Kao lay limp, a small blackened circle burned into his furs, smoking gently where the star had struck.

'Kao?' Yaz asked, her voice shaking. 'Kao?'

Nothing.

She dropped to her knees and grabbed his shoulders.

'Careful!' Erris warned. 'He could be shamming.'

Yaz ignored Erris and shook Kao. 'Wake up! Wake up, you big idiot!' He felt lifeless in her grip, a dead weight.

'Is he dead?' Thurin asked.

Erris looked grim. An acid guilt ran through Yaz. She had experimented with a child's life at stake, and her skills had failed her. A tear rolled across her cheek.

'I . . .' Kao opened one eye.

'Kao!' Yaz seized him.

'I'm so hungry.' The boy's stomach gurgled.

Yaz snorted in relief. 'Get him out of the way,' she told Erris, and moved beside her brother. She shone the starlight into his face, still turned away from the glare of her working on Kao. The star's heart buzzed, its song sounded cracked, but she drove it hard and the demons slowly leached from Zeen's head, flowing down his neck and into the narrow confines of his bony chest. She squeezed the star, compacting its energies deep within it and raised it on high. Part of her flinched from striking Zeen. Kao looked so robust that no matter how hard she had pounded the star onto his chest she had had no worries about injuring him with the force of the blow. But her skinny brother seemed so vulnerable on the ground before her. She thought of Azad, the brother who her weakness had let die. Would her strength be the death of her remaining brother?

The same scream tore from her mouth as she swung to slam the star onto Zeen's chest. Again the world-splitting crack, though this time it sounded more like the fracturing of sternum and ribs. Again the pain in her fingers. And Zeen convulsing like a fish landed on the ice, Thurin struggling to keep his head from the rock.

Something changed in the quality of the light, but Yaz only had eyes for her brother. Thurin released him and let him lie limp between them.

'Zeen?' Yaz asked.

In answer Zeen sucked in a great gasp of air, his arms and legs rising as he did it, as if he had been as close to drowning as you can get without staying drowned. He choked and gasped and turned his head, fixing her with pale Ictha eyes full of tears. 'Yaz?' Another gulped breath. 'I had a terrible dream.'

Emotions Yaz had no name for reached up from the depths of her, squeezing the air from her lungs, taking the words from her tongue, filling her eyes with answering tears. And as she raised her hands to her face the fragments of her broken star spilled between her fingers to go bouncing across the rock, a dozen and more smaller stars, all perfect spheres, a rainbow of glowing colour shading stronger around the red.

CHAPTER 32

None of them spoke much as Yaz led the way back through the Broken's territory, aiming for the city. Thurin knew the way best of course but, like Kao and Zeen, he still seemed too shaken to do much more than follow. Yaz had surrounded herself with the fragments of the hunter star, a dozen or so, none of them larger than her thumbnail. Each followed its own slow orbit about her, collectively weaving a glowing cocoon, their light sending a myriad faint shadows sliding across rock and ice. As she led them further from the Tainted's ground and the caverns grew lighter she directed the stars into her pocket, not wanting to signal her approach to any of Pome's faction.

Zeen followed close on her heels. After his purging he had hugged her like a much younger child and had not wanted to let go. Yaz had held him just as tight, as though he were an anchor to her old life and somehow together they might follow the chain back to better days. At last she had had to pull away from him and explain that they needed to hurry and to keep silent.

Yaz took them through the outer fringes of the Broken's

caverns where the air grew colder, the ceilings lower, and the stars fewer in number. She wasn't sure how much Zeen remembered or if he fully understood where they were. She hoped that his experiences would remain a bad dream and that his youth would help him shrug them off. But Mother Mazai had always said that the hurts done to us as children cast shadows as long as our lives.

The outer chambers proved echoingly empty: no distant sounds of combat, no bodies, blood, or discarded weapons. Moving through them Yaz could imagine that she was the first to have ever come here, and that when she had moved on it would be as if she had never passed through. An unearthly beauty haunted these places, these dark, star-speckled voids miles deep beneath the ice. On their own slow timescale they were as fleeting as bubbles in water. Something about the majesty of them encouraged silence.

'Where are we going?' Thurin asked.

'To the city.' Yaz smiled; it was the first bit of curiosity he'd shown since they set off. She'd wondered if he was too afraid to ask about their friends in case she told him they were dead. No doubt the vision of Petrick falling from the bridge still haunted him. 'We're going to escape with the iron collection. Quell and Maya are gathering what we'll need for our journey on the ice.'

Thurin stayed silent at that. He'd never been out in the wind before, up there, beneath the open sky, never seen the sun or the true stars. Yaz supposed that in its way the prospect was as daunting to him as being thrown into the Pit of the Missing had been to her. Part of her wanted him to ask about Quina but he didn't.

'Maya?' Kao rumbled. They had crossed a wide chamber in the time it had taken the name to sink through whatever introspection was tying up his thoughts. 'Maya, trying to scavenge while there's a war going on down here? She's too little. She's just a—'

'She's deadly,' Yaz said. 'An Axit spy here to steal the priests' secrets. She was the one that rescued me and the others from the black ice. Worry about yourself. That one will outlast all of us down here.'

She led them on through the frozen chambers and they asked no more questions.

'Stop.' Erris caught her shoulder. They weren't far from the city now, crossing a freezing, low-roofed chamber reachable only through worm tunnels twisted and squeezed by the flow of the ice. A handful of small stars and a band of glowing dust provided faint illumination. Close at hand a small clutch of red-ball fungi clung to the rock, where they looked to be losing the struggle to prove that life will find a way.

'What is it?' Yaz asked.

'Listen.'

She heard it then, in between the creaking of the ice. A faint noise, hard to make out, attenuated as if reaching them from some distance.

Zeen showed his first interest in proceedings, pointing at one of the tunnel mouths. 'It's coming from there.'

'Sounds like sobbing,' Kao said.

Yaz pursed her lips. She wanted to get to the city. She didn't know how long they had before the collection was due but knew that it couldn't be too long. She couldn't carry the whole world on her shoulders. She took a step forward in the direction she'd been going, then stopped. It might be Quina. 'Let's find out.'

She led the way, letting her stars range ahead of her in the blackness of the tunnel. The passage had been squeezed to a concave shape and at the turns it grew tight enough that Kao had to struggle through. If they were attacked in here there would be no running away. Even turning around would be difficult.

'Definitely crying,' Thurin said behind her.

Yaz made no reply. Here and there the ice bore long smears of blood.

At each turn the sounds became clearer. Not a child, or a woman. A man's grief. Yaz scrambled up an incline, slipping on the ice and only just able to make progress. The sound ahead stopped abruptly.

'They've seen the light,' Kao hissed unnecessarily from behind Thurin and Zeen.

The next turn revealed their quarry. Two of the Broken, both black-haired, one collapsed in the lap of the other, a young man, his handsome face deathly pale. The other hunched about him, shivering violently. Blood had run across the ice, more of it than anyone could endure losing. There was something familiar about the dying man.

'We're here to help.' Yaz summoned her stars back to her hand.

The one cradling the bleeding man raised his face, framed by a tangle of red-black hair. Where the other had been handsome this one was beautiful in a way that stopped the breath in Yaz's lungs. 'Kaylal!'

'Exxar.' He tried to lift his friend. 'It's Yaz.'

Exxar's head flopped to the side, his gaze fixed. Yaz crawled forward and set her hand to Kaylal's arm, corded with muscle from his work at the smithy. 'What are you doing here?' She wanted to ask how he had got so far from the ravine where they'd last seen him in Arka's band. Kaylal's parents had thrown him into the pit as a baby because he'd been born without legs. They must have thought that the longest journey he would make unaided in his life was the vertical one they'd set him on.

'Pome's side caught us. They wanted us to work the armoury again. We escaped on the way to the forge pool.' Kaylal moved Exxar towards her. 'Can you help him?'

'Kaylal, it's Thurin.' Thurin squeezed forward, his head now at Yaz's shoulder. 'Who did this?'

'We need to get out of this tunnel first.' Yaz pushed against him. 'Everybody back to the cave.' She took Exxar's feet. 'Can you guide his head, Kaylal?'

The smith nodded. He kept Exxar's head in his lap and put on barbed metal gauntlets that he had beside him, lined with fur to keep his fingers unfrozen. With the traction provided he scooted himself along after Yaz.

Yaz maintained the fiction that Exxar might still be alive, fearing it was the only thing that could draw Kaylal from his hideaway. The hope in his face hurt her, but its inevitable death would hurt her more. She wondered how she would feel in his place with Quell in her lap. Would she burn as fiercely? Would the quality of her grief differ? What if it were Thurin or Erris's body she clung to in the dark, long after whatever had made them departed?

The rest of the group had to back awkwardly out of the tunnel until they reached a wider section, all save Zeen who was able to squirm around where he stood. It took them a while to reach the cave where the others were able to help with Exxar. Kaylal flinched when he saw Erris reaching for his friend; the Broken knew all the adults under the ice, so a stranger was a big shock. Even so, with Yaz's reassurance he let Erris take Exxar.

Erris laid him on the icy stone, quickly checking his pulse and other vital signs. 'I'm sorry.' He turned his dark eyes on Kaylal, voice gentle. 'He has been dead some while now.'

'No!' Anger clouded Kaylal's beauty, mixed with disbelief and incomprehension. Some hurts are too large for our thoughts to span. They have to enter by degrees, like a knife into its wound. 'No . . .' He fought his way back to Exxar's side. Another broken denial escaped him though it came sorrow-laden and lacking conviction. 'Not Exxar. Not him . . .' His grief found echoes in all of them, and Yaz struggled to contain her own, finding her breath catching in her throat. She hadn't time to mourn the lost, not while she had others still to save.

'How did it happen?' Thurin crouched beside the smith. He put an arm about his shoulders. Kaylal tried to shake him off but Thurin wouldn't allow it. 'Kaylal.'

The rest stood and watched Kaylal hug Exxar's corpse. Yaz found her eyes misting though she had met Exxar only twice and then briefly. Thurin on the other hand had grown up with both men and had known them all his life. They were family. The sort that wouldn't throw each other away over some imperfection.

Yaz caught herself in the lie. The Broken might not have a pit but they killed each other even so. The evidence of it smeared the tunnel behind her.

'It was Bexen.'

The words took Yaz by surprise. It had been so long since Thurin asked his question she had forgotten it had been uttered, but Kaylal hadn't. Bexen, the cruel-faced gerant with the milky eye, Pome's enforcer and right-hand man.

'We escaped Pome's raiding party when some of Arka's scouts counter-attacked.' The words fell lifeless from his lips, his voice hollow. 'Me, Jonna, and Exxar slipped away in the confusion. But Bexen and Tylar caught us out by the Green

Cave. Exxar got me away while Jonna fought them. He carried me. I didn't even know he'd been cut until we got to the outer chambers. Bexen had sliced him on the leg and Tylar got him in the back. I gave her that knife two drops after she joined us, and now she's stabbed me in the heart with it.'

Thurin shook his head and stood slowly, trailing his hand across Kaylal's shoulder. 'You'll come with us.'

Yaz beckoned Thurin to her. Kaylal wouldn't last a day on the ice. Thurin must know it. She steered him into the largest tunnel that led from the chamber. She wanted to protest that they couldn't take the smith, that it would be kinder to leave him for Pome. But even as the thoughts formed she knew them for her own version of whatever it was that let the Ictha toss their children into the Pit of the Missing. Mother Mazai had among the treasures that she showed the children during the long night an image scraped onto the hide of a parchment-fish, whose layered skin allows images of several shades to be made simply by varying the depth the stylus scrapes. The image was of an old woman's face, her folds sculpted by the wind. But if you changed the way you looked at it then the image miraculously became a picture of a beautiful young woman, a whole body image of her stretching.

What the Ictha did at the pit was the same. If you looked at it one way it was a necessary compromise to the harshness of life spent on the ice. Change how you looked at it and in one sudden step it was a horror wrought upon their own children who they should love more than life, an unspeakable crime committed by a society that would be judged on how they treated their most vulnerable members. A cancer at the heart of every good thing in the lives of all the tribes.

So instead of saying how impossible it would be to take

Kaylal with them she said in a low voice, 'There are parts of who I am that I wish I could split off like the Missing did, and lose them in the ice. Life would be much simpler if I could only see things like this one way.'

Thurin shook his head. 'When Theus got that last part of himself back it didn't feel like he was adding new badness to the mix, or at least not *just* more badness. Even though the Missing only cut away what they thought lessened them it felt like he was becoming more whole and somehow that it was better that way.'

Yaz had expected Thurin to be confused by what she was saying, or perhaps offended given the horrors he'd so recently experienced, but instead he'd surprised her. 'You sound like you agree with that monster rather than with the Missing.'

'Theus spoke to me before he left. I think he knew I'd tell it to you though, so perhaps it was a message for you.' Thurin stared into the tunnel as if trying to recover the words, as if he were hearing them again. 'He said we're all of us falling through our lives. It didn't start when you jumped or end when you hit the water. Each of us plunges through our own existence, punching me-shaped holes through days, through weeks, through conversations. We're none of us one thing or the other, we're legion, there's a different Yaz inside your skull for every day of your life. We deceive others, we deceive ourselves, we keep secrets that even we don't know and hold beliefs we don't understand. And in that state of profound, fundamental, primal ignorance we still think we can sculpt the clay of our own selves; we think we know what to cut away, that we understand the consequences of excising greed. Are we so sure we don't need it? Might we not be creating new and different demons whose most frightening trait is that they truly believe themselves to be angels? Do you say everything you think? Do you do everything you feel? Any divinity we might lay claim to is in the restraint we exercise against our nature. Every one of us is bound by our own constraints, to call them all fears makes us sound cowards. Many are judgements. Balancing harm against benefit, hurt against pleasure, our feelings against another's, the now against the maybe . . .' Thurin trailed off, coming back to himself. He spat, perhaps trying to rid himself of the taste of Theus's words. 'Theus is a monster, but that doesn't mean he's wrong. It's a dangerous game to try to rid yourself of weakness. You never know what else you might be losing in the deal.' He shook his head and forced a grin. 'We're talking about Kaylal, aren't we? You don't want to take him.'

Yaz shook her head. 'We're talking about me. And we are taking him. I'd rather die trying to carry him than live with myself having left him behind.'

Thurin's grin broadened into something natural. He nodded. Then, as if to lighten the load of Theus's observations and the weight of Exxar's death: 'So, you don't want to leave him behind. I can understand why you'd feel that way. He is *very* good-looking.'

Yaz punched his arm, snorting.

'You do know he only likes boys?'

Yaz stifled a laugh. Her nerves were frayed. Both of them were on the edge of hysteria. She composed herself and turned back into the cave. The sight of Exxar's body blew away any further inclination to smile.

'Time to go. Erris can carry Kaylal.'

Kaylal shook his head. 'I can make my own way.' The stumps where his thighs should have been were bound thick with iron and hide so that he could drag himself without damage, and his arms were equal to the task.

'All right then. But if we need to run or to move quietly then Erris or Kao will carry you.'

Kaylal nodded.

'What will we do with Exxar?' Thurin asked gently.

Kaylal lowered his gaze. He had pulled the body beside the small patch of red-ball fungi. 'The gods have the best of him now. Let the ice take what's left.'

CHAPTER 33

'You did a remarkable thing, Yaz.' Erris came to walk beside her as they trekked through the ice caves of the Broken, bound for the city.

'I did?' She gave him a doubtful glance.

'All of you look defeated!' Erris shook his head. 'But you have your brother back, and your two friends. Three people freed from the taint. Didn't you say Thurin was the only one rescued in an age, and even that wasn't successful? And now here you are, walking away with all three, thumbing your nose at the odds.'

Yaz managed a smile. It was true, all of it. She had pulled off a great and unexpected victory. The Ictha said people divided into those who, at the middle of the long night, would sigh and say forty days of darkness remained, and those who would smile and say that already forty dark days lay behind them. Yaz had always thought she belonged in the half-finished camp rather than with those counting the days remaining.

She turned to Zeen, walking just behind her, and took his hand. He returned her squeeze and both smiled, without effort this time.

They reached the city cavern without challenge. Yaz led the way down the long slope, tired in every limb, still feeling grimy from her time in the black ice. The ache in her head had subsided but it still felt as though a knife were lodged between the two halves of her brain and that every now and then an invisible someone twisted it.

Behind her Thurin, Kao, Zeen, and Erris trudged along in a disordered group, only Erris with his shoulders squared and head unbowed. Kaylal hauled himself along at the rear, scraping the iron-clad stumps of his legs across the rock.

Quell came striding across the city to meet them. At his hip swung some kind of makeshift axe that let her know he had been back to raid the hunter's remains. He'd bound a large, sharp-toothed metal wheel to a short iron bar.

'Yaz!' He took both her hands in his, studying her face. 'Are you unwell?'

She shook her head then regretted the movement. 'I'm fi—'

'We thought you were still in the city!' Quell raised his voice, edging it with a hint of outrage. 'I would have gone with you to rescue . . .' He waved a hand at the others behind her. '. . . these.'

'I didn't want to risk you or Maya being recaptured.' Yaz pulled her hands back. 'It was my mistake to fix.'

'You took your friend from the city though.' Quell's pale eyes found Erris and narrowed in distrust. 'He doesn't look like the hunter you described.'

'Quell, I presume.' Erris inclined his head.

'You do presume. You took Yaz back to that nightmare of a place—'

'She took me,' Erris pointed out. 'I had no knowledge of its existence.'

Quell's face darkened. Yaz didn't remember ever seeing him angry. 'You took my—'

'Quell!' She wanted to ask 'My *what*?' though she wasn't sure how she might feel about the answer. 'Calm yourself! We have to be ready to leave. The collection is due soon, yes?'

Quell hardened his face, forcing all traces of emotion from it. He nodded, mouth in a tight line.

'The next collection isn't due for twenty-two days.' Thurin stared at Quell, challenge in his eyes. 'If there is one before then it is because this stranger has arranged it with the regulator.'

Quell's brows rose and he shot Yaz a betrayed look. 'You told him?'

'I didn't!' Yaz protested. Her words carried their own heat. Mention of Quell's deal with the regulator still felt like betrayal. The way he had kept it secret from her had soured the trust between them that she had always taken as absolute and eternal. She turned to stare at Thurin. 'How could you possibly know that?'

Thurin's mouth twisted. 'Theus told me. He saw it on him. He said the Ictha had signs of the regulator's influence all over him. He said Quell would betray you. He said the priests stand behind this one, and behind them their Hidden God.'

Yaz wondered what stood behind the Hidden God. Seus maybe? She had dropped down the pit then found new depths to fall to, and wondered if the mystery of the Missing went deeper still, perhaps without end. Maybe all life was like that; all people too. Tear off a layer, expose some new truth, but there will always be another layer. 'Quell did what he thought was best. He was trying to help.'

Thurin narrowed his dark eyes at Quell. 'Theus said—'

'A demon told you!' Quell stepped in close, full of menace now, his voice a furious hiss. 'I won't be accused of treachery by one who led us all into the black ice and tried to bury us there.'

'Hey . . . Quell.' Zeen stepped into view from behind Kao, a stumble in his legs.

'Zeen!' Quell was at his side, catching him as he collapsed.

'Zeen!' Yaz pushed her way towards her brother, but Quell was already carrying him in both arms.

'He weighs nothing. I expect he's starved is all.' Quell started walking back down the slope, argument forgotten, genuinely pleased to see the boy again. 'Come on. I'll show you the mountain of food I've collected. Zeen needs to eat at least half of it.'

Yaz followed. This was the Quell she remembered from the ice. Strong, caring, in control of himself and the situation.

They crossed the city ruins, alert for hunters. Yaz offered a prayer to the Gods in the Sea that none would come. More than anything she wanted sleep. Deep and peaceful sleep. She felt like a raw wound.

Quell's collection of fungi proved to be more of a hill than a mountain but he had done a good job in the time available. Yaz didn't point out the number of inedible or poisonous caps in the mix, they could be discarded later. How long the pile would last the nine of them up on the ice was a matter for speculation. Not long enough, she suspected, but then she had no true idea of how long would be enough.

Kao began tucking into the fungi, chewing his way method-ically through one thick grey-shield after another. Thurin picked up a handful of the less tough brown-scales and brought them to Zeen. 'They're better stewed in their own

juice with some salt. But these are the most digestible raw.'
He turned to Kao. 'Eat too many uncooked grey-shields and
you won't need a cable to get to the surface. You'll be able
to blast there on your own wind.'

Quell raised a brow at that, refusing to smile, and gestured
to a hollow nearby where the corner of a board could be
seen. 'Maya has been busy too. That's her stash. She even
got us a hot pot . . . is that what you call it? One of those
sigil things.'

A thick blanket of exhaustion settled on Yaz and she staggered off to slump down before she fell. She sat with her
back to a twisted metal beam and watched the others protec-
tively from beneath heavy eyelids, Zeen most of all. He was
the only reason she was here and she had succeeded in freeing
him, if not from this place yet then at least from the nightmare he had been suffering. It seemed unreal to have her
brother back, a dream she might wake from. Though now
that he *was* back she almost feared for him more than when
the Tainted had him. Now he was her direct responsibility,
and no part of her plans felt safe. In fact, once her mind
inserted Zeen into those plans they seemed suicidal. Crazed
at best. All that drove her on was that the alternative seemed
just as dangerous and yet lacked any hope of anything better
at the end. She had seen the green world in Erris's dreaming.
She had felt the grass beneath her hands and the rich, soft
soil in which it bedded. She had seen the trees towering,
swaying in a warm breeze that gave rather than took. A
butterfly had kissed her skin. These were true things. Quina's
wooden bead said that somewhere in this world of endless
white trees still grew, and just knowing that had sunk a hook
in Yaz's heart. For the longest time now she'd been afraid to
dream, knowing that all her paths led to the pit and thinking
that somehow she deserved it, for the weakness in her blood.

She'd borne a heavy load, uncomplaining, stoic in the way that only the Ictha are, accepting her fate because she refused to become a burden on her people. But the green dream that Erris and Quina had given her would not hurt the Ictha. It was a dream worth hunting. A dream worth dying for.

Yaz's gaze drifted across Quell, Thurin, and Erris, momentarily close together and in discussion, though she couldn't make out the words. Quell was binding together two of the boards from Maya's stash, his powerful, blunt fingers twisting the wire with a delicacy that always surprised her even when gloved. Thurin had been trying to show him a better way. The Broken had been working with this material for generations after all. He seemed to sense her watching him and turned to look her way. For a moment his black eyes held her gaze with what seemed a dark and starless passion. Erris made some observation that brought Thurin's attention back to the matter in Quell's hand, an observation that had both of them looking at him with a grudging admiration of the kind usually reserved for a leader. She wondered what they would think if she told them Erris was over a thousand years old and that his body wasn't flesh and bone but something Missing-made, like the boards before them.

She watched the three of them, her mind half dreaming. One from the world above, part of her life from her earliest memories. Solid, strong, dependable. One from this strange world below, owner of curious magics, dark, conflicted by tragedy, broken by experience. And one from the world before, a time when there had been no above or below, a mystery who had kept the company of the Missing's works for so long that even he didn't know how changed he might be.

Once she had thought she would share her tent with Quell and her life would be a slight variation on the song that sang out her mother's life and her mother's mother's and hundreds more joining her in a long chain to a time of gods when only Zin and Mokka walked the ice. Now she didn't even know how the old stories fitted with the ones that Erris told her, or with the green world they had walked together in the dreams that the city made real for him.

'Yaz?'

Yaz blinked and realized that she had been asleep. Maya stood before her, a shy half-smile on her lips, every inch the young girl rather than the shadow-weaving Axit assassin.

'Good to see you, little sister. You've done well here.' Yaz forced away a yawn. She stood stretching. 'How long have I been dreaming?'

'A long time.' Maya turned away, pointing. 'Others are coming.'

That woke Yaz up quickly, a cold wind blowing away her mind-fog. 'Who is it?' Following Maya's line she could see figures in skins coming down the long slope with spears on their shoulders. 'Didn't we have anyone on guard?' Had it been her responsibility, she wondered, to organize things like a perimeter?

'Thurin went up there to watch not long after you fell asleep,' Maya said.

Yaz tried to spot him in the group coming down. There were more than ten of them in view now, and none of the figures looked like Thurin.

'Arka!' Kaylal hauled himself from the depression where he'd been working on Maya's haul of stolen boards and other material. 'Arka!'

Yaz relaxed. With Thurin absent none of their company was better placed to recognize Arka and her company than Kaylal.

Arka raised a hand in greeting and came to the fore of her group, leading them cautiously across the scraped ruin of the city. The dozen or so Broken with her all kept low, moving between the holes that would offer them an escape into the chambers below if a hunter were to surface.

Yaz searched desperately for Quina among the shuffling, exhausted group but saw no sign of the girl.

'Yaz!' Arka looked tired. A bloody wound on her forehead would add to the collection of scars that Hetta had given her, if it ever had the time to heal. Grey streaks stood out in her dark hair where none had been before. 'Kaylal.' She reached down for his hand. 'Exxar?' She looked around at the others approaching from the stashes as her own followers came up behind her.

'Gone.' Kaylal's voice fractured around the word and he let her hand go.

'I'm so sorry, Kaylal.' Arka lowered her head. After a long silence she turned to check her people. One was the girl, Jerra, who had been with her when they rescued Yaz from Hetta. Yaz had still been wet from her drop. It seemed a lifetime ago but couldn't have been much more than a week. Jerra had graduated from her rock-and-bone hammer to an iron spear, lighter and shorter than Arka's though.

'Have you seen Quina?' Yaz asked.

Arka nodded though she looked grim.

'Tell me!' Doubt clutched at Yaz's heart. 'She's not with Pome, is she?'

Arka set her hand to Yaz's arm the way the Ictha do when telling bad news. 'A hunter took her. A hunter from the city.'

'She's dead?' Yaz's voice broke.

Arka made a pained shrug. 'Taken. The hunters take us. We've never found the bones of any they catch. Maybe they eat those too . . .' She drew a breath. 'They've been busy while we fought. It might be we've lost more to their claws than to Pome's forces.'

Yaz shook her head, not trusting herself to speak yet. Quina was too quick for a hunter to catch. She didn't believe it.

'I'm sorry.' Arka took back her hand. She looked around at Yaz's friends. 'Petrick is not with you?'

'He . . . fell.' Yaz found it hard to speak about. 'Into the chasm.'

Arka closed her eyes. Something like a mother's pain twisted her lips. 'So many gone.'

Another silence stretched between them. Yaz broke it.

'Why are you here?' She tried not to sound unwelcoming. Her plan interfered with the fundamentals of life in the caverns and might disrupt the long-held arrangement that kept the Broken alive. She didn't want Arka trying to stop her.

Arka seemed on the point of answering with some rousing speech for the benefit of her followers but instead she released the deep breath she'd drawn and her shoulders fell. 'Because Pome is winning.'

It wasn't the news Yaz wanted to hear. She pursed her lips. 'Won't the city be harder to defend than anywhere else?'

'It will.' Arka nodded. 'But the hunters here will attack them as much as us. Which will help even the odds. If we're lucky a hunter will take Pome. They might even destroy *his* hunter.'

Yaz frowned, puzzled, then realized that much of what she'd learned during her time in the city was unknown to Arka. 'The regulator made all of the hunters, not just Pome's one. I don't know how much he sees down here but you could find yourself facing Pome's forces along with the very hunters you hoped might attack him.'

Arka shook her head. 'That makes no sense. Why would the regulator have made the hunters? They're responsible for the loss of so many of the best of us. Without them we could get more iron. Lots more! And that's why we're down here.' She shook her head again, more emphatically. 'Someone has been lying to you.' She glanced at Erris, brows rising as she clearly remembered Yaz's claims about his origins. 'And this stranger. What does he want from us? Or did he follow you up from the city like Quell followed you down from the ice?'

'It was me he came here for, yes.' She hid a smile, surpressing a kind of pleased embarassment.

'But listen to me. The hunters serve the regulator. Erris saw him make them.'

Arka still frowned in disbelief but her shoulders slumped a second time. 'If that's true then we're finished.'

Yaz glanced towards the fungi heap and felt immediately guilty for wondering if Arka and her followers would need feeding. 'I guess you should ready your positions. Thurin is still on watch but you could send—'

Arka nodded. 'I left two warriors with him.'

'Well . . . if we see Pome he'll have all of us to deal with.' Yaz didn't mention that in a day at most she expected to be gone. She wasn't sure that Arka wouldn't try to stop her rather than coming with her. Arka still dreamed of restoring the Broken to what they had been when Yaz arrived. She saw herself as Tarko's heir and she wouldn't want to antagonize the regulator. If she started to believe that the priests owned the hunters that might just make her more willing to placate them. She might still let Yaz ride the cable to the surface, but alone, and bound as a tribute.

Yaz drew a deep breath. 'We'll stand with you. If we see him.'

Arka clapped a hand to Yaz's shoulder. She offered no

thanks. Her authority stood on the assumption that Yaz owed her obedience, but there was gratitude in that contact. She moved away as Erris came in close. 'Positions!' Arka gestured to Jerra and the others with her. 'As we discussed.' Together they moved away towards nearby openings leading down into the city.

Yaz watched them go, feeling unsettled. Pome was hunting Arka and her people. When he found them gone from the main caverns he would follow them to the city. She felt that she was abandoning Arka's faction to their fate, and it made her feel dirty. Jerra wasn't the only child among them, but it seemed that the caverns of the Broken weren't large enough for childhoods. Quell had said she couldn't save them all, and it was true. Lately life seemed full of ugly truths and attractive lies.

'How long does the cage normally stay down?' Yaz had gone to eat in one of the craters. This one had a rectangular shaft at the bottom of it, sheer-sided and too narrow for any hunter she'd yet seen.

'Two days,' Thurin said. 'It takes a while to load all the iron securely.' Quell had taken over his guard duty above the slope and Zeen had gone with him, though Yaz had wanted to protest. 'Sometimes three.'

'We won't have two days. Not with Arka here and Pome hunting her.' Maya bit into a large mushroom without enthusiasm.

'But the regulator is sending this cage down for you, right?' Kao asked. 'So he might just leave it there long enough for someone to get on, then haul it back up.'

Yaz nodded. 'True.'

'This means the regulator is going to be right there waiting for you up top,' Thurin said. 'With gods know how many priests. He'll want the rest of us back down here to work for him.'

'But he won't be expecting the rest of you.' Yaz offered a smile. 'And you can pick a man up without touching him, Thurin. If the regulator tries to stop us going south then you can throw him down the hole to scavenge his own iron.'

Maya and Kao nodded. Thurin looked worried. They ate without speaking, and after a short while Maya and Kao left the pair of them alone, going to join Erris who was still working on fashioning their collapsible shelter from the materials that Maya had recovered from the settlement.

'Eular wasn't with Arka,' Thurin said.

'No.' Yaz had noticed the blind old man's absence and had worried for him. 'Pome must have caught him after the Icicle Cavern. If he's wise he'll do whatever Pome asks and hope Arka can rescue him.'

'Oh, he's wise.'

Thurin said it with such conviction that it prompted Yaz to share what the old man had said to her when Pome first brought her before him. 'He predicted all this, you know.'

'All this?' Thurin raised a brow. 'That must have taken some telling.'

'Well, not *all* of it. He said I was an agent of change. That I had been dropped into the middle of something that was ready to become a new thing.' For an eyeless man it was impressive vision. Though his foresight had been blind to Theus lurking inside Thurin. 'What did he tell you?'

Thurin's pale skin reddened and he turned his head away to watch the distant star-littered ceiling. 'He talked about . . . you, I think . . . well, I'm not sure what he was saying. But I remember what he said, if that makes sense? He said when you put some people together for the first time there's a kind of gravitation, a slow spiral dance as they're drawn into each other's orbit, each opening to the other by degrees, discovering how closely their wants and hopes and passions align.' Thurin kept his eyes on the distant stars, speaking the words from memory as if he had spent many hours turning them over in his own mind. 'He said there's a darkness in each of us, afraid to show itself, wrestling with such blunt tools as words and deeds to make itself known to the darkness in another person similarly hidden behind walls of camouflage, disguise, interpretation. Honesty is a knife that we can use to pare away those layers, but one slip, go too deep, and who knows what injuries might be inflicted.' He frowned and quoted, '"The wounds an honest tongue can open sometimes take a lifetime to heal."'

Yaz could imagine the old man saying all that. Part of her thought that he could have been talking about her and Thurin, seeing a time when they might spiral into each other, but, as she opened her mouth wondering if she dare say so, a cold thought ran through her. *A darkness in each of us, afraid to show itself.* It was almost as if Eular had been speaking directly to Theus rather than to Thurin, inviting him to reveal himself. And for a moment Yaz wasn't sure quite how much Eular saw with his hollow sockets.

After a long silence Yaz opened her mouth to reply but a curious spattering sound turned her head. Not far behind her two thin threads of silver joined the distant ceiling to the floor. Where they touched the rock a constant shower of sparkling droplets danced into the air. 'What is it?'

'Water!' Thurin grinned for the first time since the black ice. 'The collection is coming!'

CHAPTER 34

'The drain shaft and the coal shaft have reached the ceiling. That's the water melted by the heat pots, all draining out,' Thurin said.

Yaz made no reply. She just watched the twin streams falling, glittering in the starlight. For the first time she thought they might actually make it back to the surface. All of them. As many as dared try.

Erris and Kao hurried back to join them, Kao looking excited rather than scared for the first time since his rescue.

'How long will it take before the worm reaches us?' Erris asked.

'Soon? Will it be soon?' Kao sounded so eager to reach the surface. It hurt Yaz's heart to know that he was too broken to live the life he wanted to have back. 'How long?'

'In a short while they'll be pouring coal into the coal shaft. The priests will make a column of coal this much around.' Thurin made a circle that both his hands couldn't quite reach around.

'And the worm makes all its heat from eating this . . .

coal? Enough to melt through miles of ice?' Yaz asked, still amazed by it.

'It's a rock that burns,' Thurin said. 'If we had a pile of it here we could make a fire so hot we'd have to leave the crater.'

'That stream's quite small, there must be so much more coming than that . . .' Yaz pushed back from the crater wall, staring at the falling water. She left Kao and Erris behind her, and joined Thurin by the narrow slot leading from the bottom of the crater down into the darkness of the city. 'Lots more?'

'Both shafts will drain soon. When the worm starts following the coal and leaving the full-sized passage behind there'll be a river of meltwater through the drain shaft. It takes an hour or more to drain, and it melts the drain wider so at the end it's quite a deluge,' Thurin said.

'You couldn't . . . you know . . . speed it up?' Yaz turned to face him. She didn't know how long they had but maybe not long enough. 'With your magic. So we could all get out of here quicker?'

'My ice-work's good.' Thurin pursed his lips. 'But not that good.'

It wasn't a noise that lifted Yaz's head, turning her gaze from the work Erris had set her to, wiring boards together. It was the stopping of a noise. Just as on the one occasion in her life when the wind fell silent it had been that pause in the world's song which hauled her from the tent, now it was the cessation of the water's patter. 'It's stopped!'

Thurin nodded beside her, his eyes still on his work. 'They'll finish filling the coal shaft soon. Then summon the worm to follow it.'

Yaz made a grim smile. 'With any luck we can be out of here before—'

'Someone's coming!' A shout rang out and Yaz stood sharply.

'Gods in the Sky!' She raised her hands in the 'why me?' gesture the Ictha used.

A lithe figure was racing across the city ruins at speed, leaping pits and swerving around the few girders in his way.

'It's Zeen!' Yaz clambered up onto more exposed rock. 'Let him through!' She could see now that Quell and two of the Broken were also running back, though they had yet to reach the halfway point on the long slope.

Zeen came in faster than Yaz had ever seen anyone run, his feet flickering against the stone. He tamed his speed but still crashed into her and hung in her arms for a moment, panting. 'Pome's coming.' He hauled in a breath. 'With everyone.' Another breath. 'And his hunter.'

Yaz stepped away from her brother to watch the other three approaching, Quell in the lead. She shook her head. Half a day would probably have seen them all gone. A few more hours maybe. But no, it all had to come crashing in right now. Maybe it was better this way. The shame of leaving the others to face Pome alone would have been hard to carry across the ice.

'Take your positions,' Arka shouted. 'Stay hidden until my mark.' She lowered herself to her chest behind an outcrop of the more stubborn rock that the Missing had poured their foundations from. In her left hand she held an iron spear, no different from the one that had seen Petrick fall from the bridge or the one that had slain Jerrig, the huge and gentle harvester.

Kaylal hunkered down beside Arka, clutching a short sword from his own forge. Without legs, though, he was unlikely to last long in the coming fight. His fierce determination lent a new aspect to the beauty the gods had given him. He met Yaz's eyes for a moment. Memories of Exxar haunted his stare, though whether it was revenge driving him or the desire to join his lover Yaz couldn't say.

Quell found cover thirty yards ahead of them. The two with him vanished into the city through a jagged crack. The first of Pome's force were just coming into view at the top of the long slope. Four slim, dark-haired hunskas, fast enough to stand a chance against ambush and perhaps to dodge spears thrown from cover. They advanced in scurries, one moment a blur of motion, the next motionless save for their heads scanning for threats.

Gerants came behind them, bundled in skins and armour plates. Too many of them but not nearly as many as she had feared. She remembered lots more. Surely Arka's followers hadn't killed them?

Bexen led from the centre of the front line. The distance was too great for Yaz to see his milky eye but his size marked him. He bore a round shield on his arm and in the other hand a sword as long as Yaz was tall. It might still have Exxar's blood on it. They came on swiftly, not running but with rapid strides, as if eager to get on with what would surely be the last battle of this insurrection.

The hunter loomed behind the first rank, dwarfing even Bexen. Yaz wondered that it didn't lead the way in. Perhaps Pome valued it above his human servants. The thing looked ill fashioned, a brutal and graceless collection of iron. On one side, three arms ended in serrated blades, on the other two slightly heavier and longer arms – one sporting a six-foot spike and the other ending in a blunt-fingered hand of banded metal that looked capable of crushing rocks.

Pome sheltered behind the hunter, betrayed by glimpses of the glowing star in his hand. Others of his band followed on, many of them the younger and the older members of the Broken who had been swept into Pome's orbit and had found themselves unable to leave it without help.

Yaz's heart was beating as fast as if she'd been sprinting

alongside Zeen. They could fight them here or run into the city and be hunted there, but either way it would be bloody. She found herself as scared as at any point since her fall. There had been no time to think when she faced Hetta or the hunters, but now, watching the approach of people who were ready to kill her, a terror rose through her in place of the anger that had helped her before. A terror that not only would she die, slashed open by the swing of a well-forged sword, but that Zeen, barely twelve and huddled behind her, would die too, run through with an iron spear. And that Kao, white-faced, his bravado gone, would spill his blood on the rocks, and Thurin, Quell, even Erris would fall beneath a flurry of blades. The horror of it paralysed her and set both hands trembling against the stone slope before her.

'This is not going to end well.' Thurin joined Yaz, leaning up against the side of the crater.

'I thought this Pome wanted Yaz returned to the surface?' Erris slid up on her other side.

'Well, he does . . .' Yaz admitted. The presence of Erris on one side and Thurin on the other released her from her paralysis. She drove back her fear, trying to keep it from her voice. 'But he wanted to send me up as a tribute to the regulator.'

'Pome wanted you delivered to the man who Quell has contacted to arrange this collection so that you might be brought to him?' Erris asked.

'Well . . . yes.' Yaz wanted to protest that it wasn't the same. Pome was doing it because he wanted something from the regulator. But she knew that Quell was also doing it because he wanted something from the priest. Only in Quell's case that something was *her* rather than a kingdom under the ice.

'So the only people here who might object to your going

are those who have given their loyalty to Arka?' Erris pressed on with his relentless logic.

'Pome is a . . .' She stretched for an insult. The Ictha used them rarely and had few to choose from. 'He is cruel and unworthy. I wouldn't want him guiding the Broken even before he tainted himself.'

'But won't Theus and the other Tainted overrun them all soon in any case?' Erris sounded sincere, as if he genuinely didn't know that he was bringing out into the light all the issues she had been hating herself for.

'It's not that easy—'

Thurin exclaimed. 'He's got more gerants at the back than at the front!'

Yaz looked away from Erris, grateful for the interruption. Pome's whole force was on the slope now. At the back were ten gerants bearing the large square shields she remembered from the meeting in the Icicle Cavern. Rather than focusing their attention ahead of them though, these ones kept glancing over their shoulders.

'I don't think they're chasing Arka at all,' Yaz said. 'I think they're being chased.'

CHAPTER 35

Pome's force closed ranks as they approached the city. Yaz watched their advance, her eyes level with the edge of the crater. Though they were just children of the tribes, the Broken seemed very different to those who had cast them down from the ice, and not just the hulking gerants. The wind hadn't sculpted their features; they wore a pitiful mix of patchwork rat skins, the ageing remains of whatever they had worn on their drop day, here and there a cloak of woven hair or a pelt sent down by the priesthood along with their payments in salt and fish. And yet despite their beggar's garb they carried in iron the wealth of many clans, all of it shaped for war.

They halted some fifty yards shy of Yaz's position, though Quell was hiding much closer, about halfway between them. Pome came out from behind his hunter and three of the hunskas moved to protect him, as if they might be fast enough to pluck any spear out of the air before it could hit home. He stood wrapped in the thickest hides the Broken had with an iron breastplate over the top. In his right hand he held a short iron rod with his star glowing crimson at the other end. Taller than most Ictha and of slighter build, with his thin brown hair and narrow face he looked a man of little consequence, but somehow, like parasitic worms, his words burrowed into the minds of those around him, swaying them to his cause.

'I am not here to make war!' he shouted. 'I have come to see that the girl, Yaz, is returned to the surface in accordance with the regulator's orders. Once she has been dispatched to the ice we can resolve our differences.'

'He's scared of me,' Yaz hissed to Erris and Thurin. 'He's worried I'll mess with his hunter again. He just wants me out of the way before he kills Arka.'

'Come out here, Yaz of the Ictha! I'm sending you home!' Pome tried to make it sound inviting but his voice was no more capable of holding warmth than the ice was. 'I'll give you a moment to say your goodbyes. Don't make Bexen come in and get you.'

'We can't beat them, can we?' Yaz asked.

'Even if we could, think how many would die.' Thurin frowned. 'And the Tainted must be hard on their heels judging by how they came in here.'

'I—' Motion between her crater and Pome caught Yaz's eye. Quell had broken cover and was hurrying over to her, trusting in Pome's period of grace that he wouldn't end up with a spear between his shoulder blades.

Quell slid over the edge of the crater, his booted feet thudding down on the rock beside her. Thurin stumbled back, narrowly avoiding being flattened.

Quell reached for her shoulder. 'Pome must have spoken with Regulator Kazik somehow, so he'll know to let me and Zeen come up with you too. It's got to be just the three of us though. I think it's that or a bloodbath. You can do more for your friends up with the priests than in a war down here.'

'But—'

Quell raised a hand to her objections. '*Think* about it. This Pome is a madman pretending to be sane. And look how many he has with him.'

A clattering from behind saved her from answering. She turned in confusion to see black stones bouncing in the puddled meltwater from the two narrow shafts.

'It's coal escaping,' Thurin said. 'Tarko normally seals the end of the coal shaft with his ice-work.'

'Tarko's dead. You'll have to do it.' Yaz glanced up at the hole, wondering if Thurin could work his will over such a distance.

'I should save my energies if we're going to fight.' Thurin looked doubtful.

'Try.' Yaz reached out to grasp his arm below the elbow. 'We won't get out of here at all if all the coal falls through.'

Thurin furrowed his brow and reached out towards the ceiling. He gritted his teeth and drew his lips back in a mask of effort. The fall of stones thinned out with just a handful more hammering into the small mound that had already formed. He grunted and they stopped entirely. 'Ouch.'

Pome's call reached them across the rock. 'Your ride is nearly here, Yaz. Come out. You've no choices left.'

The sound came of iron feet ringing on stone as the hunter advanced a few yards to underscore its master's point.

Quell held his hand out. 'We should go, Yaz.'

Yaz pulled back, her mind working furiously. There was a hard logic at work here. The same cold weighing of benefit and loss that surrounded the pit. She couldn't find the words to argue with it but that didn't stop her wanting to fight against it.

Far above them the cable and the lifting cage would be resting on the ice, waiting for the summoned coal-worm to arrive and follow the lead shaft, widening it sufficiently for the cage to follow down. The coal had fallen a great distance and the shaft behind it must be full of falling coal now backing up behind the blockage. The worm might even have started its work, pursuing its meal. But she hadn't time to wait for the cage, and even if it were here now then Pome wouldn't allow the others to join her in it, or let them take the food and the shelter they'd made. She hissed in frustration. They had come so close.

'Maybe this is the only way,' Erris said solemnly.

An idea hit Yaz, almost a physical blow. She rocked onto her heels. 'Thurin! All that coal in the shaft . . . Could you make it burn? You once told me that you thought your flame-work was stronger than your ice-work.'

A rough laugh broke from him. 'I have no idea! I know I can't set things on fire. Once it was burning I might be able to do . . . something. I don't know for sure – I've never properly used my flame-work. But we don't have any fire and—'

Erris raised his hand between them and clicked his fingers. A small flame danced on the end of his thumb as if it were an oil lamp.

Thurin's eyes widened in amazement. 'How . . . ?'

Yaz waved the question away. 'It doesn't matter. Can you burn the coal?'

'What? No! It's all the way up there and the flame . . . is . . . here . . .' Thurin seemed hypnotized by the flame. It started to flare, growing several feet tall in the instant before Erris shut it off. He looked surprised, alarmed even, and his thumb was left gently smoking.

Yaz remembered what Thurin had said about the need to use his ice-work at least every few days or the energies built inside him and burst out more strongly and with less control when he tried to use them. His flame-work had been building up for a lifetime. When he let the talent loose the results might be spectacular.

'Come with me!' She started running.

Yaz crossed the crater and scrambled out, breaking cover. She made for the coal pile that had fallen from the shaft over a hundred feet above her.

'Yaz of the Ictha!' Pome roared, spotting her at last.

Yaz ignored the shout. She splashed through the puddled meltwater and reached the coal. Behind her came Erris and Thurin but also Zeen and Quell.

'Can you burn that?' Yaz pointed at the pile. 'And lift the fire up to the ceiling, then burn the coal in the shaft?'

'I have no idea!' Thurin stared up at the two small, icicle-hung holes in the ceiling far above, one blackened with coal dust. 'And why would I want to?'

'It would bring the cage down fast,' Zeen said.

'There's no telling what it would do,' Erris said. 'There are too many unknown parameters.'

'One thing is pretty sure,' Quell said. 'If it works then we're all going to get wet.'

Behind them the hunter began to advance again, its foot-steps clanging on the rock. The gerants were coming too, making some kind of battle chant, 'Hruh! Hruh! Hruh!' A deep, throbbing sound intended to terrify.

Erris clicked his fingers again to produce another flame and crouched to hold it to the nearest coal. 'If you're going to do this do it n—'

The coal seemed to suck the flame from Erris's fingers, drawing it in as if it were a hole rather than just a black rock. For a moment Yaz thought the fire had disappeared but Thurin extended both hands, fingers splayed as though warming them at the sigil pot in the drying chamber.

In the next heartbeat the first coal turned orange, a fierce bright orange. The nearest coals were already a dull red where they touched it.

'Stand back.' Thurin's voice shook, though Yaz couldn't tell if it was with the effort of burning the piece of coal or with the effort of holding back.

She stepped away, glancing over her shoulder at the advancing line of Pome's warriors. She was about to say 'Hurry' when a wall of heat pressed against her. As she stumbled and fell she became aware that the whole heap of coals had turned from black to a fierce orange-yellow and that the roaring in her ears came from the column of flame rising above the blaze.

Thurin stood silhouetted between Yaz and the burning coal, his arms raised as if conducting the inferno. The tongue of fire licked two dozen yards into the air but still couldn't quite reach the star-speckled ice. Rather than growing the blaze had begun to shrink already, its fuel expended in one extravagant gesture.

Yaz flung out her own hand from where she lay on the wet rock and the dozen fragments of her hunter star shot from her pocket, streaking into the column of fire.

What happened next occupied only a frozen fraction of a heartbeat, making no sense until her mind unfolded it in the next breath. A dark line passed over her head. An iron spear flung at Thurin's back. The horror wouldn't hit Yaz until after the spear had struck its mark. The force behind such a missile was enough to punch a hole through a man whatever bone or flesh might get in the way. Thurin's first understanding would come after the crimson spear emerged from his ribs, flying away from him leaving a trail of his own blood hanging momentarily in the air.

But somehow a figure managed to rise beneath the spear

in the same instant it flew above them and to press upon it in such a way that it deflected upwards by just a few degrees. Zeen!

The skins over Thurin's left shoulder danced as the spear sliced through them. The wind of the shaft's passing fluttered the dark hair around his ear.

Yaz's handful of stars rose in an accelerating spiral, travelling faster than she had ever made them fly before. She pictured the fire sigil in her mind and, as the stars broke from the top of the flames, the gyre they made carried the fire with them, a twisting vortex extending the tongue of flame to lick against the ceiling itself.

'Now!' she shouted.

Thurin's release of pent-up potential, though not directed her way, shuddered through Yaz like something primal, both shocking and thrilling, filling her with want. Above them the ice lit with an orange glow as his flame-work, unused for all the years of his life, launched those long-banked energies into the column of coal. Like Thurin the coal was itself a store of energy held inert for its whole existence and was now able to release that heat in one glorious burst. Driven by Thurin's talent the fire exploded up the column far faster than any natural spread.

'Run!' Yaz shouted before the first drop of water had even hit the ground. 'Secure the supplies!'

The first instruction was for everyone. The second was for Thurin. Only someone with power over water could hope to stop their food and shelter washing away in the coming flood.

Even as she shouted, though, she could see Thurin drop, as if the release of his flame-work had hollowed him, leaving an empty skin to flop to the ground. It likely saved his life as a second spear scythed past him and another skewered the empty space where his head would have otherwise been.

The flood came so swiftly that few there would have had time to take hold of something fixed, let alone to start running. Yaz found herself swept along by a white wave of water, tumbling over and over, swiftly losing all sense of direction. She knew enough from fishing the Hot Sea not to scream or to try to draw breath.

Where the rolling beneath wild water turned into rolling to lift her face from cold wet stone she wasn't sure. She was equally unsure how long had passed between that rapid, uncontrolled spinning and the effort-laden flop that brought her groaning to her side.

The flattened ruins of the city seemed unchanged save for the scores of pools and puddles reflecting the stars above them. A muted gurgling sounded from many quarters as the thirsty depths below drank down the deluge.

Everywhere the Broken lay scattered, Arka's faction mixed with Pome's, some beginning to lever themselves up onto their arms, others still lying dazed and sodden. The gerant ranks had been swept away, the individual warriors littered here and there. Pome's hunter lay on its side, starting to scrabble for the purchase needed to right itself. Of its master there was no sign.

Water still torrented from the shaft but at a fraction of its original rate. The shaft's mouth now gaped like a crater and chunks of ice lay all around, swept along with the meltwater as they broke from the ceiling.

Amid the crash of water hitting stone after its long drop, and the hunter's clatter, and the groans of the Broken recovering themselves, there was another sound, more distant but chilling. A howling.

Yaz raised her head and without needing to gather her bearings let the blood-curdling screams lead her gaze towards the long slope.

'Tainted!' She tried to yell but broke into a fit of coughing before shouting with more force, 'The Tainted are coming!'

A ragged swarm of the Tainted were surging down the smooth stone of the slope, their numbers far in excess of Arka and Pome's forces combined. A screaming, raging horde, some armed for war with spears, shields, and bone clubs, many empty-handed, carrying nothing but the furious desire to kill.

'We have to run.' Quell came to help Yaz to her feet, still shaking water from his hair.

Yaz glanced at the gaping hole in the ceiling with no cable hanging from it. At the Broken scattered in disarray, and at the massed insanity sweeping towards them. The cage hadn't fallen; there was to be no rescue.

'There's nowhere to run,' she said. 'I've killed us all.'

CHAPTER 36

The first of the Broken to be reached by the lead runners of the Tainted were those that had been swept furthest by the flood. The lightest. Mainly the youngest, those the tribes would still call children, and the elderly.

Theus must have been watching from the heights of the slope, waiting to see how the conflict with Pome would resolve, waiting for the best time to strike, when the Broken were at their weakest. Now his minions swept over the most vulnerable of their foe, clubbing them into submission rather than killing them. Yaz saw skin hoods being pulled over faces, wires looped about wrists and drawn tight. The Tainted had a worse fate than death in store for those they captured and they were bent on captives where they could be taken without too much risk. Those who proved resistant to possession would be tortured for sport. Yaz had seen the gruesome evidence with her own eyes.

One of the most far-flung gerants rose before the charge, bearing her large square shield before her, and the advance broke around her, one Taint bouncing off her war-board with a bone-crunching impact. They closed about her though, pulling her feet out from beneath her.

Pome's hunter managed to right itself and went clanking towards the attack. Its master still lay hidden somewhere but he had clearly seen where the main threat now lay.

'Yaz!' Kao reached her side, dripping wet and desperate. 'What are we going to do?'

Yaz opened her mouth but found no words. She didn't know what they were going to do. The Tainted were sprinting towards them, just fifty yards away, grinning, howling, frantic, weapons raised. Yaz had nothing but her empty hands. Even her stars were gone.

'Yaz!' Kao repeated. Despite his fear he balled both fists and braced himself for the impact.

Yaz looked past what lay before her. It was hard to see the river that runs through all things with scores of maniacs charging straight at her, but she saw it, its bright waters flowing through the strange angles that lie behind the world. Even as she reached for the power she shuddered to think of the carnage to follow. She doubted it would even save her. The Tainted would leap over the shredded remains of their front ranks and come at her through the gore.

For a moment Yaz thought the noise she heard was some new horror rushing at her through the Tainted's charge, or even that it came from the river itself. Within the space of two heartbeats the sound swelled behind her, a crashing, wooshing noise that drove a wind before it, and then ended with the loudest boom in the world.

The Tainted faltered but kept coming, forced on by their own momentum.

'Run!' Yaz grabbed Kao's arm, hauling him around.

In the place where the coal had fallen a huge piece of ironwork now lay at an angle, partly supported by a cable that led off into the great hole funnelling up into the ceiling. The sudden melting of the shaft must have taken the priests by surprise or been seen as what it was, a cry for rescue, and led to them dropping rather than lowering the cage into which the Broken would load their scavenged iron.

The cage was a tube about two yards wide and six yards tall, large enough to fit a dozen people if they could cling at different heights on the inside without having fingers and toes crushed by the passing ice. Failing that then maybe five or six could cram in together at the bottom, but getting in would require climbing up the slanting outside, and once inside they would be helpless, exposed to any attack until the thing was eventually hauled back up into the ice.

When running for your life it pays to keep your attention on the ground in front of you. Something snagged Yaz's foot and she went down hard. The air exploded from her lungs. Her crossed arms saved her face from striking the stone but the impact still left her vision crowded with new lights and her mind full of fuzz. She was dimly aware of Kao catching up and thundering past her.

By the time Yaz managed to roll and sit up, the leading Tainted were almost on her, their shrieks filling her ears. The nearest, ahead of the dirty wave washing towards her, was a thin man with long, matted hair streaming behind him and a wild gleam in his eye. He had blood around his mouth and chin, running down a filthy neck. Probably not his own blood.

Paralysed in the moment Yaz could do nothing, she hadn't even time to be afraid. Something large and dark passed over her. The ragged man reversed direction as something far more solid hit him. Kao crashed in among the first of the Tainted with a roar, bringing four or five of them down. As he rolled to a halt he managed brief eye contact and in that moment yelled at Yaz to run.

Yaz gained her feet and staggered back. Kao had vanished beneath a heap of snarling Tainted. He surged up once, shedding bodies, but more piled on, bringing him down again. Further back the Tainted's gerants were drawing closer, led by the older red-haired gerant that Theus had possessed when he left Thurin.

Although she could do nothing for the boy Yaz found herself unable to abandon him. Any energies she took from the river that flows through all things and flung at the Tainted would break Kao as well. Her power was a blunt weapon.

On all sides the Broken, scattered by the flood, were going down in isolated ones and twos beneath the attack. One of Pome's gerants had made a stand before a corroding girder, skewering a Tainted on his iron spear, then a second, then swinging both spear and impaled bodies as a club to sweep others from their feet.

Another fleet-footed Taint, clearly part hunska, leapt over Kao and his attackers, coming straight at Yaz. Erris came out of nowhere to fell the man with a punch. The next three to come at her fell to a blindingly swift combination of kicks and punches that Erris executed with a dancer's grace.

More attackers flanked them. The sounds of battle rang out across the ruins, a dozen different fights, with knots of defenders holding out here and there. In the midst of the Tainted, like an island that the sea has swept around, Pome's hunter flailed bloody limbs. Theus and six other gerants had brought with them thick, rusty lengths of chain and swung them at the hunter, careless of any others who might be hit. The clatter and boom of their assault could be heard even above all the screaming and dying in between. They weren't trying to batter their enemy to death though. They swung to snare and entangle. When a leg or arm became trapped then other gerants would join in to haul at the hunter, seeking to unbalance it and drag it across the rock.

Arka and a knot of her faction had emerged from one of the larger entrances to the undercity not far from Yaz, and now battled to hold their position. They stood with shield on arm, swinging hide-wrapped iron bars, trying to club down the Tainted. Even as Yaz glanced their way, the woman beside Arka, a harvester named Mirri, fell backwards into the hole, grappling with two assailants, neither older than twelve.

Erris fought like ten demons, felling even the biggest Tainted as if they were children while twisting from the thrust of spears and the swinging of blades. Those he felled seldom rose again but even as they lay groaning they reached to snare his ankles or rolled to trip him.

Despite his efforts Erris couldn't defend on all sides and Yaz fell beneath a raging, blood-soaked woman foaming at the mouth. Erris kicked the woman clear but a near-identical Taint caught him in the side of the head with a wild swing of her bone club. As Erris twisted away to deal with some new threat Yaz found herself looking up from the ground at the descending foot of a large man, part gerant.

The stamp that might have crushed her head never arrived. The man fell back spraying crimson to reveal Quell swinging his makeshift axe at another attacker. Yaz got to her feet and raised her trembling blood-speckled hands before her. Quell had killed a man. The look his face bore made a stranger of her oldest friend. The carnage she had feared so much unfolded on every side. And as the Tainted died, the demons inside them would surely find fresh blood and bone to wear. Soon they would be tainting new victims, sliding in past their rage as they joined the fight and flung the wells of their most primal emotions wide open.

All around Yaz her friends were fighting and dying. She had no idea where her brother was, where Thurin or Maya were. It was like when the dagger-fish took Azad from the boat in front of her. A disaster seemingly dragging itself through the heartbeats and yet still too swift to stop. A nightmare that could be turned around if only she had the strength, if only she weren't broken. But she had nothing to strike with and even her enemies were innocent victims of the black ice. Her only strength lay in the river that flows through all things, and that was an axe far larger than the one that Quell was swinging. If she used it then friend and foe alike would burn.

Another wave of Tainted charged in while Erris and Quell were still engaged off to Yaz's left and right. More screaming lunatics flung themselves at Yaz and yet somehow they deflected away before reaching her.

'We need to get down into the undercity.' Thurin stepped up beside her, wet black hair framing his pale face. Another Taint leapt at them and Thurin slapped him aside without making contact, the power of his magic hauling on the water inside the man.

Theus and his core of tainted gerants came through the rest of the Tainted as though they were wading through chest-high water. Somehow they had finished with the hunter. When they reached Yaz there would be no stopping them.

Even as Thurin shouted again about the undercity a fallen Taint lunged up to catch him around the knees and bring him to the ground. More of the Tainted closed in. Yaz swung a fist and found she still had enough strength in her arms to fell the first of them.

The attack that brought Yaz down came from behind. Two impossibly strong hands clamped to either side of her head and hauled her back. In the next instant she was falling. She never hit the rock. Instead she found herself pressed to warm soil, grass around her face, the slow buzz of something passing by her ear. An insect. A bee! Erris's names rose to her tongue.

She lifted herself and found Erris sitting nearby, resting his forearms on his upraised knees. Behind him blue sky, puffy white clouds, distant trees. And although he looked the same, something about the rich brownness of his skin and the tight black curl of his hair seemed more real than the body he had made to leave the city with her.

Panic seized her. Images of the Tainted howling past bloody teeth. 'Where—'

'I'm sorry. I can't save you. There are too many of them.' Erris offered a sad smile.

'You've killed us!' Yaz gasped in horror.

Erris shook his head. 'Time is passing much more slowly here. We are close enough to the city to reach the void. But only because it remembers us. In many senses part of us never left.' He raised a hand against her next question. 'We have time to talk and to still go back to the fight before we hit the ground. Or we could accept the inevitable, ask the city to take us back, and if it does, stay here, abandoning our bodies. But we do need to decide. If we are destroyed up there without making the proper transfer then we will face the final death. And there is barely enough time to make that crossing from the flesh to the void star.'

'I thought the city wouldn't have you back.'

'Never heard of the prodigal son?'

Yaz met Erris's gaze. 'I can't leave them.'

'Would any one of them wish you to die alongside them if they knew you could escape?'

'You could bring them—'

'I can only bring you because of the days the void star had to store your data.'

'I don't know what that means.' But she knew it meant no.

Yaz sat, her heart still pounding, limbs trembling, but calming beneath the sun's warmth and the soft touches of the breeze. Soon she would be dead, or worse. If Erris told her that this was free time, passing in a moment as she fell, then why not enjoy it? She slipped the skins from her feet and curled her toes in the grass. She had imagined doing so since her first visit, but the reality, if she could call it that, was beyond her imagining.

'Stay here. With me.' Erris's smile was already sad, as if he knew her answer.

Yaz looked at the grass beneath her hand, a daisy nodding its head between her outstretched fingers, a tiny black . . . something . . . an ant – the word came to her – crawling between stalks that were as big to it as trees were to her.

'The Missing lost something of themselves when they cut away their evils. Something they didn't think they needed and that Theus thinks they did.' She drew a deep breath, marvelling at the quality of the air. 'If I leave my friends to die, even if I can't help them, even if they would tell me to go . . . I would leave something of myself with them that I *know* I need. And even this place wouldn't be able to make me feel right. Not even you. And in time I would be a poison to you, to this place, to all of it.'

'But—'

'Even this place has its darkness, hiding behind what we can see.' Yaz knew that it was Vesta who had made this green memory for Erris. But she also knew that Seus haunted the city's veins. 'You said yourself that Taproot is seeking to draw me into his plans. That makes me Seus's prey, part of whatever game they're playing between them.' She patted her hides, finding them dry, just as the city remembered her, as if the recent flood had never happened. Her fingers sought something above her collarbone, then pulled Elias Taproot's needle free from her jacket. She held it out. 'This followed me here where the water couldn't follow.' The needle might be small but its significance was not. Its sharp truths could pop the sweet dream that Erris wanted to keep them in, just as easily as it could pop any other bubble. 'There's nowhere for me to hide, Erris. Trouble's coming for me one way or another, so I had best face it head on.'

'Stay.' Erris pressed his lips into a tight line. 'Whatever happens here it would still be better than having your brains dashed on the rocks. Or being eaten alive by those creatures. Or used to house old evils in service to Theus's search. You saw what he did, what your life would be. Mining the ice in the dark until your body grows old and fails.'

'There's still a chance though. It doesn't matter how slight. I can't leave them while there's still a chance.' Yaz knew she couldn't leave them even when the last chance had long gone, but it seemed easier to speak as if she would.

'What chance?' Erris asked.

'I'm a . . . what did you call it? A quantal? Like the priests. I can reach for my power.'

'That would be like setting off a bomb.'

Yaz frowned in confusion.

'You might destroy half of the Tainted but you'd shred your friends too, and maybe yourself.'

Yaz looked out across the meadow. Butterflies were dancing among the flowers, all wings and flutter. Hidden birds sang out their tiny hearts, filling the air with a chaotic beauty. A lone tree stood amid the waving grass, its branches fingering into space, leaf-clad, swaying in a slow dance that struck an echo in her chest, something old and deep, a kind of peace she had never known.

'Do you think the world still has these things in it?'

Erris shrugged. 'It's possible. Near the equator. But if the ice hasn't advanced from both poles to join hands then it's only a matter of time. Our star . . . our sun . . . was dying when the tribes first arrived here. They thought we might have a hundred thousand years or longer. But the death throes of a star are hard to predict and it faded faster than they thought. Fewer than a hundred centuries to go from this' – he gestured about them – 'to endless ice.'

She took in a deep, slow breath. 'Can you show me the battle?'

'I was going to show you the coral reefs off the Kondite Coast. A sea warm enough to swim in, a riot of colour and wonder beneath the waves, and beaches of golden sand. We could take a boat and sail—'

'I need to see the area around where we were standing . . . are still standing.'

Erris furrowed his brow. 'You're just torturing yourself, Yaz.'

'Please.'

He sighed and waved away the world about them, painting in the battle as they had left it but frozen in time. His recollection was remarkable, though in the areas shielded from his vision things grew grey and misty, the figures indistinct with just an impression of numbers.

Erris helped Yaz to stand. 'We can walk around. They're not solid.' He swung a foot through a muscular Tainted wrestling with Kaylal on the ground.

'This isn't how I look!' Yaz found herself in the act of punching the Taint who had leapt at her, her fist frozen in the moment it met his cheekbone. She glanced around at Quell with his axe flung back, a spray of blood droplets hanging in the air behind the blade. At Thurin grappled around the knees and falling, his mouth caught in the moment of surprise. They both looked like themselves. But her face . . . was not her own, surely? Not the face she felt beneath her fingers? The fat that the Ictha needed to survive the northern cold had melted from her bones, she looked frail but fierce, the new angularity of her features carried a hardness with them, a threat, and the determination in her white-on-white eyes shocked her. A new person revealed beneath the old as time cut closer to the bone, like the world of the Broken that would be revealed if the ice were pared away. Yaz studied herself a moment longer. If she were one of the Tainted she would think twice about throwing herself at someone with that look.

'Zeen?' Yaz spun around, finding no sign of him in the confusion of bodies.

Erris shook his head. 'I didn't see him. But he's fast enough to stay out of trouble.'

'He's a boy with his head full of being a man. He's stupid enough to get into trouble.' The thought of Zeen lying out there, wrapped around a wound, was a cold wind through her heart. She spun again, noting the occasional outcrops of harder rock, the bent girders, and here and there a gap in the battling crowd where a hole or fissure must lead down into the chambers beneath their feet.

Yaz set off towards the wedge of tainted gerants advancing behind Theus as he led them through the rest of his forces. She felt strange, passing through people, as if she were the ghost not them, as if she were like the first daughter of Zin and Mokka who still haunted the ice, less substantial than the wind.

She reached the red-haired gerant, his face less bloodcrazed than the others, a cruel and eager pride on blunt features, green eyes staring out from beneath a heavy brow.

She turned to Erris as he caught her up. 'Can you show me the undercity? I mean how it lies beneath the stone?'

Erris frowned in concentration then nodded. The Tainted and the Broken faded into smoky memories, even the stone beneath their feet became translucent and shining through it she could see a confusion of chambers and tunnels stretching down into untold depths. In some places you would have to mine through fifty or a hundred yards of rock to find a void. In others the nearest chambers almost touched the surface. In others they did touch the surface, and those were the holes down which the recent flood had drained in a remarkably short time given the volume of water.

Yaz made a slow turn. Thurin had wanted them to escape to the undercity but even if the nearest entrance were just yards away, and it wasn't, it would still be too far with all of them already grappling the foe. Yaz tried to see if there were some way she might direct any power she took from the river into the rock to forge a new escape route. But the nearest chamber that lay close to the surface was nearer to Theus and the advancing gerants. They would reach it first.

'Send me back to the fight,' Yaz said. 'I mean, wake me up, or whatever it is you do.'

'I'm not sending you. If we go we'll go together.'

'I thought . . .' Yaz frowned. 'I thought you had coral reefs to see.'

Erris smiled a slow, regretful smile. 'I had coral reefs to show you. I have spent too long alone in such places. The only joy left is in sharing them. I would rather share your last minutes than spend another eternity in sunshine and green fields by myself, Yaz.'

Yaz didn't know how to answer that. 'Keep them off me for a few moments more. I'm going to try something.'

Erris nodded. He reached for her face, one warm hand

shaping itself to the curve of her cheek; some urgent and unexpected need swelled within her and she opened her mouth to speak, but suddenly everything was screaming and falling again.

Yaz's fall ended with a sharp pain and a sudden loss of breath. The Taint that had brought her down clung to her legs while a howling child no older than Zeen hurled herself at Yaz's face, biting and clawing.

A heartbeat later the girl sailed away, plucked from Yaz by Erris and thrown into the advancing masses. He hauled Yaz to her feet while kicking her other assailant clear.

'Make it fast!' Erris pivoted to kick a large man high in the chest, sending him tumbling back before he could swing the ice-hatchet in his hand.

As Erris threw himself into the oncoming lines, kicking, twisting, and punching, Yaz tried to see past them as she had in the vision she had so recently shared. The river that runs through all things was there before her, thin, ethereal, but within reach if she could just stretch . . . She extended her arms, her eyes defocused, fingers straining. The river eluded her, like a sneeze that was there but wouldn't quite make itself known. The screaming and roaring and falling bodies made it hard to find. She needed her stars but they were gone. She needed time but the booming voices of the gerants flanking Theus told her that she had none.

'I can't . . .' It was too soon, and her work in the black ice with the hunter's star must have used the same muscle as reaching for the river because it seemed to retreat before her. Her friends were dying. Innocents were falling on all sides. '*I can't.*' And suddenly she could. Suddenly the river was beneath her fingers, swirling around her hands, flowing through her, filling and flooding her, trying to tear her from the moorings of her flesh.

With a cry Yaz pulled free. Even in the depths of their madness the Tainted knew to draw back as Yaz shuddered with the raw energies that pulsed through her. To her own eyes her flesh shone with a golden light. Time fractured around her, different possible Yazs trying to fall in every direction at once. The pain was as nothing she had experienced before and with a shriek she released the borrowed power before it destroyed her. She flung it forward in a thick beam of brightness that cut through several Tainted before it reached the rock just before Theus's feet. The stone absorbed the bolt, glowing with the same spreading gold that Yaz's hands had shown, and shattered rather than exploded. A great sheet of rock fell in broken pieces taking Theus, his gerants, and a score of other Tainted down with it, falling into the chamber that had been hidden beneath their feet. The sound shook the ground as if the ice sky itself had fallen, raw, violent, bigger than mountains. The hole was a rough rectangle with jagged edges, many yards on each side, and dust rose from it in a big curling cloud, wooshing up towards the icy heavens.

CHAPTER 37

The dust cloud rolled over Yaz, taking the ice sky away and most of the light with it. The boom, louder even than that of the collection cage hitting the floor, had for a moment stolen everyone's voice. An eerie silence, as tenuous and fleeting as the dust cloud itself, hung in the air.

At first it was groans and calls to friends that nibbled away at the thickness of the silence. Yaz called for Erris and found her voice distant as if the crash of falling stone had deadened her hearing. The snarling of the Tainted came next, orienting themselves in this unexpected grey world. Yaz found a pair of bodies resuming their struggle and hauled the thinner one away to reveal someone familiar. 'Quell?' She coughed on the dust, trying not to choke. The man looked almost like Quell beneath the grey.

'Yaz!' It was Quell. He gripped her arm and used her as support while he clambered to his feet.

'Get to the cage,' Yaz said.

He nodded, uncertain of the direction, then set off, pulling her with him.

'Wait. Thurin is close.'

The howls were rising again from many directions. The sounds of renewed fighting echoed out, fresh screams of pain and anger and fright.

'Yaz?' Against the odds Thurin stumbled from the sifting clouds.

'The cage,' she said, and let Quell pull her on. 'Erris! The cage!'

Thurin limped after them. Glancing back she saw the left side of his face ran with blood, so dark as to look black in the half-light.

By the time Erris jogged into view to join them the dust had settled enough for a good ten yards of visibility. They passed ghost-grey people identifiable as the Broken only by the fact that they didn't run madly to attack them. Quell led on, taking Yaz further from the front line where the flood had swept her, back past the positions Arka's followers had established.

'Zeen! Maya? Kao?' Yaz called the last name without hope. The boy had been among the first to go down, throwing himself at the Tainted to save her. 'Kaylal? Arka?'

They reached the cage, looming above them, a thing as alien as the hunters, having no place on the ice. It still leaned at a steep angle, supported by the forking cable at one end and by the edge touching the rock at the other. The cable end was high enough that Yaz couldn't reach any of it with outstretched arms.

'If we climb on it they'll have to come up at us,' Yaz said.

'Or bring us down with spears,' Thurin said.

'I have this.' Quell had picked up one of the big gerant shields on the way: a grey board as dust-covered as he was. 'We can hold out until they haul the cage back up. Maybe.'

'We've no food or shelter,' Erris noted.

'No.' Yaz hung her head. It had taken the only member

of their group not to need either of these vital things to point out their absence. The boards and fungi had doubtless been washed away and swirled down into the undercity through a dozen different holes, along with the last of any remaining hope.

'They're where we left them,' Thurin said. 'I convinced the water to leave them behind.'

'Thank the gods.' Yaz blinked at Thurin, amazed and elated in equal measure. His ice-work had advanced seemingly in leaps and bounds. When they first met he'd showed off by lifting a puddle. Now he steered the currents of a wild flood and threw grown men through the air. 'We need to load it. Quickly. And search for the others.'

Quell opened his mouth to speak but at that moment the cage began to straighten up. 'They're hauling it back!'

'No,' Thurin said. 'They'll lift it a little off the ground. So they know it's vertical and easy to load.'

'How do they know?' Yaz asked, ready to grab the bars should it start to rise beyond reach.

The cage straightened but instead of rocking on its base it scraped across the ground then began to swing free beneath the still-rising cable. A moment later it stopped rising and just hung there swinging slowly.

'They must be able to tell by the weight on the lifting mechanism,' Erris said. 'Let's hurry.'

With the dust settling all around them and visibility heading back to normal the four of them hurried to get the stashed food and shelter. They worked in pairs, heaping fungi onto stacked boards then carrying the loads to the cage. The Tainted and Broken had resumed their fights, knots of Arka's and Pome's factions struggling against the possessed intruders from the black ice. Even with Theus and his gerants removed from the battleground along with a score or more of others the Tainted still had more than twice the combined numbers of the Broken factions. The pause had, however, allowed the Broken a moment to organize their defence.

Guilt dogged Yaz's steps as she worked. They were preparing their escape while others fought and kept the enemy from them. Worse still, Zeen was still out there. But without the cage and supplies she had no salvation to offer her brother even if she could find him. She knew though that she would not be leaving without him.

Yaz and Quell were returning to the cage with their third load before the first band of Tainted came running at them. Quell set down his end of the boards, spilling fungi, and raised the bloody axe hanging at his hip.

Yaz looked at the five Tainted sprinting towards them across the wet rock. Two ragged children, two painfully thin women, their dirty hair flying out behind them, and a man of more solid build, his chest bare and bleeding from several long cuts. She could already imagine the ruin that the swing of Quell's axe would wreak. 'Couldn't we . . .' She raised her fists and mimed a punch.

'They want to kill us, Yaz!' Quell readied himself for his strike. 'There're more coming.'

'Please!' The feeling Yaz put into the word was aimed at the gods as much as at Quell. It wasn't his fault they were in this impossible situation. It wasn't his fault she had jumped.

Despite his shorter legs it was the smallest of the two boys who reached them first. A child with a touch of hunska in him. Zeen had been just like him until she drove out the demons. Yaz stepped in front of Quell to intercept the boy, swinging a punch. The boy proved too fast, ducking under her swing and leaping onto Yaz, tearing at her face.

The boards went skittering across the ice as Yaz grabbed the boy and rolled, scattering and crushing carefully hoarded fungi. She got on top of her attacker and banged his head against the rock, once, twice, until the fight went out of him. A sharp pain in her shoulder told her another child had leapt on her. Yaz got to her feet, rearing up beneath the second attacker as a third hammered into her. Close by, Quell felled a man, clubbing him two-handed across the chest, his axe abandoned.

The Tainted came too quickly and there were too many to be fought off. Food and shelter were kicked aside, trampled, her last hopeless plan in ruins. Yaz managed to shrug off the child on her back, crying out as the girl's teeth lost hold of her shoulder. The child fell to the ground and as the girl rolled to grab Quell's leg Yaz saw that it was Jerra, the girl with the short brown hair who had arrived with Arka an hour before, now host to one of the devils from the black ice.

Another of the Tainted tackled Yaz immediately and for a time punctuated by blows and screams they wrestled each other, rolling back and forth, locked in a vicious struggle. Finally Yaz banged the man's head against the rock, hard enough to take him out of the fight.

A cry rang out as she raised herself. A cry that cut through the noise, not because it was louder than the din but because she had known that voice all her life and never heard terror in it. Her eyes found the knife in Quell's side, buried to the hilt which was still gripped by the grimy hand of the young girl grappling him. Jerra had stabbed him. Jerra who had lowered the rope to save her from Hetta. Even as Yaz looked, Quell was falling, hauled down from behind by a heavily muscled ice-miner, another of the Broken newly overwhelmed by devils freed from the Tainted he'd killed.

'No!'

The Tainted closed on all sides. If Thurin and Erris were still fighting they were lost in the press of bodies.

'No.'

A slow calm closed around Yaz, deadening the screams and shouts. Another Taint hammered into her and although the impact shook her it didn't reach her core. The world slowed again, as it must for a hunska in the throes of their quickness, though it gave her no liberty to act.

'No . . .' She kept eye contact with Quell as he dropped. His hand wrestled for control of the knife whose blade reached deep into his flesh, but his pale-on-white Ictha eyes held hers.

'No.' The same denial that had wrapped her when the regulator pushed Zeen into the pit now owned her once more. She had fallen from her life and now the dream of freedom lay broken. It had always been a dream, like the green ghost in the south taunting her with ancient memories of softer times. But the ice held them. The ice was truth. And now at the end of things she found herself too cold for dreaming.

Another half-felt impact and she too was falling. She saw only the river that flows through all things, impossibly distant, the thinnest of lines far below her, too far to reach. The river couldn't be touched twice in a day let alone twice in the space of minutes. When she *had* touched it twice in a day it had been the stars that allowed it. The stars brought it closer.

As she fell Yaz became aware of the stars, constellations of them, watching her from the ice-locked heavens. Stars like dust. A line joining each of them to her and her to each of them. Stars above her in the ice. Stars below her in the undercity. Stars on every side. A million threads with her held weightless at the centre.

The river lay too far below her and too thin, but she was falling. Hadn't Theus said that, ancient in his darkness?

Hadn't he told Thurin that we fall through our lives? Yaz fell towards the river and with each moment it grew closer. Somewhere far away there were screams and howls. In that place there was pain and the dying of friends.

'No.'

Yaz couldn't reach to touch the river. But she could dive into it. And she did.

In the black skies of the long night when the dragons no longer lash their aurora tails across the heavens and only the uncountable crimson eyes of the dying stars bear witness, there comes from time to time a white and shooting fire. It is as if one of those low-banked hearths has gathered all its fuel in a last blaze of defiance and hurled itself from the impossible heights to burn a brilliant path towards the ground.

Mother Mazai had a tale wherein once during her youth a white light reached in through the hides of her family's tent and rolled their shadows across the far walls. And scrambling from their beds into the killing cold Mother Mazai's family had watched, ankle-deep in the dry ice of the polar night, as a ball of blinding whiteness carved through the sky, shaking the ice with thunder until it fell from view with one last crash that set the powder ice dancing into the air.

Mother Mazai said her own grandmother had gone to find where the star had fallen. She went alone, wrapped in so many hides a hoola would have run from her if any such roamed so far north. There was no sense in it, Mazai said. It was not the Ictha way to spend precious energy in the long night, but her grandmother said she had seen the end of her days approach and that the Gods in the Sky would want one of the true people to stand witness to the fall of this star. And so she went.

She returned long after they had given her up for dead, and she died soon after for the cold had its teeth too deep in her for the warmth of the tent to draw them out. But before she fell asleep that last time she said she had found the crater where the star fell and that it was as large as the wandering seas, and in all that great wreckage of ice there was only darkness. The light that had lit up the world was gone. Wholly spent in one last defiance.

Yaz knew she was that star.

She stood and her flesh was burning. The Tainted fell away screaming. She held a thousand times more power than she could possibly contain and direct. It would burst from her in every direction taking her bones with it. But like the shooting star she would have defied the darkness if only for a short time, and when her moment of glory was done there would be nothing of her for the darkness to claim.

Even in her instant of release Yaz thought of the ones she loved. The lines that joined her heart to theirs radiated from her. Quell, her foundation, Thurin, as broken as she had become, Erris, both ancient and young, Zeen, her last tie to family, and all the other friends around her. But growing stronger and more clear than even these connections were the million threads that joined her to the stars. The power in her made each star in the ice above and city below known to her with a clarity she had never experienced before. She knew their position, their song, their nature. Even the void star, further below her than the surface of the ice lay above her, even the void star echoed her song. Even its heartbeat quickened in response. Those million threads thrummed and sang with power, a celestial harmony leeching energy from her through uncountable pinpricks.

'No!' Yaz raised both arms, fingers splayed. Above her the ice lit, alive with the colours of every star from those that would cover a thumbnail to those that could be lost among grains of dust. Beneath her the dark, dead chambers of the undercity knew light once more as the script walls burst into brilliance and the stars as yet unscavenged began to burn with a new fire. Light woke in rooms that had stood for millennia in silent, unbroken blackness. The shadows ran from galleries where the last flame had been borne in the hands of the Missing.

Yaz found herself at the midst of a constellation, of a galaxy, and as she shouted her denial every star orbited around her centre. Each one carved its own curved path through the ice, burning with heat stolen from the river in which she swam.

'Come!' Yaz roared, and the closest stars answered, tearing from the ice to swarm through the air in shimmering tendrils.

The stars broke upon the battlefield like a deluge, a rattling flood of light, surging in response to Yaz's desire. She wrapped the Tainted in cocoons of glowing stars, flexible dusty skins studded with larger stars.

'Go!' Yaz commanded, feeling through the stars as if they were somehow extensions of her own hands, feeling the number and disposition of the devils in each of their victims. 'Leave!' She struck as she had struck with her hunter star against first Kao's chest and then Zeen's, but now with many thousands of lesser stars and with far greater clarity. The pulse of light as the stars gave out the last of their stolen energy was enough to burn out many of the smallest, leaving nothing of themselves behind.

Yaz fell to her knees amid the shimmering drifts. With the last of her strength she flung her arms out to her sides and drove the stars back. The drifts drew back towards the outskirts of the city, leaving a battlefield littered with bodies.

A silence reigned and Yaz lay spent, unmoving, her gaze fixed. It seemed an age before anyone spoke and before they did not a single thought passed across the clean white field of Yaz's mind. At last the bodies began to move. Beside Yaz the girl, Jerra, freed from possession now, rolled onto her back, groaning. 'What? What happened?'

CHAPTER 38

Yaz had saved them. A smile found its way to her lips, even as she lay hollowed out on the rock. If Yaz had achieved nothing else, if the last of her life's energy trickled from her limbs as she lay on the cold stone, she had done this one good thing. She had driven the devils from those claimed by the taint. She had ended the battle that saw son turned against father, mother against daughter. She had reunited two great halves of the Broken, and mended families torn apart by ancient evils.

In a fog of wonderment the newly cleansed Tainted began to gain their feet. Friends and family long parted found themselves in each other's arms once more.

'It's started rising again!' Kao's shout startled Yaz out of her daze. She turned as quickly as her fragile body would allow. She felt as though she were a collection of broken parts, her bones turned to brittle ash. The power that had flowed through her left a burned-out feeling. If all that energy hadn't found an immediate exit she would have been blown apart by it. The stars had saved her.

'The cage . . .'

The cage hadn't stopped. They were still hauling it back. Slowly but without pause.

'They're not supposed to do that!' Thurin hobbled towards her, holding his arm.

'We should hurry then.' Erris had already collected several boards, still wired together at the edges. His white tunic, now smeared with dirt and blood, had been half torn from him revealing the musculature of his chest and belly. He strode urgently towards the rising cage, now hip height above the ground.

Yaz's sense of success turned to panic. Zeen was still out there! 'You three do it. I'm going to look for—' Yaz broke off, remembering Quell. Somehow the vast energies she had employed had temporarily wiped from her memory the horror that had driven her through whatever barriers she had overcome in order to call on them. She spotted Quell as one of the Tainted who had been attacking him, the same child who had driven the knife home, now moved aside from trying to tend his injuries.

'I'm so sorry.' Jerra wiped at her grimy tears.

Yaz shouldered her aside. It was as if the idea that Quell might die had been too big to fit in her head, blasted from it by the very plunge into the river that it had precipitated. The knife was still buried to the hilt in his side, no part of the blade showing. She took Quell's hands, their eyes meeting again. There were no words to say. The Ictha had no healing save for minor cuts. To become injured on the ice was to die. Living without injury was struggle enough. It was the same hard fact and same cruel logic that saw children thrown into the Pit of the Missing.

Yaz reached to pull the knife out.

'Don't.' Jerra caught her arm. Her hair was still dark with the flood and guilt haunted her eyes. 'He'll bleed to death.'

'Take it out.' Quell gasped through gritted teeth. 'Going . . . to . . . die anyway.'

Another of the Tainted, blinking, still disoriented, reached to stay Yaz's hand. 'It's a bad wound, but if we stitch it and bind it' – she tilted her head as if trying to judge what the knife might have reached – 'and keep it clean . . . he stands a chance. A good chance maybe.'

A dark shape loomed over them. 'She's correct.' Erris knelt beside Yaz. 'We don't want to remove the blade until we are ready to deal with the wound. I suggest your new friend helps you move Quell to the cage.' He softened his voice and added, 'Quickly.'

Erris hurried back to the business of loading food and equipment. He and Thurin pushed through the wandering crowd, made rough by fear of the cage leaving them behind, seemingly the only ones there with any purpose. The rest of the Broken were too overwhelmed to notice what Yaz's friends were about. They were busy tending to their wounded, weeping over their dead, and discovering those who they'd thought lost forever months or years before.

Members of Arka and Pome's factions were scattered and intermingled but their fight seemed forgotten, washed away by a flood of water and the falling of stars. The Tainted, returned to their senses when Yaz's last effort burned the devils out of them, were now the glue that joined the two pieces of the Broken together, the joy of their reunion stronger than recent disputes of which they knew nothing. Yaz had no idea how long it would last. Long enough, she hoped.

Yaz, with help from Jerra and the woman, bent to carry Quell by his arms and legs but as she began to pull Yaz saw the pain it would cause. She set the woman to watch while she and Jerra got boards onto which they could roll Quell and then drag him to the cage. She wanted to stay with him, to talk, to tell him he was going to survive, but there wasn't any time, the cage was leaving. Before long it would be shoulder high from the ground and for all Yaz knew the priests might soon start to haul it up at speed.

'Let's do this.' Yaz had found the boards. With the woman's help she slid them under Quell.

The strain required to move the solid Ictha proved too much for Yaz, burned out by her miracle with the stars, and for the woman starved and weakened during her time in service to Theus. Jerra was stronger than both but too small to make the difference. Yaz's fingers slipped from the board beneath Quell's shoulders and she fell back cursing, weeping with effort.

As she sat up Yaz found a hulking shape coming towards her, unrecognizable in the dimmed glow from the ice ceiling high above them.

'I'll do it.' Kao bent to take hold. His thick arms bore a dozen bleeding bite marks and cruel nail furrows. His hair stood at odd angles, some having been torn out in clumps, and his hides were ripped in several places. But he still had his strength and soon had Quell scraping across the rocks, gasping at the jolts.

At the cage Thurin was already inside, receiving fungi, boards, and other equipment as Erris brought it. A dozen or so former Tainted stood watching in confusion, their minds perhaps unsure of reality after the sudden departure of the devils that had ruled them for so long. An emaciated fair-haired young woman approached the cage as Kao reached it, dragging Quell.

'Thurin?'

Thurin positioned the heat pot Erris had given him, setting it on a stack of boards. He turned to the woman. 'Klendra?' A smile of astonishment cracked his bloody face. Seeing Yaz he pointed to the blonde girl. 'She's cave-born. We grew up together.' He rubbed his eyes as if to clear his vision and looked at Klendra again. 'Is it really you? They took you so long ago! You were six? Everyone thought you must be dead ages ago.'

Yaz wanted to shout that there wasn't time for reunions. Part of her wanted to shove the girl aside. And other voices within her skull cried out to shame that first voice. Exhaustion was showing her what the stars did to other people. She understood that she wasn't the selfish voice, or the kind one, she was the sum of a multitude, normally joined so close that the seams didn't show, but liable to fall apart under stress. Everyone was. A mix, a recipe, the sum of their parts and more.

Erris had swarmed up the outside of the cage and now motioned that he was going to drop the load of boards he'd brought across. 'Sorry to be insensitive but we're on a clock here.'

Thurin looked up. 'A what?'

'In a hurry.' He dropped the boards for Thurin to catch.

Yaz called out to him. 'Erris! Help me with Quell. I can't lift him like this.'

Erris landed beside them, making the fifteen-foot drop from the side of the cage seem nothing. The bottom of the cage was already approaching shoulder height above the ground.

'Do you know what to do for Quell?' Yaz asked, thinking that in the warm years into which Erris had been born there might have been time to heal the sick rather than discard them.

'I'll have a look at it on the way up,' he said. 'How long was the blade?'

Quell shook his head. 'Feels like it's long enough to poke out the other side.'

Erris pulled himself back onto the gently swinging cage and Kao, with Yaz's help, lifted Quell towards him. Erris took hold of Quell from behind, reaching one arm under his armpit and across his chest, then began to climb, as if Quell were a small child and his considerable weight was nothing. Quell panted through his teeth, clearly in great pain, but made no cry, just a groan as Erris lifted him over the top of the cage, avoiding the lifting cables.

Yaz turned to make a quick study of Kao. 'I thought they'd killed you.' She found her voice thick, tears in her eyes, surprised at how glad she was to be wrong. 'Come on. Quickly. We need to find Maya and Zeen and—' She wanted to say Kaylal, she wanted to say Arka, and even Jerra, she wanted to say all of them. But the cage was leaving too fast, and even if they had time it wouldn't hold many.

'I'll find them,' Kao said, and immediately rushed off, shoving through the growing crowd of onlookers. They looked unusually similar, all of them grey with the dust that clung to their wet hides, their hair, and their skin. Kao swung his head this way and that, his height offering him a better view. He called for Zeen, at first in a tentative almost-hiss as if afraid someone might hear him.

Yaz set off in the opposite direction, pushing her way through the dazed survivors as gently as time allowed, which wasn't very. They almost seemed to be ghosts, haunting the ruins, but those who had been Tainted had more in common with ruins than with ghosts. They had been haunted but now stood empty. She hoped they could rebuild their lives.

'Zeen!' She shouted her brother's name. The first loud sound since the howling fight and the falling of stars. The greetings and reunions within the grey and milling crowd had been muted, muffled by wonder, as though everyone worried that this was a dream from which too much excitement might wake them. 'Zeen!' Yaz had no such worries.

She glanced back to the cage. Erris was gone from it, Quell was lying at the bottom coming into view above the heads of the crowd. Thurin stood beside Quell, looking worried. He cast about then found her. 'Hurry!' he yelled. 'We'll be out of reach soon!'

Yaz started back reflexively, but someone caught her arm. For a moment she tried to tear herself free, thinking it an attack.

'It's me. Arka.' Her scars were just visible beneath the layer of damp, grimy dust. 'You're going back.' Not a question.

'Yes.' Yaz relaxed a fraction, glad to have told the truth. 'Have you seen Zeen or Maya?'

Arka shook her head as if the question were a distraction. 'Pome must have arranged this collection with the priests. Gods know how he speaks to them but it seems that he can.' She furrowed her brow. 'But I can't see Pome anywhere, and those you've returned will stand with us. It's going to be all right here. You don't have to go back to the priests. Not any more.'

'I'm not going back to the regulator. I'm going back to the ice, and I'm taking anyone who wants to come with me.'

Arka stepped back, eyes widening. 'To die in the wind? That's madness. The priests will be waiting for you, and even if you could escape them there's nothing up there for our kind. We're broken.'

'We're going to try. Quina—'

'Ha!' Arka barked the laugh, turning the heads of those nearby. 'You've been sold that old tale of the green belt around a white world. Next you'll be telling me the one about the moon that keeps it warm!'

Yaz didn't know what a moon was but she didn't have time to ask. Glancing back she saw that the cage was rising above the heads of those around it. Even as she watched, Erris swung onto it, seemingly unburdened by yet another load tied to his back. He turned and called to her with real urgency. 'Hurry!'

'Zeen!' She bellowed his name and more faces turned her way.

A fear was growing in Yaz. The fear that her brother lay dead or dying among the ruins, perhaps broken-backed, wrapped around a girder by the power of the flood, or swept down some drain to the undercity and drowned in the dark. Even if he lived this chance wouldn't come again. Whatever precautions were taken up there on the ice they would be doubled and doubled again after Erris and Quell and Thurin arrived there equipped for a journey.

'They say set a gerant to find a needle,' Arka said beside her. 'You need height to find someone lost in a crowd.'

'He should have heard me . . .' But Yaz took the point. She turned her back on Arka and started returning to the cage. As she pushed her way through she saw Erris leaning over the top to pass his load to Thurin. Kao beat her back and the cage swung with the addition of his weight as he began to climb it. She hoped he had Zeen with him but he seemed to be alone.

By the time Yaz laid her hands on the bars and saw Quell, deathly pale, staring at the great hole above them, she had to reach up to snag the cage. Shockingly, she barely had the strength to haul herself up so her foot could find a hold on the underside. The effort nearly broke her. Touching the river twice had left her in ruins, though by rights she should be dead.

She would look for Zeen from the top. If he was lying

hurt or unconscious she would see him and send Erris to recover him. If she couldn't see him she would jump back down. Whatever the cost she was not leaving without her brother.

She reached the top of the rising cage and hung exhausted for a few deep breaths as Erris and Kao began climbing down inside. The noise of the crowd surrounded her, still ringing with the joy of reunions, the hurt of wounds being cleaned, the weeping of the bereaved, the groans of the dying. But something had changed. A muting of conversation rippled out and Yaz turned her head in the direction it came from.

The Broken parted before Bexen, Pome's enforcer, the largest gerant on the field of battle, the starlight reflecting dully on his iron breastplate. His good eye and the milky one both stared in Yaz's direction, bright with malice. As the people hurried to get out of Bexen's way Yaz saw Pome beside him. He still held the red star that had given him control over his hunter. He clutched it in his bare hand now. The left side of his face had been scraped raw and torn, as though he had been dragged some distance across the rock, perhaps refusing to let go of his star when it moved to obey Yaz's will along with all the others.

The last few people cleared from their path, revealing Zeen, helpless in Bexen's grasp: one huge hand wrapped about his neck, the other holding a notched black iron blade close by. Two other gerants came behind them, glaring at the crowd as if challenging them to make a move.

'Yaz of the Ictha.' Pome wore a tight, victorious smile. 'Your companions will exit that cage and you will put your hands through the bars for your wrists to be bound. If this is not done Bexen will kill the boy and your friends will be dispatched with spear thrusts.'

'Let him go!' Yaz shouted. But Pome's smile only widened.

He lifted his star, the scarlet glow leaking between his fingers. The light of it cast his face in shadows and blood.

'Yours is not the only rising star.' He lifted his voice, speaking for the crowd, his magic letting his poisoned words find a home in some of the hearts that would otherwise reject them. 'The girl, Yaz, must return to the surface as the regulator has stipulated and answer for her crimes there. I don't need to remind you that without the goodwill of the priests we would have no fish, no salt, and no skins. You are all too young to know but Eular remembers a time without salt. It's a slow, ugly death. It takes about ten days before it starts to hurt, and quite a few more days to die, but after the first twelve days you'll wish you were dead.' He nodded to one of his gerants. 'Go bind her hands.'

Some of the Broken had looked angry at the threat to a child's life, but now that anger wavered, torn by self-interest, swayed by Pome's influence. They couldn't live on fungi alone, and rats were too scarce. The priests might be miles above but they could reach down and wrap their hands about the throats of the Broken just as Bexen was doing to Zeen.

Each moment the cage edged its way higher. The bottom of the cage had cleared the Broken now, above the reach of those of regular height. The gerant coming to tie Yaz's hands outside the cage. Yaz would have to drop down on the inside and push her wrists through the bars to comply.

'I should leave.' Thurin began to climb out, his face grim but forcing a smile. 'Pome ought to let you take Quell back. The priest sent your friend to get you after all.'

Erris, already near the top of the cage, swung himself back out and began to climb down. 'I'll find you again, Yaz.'

Thurin snorted and pointed at the hole above them. 'Good climber, are you?'

Erris smiled. 'I have a knack for getting out of places I don't want to be in.'

Kao hung where he was, halfway up the inside. He watched her, blue-eyed beneath his mass of dirty blond hair. He exhaled a long sigh. 'The Golin wouldn't have me back anyway,' he said, his voice thick with a boy's heartache, and with one more sigh he began to haul his man's body back out of the cage, every limb sporting cuts and bites he had taken saving her from the Tainted.

Yaz couldn't let them go but she saw it was no good to argue with any of them. Instead she addressed the Broken, hoping to turn them against Pome.

'The priests need you as much as you need them,' Yaz called as she clambered into the cage. To her own ears she sounded like a nervous girl trying to argue with an elder, but she pressed on as she began to climb down to where Quell lay curled around his knife wound. 'They need the iron you scavenge. It's how they influence the tribes and gain their favour. They need the trade. It's not done out of kindness. They trapped you here for their use.'

Pome laughed. 'Do you think they will run out of iron before we run out of salt? Which need is more urgent?' The humour dropped from his face leaving something ugly behind it.

For a moment despair swamped Yaz, darkening her mind. But the darkness took on a shape as it swam across her thoughts. 'Wait!' she shouted. 'There's a whale! We found a whale locked in the ice. One of the great whales, enough to feed all of you for years. It's in the furthest cavern of the black ice, but I cleared the demons from it. You don't need the priests.'

She felt the change in the crowd. Rumbles of 'She cleansed the Tainted', 'They should be allowed to go', 'We don't owe the priests anything'. Rebellious faces turned Pome's way. Some of Arka's faction started towards him and for the moment nobody seemed inclined to stop them.

Thurin paused at the top of the cage, clinging to the outside, ready to go down.

'Uh, Yaz?' Kao, white-faced, now dangled beneath the cage, his toes almost scraping stone. 'What should I do?' The distance he had to fall wasn't growing very fast but for someone of such heavy build a drop of even a few feet could hurt.

Before Yaz could answer Pome snarled and raised his crimson star above his head again. 'This is not open for debate,' he roared.

The star flared and with a clanking and a grating of metal on stone, hunters began to emerge from cracks and pits all across the ruins. Three, four . . . half a dozen iron behemoths. Some within the great halo formed by the drift of stars and stardust, some outside it.

Pome shouted, all traces of persuasion gone from his voice: 'You *will* obey the priesthood. All of you. As far as you lot are concerned I *am* a priest. I rule here now and my word is law.' The wrist that had emerged from his skins as he had raised his arm lay mottled with the stains of demons, not from the black ice, not pieces that the Missing had cut away, but devils of his own making, split from him by the too-fierce light of the star that he lacked the skill to properly handle. These were parts of Pome's madness now given their own voice, and their influence was all the stronger for it.

The hunters had all emerged now, standing motionless, the red glare of their eyeholes sweeping the crowd for dissent.

Pome focused back on Yaz. 'I'll count to ten. If the others aren't out of the cage by then and your hands are not presented for Rakka to tie then Bexen will kill the boy.'

He drew a breath. 'One. Two.'

Erris reached the bottom of the cage on the outside. Yaz dropped painfully beside Quell on the inside. The gerant, Rakka, more than a foot taller than the dangling Kao, stood below, raising the looped hide strips he would use to bind her hands.

'Three. Four.'

Yaz thrust her hands out through the square gaps in the cage. Rakka had to reach up at arms' length. He set the loop about her wrists and drew the knot tight, trapping her hands outside.

Erris hung from the bottom of the cage and dropped lightly to the ground.

'Five. Six.'

Thurin hung below the cage. He looked up, despair in his dark eyes even though he had never known the surface. 'Yaz . . .' He dropped away, landing less well than Erris and falling to hands and knees at the older man's feet. The cage jerked, starting to rise faster.

'Seven. Eight.'

Kao hung beneath the cage, his toes nearly a yard above the ground.

'Let go.' Rakka punched him in the stomach.

'Nine.'

'Yaz?' Kao wheezed.

Bexen tightened his grip on Zeen's neck, a grin cracking his brutal face. Yaz opened her mouth to tell Kao to drop, but a spray of crimson across Bexen's shoulder stopped her. Something long and thin emerged from just above his collarbone, clearing the top of his breastplate and grazing his chin, coming level with his left eye. That eye and the other one widened. The cruel mouth beneath them went slack. And with a clatter of metal he collapsed, dragging Zeen down with him.

Maya stood revealed behind him, shedding shadows. She climbed over Bexen's transfixed body before Pome could react and tugged the gerant's fingers clear of Zeen's neck.

'Catch him!' Pome roared, but Zeen was away and weaving through the Broken with a hunska's swiftness.

The six hunters lurched into action as one, their metal feet gouging the stone to accelerate them forwards.

Yaz gritted her teeth against the pain that made her head feel like brittle ice waiting to shatter, and with the last effort remaining to her she reached out. The star in Pome's hand jerked forwards. He got both hands on it, braced against the pull . . . and held. Yaz cried out in despair, having no more to give, but a moment later a dark shape rolled from among the nearest onlookers to knock Pome's feet out beneath him. Kaylal! The legless smith tried to grapple Pome but Pome managed to keep one hand on the star and it dragged him clear. Devil-darkened fingers refused to release the star even as it hauled him across the roughness of the rock, trying to fly to Yaz's outstretched hands.

Yaz bowed her head in defeat but even as she did so Maya leapt forward, evading the gerants behind her. With one slash of a heavy knife she cut Pome's hand from him. The star flew free, the severed hand tumbling in its wake. In a crimson streak it sped through the air on a rising curve to hammer into Yaz's outstretched palms.

Yaz's vision dimmed as she strained to send a word of negation to the hunters through Pome's star and the great mechanisms ground to a halt. She collapsed beside Quell. A trickle of his blood ran across the boards beneath her neck and she watched the drops fall from the cage. They had a frightening distance to fall. Past Kao, still hanging white-knuckled beneath the cage and carrying on for another four yards beneath his kicking feet before splashing on the bedrock.

Erris, Zeen, and Thurin stood beneath staring helplessly, watching Yaz being hauled away. Unchallenged by Pome's remaining gerants Maya had hauled the iron rod from Bexen's toppled corpse and, trailing the bloody, nearly five-foot length of it, she was racing to join the others.

A warm tear rolled from Yaz's cheek and fell like the blood. She had failed. If instead of following Zeen into the pit she had stayed and watched the regulator throw more children down how would things be worse? She would have been alone in his bony clutches and Quell would have stayed with the Ictha. And now? She was being delivered weak and alone into the priest's hands, a package they had bartered for with salt and stars. And Quell would be given back to the Ictha, wounded, not fit for life on the ice.

Beneath her Zeen was retreating at an increasing pace. Maya, a friend who had saved them so many times, was also now abandoned in this hole. And Thurin, and Erris. Both of them had infinitely complicated her life but she found that losing them was tearing her apart as if each owned a separate piece of her heart.

Erris was doing something. One moment he had been talking urgently to Thurin and in the next he became a blur of motion. Somehow he climbed Thurin, and in a leap that sent the other man sprawling to the ground he launched himself skywards. The jump should have been impossible but Erris wasn't made of flesh or bone. Somehow he got his fingertips to the toe of Kao's boot and found enough purchase to hang there. Kao yelled in pain but didn't surrender his grip on the bars.

As Thurin got to his hands and knees little Maya used him as a step to execute her own leap. Even with Erris hanging below Kao the vertical distance was too great for her to jump but she thrust her bar out above her and with inhuman skill Erris caught the very end of it between his heels. Held by such a tenuous bond Maya swung at the far end of more than a yard of bloody iron and rose with the accelerating cage.

Thurin got unsteadily to his feet, still bent over, and formed a cup with both hands. Zeen stepped into it. With a howl of effort and unsuspected strength Thurin threw the boy into the air.

'No!' Yaz shouted. It was like the game where you stack ice blocks impossibly high, each person adding one in turn until the teetering structure eventually falls. The chain beneath her was already longer and more fragile than anything that was likely to endure. To expect Zeen to join it . . .

The boy caught his arms around Maya's ankles. The impact made her grunt and sent her swinging more wildly. The slippery iron between Erris's heels worked back and forth. For a heartbeat it looked like everything might impossibly hold together. And then with a shriek of anger Maya lost her grasp on the rod.

She should have fallen. Somehow she didn't. On her face frustration turned to surprise. Her hands reached up and took new hold.

Back on the ground Thurin stood with his own hands raised and Yaz understood. He had used his ice-work to take hold of the water inside Maya and lift her and Zeen who hung from her ankles.

The cage jolted. Far above, whatever was hauling them up began the task in earnest and they began to rise faster still. Yaz locked eyes with Thurin for an aching moment before a groan from Kao demanded her attention.

'Can't hold . . . much longer.'

Kao started to breathe in short desperate pants. Even after

his beating Yaz had thought the gerant equal to the task of supporting a man and two children in addition to his own muscular body. But Yaz had never considered what the body Erris had built for himself might weigh.

'Hold on, Kao!' Yaz wanted to reach down between the board stacks and set her hands to Kao's bloodless fingers but with her wrists bound outside the cage she could offer only words as comfort. The strength left to her was barely enough to get her to her knees though once she might have been able to tear free of such bonds.

Beneath Kao the human chain that ended with her brother swayed dangerously. Erris frowned in concentration and slowly, very slowly, brought his knees up, still with the end of the iron rod trapped between his heels. Impossibly he brought his knees to his chest with Yaz expecting Maya and Zeen to fall away at any moment.

To the accompaniment of Kao's puffed breath, and now an agonized keening, Erris released one hand from Kao's foot and reached down to take a grip on the rod that Maya had killed Bexen with.

Erris raised the rod and its burden of two children one-handed while straightening his legs again. Grim-faced and hurting almost as much as Kao was, Maya transferred her grip to Erris's ankles.

Erris discarded the rod. Yaz hoped it would miss any of those beneath them, craning their necks to watch. 'Zeen. Climb up,' Erris ordered.

Kao's eyes bulged bloodshot from their sockets. 'Gods in the Ice!' His gasp was hardly audible.

Zeen began to climb Maya, the sheer terror of the fall beneath him overriding the Ictha shyness around close contact. He clutched her with an intimacy that would make married Ictha blush in private. Even so he looked precarious, poised to drop, risking his life time and again on the strength of patchwork skins and the stitches holding them together. Twice something tore and he slipped back with a despairing shriek only to catch himself again, both arms hugging Maya's waist then neck.

Above them the yawning throat of the ice shaft loomed, fringed by dripping icicles. Bands of glowing stardust marbled the first twenty yards of shaft and above that all was darkness. Zeen reached Erris, who grabbed his wrist and lifted him to where he could use both hands to grip Kao's leg.

Yaz met Kao's despairing stare. 'Hold on, just a little longer!'

Before Zeen was halfway done climbing Kao Erris lifted Maya to pursue him. They both reached the cage together and hung from the bars, relieving Kao of some of his burden. Next, Erris began to climb up Kao.

By the time the cage entered the shaft Maya and Zeen had moved hand by hand to the edges of the cage bottom, still looking ready to fall at the slightest bump. It was Kao who fell though, dropping away with a despairing wail as Erris reached his neck. Quick as any hunska Erris shot a hand out to grab the cage bars even as the pair of them dropped. The whole cage jolted and Zeen cried out in fear. Yaz's own scream died in her throat as she saw that Erris now had Kao's thick wrist clasped in one hand while the other kept them both secured to the cage.

Maya managed to get herself from the bottom of the cage onto the side, holding to the bars with hands and feet while the walls of the ice shaft came closer and closer as they rose. She cut the bonds on Yaz's wrists as she passed.

Gathering her strength Yaz moved the board stacks a little then helped Zeen with the transition to the side of the cage, making sure she had hold of him while he reached and strained.

Finally, with the dark now broken only by the red glow of the star Yaz had taken from Pome, Erris showed more of his inhuman strength by climbing the outside of the cage using only his hands while carrying Kao locked between his legs. At one point the ice wall came in close enough to touch them and Yaz feared both would be scraped away. But Erris held on and soon added himself and Kao to the crush inside the cage.

Ice walls slid past with surprising speed, glistening in the red light. Yaz had dimmed the star to a glimmer to lessen its impact on the others. For quite some time Kao lay groaning, incapable of motion. Quell beside him made no sound but lay beaded with sweat, watching Yaz through eyes slitted with pain. Maya crouched against the bars, as far from the others as she could get. The darkness seemed to flow around her as the cage rose, making her indistinct in that strange shadow-work way. Zeen sat beside Yaz, as close as his tolerance for the star's radiance would let him. He said nothing, only hunched around his worries. Alone of them Erris stood, untroubled by his exertions and showing no sign of the recent battle save for the rips and bloodstains across his tunic and trousers. Yaz noted that neither of these garments . . . the word 'cloth' floated across her mind . . . were suitable for the surface. Though none of them, even in Ictha skins, would survive long in the wind, damp as they were.

'Well,' said Erris eventually. 'We made it.'

'Thurin didn't.' Yaz could hardly believe they had left him behind. The idea didn't want to fit into her mind.

Erris inclined his head. 'I'm sorry. Thurin proved himself brave and resourceful. Without him Zeen would not be with us.' He paused for a long moment then shook his head and managed a smile. 'Still, even without one of our number you have accomplished great things here today, Yaz. Think of it. Your brother and two friends recovered from the heart of the black ice. Taken back from Theus himself. Six of us headed to the surface through a hole you helped put through two miles of ice. The Tainted freed from the horror that ruled them. Theus's power broken!'

'And Pome's,' Maya said. 'You made the Broken whole and brought them peace.'

'Peace and food,' Kao said. 'An entire whale! I never tried whale.'

'But Quell . . .' Yaz turned to him, still horrified by the hilt jutting from his side.

'They're right, Yaz.' He managed a weak smile. 'And you were right to ask me to drop that axe.' A glance towards the knife. 'I'd rather this than living with the memory of children that I cut down to save myself.'

Yaz found her eyes blurry with tears and her throat too tight for reply. She shook her head and reached out for his hand.

They sat like that for a long time.

The ice walls seemed to slide by quickly in the crimson light but either that was an illusion due to proximity or the hole was deeper than even they had thought, because the first hour passed with no sign of daylight from above.

Yaz's pain and exhaustion ebbed slowly. Strength crept back into her limbs. She began to realize that despite it all, despite the losses and setbacks, she had won. They had won. The Broken had won. It might even be possible to convince Regulator Kazik to set right what had gone wrong. Quell could be healed. Erris had said so.

And once on the ice they had both shelter and food to

carry south with them. She touched the needle at her collar. If the journey proved too hard then, as a last resort, Elias Taproot was out there too and she could find him. Perhaps they would need his help, but she hoped not. She didn't want to get drawn into his battle with Seus. The green world was a haven, a dream of peace. She wasn't going there to make war.

'How long?' Kao raised his head from the boards. 'Before we get there?'

Yaz looked up. She had seen only velvet blackness before but now it seemed that a single tiny star shone directly above her, a lone point of light in all that dark. 'Is that . . . the sky?'

Even as she said it she thought of Thurin, who had never in all his life seen the light of day.

CHAPTER 39

'We need a plan,' Yaz said.

The faint point of light had become a distant circle of sky. Yaz knew they didn't have too long before they were hauled out into the daylight like fish drawn from the sea in the regulator's iron net. They had perhaps another half- or quarter-mile to go.

'Didn't we have one already?' Kao asked.

Yaz scowled. 'I *planned* on not arriving with all my powers spent, or Quell with a knife in his side, or without Thurin and his ice-work. Now we need something new or the priests will catch me and throw the rest of you back down the Pit of the Missing.'

'What do you suggest?' Erris asked. 'The last time I saw the sky the place we're going to was above the clouds. So assume I have no idea what to expect.'

Yaz pondered. 'The element of surprise is supposed to be important when making war. Isn't that what the Axit say, Maya?' She glanced around. 'Maya?'

Suddenly they were all looking for the girl. 'Maya?'

'I would say', Erris commented dryly, 'that Maya agrees with you.'

'But where could she be?' Yaz continued searching, arms outstretched as if the girl might have made herself invisible. 'It's a cage!'

Erris pointed up. 'She's climbing the cable. The priests know when the cage should get there. They'll be ready for us then. Maya is going to arrive ahead of schedule.'

'We should too!' Yaz exclaimed, though even as she said it she found herself daunted by the idea of hauling herself up hundreds of yards of icy cable.

'I think you should.' Erris nodded. 'It's you they're expecting. You and Quell. Then if they spot you they'll be in the middle of dealing with you when we arrive and they won't be expecting us.'

'You're coming up with me though, right?' Yaz suddenly had no idea what she might do when faced with the regulator once more. 'What will I say?'

Erris shook his head. 'I need to take this knife out of Quell and stitch him up. We'll probably have to move him quickly and if we do that with the blade still inside him it will do all sorts of extra damage.'

Yaz blinked. 'You couldn't have done that during the first half of our journey up?'

'There's going to be a lot of blood, Yaz. Once it's done we're going to need to get him lying down and warm as soon as we can if he's to live.'

Yaz tried to imagine how that was even vaguely possible. She stamped down on the doubt and looked up at the cable instead, stretching away to the distant circle of light.

'I should come too,' Zeen said. Over the course of their long ascent his mood had changed from wild optimism

461

fuelled by the excitement of their escape to a pensive accept-ance that although they were going back to the ice and the sky and the wind they were not going back to their lives. At first he had even thought that their parents would take them back, that their mother would open her tent to her two surviving children despite the regulator's judgement and the rulings of Mother Mazai. Yaz had tried to be gentle. The judgement had changed how their world saw them. The fall had taken them from their past and simply climbing back out could not change that. More than this though were the changes that had undeniably been wrought in them during their time below. With every challenge Yaz's quantal blood had worked its magic, saving her but making something new of her. She had grown both stronger and weaker each time, as though the threats and fear and hurt had torn first one skin from her, then another, revealing a different creature beneath. Zeen too had changed beyond recognition, his speed a part of him now, evident in every move in a way it had not been before the fall. Before the regulator's shove Zeen had been merely quick, now his hunska blood owned him and his swiftness was inhuman. These gifts had come at a price: the strength of the Ictha had bled from them, and the northern nights would eat them alive.

'I should come too,' Zeen repeated.

'You don't know how to climb.' Yaz was grateful that a simple answer lay to hand.

Without further discussion Yaz clambered up the side of the cage and then with more trepidation reached up to where the four supporting cables, which led to equally spaced points around the cage's edge, met together and twisted into the single thick cable stretching directly upwards. She set the red star orbiting her in a slow spiral and glanced down one last time to see Zeen and Kao staring up at her. Erris was already kneeling beside Quell, bent across him hiding both their faces.

With a prayer to the Gods in the Sky Yaz took hold of the freezing cable. She grunted with effort as she hauled herself up; then locked her legs about it and began to climb. Her time in the undercity with Arka and her days alone there had taught her all about climbing cables, except perhaps what to do when they are filmed in ice and so cold that they leech the feeling from your fingers within the first ten yards.

She was thankful that enough strength to climb had returned to her during the long journey to the surface. Even so she made only slow progress. However slow her progress though, each time she reached up the cable she put distance between her and the cage.

Yaz would not have made it far but for the fact that Maya had preceded her and, like many marjals, she had some minor talent for ice-work: at least enough to break away the cable's ice cladding at the places she wanted to hold on. Yaz took advantage of these clear spots and continued to climb until her arms began to tremble with the strain and her hands felt as if they belonged to a stranger. Looking down she was surprised to see the cage had entirely vanished into darkness.

Above her the circle of sky loomed larger and closer than ever, a bleak blood-tinged white offering no hope of warmth. She had half expected to see Seus's dark form reaching across the heavens like a skeletal hand, as it had above the freezing forest where she had found Elias Taproot. But even the bare sky felt like a threat.

During her time in the close confines of the caverns and the undercity Yaz had mourned the loss of her open spaces, the aching distances of the ice plains, even the unending song of the wind. But now, hauled inexorably from her hole out into the daylight, Yaz found herself daunted by that same wide emptiness she had wanted back.

Only a short time remained. She could now see the frame that presumably supported the cable. Maya must already have reached the surface ahead of her. Yaz brought the star into her sleeve and began to worry about the mechanics of her arrival. It hadn't occurred to her until now but it seemed that the cable must be wrapped across some kind of wheel on the frame above. If Yaz failed to release her hold her hands would be destroyed. If she did release it she would fall back down the shaft, dropping a distance that would kill both her and whoever she landed on.

Yaz experimented with climbing back down, trying to mark her position against the shaft wall. At the fastest rate she felt safe with, her descent was still exceeded by the rise of the cable. Increasingly desperate she tried to judge the width of the shaft. Would it be possible to jump to the side? She would have to land almost entirely on the ice or she would slide back down the hole. Given her current weakness it seemed unlikely that she could make it. Would she have to scream humiliatingly for the priests' attention and hope that they would be able to stop the cable in time?

Gods in the Sea! She was such an idiot! Yaz's terror grew moment by moment. The circle of sky was rushing at her now, growing larger with each heartbeat. Soon it would be the whole world and the time for thinking would be replaced by a need for action.

'Maya made it,' Yaz whispered. The girl's body hadn't dropped past her, not even a scatter of severed fingers, so somehow little Maya had figured out a solution.

Yaz could hear the creaking of the wheel now and see it on its great iron frame, devouring the cable yard by yard, directing it through a sharp turn to angle down at the ice where some great mechanism must be winding it onto a spool. Yaz wondered if she could reach out to the cable after it left the wheel, but the distance looked too great and her arms too leaden to lift her.

And suddenly she was level with the ice, slitting her eyes against the light, with no time left to think. The wheel was huge, the cable hauling her swiftly towards it. With a strength born of terror Yaz released one numb hand from the cable above her and took a hold much lower. Crying out with effort she lifted and twisted her tired body and set both feet to the cable between her two hands. If her grip failed a fatal fall waited. She thought perhaps that her top hand might be frozen to the metal and that that might be all that was keeping her from the drop.

The clanking filled her ears. The wheel brought her racing towards it a good twenty feet above the ice, tall enough for all of the cage to be lifted clear. Straining every muscle Yaz thrust as hard as she could with her legs while clinging desperately to the cable. Tension built rapidly. The wheel was on her, her frozen fingers racing towards the narrowing gap between the iron rim and the cable. Yaz tried to let go and found she couldn't. She saw her hand pulled past the bottom of the wheel, inches from mutilation. She screamed with effort, legs straining and found sudden release. The force flung her outwards; the blackness of the shaft yawned beneath her. She hit the slick, sloping ice at the edge of the shaft where the coal burn had melted it away. She would have slipped back into the hole but her momentum carried her on, rolling and sliding to a halt on the raw ice. Without the wind that now pressed on her back she would never have made it. The Gods in the Sky loved her. Though lying there with her body feeling like one huge bruise and unsure how many of her bones remained unbroken Yaz couldn't find it in her to thank them. She hauled her right arm towards her face, terrified that the thing that had broken her grip on the cable had been the removal of her fingers. But no, they were still there, abused but whole.

Yaz levered herself up, gritting her teeth against sharp pains all along her side. The fall had left her vision blurred but she could see enough to spot that her star had rolled from her sleeve and lay some yards ahead of her glowing dully on the ice. She wasn't sure which would hurt more, compelling the star to her or crawling to get it. The shockingly cold wind clawed at her, icy fingers finding a way through her damp hides to filch every last scrap of warmth from her body.

She spat blood onto the ice and crawled. The clanking of the wheel accompanied her progress. By the time she closed her numb hand around the red sphere Yaz's vision had cleared enough to see her surroundings. Empty ice stretched away before her, mile upon mile until it met the sky in a white infinity. Encompassing the star in both hands and grateful for its warmth she got painfully to her feet like an old woman of fifty.

Yaz had expected to see the Black Rock. She shook her head to rid it of the fog that had filled it when she hit the ice. Some bone in her neck screamed in protest, almost making its echo burst from her mouth. Carefully, leaning into the wind, she turned her body, keeping her head still to avoid further agony. The mountain came into view, the Black Rock, rising from the ice like the tip of some vast spear driven up from below. She turned a little more and the lifting frame then the winding gear both came into view. The winding gear was another iron framework, taller than a man and filled with large many-toothed wheels. Five figures in the black hides of the priesthood stood to either side turning great handles, although many more could fit beside them to help if the load was a heavier one.

It seemed impossible that they didn't see her but apparently their labour wholly occupied them, and whatever method they used to gauge their progress told them the cage would not arrive for a little while yet.

The wind had her shivering already. The changes wrought on her down in the caverns of the Broken had left her shockingly vulnerable. She hunched over her star, willing more warmth from it, and laboured around to complete her circle.

The long-expected sight of the regulator still startled her and halted her turn. He stood five yards off, hunched against the wind, the trailing strips of his cloak fluttering about him. The symbols burned across his face and scalp were familiar now, the script wall of the Missing had driven him from the undercity and left its mark upon him.

'Yaz. Welcome back. And you've brought my star, I see.'

The slight smile on the regulator's lips was enough to ignite her anger. 'You throw children into that hole to be your slaves!' The long-banked outrage burst from her mouth. 'You use up their lives in the dark, and just for the iron that gives you power over my people!' Yaz found herself pointing in accusation.

Rather than show any shame the regulator threw back his head and laughed. 'That's rather melodramatic, young Ictha.' He fixed her with white-on-white eyes. 'I hear it's warm down there, and quite well lit. And most of them don't get worked to death. The hunters take them!'

Yaz's anger flared into rage, burning bright, fuelled by that same deep sense of injustice that had dogged her throughout her time in the pit and had underwritten so many of her actions over the past few days. Her hand reached for the dagger-fish knife at her hip and finding it gone she began to advance on the man with her bare hands, ready to brain him with the star. Kazik had tossed Jaysin into the pit just to carry a message, delivering a scared little boy into the clutches of a monster like Hetta. He'd thrown generations of Jaysins into that hole, tearing their young lives apart to add comfort to his own. A red haze filled Yaz's vision as if she had brought a devil of her very own up from the black ice.

'Mine, I think.' The regulator pointed to the star in Yaz's raised hand and without warning it jolted towards him.

'No!' Yaz managed to hold on though the initial yank nearly took her shoulder from its socket. Mustering what little remained of her strength she leaned back, hauling on the star with both hands as it strained towards the priest. A new noise was coming from the shaft now, a deep thrumming sound from the cable but rising swiftly in pitch, a sign that the cage had nearly arrived.

The regulator snarled and his face twisted with effort.

Yaz found her feet slipping. She added the muscle in her mind to the contest. A bright pain blossomed behind her forehead and she tasted blood behind gritted teeth but slowly she bent the star to her will. A slow horror crept over Kazik's face. Disbelief at being bested by a mere girl barely woken to her talent. He redoubled his efforts, and Yaz fought him.

All thought of escape left her. She advanced again, the star raised and burning brighter and more crimson than the sun. 'You're a monster, old man, and I am going to end what you do here.'

A gentle voice spoke to her left, a man's voice creaking with age. 'Well, we can't have that, can we, Regulator Kazik?'

The star blazing in Yaz's hand went out. It didn't merely

dim. It turned a cold, smoky grey. Its song ceased. Its heart-beat stopped. And in an instant it became so heavy that she dropped it, crushing the ice where it landed.

Yaz turned uncertainly, trying to twist her neck to see but unable to do so without fainting from the pain. She couldn't tell if the priest who came into view as she turned had been there all along, watching her struggles, or if he had somehow materialized out of the air. He stood thin and bent with age, robed in black hides and hooded against the wind, less tall than Kazik, frail with age.

'Hello, Yaz.' He pushed back his hood. 'I told you you'd be an agent of change.'

Eular, his thin white hair streaming in the wind, regarded her with eyeless sockets and a sad smile. 'You misunderstand the purpose of the pit though.' His smile was the same gentle one he had used back in the caverns, almost kindly. 'It's not iron we're most interested in mining, or even the star-stones. It's the Broken.'

'But . . . You?' Yaz stood dumbfounded.

'Did you bring 'Theus with you?' Eular asked.

''Theus? No! I destroyed him.' Yaz looked between Regulator Kazik and Eular, still unable to understand.

Eular nodded. 'A pity. You know, the city once told me that very long ago one of the Missing predicted that Prometheus, our broken 'Theus, would be the greatest of their kind. The one who made the prediction was part of the faction that rejected technology and styled herself a witch, but she saw the future better than any of them. She said he would "bring the fire", whatever that means. But in the end they persuaded, or forced, him to ascend with the rest of them, and left the unwanted pieces behind.' The old man pressed his lips into a thin line. 'Destroyed, you say?' He shook his head. 'Ah well.'

Yaz could hear the rattle of the approaching cage, very close now. 'I don't understa—'

'Sleep,' Eular suggested.

The exhaustion that Yaz had held at bay so long overwhelmed her. A black sea drowned her. And the last voice that reached her as she sank to the ice was Eular's, though his words weren't aimed at her.

'Let's take her home, Kazik.' A pause. 'Oh, and have them drop the cage.'

ACKNOWLEDGEMENTS

As always, I'm very grateful to Agnes Meszaros for her continued help and feedback. She's never shy to challenge me when she thinks something can be improved or I'm being a little lazy. At the same time her passion and enthusiasm made working on the story even more enjoyable.

I should also thank, as ever, my wonderful editor Jane Johnson for her support and many talents; Natasha Bardon, Vicky Leech and the sales, marketing and publicity crews at HarperCollins. And of course my agent, Ian Drury, and the team at Sheil Land.

Turn over for chapter one of the second novel
in the Book of the Ice series:

THE GIRL AND THE MOUNTAIN

Coming April 2021

CHAPTER 1

Thurin

There had been a great fire and there had been a great flood. Both are forces of nature that sweep clean, that wipe the slate and promise a new beginning. Thurin had been the cause of the fire and of the flood. And yet both had failed to wash away his desire to be with Yaz of the Ictha: the girl for whom the stars shone brighter.

Thurin stared up at the miles-long hole stretching vertically through the ice to a world that he had never seen. It seemed impossible that he had driven the fire that melted it. The release of his fire-talent, of energies that had built inside him for years and years, had hollowed him. The subsequent battle with the Tainted had left him bruised, bitten, and torn. And almost immediately after that he had used the full extent of his ice-work in a desperate attempt to ensure Yaz's brother joined her escape.

Even as he wondered what it was that still kept him upright, Thurin found himself collapsing to the floor. The last image to remain with him was of Yaz's impossibly white eyes locked on his as the cage rose ever further and vanished into darkness.

*

'Wake up!'

Thurin rolled to his side, groaning. A pleasant heat wrapped him and for a beautiful moment he thought himself at home in his mother's house within the settlement. He tried to cling to the illusion but it slid through his grasp, leaving only pieces of the darker dreams that had haunted his sleep, ones in which Theus stood above him pulling puppet strings to make him dance to a tune that was not his own.

'Still with us? Good.'

Thurin cracked open an eye. A fierce glow, distorted by his blurry vision, stole detail from the scene but he saw enough to tell that he was lying in one of the forge sheds. Lengths of chain and a variety of tools hung from the support beams. 'Kaylal? That you?'

'It is.' The young smith clapped a hand to Thurin's shoulder. 'Takes more than a hundred screaming Tainted to put me down.'

Thurin struggled to sit. All of him hurt. Bites and scratches that he hadn't noticed before now cried for his attention. 'You're all right?'

'Well, I lost both legs . . .'

Thurin smiled at the old joke. Kaylal looked as bad as he felt, both eyes blackened and puffy, his ear torn and bleeding, bruising round his neck. Still, the greatest of his hurts was the loss of Exxar. The rest of his wounds would heal. 'It's good to see you. How did I get here?'

'Arka had the wounded carried to shelter. The worst of them are at the settlement.' Kaylal hauled himself up a chain to gain his work stool. 'Your friend Yaz left in spectacular fashion, I'm told.'

'She's your friend too.' Thurin scowled, angry at his own evasion.

Kaylal shook his head. 'I lost Exxar and there's no getting

him back. Yaz has only been gone half a day. She's up there.' He pointed. 'It's a journey that took even me almost no time at all.'

'I'm told it's harder on the way up.' Thurin stood, groaning at the stiffness in his limbs.

'Seriously, though, you need to do something, Thurin. I saw how you looked at her. What will it be like spending the years to come always wondering where she is, what she's doing?'

Thurin stretched, imagining he could hear his leg bones creaking. He knew Kaylal was right and it scared him. He moved closer to the forge pot, still radiating residual heat despite being empty. 'The Broken need me.'

'That's just an excuse. We have Arka. We have our people back from the taint. And if this whale is really there . . .'

'It is. Getting it out of the black ice will be a problem, but I saw it. I never believed the stories when they said how big those things are!'

Kaylal grinned. 'I want to see it too!'

Thurin echoed his friend's smile. It seemed madness for the two of them, neither having any memories of the ice, to be discussing his going to the surface. But if ever there had been a time for madness it was here in the days since Yaz's arrival.

'I don't know how to follow her.' Thurin said it in a small voice. It seemed a sorrier excuse than being needed here. But the truth was that two miles of ice was a daunting barrier. It wasn't as if anyone had ever overcome it before Yaz made her escape.

Kaylal laughed. 'They say you're the one who made that hole in the first place. If that's true then surely you can get yourself up it. I doubt they've been able to close it off yet.'

Thurin frowned. 'Maybe . . .' He bit his lip. 'It would be dangerous though. Very.'

'Oh, well. Better stay then.' Kaylal took down one of his hammers and began to inspect the open chain links scattering the table before him.

'Heh.' Thurin shook his head. 'Everything has been dangerous since she came. I guess I've got a taste for it now.'

Kaylal reached out behind him and took hold of something dark and heavy that he tossed to Thurin.

'Exxar's cloak?' Thurin stroked a hand down over the garment: double-layered rat-skin. It had taken an age for Exxar to barter for the furs.

'He was never warm enough.' Kaylal managed a smile.

'I can't—'

'Take it. I heard it's chilly up there.'

Thurin swirled the cloak around his shoulders and started towards the door. He paused to set a hand on Kaylal's shoulder. 'You'll look after them all for me, won't you?'

'I will, brother.' Kaylal put down his hammer and laid a calloused hand on top of Thurin's. 'And we'll be here if you need a place to come back to. Now go and get her.'

Thurin returned to the city cavern, passing through cave after cave where the Broken wandered in numbers greater than he'd ever seen them. Those reclaimed from the taint outnumbered the Broken who had remained free, but they were intermixed now, families reunited. There were greetings from people who remembered Thurin as a baby, and others he recalled from his childhood. Some, taken more recently, rushed to hug him, trying to drag him off to this or that celebration. The joy that Yaz had left in her wake was just starting to sink in. The Broken were only now beginning to truly believe that this was no dream, that it was something real that couldn't be taken from them.

Each invitation, each reunion, weakened his resolve; each

was a hook sunk into his flesh and needing to be torn free if he was to continue to his goal. It would be so easy to stay, so easy to resume the familiarity of his life, to enjoy the improved future within the company of his extended family. But Thurin knew that if he turned from his course, if he surrendered to what was easy, then Yaz would haunt him all his life, however long it might be. A great 'what if' hanging over his head year after year.

And so he came to the city cavern and crossed the puddled expanse of stone, the iced-over remnants of the flood cracking beneath his feet. He walked among the abandoned wealth of iron, the wreckage of broken hunters, discarded armour, weapons cast aside. He gave a wide berth to the pit into which Theus and the other tainted gerants had fallen when Yaz collapsed the floor beneath them into a chamber of the undercity. He assumed that the pit remained full of the bodies of those who had fallen amid a tumult of shattered rock, but he had no wish to see the truth of the matter for himself. The families of the dead would come for them soon enough.

Thurin spotted a lone figure poking among the debris of Pome's hunter, Old Hanno, who after Eular had to be the oldest of the Broken at well over fifty. He raised his hand in greeting. Apart from the two of them the ruins stood deserted.

Thurin came to a halt beneath the wide throat of the hole that stretched up through the roof of the city cavern to the surface of the ice, allegedly miles above. The stardust marbling the ice illuminated the first twenty or thirty yards of the shaft in a dim multi-hued glow. Beyond that, only darkness, no hint of the sky that the stories told of. Most of Thurin's friends had memories of the surface, but none of their words really painted a picture in his mind, or even made sense. What held this 'sky' up? How high above the ground was it? Where were the walls? Thurin sighed and guessed that if his plans succeeded then he would soon see for himself and being an adult he would understand what the Broken had failed to explain from their childhood recollections.

A deep breath calmed him a little. Another deeper breath, exhaling the tension. Thurin's power to work the ice came from his marjal blood. Next to shadow-work the elemental skills were the most common to manifest in marjals. He had been strong with water and ice since his early years. By the age of ten he had been able to weaken the cave walls, allowing the gerants to dig through much more swiftly in their hunt for stars. The talent had slowly strengthened as he grew and used it daily with the mining crew, but it still hadn't been anywhere near as strong as Tarko's.

That had changed when Thurin returned from the Tainted. Something had shifted within him; some barrier had broken. He found himself capable of new feats. And in the week since Yaz's arrival it had seemed that some hitherto unsuspected barrier had broken each day. In the fight with Hetta he had held her off by seizing the water that suffuses all humans. Yaz's arrival had heralded a sequence of life-or-death situations, and in each new extremity Thurin had clawed his way to some fresh height, unlocking more strength, his ice-work at last becoming equal to that of their former leader. Perhaps even surpassing it.

Another deep breath and Thurin reached for his power. The idea had come to him when he thought about how he had saved Zeen. The boy had lost his grip as the cage accelerated upwards towards the shaft. Thurin had reached out with his ice-work, his mind taking hold of Zeen's blood. Thurin had lifted the boy and sent him in pursuit of the cage, letting him grab the bars once more.

Now Thurin turned his ice-work inwards, taking hold of the water in the blood that ran through his own veins, the water that suffused his flesh. You only had to see how solid a corpse would freeze to know how much of us is water. With a small grunt of concentration Thurin lifted his feet clear of the rock. It was easier than he had feared, yet still hard enough to make him worry that sustaining the effort for as long as was necessary might be beyond him.

He rose slowly into the air with the sense that he was balancing on the narrow top of an invisible, ever-growing tower. The pressure needed to raise his bodyweight pushed back on some elastic part of his mind, some focus of his talent that would stretch and stretch again, providing whatever effort was demanded of it . . . right up to that moment when suddenly too much had been asked and without warning it might snap.

Empty yards piled up beneath his feet. The ground grew more distant, the roof closer. With the ice ceiling looming above him on every side, Thurin found himself seized by a swift and unexpected terror. The distance yawning beneath his feet seemed to exert a pull all of its own. The invisible tower on which he balanced became an unstable stack of loosely connected parts, piled way too high. The rocky expanse bearing the city's scars demanded that he rejoin it with crushing speed.

A panicked burst of power sent Thurin rushing into the shaft, and in its rapidly narrowing, rapidly dimming confines the distance beneath him was quickly tamed. Within a short time, all that could be seen below him was a shrinking circle of light that yielded no impression of the fall it concealed.

Within a hundred yards the darkness wrapped Thurin completely and from then on he was simply a dot of warmth rising blind through the night, grazing the ice walls from time to time, and wondering if the seemingly endless shaft would spit him out into the world above before gravity's pull overcame his willpower and dragged him screaming back to a quick but ugly death.

Up, always up. Thurin lost track of time. The pain built behind his eyes until he also lost all sense of where he was going and why. Up and up. And the hurt kept getting worse.